A Night Owl Slips in

This is a work of fiction. Names, characters, organizations, places, events, and incidents are either products of the author's imagination or are used fictitiously. Any resemblance to actual persons, living or dead, or actual events is purely coincidental.

Copyright © 2021 Douglas Lumsden
All rights reserved.
ISBN-13: 9798485753832

No part of this book may be reproduced, or stored in a retrieval system, or transmitted in any form or by any means, electronic, mechanical, photocopying, recording, or otherwise, without express written permission of the publisher.

Cover design and art by Arash Jahani (www.arashjahani.com)

A Night Owl Slips into a Diner

By

Douglas Lumsden

To Rita. Always.

Books in this Series

Alexander Southerland, P.I.

Book One: *A Troll Walks into a Bar*

Book Two: *A Witch Steps into My Office*

Book Three: *A Hag Rises from the Abyss*

Book Four: *A Night Owl Slips into a Diner*

Contents

Chapter One 1
Chapter Two 14
Chapter Three 29
Chapter Four 40
Chapter Five 52
Chapter Six 67
Chapter Seven 82
Chapter Eight 93
Chapter Nine 108
Chapter Ten 119
Chapter Eleven 132
Chapter Twelve 142
Chapter Thirteen 152
Chapter Fourteen 164
Chapter Fifteen 175
Chapter Sixteen 189
Chapter Seventeen 201
Chapter Eighteen 212
Chapter Nineteen 226
Chapter Twenty 239
Chapter Twenty-One 250
Chapter Twenty-Two 262
Chapter Twenty-Three 274
Chapter Twenty-Four 283

Chapter Twenty-Five 292
Chapter Twenty-Six 301
Epilogue 311

Chapter One

Breaking into Redhorn's data files turned out to be a lot less trouble than I thought it would be. I'd spent the morning scheming up ways to steal the information I needed, discarding one idea after another. I'd thought about breaking into the office during the night and installing a surveillance camera, but dismissed the idea as too inefficient and too risky. I considered summoning an air elemental and sneaking it into Redhorn's office to watch him type his passcode into his computer, but concluded that observing and memorizing keystrokes was beyond the capabilities of even the cleverest air spirits. I didn't even think that Smokey would be able to manage it, and Smokey was one of the smartest air elementals that I'd ever worked with. Certainly the best trained. I went online and researched some sophisticated gadgets designed to divine computer passcodes in various ways, but decided that they were too unreliable, especially for the amount of dough they would set me back. By lunchtime, I was ready to drag Redhorn into an alley and beat the passcode out of him. I decided to hold that option as a last resort. In the end, it turned out that I'd been overthinking the whole problem. All I actually had to do was peek over Redhorn's shoulder and let him show me the way past the walls that guarded his most precious secrets. I told myself that his carelessness absolved me of any trace of guilt I might have felt. I mean, it's not stealing when they insist on giving it to you for free, right?

I was waiting outside his office when Redhorn returned from lunch. The middle-aged senior engineer stepped out of the elevator and turned down the hallway with the deliberate upright stride of a man who had washed down his meal with at least one too many martinis. His forehead glistened beneath the brim of his homburg, and his horn-rimmed glasses had slid halfway down the bridge of his nose. He was wearing an expensive wool suit that had probably made him look pretty dapper when he'd picked it up some five years and fifteen pounds ago, but since then it had lost much of its luster and picked up a few wrinkles. The jacket hugged his shoulders, and he left it unbuttoned in order to give his expanding boiler some room to grow.

When Redhorn saw me, his florid mug scrunched with curiosity as he tried to recall who I was and why I might be standing in the executive wing outside his locked office. After a moment of intense concentration, his eyes lit up in what looked to me like alarm. "Southerby, isn't it?"

"Southerland," I corrected him. "Alexander Southerland. From procurement?"

"Quite, quite." The engineer took a long, deep breath before visibly composing himself. "Well.... You wanted to see me?" He spoke with measured precision in an obvious attempt to keep from slurring his words.

"Mr. Brantley told me to ask you for a copy of a blueprint. I've got the number right here." I held up a clipboard with a pad of official looking forms attached. "He wants you to email it to me."

Redhorn frowned and looked confused. He cleared his throat and scowled. "Fuckin' Brantley." He sighed and extended a hand.

I pulled the clipboard to my chest. "I'm supposed to wait while you send me the email attachment. It should only take a second."

"What? Fuck that. Tell Brantley I've got my own work to take care of. Leave me the paperwork and I'll get to it later this afternoon." Redhorn reached into his pants pocket and pulled out a metal ring holding too many keys.

"Mr. Brantley told me to get started on the blueprint right away," I told him.

"Brantley can go fuck himself." Redhorn fumbled with the keys, muttering under his breath, but his hands were shaking and the keyring slipped from his grasp. Seeing it coming, I reached out and snatched the keys out of the air before they could fall to the floor. I held them out for Redhorn, who ripped them out of my hand as if he'd caught me picking his pocket.

The engineer glared at me over his glasses. "Quick little bastard, aren't you!" He drew in a breath, and his features softened. He glanced at the keyring in his hand and then turned back to me with the hint of a smile. "That was quite impressive. What are you, some kind of magician?"

I didn't have a response for that, so I said nothing.

Redhorn turned his attention back to the keyring and found the key he was looking for. "All right, all right," he grumbled. "Let's get this over with." With a resigned sigh, he unlocked his door and led me into his office. Once inside, he dropped into the padded chair at his desk with a grunt and slapped at the space bar on his computer to wake it up. After a few seconds, an image of a sailboat cruising on the blue waters of the Bay filled his screen. Redhorn didn't strike me as an outdoorsman, and I guessed the picture was more fantasy than reality for the frumpy engineer. In the center of the image was a rectangular box with a cursor blinking on the left edge. I stood behind Redhorn and kept my eyes on his fingers as he tapped the buttons on his keyboard, one at a time, making sure to get each keystroke right. A row of asterisks filled the box on the screen, but I'd seen the ten characters he'd actually typed: R-3-d-&-H-o-r-n-y-!.

Probably his high-school nickname.

Picking up the passcode like that isn't as easy as it sounds. But as a professional snoop with magically enhanced awareness it was right in my wheelhouse. I committed the passcode to memory and knew it would be there when I wanted it.

Redhorn glanced back at me and asked, "You say Brantley wants me to email the print to you?"

"That's right." I held out the clipboard.

Redhorn took it from my hand. He adjusted his glasses on his nose and stared at the official interoffice request that was clipped to the board. His head jerked in my direction. "This is for the regenerator! What's Brantley want this for? Most of this project is still classified."

"He wants me to run a cost analysis on the components."

The engineer glared at me for a few moments, as if he suspected that I was trying to pull off some sort of prank, which, essentially, I was. Then he sighed. "Sounds like a swell time. What's your email address?"

I spelled "Southerland!A" out for him.

Redhorn put the clipboard down on his desk and went to work on his keyboard. After half a minute, he handed the clipboard back to me. "Okay, you've got it. Tell that motherfucker Brantley that I won't let him skimp on material for this one, no matter what Leaflock says. The device won't work for shit with bargain-basement parts. Oh, and you're not going to be able to cost item fourteen. That's the RAA. I haven't released it yet, and when I do it will be proprietary information. Top secret from everybody but Leaflock. Brantley knows that already, so it shouldn't be an issue." The engineer's voice sounded clearer now that he was settled in and working.

I nodded and tried to look concerned. "Okay, thanks."

"Yeah, sure." Redhorn looked up at me and met my eyes for the first time. He frowned and asked, "That's all you needed?"

"That's it." I turned to leave.

Redhorn stopped me. "Hold on a second. How long have you been with us, Southerby?"

I stopped. "Southerland. A few weeks. I started at the beginning of the month."

"Brantley hired you?"

"Mr. Leaflock hired me and assigned me to Mr. Brantley."

Redhorn's eyebrows lifted above his glasses. "You were hired by the Big Cheese himself?" He looked me up and down. "You ain't no gnome, so you can't be related. Where'd he find you?"

I shrugged. "I sent in a resume. I guess he liked it."

A humorless smile appeared on Redhorn's face. "Hmm. What did you do before you came here?"

I wondered why I was getting the third degree and thought that Redhorn might be on to me. "I did some work back east," I told him. It wasn't a lie. I *had* done some work east of Yerba City after leaving the army some nine years earlier. I'd been a dishwasher at a restaurant in Missouri Province for a few weeks. Before that, I'd been a bouncer at a bar in Aztlan for a couple of months, although technically speaking that was more south than east.

I wasn't sure what was going on behind Redhorn's thick glasses and sweaty brow. He seemed to be trying, and failing, to come to some sort of decision. After a time, he nodded slowly. "No shit? Huh! Well, welcome to the factory, such as it is. Hope you like hard work and low pay. The cheap bastards around here toss nickels around like manhole covers. Tell Brantley that if we keep filling our products with shit, we're going to keep producing shitty products. Not that that shithead'll give a shit." Redhorn's cheeks puffed as he belched through pursed lips and filled the confined space of his office with the fragrance of recycled gin and vermouth.

I coughed into the back of my hand. The engineer looked up at me with a sheepish grin. "Sorry about that."

He hesitated, looking like he wanted to say something more, but not knowing how to begin. He opened his mouth to speak, but then abruptly swiveled his desk chair and began to gaze through his window, which offered a scenic view of the nondescript gray office building on the other side of Gold Street. I waited to see whether he would break the silence. Just as I was about to give up and leave him to his thoughts, he began to speak, more to himself than to me. "We had a dream once. Leaflock and me. He was my student, you know. When I was teaching at YCIT. I could see right away that he was special. He was a brilliant student, sure, but I've seen my share of brilliant students. There was something different about Leaflock, though. He could take the material that he was learning and twist it, make it jump through hoops, make it do things that nobody else had thought of. I have to admit that I was more than a little mesmerized by that little gnome. He told me about some of his plans, and I knew right away that I wanted to be a part of them." Redhorn snorted. "His enthusiasm is contagious that way. I took a big chance when I quit my job and helped him launch this company, but I did it because I had faith in his vision. We were going to use his ideas to build useful utilitarian products and make a lot of money. My wife thought I was crazy, and maybe I was. We did it, though. My faith in him paid off. We got rich, and we helped a lot of people. We built a solid business. Rock solid. Hired lots of good people and made money hand over fist."

Redhorn turned back to me then, swiveling in his chair. A rueful smile was on his face. "That's how it began. We were a good team, him and me. Leaflock's a genius. He really is. Not all that practical, though. That's why he needed me. I helped him to convert his ideas into products that worked." He sighed, and his eyes drifted. "And then things got... complicated."

I waited until I was sure Redhorn had finished speaking. "Right," I said. "Well, thanks for the welcome. I'll leave you to it."

Turning to go, I lingered long enough to take a last look at Redhorn, who was staring at nothing with drooping eyes and a sagging mouth, looking as if he'd just received a fatal diagnosis from his doctor. I left the office then, thinking that ol' R3d&Horny! was having himself a real shitty day. I didn't have the heart to tell him that it was likely going to get much worse.

***

I had taken an instant dislike to Morgan Leaflock, the brilliant gnome at the head of Leaflock Services Corporation. I wasn't sure why, at first. Maybe it was because I'd never seen a man so in love with himself and so contemptuous of anyone who wasn't him. Yeah, that was probably the reason. But he was a client with money, so I tried to play nice. He'd hired me, not because of any expertise in materials procurement or cost analysis, or even because of my dishwashing skills, but to find out who was selling proprietary information from his electronics engineering firm to his competitors. Two of his company's design improvements had already found their way into the hands of his rivals, and Leaflock was desperate to plug the leak. He'd complained to his lawyer, another gnome named Robinson Lubank. Rob Lubank was also *my* lawyer, as it happens, and he referred Leaflock to me. The timing was good: my last client had stiffed me on my fee on his way out of town, and my bank account was gasping for oxygen.

Like all gnomes, Leaflock was about three and a half feet tall, give or take, and sported a pair of sizable mouse-like ears. His spindly limbs, sunken chest, and rounded bloat of a belly gave him the appearance of a great four-legged spider. His pale gray eyes were buried behind heavy sagging pouches, but they were alive and filled with energy. Leaflock wasn't yet twenty-six, but the company he'd started in his studio apartment just five years earlier had already captured the attention of major investors all over the globe.

"We're right on the verge of a breakthrough that will put this company into orbit!" The palms of Leaflock's hands pounded out a rapid bongo beat on his desktop as he explained to me why he needed the services of an independent private investigator. "I've got something coming out that will revolutionize the medical industry. Once it passes its initial test, it's going to impact the world like the discovery of fire! It's going to change *everything*!" The gnome frowned and slammed his palm on his desk. "But only if I can keep our research and development in house!" He fidgeted in his chair while he explained the situation to me, a perpetual-motion machine that couldn't sit still for more than three seconds without blowing a gasket.

"Do you have any idea who might be stealing company information?" I asked.

"If I did, I wouldn't need *you*, bright boy! I've got fifty-four employees, Southerland. I work them hard, pay them no more than they're worth, and they all think that I'm a son of a bitch. Any one of them could be selling me out. Find out who the turncoat is. Do it right and make it quick." Leaflock sat back in his chair and folded his hands over his paunch. "Now, what's this going to cost me?"

Predictably, the tightly-wound gnome, who seemed to burn agitated indignation like fuel, had objected to my rates, and his face grew red as he railed against them for the better part of ten minutes. During that time he called me a chiseler and an extortionist, and he accused me of jacking up my rates because of the common prejudice that all gnomes were rich. I had not, in fact, increased my standard fee, but the more I listened to him rant, the more I thought it might not have been a bad idea. He informed me that private investigators were detestable little creepers who made their livings by turning up stones to expose the worms and maggots that hid beneath them, and that people in my profession were, at best, necessary evils. He told me that charging as much as I did for such unseemly work was a crime, and he asked me how I managed to sleep at night. For my part, I let it all slide, maintained a poker face, and remained polite. I needed the dough, and I regarded his verbal abuse as nothing more than negotiation tactics. I'd heard it all before, although maybe not with the same level of vitriol that the frenetic gnome brought to the table. I held firm, until finally, with an exaggerated show of reluctance, Leaflock signed my prepared contract and coughed up an acceptable retainer.

The next day, I found myself behind a small wooden desk in an open workstation sharing a crowded office space with a dozen tired-looking drones. Brantley, my supervisor, was mystified by my sudden appearance in his department and hard-pressed to find anything for me to do. That was fine with me, as I wasn't remotely qualified to tackle any of the work delegated to his section. After some fuss, he assigned me some tedious data-entry projects that no one was depending on and forgot about me. I spent the next few days getting to know my co-workers and listening in on the office gossip. By the end of the first week my office mates were including me in their group gripe sessions, and by the third week, I was confident that I had found the man leaking company info to Leaflock's competitors. I spent the next few days compiling a detailed summary of my investigations. It revealed a story of a meteoric rise and the heavy toll that sudden success can have on interpersonal relationships.

Inyon Redhorn had been with Leaflock from the beginning. Seventeen years older than Leaflock, Redhorn had been the young gnome's engineering professor at Yerba City Institute of Technology. It was Redhorn who had first realized that the bored and indifferent student with only an average academic record possessed natural gifts that his unimaginative teachers had failed to spot and were neglecting to develop. Professor Redhorn recognized the young prodigy's potential, and he adopted the student as his protégé. Redhorn took

Leaflock out of his class and gave him private lessons, encouraging the boy to give his natural instincts and unorthodox ideas free reign. The young gnome's intellect blossomed and flourished, and, with his mentor's support, Leaflock developed plans to leave academia and begin his own business. At his protégé's invitation, the professor quit his job at the university, helped Leaflock secure a business loan, and joined the ambitious youngster's brand new start-up engineering firm.

The two of them worked well together. Redhorn was a steadying influence on the hyperactive phenom and a competent designer in his own right, though he lacked the creative flair of his younger compatriot. Leaflock's gift was a knack for finding creative strategies for doing more with less, and, with Redhorn's practical guidance, the boy genius designed a critical innovation in gas-detection technology that allowed production of a less obtrusive and inexpensive smoke detector. Leaflock negotiated a deal with a major hotel chain, and Leaflock Services was born. Within a week, the young entrepreneur, just into his twenties, put together a small, eager young sales team that marketed his smoke alarm to office buildings, apartment complexes, and hospitals, and his fledgling company took off like a rocket to the stars.

Before his twenty-first birthday, Leaflock found himself wealthy beyond the dreams of the average dreamer, but the enterprising and audacious young gnome was just getting started. He never stopped pushing for other innovations, and, over the next three years, his company filed several major patents. Redhorn was with Leaflock every step of the way, providing the stabilizing hand and mature restraint that kept the impulsive young visionary from flying headlong into the sun. When the company took off, Redhorn found himself making ten times as much money as he had been earning as a mere professor of engineering at a major seat of higher learning.

But Leaflock never made Redhorn a partner in his company, and Redhorn's earnings were a fraction of what Leaflock was taking in. The highest title Leaflock was willing to give to his former teacher was senior engineer, and Redhorn received a steady salary rather than a percentage of the company. He even had to buy his own stock options. Leaflock built Leaflock Services in his own image and for his own benefit. He surrounded himself with qualified experts, like Redhorn, and delegated essential responsibilities as required. He listened to and accepted sound, prudent advice. He publicly bestowed credit where credit was due and told his employees that he regarded them as family. In truth, however, even as it grew in size and value, Leaflock Services remained an extension of the fertile mind of its founder, and Leaflock regarded his employees as the mere background music for his own virtuoso performance. Morgan Leaflock was Leaflock Services, and Leaflock Services was Morgan Leaflock. The company's logo, a stylized padlock in the shape of a leaf, left no doubt about that.

A few months after Leaflock Services lit up the landscape of young innovative high-tech firms, Redhorn realized that the rocket ship he was riding was streaking away into uncharted space. While the engineer was helping to convert Leaflock's ideas for new smoke detectors into marketable products, Redhorn had regarded himself as an essential accomplice in the whiz kid's schemes and a vital part of their shared success. Once the company had been established as a major player in the design engineering field, Redhorn set his sights on developing major modifications in the company's signature gas detection products with the goal of producing an inexpensive residential line of detectors that could be marketed to middle-class homeowners. The engineer envisioned small, efficient Leaflock brand smoke alarms mounted on the ceilings of every home in Tolanica, and he believed that his new designs would engrave his name alongside his former protégé's as a driving force in the company. He even hoped to be made a full partner. Redhorn spent several months working on his new designs, keeping them under wraps for what he hoped would be a grand unveiling. He had taken great pride in the results, which he thought were going to push the company to another level.

When he'd tried to present his plans to the man he'd assumed was a kindred spirit, however, Redhorn discovered his real place in Leaflock's scheme of things. Leaflock dismissed his former teacher's ideas out of hand, declaring that they lacked vision and cheapened the company brand. He told his pragmatic engineer that his company was done with "toys and trinkets," and that he had moved on to bigger things. The mercurial young gnome had been struck by a revelation so grand that it could scarcely be put into words, and he was redirecting the production of his company to the fulfillment of his new vision. While Redhorn listened in silence, the boy phenom launched into a vague and chaotic description of a new top-secret product that had left his former teacher's head spinning. The excited company head would only give his chief engineer the barest hints of his bold new schemes, overwhelming Redhorn with the unprecedented magnitude of his grand plan, and repeating over and over again that Leaflock Services was going to shock the world. Afterwards, the stupefied Redhorn, unsure of what his role in his company head's new direction would be, had left Leaflock's office, walked straight out of the building, and turned into the first bar that he could find, a businessman's watering hole called The Green Olive.

Redhorn had been crestfallen. He had no doubt that the unstoppable Leaflock would be able to bring his big dream to fruition, but where would it all leave the conservative engineer who had discovered the distracted young student, recognized his brilliance, and taught him how to realize his potential? For the first time, Redhorn saw himself not as an essential administrator of an apparatus that he had helped design, but as a worn-out cog in a mechanism that had become too massive for him to comprehend. He felt unappreciated. He felt discarded. He felt old and he felt small. Above all, he felt betrayed.

Redhorn began to regard himself as the victim of an unjust universe, and this injustice tore a hole in his ego that he attempted to heal with dry martinis and cheap sex. He became a fixture in The Green Olive, especially after his wife, Lindi, spotted a couple of suspicious charges on his credit card statement from an account that turned out to be a downtown "health spa." When Lindi petitioned for the deed to their luxury Westside condo in the divorce settlement, Redhorn moved into a midtown apartment within easy walking distance of his office and his favorite bar rather than contest her demands. He sold his car and saved a fortune in daily parking fees.

I'd pieced together Redhorn's profile from material gathered from a variety of sources. What I didn't learn from the office staff at Leaflock Services, I learned from the loose-lipped barkeep at The Green Olive, and what I didn't learn from either of these two sources, I learned from Lindi, a savvy broad with a sweet face who had in the wake of her divorce burned her wedding album, dyed her hair a rich shade of auburn, and lost twenty pounds with hot yoga and a kickboxing class. Other than the condo, the only holdover from her marriage was a teenaged son who boarded at an elite private school in the Peninsula just a fifty-five minute bus ride away.

Lindi had been happy to talk about her ex, and it was clear that she wasn't so much angry with him as disappointed. "Inyon is a brilliant man. He really is. And it's not my fault he's going to let all that brilliance waste away while he burns out his brain with cheap gin. Blame his boss for that, not me. But most of all, it's Inyon's own fault for being such a puppy dog." Lindi spoke around sips from a cup containing coffee, chocolate liqueur, and cream in roughly equal measures. "Without Inyon, that sneaky little bastard Leaflock would still be playing video games in his mother's basement. Everyone thinks Leaflock is a genius, and that he kept Inyon around as a kind of pet, like he was a fucking monkey or something. But let me tell you! Leaflock is big on ideas, but not so big when it comes to making those ideas work. That's where Inyon came in. He took Leaflock's big dreams and designed the means to make them real. And then that fucking juvenile delinquent would take all the credit! And all the money, too. I told Inyon, 'You're just as smart as he is. Come up with your own ideas! Make something of your own!' And then when he *does* design a line of new products—thanks to my encouragement and support—when he makes something that he can put his own name on and walks into Leaflock's office to tell him about it, the arrogant little prick won't even give him the time of day! I kept telling Inyon, 'What are you, a man or a puppy dog? Stand up for yourself!' But, Inyon's more puppy than man. What do you do with a mug like that! What was I supposed to do? Well, it's out of my hands now. He can rot for all I care. My life's just getting started!"

    Having acquired Redhorn's passcode, I waited for the engineer to leave for the day and made my way to his office. Breaking in didn't require my handy set of picks; the locks at Leaflock Services were so cheap that I could defeat them in two seconds with an ordinary letter opener. Once inside, I shut the door and used R3d&Horny! to gain entry into the senior engineer's computer. I scanned his folders, looking for documents that might contain evidence of illicit activity, but nothing leaped out at me. I opened his in-house email account, but found no smoking guns in his office correspondence. I clicked on the icon for his outside email server and scanned his personal messages, but, aside from some salacious online conversations with dames he'd hooked up with on various dating services, I didn't find anything interesting. I was certain that Redhorn was my culprit, but it was apparent that he'd been too careful to leave any obvious incriminating information on his hard drive. I guess that would have been a lot to hope for, but I was often surprised at the carelessness of white-collar criminals.

Time for a deeper investigation. My next step was to access the internet and look at Redhorn's browsing history to see if he'd been using a more discreet online email network. Nothing. I looked for messaging services and chat cafes with private rooms. No dice. I spent a fruitless hour scanning his social media outlets, but, besides discovering that he liked to spill his guts on a well-known conspiracy board catering to dimwits and wingnuts, I came up empty. Was Redhorn too cagey to leave inculpatory evidence where just anyone could find it? Maybe. But I wasn't just anyone. I'd been a professional investigator for nearly a decade, and, if there was a cache of secrets buried somewhere in his computer, I was going to dig it up.

I needed a drink. Figuring that the disgruntled engineer would have something at hand, I started opening desk drawers. When I opened the middle drawer on my right, I discovered a half-filled pint of high-end rye. I found a glass, too, but I held the bottle up in a toast, and with a muttered "To corporate espionage," took a jolt straight from the bottle. The familiar burn of the whiskey on the back of my throat forced a jet stream of cooling air up my nostrils, which ripped the fog from two hours of fruitless investigation out of my brain and caused my drooping eyelids to pop wide open. Say what you want about Redhorn, the man had good taste in booze.

I capped the bottle and returned it to the drawer. I'd dug as deep as I could with the tools at hand, but now I needed a bigger shovel. I went online and downloaded an app that would allow me to rummage through Redhorn's trash.

What I knew about computers could just about fit inside a thimble, but I could read instructions, and over the years I'd learned how to operate a few useful tools. I used to assume that when I deleted a file, it disappeared without a trace. Turns out that's not the case, at least not right away. Typically, the information stays somewhere in the computer's hard drive until it is overwritten, which means that it can exist undetected for quite some time. Leaflock Services provided its employees with an emailing service that used a PST, or Personal STore, file format. Even if an email was "permanently" deleted from the server's trash bin, the file didn't just vanish into thin air. Instead, it lingered somewhere, unseen, sometimes for long periods of time.

The app I had downloaded had the power to sift through data and find these deleted files if they had not been overwritten or corrupted beyond recognition. It was a pretty handy piece of software for a man in my line of work, and, even though I couldn't begin to tell you how it worked, I had made an effort to learn how to use it. Working slowly and with much deliberation, not to mention a few false starts and wrong turns, using the app took time and patience, but that was okay. I had plenty of both.

I did okay. After a couple of hours of mining loose fragments of data from a scattered collection of no-longer-labeled files, I was looking at a substantial pile of gold nuggets. Redhorn was my culprit all right. I had all the proof I needed.

The poor sap. I thought about the defeated look on his face when I'd left his office earlier that day. I wondered if he had seen this coming. He'd lost an important part of himself when the man he considered his friend, partner, and personal discovery had revealed the true nature of their relationship. He'd made bad personal choices, which had cost him his wife and family. And now his poor business decisions were about to cost him his career, and maybe his freedom. I couldn't help feeling....

I snapped myself out of those thoughts. Redhorn's choices were his own. His wife had concluded that he was more puppy dog than man. Maybe he was, but that was no concern of mine. A job was a job, and I had an obligation as a professional to do it to the best of my ability.

I loved my work. It was a new challenge every time. I was good at it, and it gave me a sense of fulfillment.

But sometimes it felt like I was kicking puppies.

Chapter Two

"Alkwat's flaming balls!" Leaflock slammed the palm of his hand on his desktop. He leaped to his feet and began to pace. I could almost see steam shooting out his oversized gnome ears. "That son of a *bitch*! How could he do this to me? After everything I've done for his sorry ass! Alkwat's flaming pecker! I'll kill the son of a bitch! I'll fuckin' kill him!"

The volatile gnome was not taking the news of his senior engineer's treachery well. After circling his desk chair and taking his frustrations out on his desktop one more time, he plopped into his seat and groaned. Waving a hand at the open tablet in front of him, he asked, "Are you sure about this? This is Redhorn? No chance the traitor could be anyone else?"

"It's him all right. The data came from his discarded emails. Redhorn had easy access to the blueprints that he attached to the emails to the buyers. The other emails indicate payment arrangements. It wouldn't be hard to check Redhorn's bank account and see if he received the payments. I could do it if you want me to. I could also track down the buyers if you want. I could trace the email accounts and find the sources of the dough going into Redhorn's account."

"Fuck that." Leaflock waved a hand at me, as if brushing away a fly. "It's just a matter of tracing some electronic communication, and I can do that as well as anyone in the realm. You've given me what I needed: the name of the traitor holding the knife that's stabbing me in the back." The tops of the gnome's rounded ears reddened as his hand clenched into a fist. "So Redhorn's the rat who's been leaking company info. He's been selling off my designs for a couple of months, at least, and now he's emailed the blueprint for my top-secret developmental cell regenerator to a competitor, or to someone who was going to sell it to a competitor, and he was doing it for money. I've staked the future of this company on the success of this device! If it falls into another company's hands, I'll be ruined! And now, thanks to that rat, the secret's out there. A lot of it, anyway. Good thing that blueprint doesn't include the most important component."

The gnome held out one of the printed copies of the email messages that I had brought to him. "And you're sure there's no response to this message?"

I read the message: "Need RAA formula. Name price." The message had been sent by someone identifying themselves only as "Nocturnal" from an overseas-based email service that ensured anonymity for its users.

Looking up, I shook my head. "No. The message was received yesterday, and if Redhorn had responded, the chance that my software would have been able to recover it is high, almost a hundred percent. But I didn't find a return message, which means that Redhorn probably didn't send one yet. Of course, he could have called him on his cell phone, or on a burner."

Leaflock allowed himself a sigh of relief. "Well, that's encouraging. But I'll dig through that email trash myself, just in case your app missed something. I'm sure it's a fine app, but I've got a few tricks of my own."

I kept myself from rolling my eyes. "Knock yourself out."

Leaflock shot me a glance. "No offense, but let's face it. If you were really an expert with data systems you wouldn't have to chase down cheating husbands in order to pay your bills."

I gritted my teeth and let that one pass in silence. But the insufferable jackass was close to using up his free shots.

"And you didn't find that drive I told you about in his office? The special one?"

"Nope." Leaflock had asked me to search the engineer's office thoroughly for a green USB flash memory drive stamped with the company logo. I'd given the office a good going over, but come up empty.

"Are you sure you looked everywhere? Every nook and cranny? You turned over every stone? It's green, like a leaf. And it's got the logo on it. You didn't see anything like that?"

I envisioned the gnome's severed head at the end of a pike and didn't respond.

"Fuck! He must have taken it out of the building." Leaflock was livid, and his face looked ready to pop. "The flash drive itself is worth a fortune. I've only got six of them. I programmed them myself, and they're protected with my own security software. And they're enchanted. The files downloaded onto these drives become tightly encrypted. Any attempt to access the contents of the drive without the right key code will trigger a spell resulting in the instant obliteration of the data files. Even an attempted screen capture will destroy the files. You can't even photograph the screen with a camera, because the image won't take. I designed the drives myself with the help of a witch I know, and they're absolutely foolproof."

"Well, I didn't see anything like that in his office." I assured him.

"Alkwat's balls! If Redhorn needed dough that badly, he could have just asked me. How could he do this to me? The son of a bitch hasn't been the same since his wife left him, but that's no excuse for selling me out." The gnome looked up at me. "Get over to his place and search it. I need to recover that drive before he delivers it to one of my competitors. Do it tonight."

I shook my head. "I've done what you hired me to do, but I've had enough. Get someone else to handle your breaking and entering. My job's done."

Leaflock reacted as if I'd slapped him in the face. "Fuck that! The job's done when I say it's done."

It had been a long day, and I was getting more than a little tired of the autocratic, narcissistic gnome. I'd seen my share of insufferable jerks like him, pricks who believed that their success entitled them to royal treatment, and who expected less fortunate saps to dance to their tune whenever they were in a mood to start whistling. Or maybe I was just feeling a little guilty about my own role in putting the arm on Redhorn, an already beaten man who, to my way of thinking, deserved a better fate than he was heading for, despite his transgressions. I couldn't help feeling sorry for the lug, whose biggest crime, to my mind, was putting too much faith and investing too much emotional trust in the wrong guy. "You've got it wrong, Mr. Leaflock. The job's done when I've fulfilled the terms of our agreement to my satisfaction. You hired me to find out who was selling your company secrets, and I've done that. I'll be expecting a check for my services by the end of the month."

Leaflock seethed for a few moments. "Fine! But I need that drive. It's very distinct, so it won't be hard to find. Consider this a new job. Same rates."

"Sorry, Mr. Leaflock. It's been nice working with you, but we're through."

The gnome pounded his fist onto his desktop. It seemed to be his go-to move when he wanted to remind the world that he was a dangerous individual. "It's one night's work, you son of a bitch! Are you trying to tell me that you're too good for it? Cut the crap! This sort of breaking and entering shit is meat and potatoes for slimy window peepers like you."

"Not this window peeper. Not this time." I put my hat on my head and started to head out the door.

"Get back here, Southerland!"

I stopped and turned to meet the gnome's eyes. "Look, Leaflock. You could have avoided this whole mess if you had treated Redhorn with the respect you owed him. He was your mentor and friend. He quit a good, respectable job to help you start and build your company. From what I've seen, you wouldn't be where you are without him. But you got big. You got successful. And you treated him like a flunky. It's easy to see why he turned on a self-centered asshole like you."

Leaflock's face turned the color of a ripening tomato. "Fuck you! Fuck you and the horse you rode in on, you son of a bitch! Who the fuck do you think you're talking to!" He pounded the desk with his fist, not once, but twice in rapid succession. He was going to break a knuckle if he kept it up. "I built this company! Me! And no one else! That no-talent motherfucker rode in on my coattails. Without me he'd still be grading papers and putting a bunch of useless students to sleep with his boring lectures. You know what my former college instructor is? A plow horse. A fuckin' mediocrity with just enough wit to follow a straight line from one end of a field to another. He's never had an original idea in his life, and now he's nothing but a fuckin' juicehead. Just a sad old drunken has-been. Worse—a never-was! I should have fired his ass years ago, but I propped him up and carried him for old time's sake. I would have made him rich beyond his puny imagination with my new project. But how does he repay me? He turns on me! Sells me out! Well fuck him and fuck you!" Leaflock pointed at the door. "Get out of my office, you fuckin' ingrate! You'll get your money, don't worry about that. The staff's gone for the weekend, but I'll get a check out to you first thing Monday morning. Now beat it! Scram! If you're not out of here in two minutes I'll have security throw you out."

I had the distinct feeling that I'd overstayed my welcome, so I left.

***

I was in a shitty mood when I walked out of the offices of Leaflock Services. Another job well done, Southerland. You caught the bad guy and saved your client's business. This called for a celebration! I spotted The Green Olive down the street and, without thinking about it twice, headed in that direction.

I hadn't taken two steps when I heard an oddly clipped moaning sound from somewhere overhead. Looking up, I spotted a bulky shape perched on top of a streetlight. I stared at it, and it emitted another of the clipped moans that had caught my attention. I blinked. Was that an owl? I'd heard of owls, of course, and I'd seen pictures of them. I'd seen them in movies and on television shows. But I'd never seen a live owl in Yerba City, or anywhere else for that matter. It was a beautiful creature, huddled up there on its perch, with black, white, and orange feathers on its wings and chest, white feathers around its curved beak, a bright orange circle of feathers around each of its large yellow and black eyes, and orange and black feathery tufts above each of them. The bird stared down at me with its intelligent-looking peepers like it could see what was going on in my mind. Maybe it was just my shitty mood, but I had the distinct impression that it didn't approve.

"You want something from me, too?" I asked the owl out loud. "You want me to torpedo a nice little dove for you like I torpedoed Redhorn? You want me to shoot down a pigeon that's had the gall to fly across your path? Well? How much dough are you willing to pay me? Because I'm a professional, and I don't do your dirty work unless you give me some motherfucking dough."

"Fuckin' right, boss." I jerked my head toward the sound of the guttural voice and laid eyes on a disheveled dwarf lying on a flattened cardboard box. "You tell 'em. Yer a perfesh'nal! No dough, no go, and don' let 'em tell you diff'rent, boss!"

I felt blood rushing into my cheeks as I stared at the down-and-out dwarf, face almost entirely obscured by his matted beard and knotted head of long hair. He was covered from the waist down by a stained khaki blanket that was probably a souvenir from his stint in the army. The threadbare covering didn't look thick enough to keep the damp Yerba City fog from penetrating into his bones.

"Say, boss. Got a taste of sumpin for a fellow vet? Jus' a little sumpin for the chill?"

I checked the pockets of my coat, but I'd left my flask at home. "Sorry, bud. I can't help you tonight."

The dwarf nodded with resigned acceptance. "Don' worry about it, boss. I'll get by. Sunny days ahead, they say." His eyes lifted to gaze at something over my shoulder, and his features twisted into a scowl. I glanced back, but saw nothing out of the ordinary, except for the owl staring down at us from the top of the streetlight.

I looked back at the dwarf, who began to shout into the night sky. "Why doncha fuckin' leave me alone—you fuckin' *asshole*! Yeah! Yeah, that's right! I'm talking to *you*, you fuckin' slimy flying fuckin'... fuckin' *snake*! Quit talking' to me! Let me fuckin' sleep, you scaly pile of exter..., exer... you fuckin' pile of shit!" The dwarf looked for something to throw, couldn't find anything, and settled for thrusting at the sky with his middle finger. Then he covered his face with his arm and curled up into a fetal position.

Overhead, I heard another clipped moan from the owl. I looked up and watched the bird spread his wings and fly off into the night. I looked back at the dwarf, who lay facing away from me, huddled beneath the blanket that was now bunched around his chest and shoulders, exposing the lower half of his body to the cool night air. One foot was covered with a worn leather army-issue boot with a hole in the sole. The other leg ended at the knee.

The dwarf had sought help from the wrong joe. I had nothing to offer him. I was no good to anyone, not unless they could afford my fee. I pulled the collar of my coat up over my neck and stared straight ahead as I made my way to The Green Olive, striding down the sidewalk like a jive jasper with somewhere important to go.

When I was inside the bar, I took a good look around the lounge, telling myself that I wasn't looking for anything or anyone in particular. I found an empty stool at the bar, and the bartender set a coaster in front of me. It was the same barkeep who had told me much of what I'd found out about Redhorn. He seemed eager to see me, probably hoping to spill more dope on the poor sap in return for my generous tips. I ordered a whiskey, straight, and turned away from him. I knew more about Redhorn than I wanted to, and I didn't feel like doing a lot of yapping. The barkeep took the hint and left me alone.

My attention was drawn by a news broadcast coming from a television mounted above the bar. The news anchor was babbling about a "monumental" event from earlier in the day when Lord Ketz-Alkwat himself emerged for a ceremonial flyover above the streets of

Aztlan. The anchor cut to a pre-recorded video of a live report of the event from a young and attractive female reporter.

"And there he is, our glorious Dragon Lord, taking to the skies." The reporter's quavering tone told the viewers that she was captivated by the sight. "Isn't he magnificent? This rare appearance by the leader of Tolanica. I'm telling you, my heart is soaring right up there with him! What a wonderful sight to behold."

The camera followed the Dragon Lord as he circled majestically above his capital city.

The reporter lowered her voice and injected it with a tone of adoration. "Lord Ketz-Alkwat is rearing back his mighty head... and... Oh my goodness, would you look at that! He is letting loose a burst of flame into the sky! And there goes another one! Such splendor, ladies and gentlemen. Such grace. The people here on the street are waving the Tolanican flag and chanting the Dragon Lord's name. What a sight. What a glorious day. I ask you, who among us is not moved by this display of magnificence? Who among us is not overcome with pride? What a day to be a Tolanican!" The worshipful commentary continued until the Dragon Lord circled and slithered back into his island compound just off the mainland coastline. The breathless reporter sounded as if she might swoon at any moment, but, with a visible effort, she managed to hold her composure until the cameras quit rolling.

None of us in the bar were as impressed by the rare appearance of old Lord Ketz as the reporter had been, or pretended to be. Ketz-Alkwat had established the Realm of Tolanica some six thousand years before any of us had been born, and he'd been ruling it ever since. To us, he was a simple fact of life, like the sun in the sky. I found it hard to believe that the immortal Dragon Lord had any interest in me as an individual, or in any of the humans who popped into and out of existence in the blink of one of the eyes in that "mighty head" of his, while he himself lived on and on.

When the story was over, the bartender asked me if I wanted another glass of whiskey, and I told him to keep 'em coming. He filled a glass for me and left the bottle. I climbed inside and stayed where I was until, hours later, the barkeep threatened to slap me upside the head with a blackjack and dump me in the alley if I didn't leave.

***

"Th'fuck you talking about, Southerland?"
"Uhhh.... Huh?"
"Alkwat's balls! Are you asleep?"
"Mebbe. Lemme check."

I was holding my phone up to my ear and in the midst of a conversation with Lubank that I couldn't remember starting. "Ummm, yeah," I muttered. "I'm still asleep."

"Well wake up, numbskull! The cops will be banging at your door any second now. You want them dragging you down to their clubhouse in your jammies?"

"I don't wear pajamas."

"Ewwwww! Get out of your damned bed and put some fuckin' clothes on!"

"Jus' a sec." I forced my eyes open and blinked, trying to bring the outside world into focus. My head felt like it was filled with lead, and a sour odor was forcing its way into my stuffed-up nose like a jackhammer. "I don't think I'm in my room."

"What? Where the hell are you?" Lubank was shouting loud enough to wake the dead, and it was starting to work on me.

I rubbed my eyes with my free hand and took a look around. "Looks to me like I'm inside a car. Laying on the back seat."

"A car! Whose car!" Lubank sounded apoplectic, but that was pretty much where he lived most of his life.

"Must be the beastmobile. I've never seen another car with this much room." The beastmobile was my own sweet ride. I'd purchased it from the owner of an escort agency, and the back seat was large enough for me to stretch my six-foot one-inch frame from one end to the other and still have inches to spare. "I must have crawled in here after they eighty-sixed me from that gin joint last night. I don't think I was in any shape to drive. Oh, shit!"

"What!"

"Looks like I tossed up last night's booze party all over my back seat. Guess that explains the smell."

"Terrific! Tell me, sunshine, are you in any shape to drive to my office? You need to be off the streets, and you don't want to be anywhere near your place right now. The bulls are probably kicking in your door even as we speak!"

"Let them. We'll sue."

"Who's this 'we' you're talkin' about, loser? I ain't suing the YCPD on behalf of some drunken bum! There's no moolah in it. The city's got that department running on a shoestring, and they ain't got a pot to piss in. It's no wonder crime is rampant in this town. An honest citizen can't walk the streets at night."

"What would *you* know about being an honest citizen, sleazeball?"

"Hey, *hey*! That's no way to talk about the only man standing between you and a lifetime in the slammer. You're in it up to your neck this time."

"Me? Why? I haven't done anything." I sat up and squeezed my eyes shut to hold back a wave of dizziness as the blood drained from my head.

"That's not the way I hear it, peeper. You better get over here right away. Better the cops find you here with your attorney than hungover, alone, and helpless. You know how those fuckin' bulls are when they smell wounded prey. And try to cook up a reasonable alibi on your way over."

I took a handkerchief out of my pocket and wiped slime off my cheek and chin. "Alibi for what?"

"Never mind—just get here!" With that, Lubank disconnected the call.

I stared at the phone for a second, and then tucked it into my pocket. I wondered what had happened during the night to set the coppers on my tail. At least my mouthpiece seemed to be clued in. The sooner I got to his office, the better, but first I had to figure out where I was and whether I was prepared to go out in public. I was still wearing my slacks and shirt from the previous day, with my tie loosened at the collar. I'd been using my coat as a pillow, and I tried in vain to shake out the worst of the wrinkles before giving up and putting it on. I'd been lucky: the vomit had only settled on the inside liner where the stain wouldn't show, and the outer part of the coat was clean. I was relieved to see that my Albion leather shoes, the only high-quality clothing I owned, were in good shape. I'd kicked them off before stretching out on the back seat and found them resting unharmed next to my hat on the floorboard. Fortunately, I'd confined my upchucking to the other side of the car. I put the shoes on and tightened my tie. Then I grabbed my hat and climbed out of the car... just in time to void what remained of last night's whiskey binge onto the pavement.

When I was finished my stomach was empty, but my bladder was still full. I coughed, spit, and took a quick look around at my surroundings. I experienced a sense of mild relief when I found that I was in the underground parking lot of the building that housed Leaflock Services. After the bartender at The Green Olive had given me the bum's rush, I'd at least had the wherewithal to find my car and the sense to refrain from taking it on the road once I'd found it. No one was around, so I sidled up to a girder and relieved myself, being careful to keep my Albions dry. I needed to rinse out my mouth and wash my face. I also needed a cup of strong black coffee the way an abandoned puppy needs love. But I figured I could hold out until I got to Lubank's.

By the time I'd parked the beastmobile in the vicinity of Lubank's office some thirty minutes later, the rancid odor from the puke on my back seat was causing my guts to clamp down tight on the last remains of bile trying to climb its way up my gullet. I didn't have any way of cleaning up the mess at the moment, but I thought that I might be able to do something about the smell. I visualized the appropriate sigils that allowed me to search the area for an air elemental. I found one that was the size I needed and summoned it. Soon, a twenty-inch funnel of whirling wind was whisking the sour air from the car's interior out through the back window, which I'd cracked open an inch. I smiled to myself. Back in my school days when my teachers were training me in the arts of elementalism, they told me that someday I'd be using my miraculous skills to alter weather patterns for the good of the planet, or to aid in spectacular feats of engineering, or to help fight great wars. I wondered what they'd think about me calling up an elemental to air out my car and make it smell a little less like fresh puke. Maybe they'd be pleased that I'd found such a practical use for my talents. Sure they would.

A ten-minute walk in the cool morning breeze drove away enough of my hangover to make me think that, despite my dubious start, I might be able to make it through the day. My elf-enhanced healing powers helped, too. By the time I'd reached the law offices of Robinson Lubank, I was feeling something close to decent. Then I stepped through the office door and broke into an uncontrollable fit of hacking that brought back the pounding in my temples and once again caused my guts to clench. The reception room was shrouded in a thick haze of smoke originating from a cute curvy blond-haired doll in a too-tight dress sitting behind a desk.

"Hi, sugar! Pardon me for saying so, but you look like something the cat dragged in!" The doll removed a cigarette stub from her polished red lips and used it to light the end of a fresh stick, which she puffed into life. She jammed the used-up stub into an ashtray that was already filled with the remains of several predecessors.

"Hello beautiful," I managed once I got my coughing under control. "I feel about as good as I look. It's possible that I might have had one too many last night. Maybe six or seven. Got anything for me? A little hair of the dog?"

"In your condition? You'll have to settle for some strong coffee. Then maybe we'll see what else we can come up with, loverboy." The curvy dish flashed me a sultry smile that would have made a holy hermit swear off enlightenment.

I groaned. "Gracie.... Did Rob warn you that I crawled out of a pool of puke this morning?"

The doll-faced siren giggled. "Good thing I know how well you clean up. C'mere, sweetie. Let me take you into the rest room and I'll freshen you up. I just put the coffee on, and it'll be ready in a minute. My hubby's on the phone, but he'll want to talk to you as soon as he's off." She shook her head and grabbed my elbow, pulling me in so that my arm pushed into her full breast. "You in trouble again, baby? What are we going to do with you, you bad boy. Whatever are we going to do."

Gracie cleaned off my face and scrubbed at my shirt and tie with a wet paper towel, fussing over me all the while like a mother hen. When she'd done what she could, she poured me a cup of mud, which tasted to me like the elixir of life. She flirted shamelessly with me the entire time and laughed when I became too embarrassed to keep pace with her rapid-fire string of double entendres. By the time Lubank emerged from his inner office, I was actually starting to feel almost alive again. Sixty-five percent, maybe.

Lubank took one look at me and rolled his eyes. "All right, Southerland. If you're done trying to seduce my wife, get into my office. You come, too, Gracie. Your boy toy is going to need all the help he can get."

Gracie winked at me. "Sure thing, baby. I'm always up for a little double-team action."

I shook my head in Lubank's general direction. Gracie, the chain-smoking angel with the effervescent smile, the delightfully bouncy body, and the playful patter, couldn't have been a more striking contrast to her perpetually irascible runt of a husband, and not just because marriages between humans and gnomes were as rare as bankers with hearts. Lubank was dressed in his typical office uniform: a green and yellow checked three-piece suit that was too loud and a dirt-brown hairpiece that lay on his dome like a dead gopher. A cigarette dangled from his bottom lip, and a half-inch of ash hung precariously from its tip. With a groan, I rose from the chair I'd been slumped in. "What I could really use is some bacon and eggs. Breakfast somehow got by me this morning."

"Th'fuck, peeper! This place look like a diner to you? I got a doughnut in my office. Half a doughnut, anyway. It's in the trash, but you can fish it out. Now get in here before the cops come breaking down my door looking for you. Don't you know that you're a wanted fugitive?"

"That's news to me, Lubank. What is it I'm supposed to have done?"

"Besides stabbing me in the back and embarrassing me? Yeah, let's start with that, you bastard!" The gnome led me into his office, and Gracie came in behind me with a pen and notepad.

Once inside, Lubank settled into the chair behind his desk and threw his cigarette into his wastepaper basket where it bounced off the top of a half-eaten chocolate doughnut resting on top of a pile of other trash. Gracie perched her shapely rump on a corner of the desk, and her dress creeped up her gams to her knees.

I fell into a cloth-covered chair and took a long sip of my coffee. "All right, Lubank. What are you talking about? I stabbed you in the back? It couldn't have been me. I was sleeping off a night of hard drinking when you called me, remember?"

"I'm talking about the way you're sticking it to the client I set you up with out of the goodness of my heart."

"You mean Leaflock?"

"Yes I mean Leaflock, you nitwit! Who th'fuck do you think I mean? You're screwing him over, and now he's royally pissed at me for sending you his way! What kind of fuckin' game are you playing at, you dumb fuck!"

I sat back in my chair and shook my head. "I don't have the faintest idea what you're talking about. I'm not screwing over Leaflock. I did what he hired me to do."

"Yeah, you gave him the bastard that was selling him out. Redhorn, right? He told me that. Nice going. But that's not *all* you did, bright boy."

"I might have told him off a little. I might have even called him an asshole. But he had it coming."

"Brilliant business decision, peeper! Pissing off your clients is a *great* way to attract new business. No wonder you have to dress like a bum!"

Despite Gracie's best efforts, the vomit had left distinct brown stains on the front of my shirt and tie. "These looked a lot better when I put them on."

"But the worst part of it," Lubank continued, ignoring my response, "was that you made *me* look bad for recommending you to him. What do you think people are going to say about me when all this gets out?"

"Right. Because it's all about you."

"You bet it is! Tell him, Gracie."

Gracie beamed at me. "Robby is getting an award! The Yerba City Gnomes' Businessman's Association has named him Defense Attorney of the Year. Isn't that wonderful?"

I nodded at Lubank. "Congratulations. Those blackmail files of yours are really paying off."

Lubank scowled back at me. "Leaflock sits on the executive committee. If he's pissed enough off he might rescind the award!"

"Don't worry. I'm sure he can be bought. Besides, I found his guy. Hell, I probably saved his company."

"Is that right, wise guy? Well Leaflock says you ran off with a valuable secret formula. I was on the horn with him all morning, apologizing to that jacked-up jeebo for saddling him with a lousy window peeping punk who walked out of the building with the keys to his kingdom! Did you really think you were going to get away with that?" Lubank clenched his jaw and glared at me.

"I don't know what you're talking about."

"He told me that you copped something called RAA."

"I don't even know what that is. He's lying."

Lubank's face relaxed by a degree. "Well, I told him that you might have a smart mouth, but that you were too much of a professional to steal from a client. He's madder than a fuckin' hornet, though. You're lucky he just set the blues on you instead of putting out a contract. He might do it anyway."

The stubble on my neck was beginning to itch, which reminded me how badly I needed a shave and a shower. "Leaflock is too much of a cheapskate to hire a hatchet man. Not when he can call the cops for free."

"Yeah? Well…, actually you're probably right about that." Lubank tried to pop another cigarette out of his pack, but it was empty. Frustrated, he crushed the empty pack into a ball and threw it in the general direction of his wastepaper basket, missing it by three feet. Without a word, Gracie removed her cigarette from her mouth and, reaching across the desk, slipped it smoothly between Lubank's lips.

Lubank took a long, slow puff and let a stream of smoke drift from his nostrils. He turned to Gracie with an easy smile. "Thanks, doll." Then he turned and stared into my eyes like he was trying to peer into my soul. "You didn't scoop up an enchanted flash drive on your way out of the building last night? Leaflock says you did. If he's right, you made a real dumb play, peeper."

"You know me better than that. Leaflock's got a beef with me because I told him that he could've saved himself a load of grief if he had just treated Redhorn with the respect he deserved. Redhorn quit his job so that he could help Leaflock get started. He did it because he had faith in Leaflock. He believed in him, and he thought that they were friends. But Leaflock's a self-entitled little prick who thinks he's better than anyone else. I more or less told him so, and he flipped his lid. Now he's setting me up just to get even with me for standing up to him."

Lubank nodded slowly. "And you don't know anything about this whatzahoozit? This RAA?"

"I don't know what it is exactly. I know that it's part of a device that Leaflock thinks is going to make him millions. Apparently it's a top secret formula of some kind, but beyond that?" I shrugged. "Leaflock was concerned about a special green flash drive. I think it must contain information about this RAA. Leaflock had me search Redhorn's office for it, but I came up empty. He wanted me to look for it at Redhorn's apartment, but I turned him down."

Lubank's eyes opened wide in surprise. "You turned him down! What for?"

"I told him that the job was done. I'd fingered Redhorn as the guy selling off his proprietary information, and that's all he'd hired me to do. I didn't like Leaflock's attitude. I told him that if he wanted someone to break into Redhorn's apartment, he'd have to find another mug."

Lubank studied me for a few moments longer and then nodded. "All right, that should work. Stick with that story."

"What story? It's the truth."

"No one gives a shit. What's important is that you didn't find a flash drive in Redhorn's office, or anywhere else in that building. And you didn't go to Redhorn's home and search it. You've never seen a fuckin' green flash drive with the Leaflock Services logo on it. And you absofuckinlutely positively do *not* know what RAA is. Got it, genius?"

"Got it. We're going with the 'I'm totally ignorant' defense."

"Good thing you're such a natural."

Gracie smiled at me and shrugged.

I opened my mouth to say something scathing and witty to both of them, but we were interrupted by a voice that rang in from the reception room. "Anyone home? Mr. Lubank?"

"That'll be the cops," said Gracie in a low voice. "I'll take care of them."

Lubank slid out of his chair. "That's okay, doll-face. Tell them I'm surrendering my client peacefully. I'll go with loverboy to the station and make sure they don't mess up his face too bad. They've got nothing on him anyway, so he should be out of there by this afternoon."

Chapter Three

As it turned out, Lubank had been a little optimistic. More than a little. I spent the whole day at the station. It was getting close to eight o'clock by my reckoning, and I was still cooling my heels in a holding cell waiting to be interrogated. Lubank had been in and out to say hello a few times, telling me that he was looking out for me and to be patient.

"The good news," he explained to me, "is that all of these hours are billable, so you'll owe me a fortune by the time this all gets resolved."

"How is that good news?" I asked him.

"It's good news for me."

"What about *me*?"

"Who the fuck cares?"

"Gee, thanks pal." I stretched out on the bare mattress and crossed my arms behind my head. "Tell them that if they don't feed me in fifteen minutes I'm going to break out of here and walk across the street to The Acorn Grill. They can interrogate me there over a plate of fried calamari."

Lubank rose from the chair he'd been sitting in and moved toward the entrance to the cell to peer through the barred door. "Relax, peeper. They're just waiting for a prosecutor from the D.A.'s office to get here. Shouldn't be long."

Right on cue, I heard the clang of a door opening down the hall, followed by the sound of approaching footsteps. Two uniformed cops soon appeared, and one of them opened the cell door. As I stood to go, the second cop brushed past Lubank and pulled a set of cuffs from his belt.

"Not so fast there, cowboy," the cop said. "Let's see your hands."

Lubank stopped halfway through the open door. "Th'fuck, officer. Is that necessary?"

"Orders from the A.D.A. Sorry." The cop sounded anything but as he clamped the bracelet around my wrists.

"Which A.D.A.?" Lubank demanded.

"Costano."

"Costano!" Lubank sounded incredulous. "She's not usually such a hard-ass, and it's not like my client is being charged with a violent crime. What's the deal?"

"She's not alone." The officer shot a glance toward the door, as if making sure that no one had dropped by unexpectedly. "Deet is with her."

"Deet? Oh shit." Lubank's eyes went wide, and for a moment I thought that his cigarette was going to fall out of his open mouth. He quickly regained his composure and drew in a slow breath.

I looked past the officer to Lubank. "Who's Deet?"

Lubank met my eyes. "Officially, Deet is a liaison from the Office of the Tolanican Attorney General."

I nodded. "Let me guess. Leea?"

Lubank's face went blank, and when he spoke his tone had lost its usual feisty edge. "You've really stepped in it this time, Southerland. Take my advice. When they get you into interrogation, play it straight up. None of your smart lip. Trust me, Deet has no sense of humor."

"He's dangerous?"

"Deet's not a he. Not a she, either. Not even a they, and damned sure not an it. Just Deet. Deet will neither accept nor tolerate sex-related labels, not even neutral ones. Deet believes that the root of all social and economic evil is the practice of using gender as a primary means of identifying individuals. I believe such people are referred to as 'pomosexual,' with a 'p.' And, yes, Deet is dangerous. Like a massive fuckin' coronary is dangerous. When you talk to Deet, imagine that you are talking to the almighty Lord Ketz-Alkwat himself, and you *might* walk away with your tiny little genitals intact. If you're lucky."

I didn't say anything in response, but my mind was racing. Leea. The Lord's Investigation Agency, or LIA. The highest investigative and enforcement agency in the Realm of Tolanica. Leea was Dragon Lord Ketz-Alkwat's secret police force, answerable only to Lord Ketz himself. The agents of Leea were everywhere and nowhere, always present, seldom seen. You defied them at your peril, and those who did risked disappearing so completely that their own mothers would forget having given them birth. As the officers led me to the interrogation room, I practiced every technique I knew to slow my heartbeat and calm my thoughts. I focused on willful ignorance and non-resistance, which were sure to be my best weapons in the coming ordeal.

The officers led me to an unmarked door that I knew would open into one of the department's sweatboxes. Inside I would find a metal table bolted to the floor and lightweight metal folding chairs on either side of the table. One-way glass would cover one of the walls, and a camera would be mounted near the ceiling in a corner of the room. I would be able to detect the faint odor of the bleach that had failed to entirely eliminate the bloodstains on the cement floor and walls. The station had a number of these interrogation rooms, and I'd been in most of them at one time or another. Or maybe I'd been in the same one each time. I didn't know. They all looked the same.

The professionally groomed woman seated on one side of the metal table was writing something on a notepad and didn't so much as glance my way as I was led into the room to a chair directly across from her. An officer uncuffed the bracelet from my right wrist and attached it to a bar built into the underside of the table. Lubank took the chair next to me and placed his briefcase on the tabletop.

Without looking up, the woman, speaking in a pleasant, but distracted voice, said, "Hello Robby. Nice to see you again."

Lubank's response was polite enough, but it contained little emotion. "Hello, Luisa. Pleasure as always."

The officers left us to fend for ourselves in the sweatbox, taking care to avoid glancing in the direction of the unmoving figure leaning with crossed arms against the wall near the far corner of the room behind the Assistant District Attorney.

I forced myself to look at Deet, who eyed me in return. A slinky five-foot eight or nine, Deet was dressed in a loose gray suit with a white shirt and a gray tie. Deet's head was completely hairless: no hint of stubble on the bald head or on those chiseled jaws that looked sharp enough to cut diamond, no eyebrows, not even eyelashes. High cheekbones and an oddly flat nose highlighted a face that looked smooth as an eggshell and was the color of bamboo. The pursed lips were too red to be credible; they appeared to have been permanently tattooed with rose-colored ink. Unblinking ebony-colored peepers cut straight into the back of my brain like the blast from a double-barreled shotgun. I'd looked into a lot of menacing faces in my thirty years. I'd seen the mug of a mean drunk, twisted by shame and frustration into bestial rage as he came at me with clenched fists. I'd seen the cold dead eyes of enemy soldiers, desperate to make me die for my realm before they died for theirs. I'd looked into the malevolent glares of powerful witches and unearthly demons, at the deadly stare of a snarling four-hundred pound manticore, and into the glowing red eyes of a sadistic troll as he held the tip of an icepick an inch away from my eyeball while I was drugged and bound. I thought of myself as a tough customer, and it took a lot to unnerve me, but, as I met the probing gaze of those icy black eyes, I was aware of the hairs on my arms rising and standing at attention. I endured that gaze and knew with absolute certainty what it would be like to be a bug pinned to the bottom of a killing jar, waiting to be categorized and tucked away on a shelf.

I blinked first. I had to. Those ebony eyes would blink about the time the earth fell into the sun.

My interrogation began, and it was as long as it was pointless. Assistant District Attorney Costano asked me why Leaflock had hired me. I told her that I'd been hired to find out who was selling proprietary information.

"And you discovered that it was Redhorn?"

"Yes."

"And you told Leaflock that Redhorn was the man selling his company's information?"

"Yes."

"And you have no doubt that it was Redhorn?"

"No doubt at all."

"No one else was involved?"

"Not likely. Certainly not to my knowledge."

What did I know about Redhorn's schemes to sell Leaflock Services's proprietary information?

Only what I had seen in the emails that I had fished out of Redhorn's hard drive.

And what had I seen?

That Redhorn had sold proprietary information to Leaflock's competitors on at least a couple of occasions.

"Including the blueprint for the cell regeneration device?"

"Yes."

Costano paused to write something on her notepad. Probably a reminder to pick up a loaf of bread on her way home. Then she began to ask me about my investigation on Leaflock's behalf and how I had concluded that Redhorn was the one who had been selling company information. I was reluctant to talk about Redhorn, but Costano was persistent. It took a little more than an hour, but by the time she was done with me, the A.D.A. knew everything that I had found out about Redhorn over the course of my investigation.

When she was satisfied that I wasn't holding anything back, Costano changed course. She asked me whether I had searched Redhorn's office for a green memory drive.

Yes, I had.

Did I find it?

No.

Had I done a thorough search?

Yes, I'd tossed the place pretty good.

"Did you look to see if anything had been taped under the desk drawers?"

"Yes."

"And under the file cabinets?"

"Yes."

Had Leaflock asked me to search Redhorn's apartment?

"Yes."

"Did you?"

"No."

"Why not?"

"Because breaking and entering is against the law." (This response brought a brief smile to Costano's lips.)

She asked me more questions about the memory drive, but I didn't have any satisfactory answers.

We'd been at it for a couple of hours, and Costano was looking as tired as I felt, so we decided to take a short break. I was allowed to use the restroom—I was verging on desperate by then—and then hustled right back to the interrogation room as soon as I was finished. Lubank was waiting for me, and he launched into a long salacious story involving a troll, an adaro, a human woman, and a dwarf that could have been male or female. The punch line had something to do with the fact that both male and female dwarfs have long, thick beards. It was a stupid joke, not funny at all, but it ate up the time. No one brought anything to eat or drink, not even when Lubank kicked up a fuss about it and I faked a dizzy spell. Neither of us really expected anything, but it was worth a shot.

After about twenty minutes, Costano and Deet returned to the sweatbox looking well fed and refreshed. Assholes! Deet returned to the space in the corner of the room and seemed to disappear into the wall. Costano returned to her chair. Without preamble, the assistant district attorney asked me what I knew about RAA, and I stuck to the story Lubank had given me: I'd heard Leaflock mention it, and I knew that someone had wanted to buy it from Redhorn, but I had no idea what it was or who he was trying to sell it to.

Did I know what the letters RAA stood for?

No.

Had I tried to guess?

"Red-Assed Acrobats? Rear Admiral Arsonists?" No, I had no idea.

Had Redhorn talked to me about RAA?

No.

Was I intending to sell information about RAA to Leaflock's competitors?

No, I didn't have anything to sell.

Was I working with Redhorn to sell information about RAA to a third party?

No, I wasn't conspiring with Redhorn in any way.

Did I know whether Redhorn had already sold RAA to a third party?

No, I had no knowledge about that.

And on and on and on.

Costano was a seasoned operator, and, despite being the target of her inquiries, I took a professional interest in her work. In my judgment, the A.D.A. was doing a competent, workmanlike job, but it seemed to me that something was a bit off. She was playing it by the book, asking all the right questions and using all the standard tricks of the trade, but, even though she kept at me for the better part of the evening, I never got the impression that her heart was really in it. She had to have known about my background: that I'd served my time in the Tolanican army, and that a good part of my training had included techniques for resisting interrogation. She knew that her routine line of questioning had no chance of breaking me if I was lying to her or holding anything back. Sure, I was tired, and I was hungry, but I'd been grilled much harder than this, probably in that same room. Costano hadn't even brought in extra muscle to knock me around. Hell, she hadn't even threatened to revoke my investigator's license, and they usually *started* with that. Either Costano was doing one hell of a job of setting me up for a sucker punch, or she was simply going through the motions.

Turns out that she was setting me up, all right, but she wasn't the one who delivered the blow. When the gut punch came, it came from Deet. After hours of dancing with the A.D.A., I'd all but forgotten about the still and silent presence in the corner of the room. But Deet hadn't gone anywhere, and, when the opening presented itself, the Leea agent struck.

Costano had been trying a new angle. "When you went to The Green Olive, were you planning to meet Redhorn there?"

"I just wanted a drink. I went to The Green Olive because it was the first bar I saw when I left the building."

The A.D.A. leafed through her notebook and pretended to read over a passage. "According to what you told me earlier, you knew that Redhorn was a regular at The Green Olive, and that, in fact, you learned much of what you know about Redhorn from the bartender who works there."

"That's right."

"So when you stopped by The Green Olive last night, you did so with the hope that Redhorn would be there."

"No, the bar just happened to be handy."

Costano looked up from her notebook and locked her eyes on mine. "Come now, Mr. Southerland. You had to know that there was a good chance that Redhorn would be there. He was there *most* nights, and you knew that."

I shrugged. "I wasn't thinking about it. Like I said, the bar just happened to be nearby."

Costano lifted her eyebrows in an exaggerated way in order to show me how skeptical she was. "Really? I'm supposed to believe that you walked into Redhorn's favorite bar with no expectation of seeing him there?"

Lubank cut in at that point. "Asked and answered, counselor. I'd like to remind you that my client hasn't eaten anything since lunch, and, for that matter, neither have I, although it appears that others in this room have. My client has made it clear that he didn't go to The Green Olive to meet with Redhorn. He went there to get drunk, and his subsequent behavior demonstrates that he did a damned fine job of it."

When the new voice sounded, it was so unexpected that for a few seconds none of us knew where it was coming from. The voice was a clear, almost melodic contralto that could have been either male or female. It contained no menace, no emotion of any kind, really, though it was not pleasant. It was a government functionary's voice, like the voice of a clerk explaining that you are in the wrong office and will need to go to the one on the next floor.

"Mr. Southerland was not in The Green Olive to meet Mr. Redhorn," the voice said. "Mr. Southerland was there to provide himself with an alibi. Mr. Redhorn is dead."

***

Deet and Costano were staring at me, looking for a reaction. Even Lubank was gaping at me, openmouthed. When I'd arrived back in the provinces after my military discharge some eight or nine years earlier, I'd prided myself on my ability to hide my reactions and emotions, to maintain a poker face under stress and when taken by surprise. These skills had increased when an elf, a creature thought by most of the general public to be extinct, had performed a bit of elven enchantment on me that had, as he put it, "enhanced my awareness." Afterwards, I discovered that I was able to perceive my surroundings in a way that I couldn't quite understand, but that mimicked improvements in my senses of sight, hearing, smell, taste, and touch. The elf's magic had also increased my brain's ability to sense my body's inner workings. One convenient result of this development was that my body healed at a rate that was, well, magical. As I grew more and more accustomed to my new abilities, I found that my control over my physical responses to outside stimuli was becoming rather impressive.

For example, when Deet informed us that Redhorn was dead, I felt the surge of adrenaline that poured out of my adrenal glands into my bloodstream. I became aware of my nostrils wanting to expand in order to admit increased oxygen into my lungs. I also knew that my pupils were preparing to dilate in response to the "fight or flight" message that it was receiving from my brain's control center. In that moment of awareness, I did something that up until that point I didn't know I was capable of doing. I canceled the alarm signal that my brain was transmitting. I belayed all orders to panic. I assumed control of my command center and changed the "fight or flight" message to "rest and digest." My body responded accordingly. The gates in my adrenal glands closed, cutting off the surge of adrenaline before it could saturate my bloodstream. My lungs stopped demanding extra oxygen, so my breathing remained even, and my nostrils had no reason to flare. My command center no longer demanded extra alertness from my vision, so my pupils remained steady.

My only visible reaction to Deet's revelation was a slight nod of my head, as if I'd just been informed that fog would be rolling in from the west at sunrise, and I might be needing a jacket.

Lubank's response was more dramatic. Leaping to his feet, he yelped out a strangled "What!" He reached up and straightened his hairpiece, which had slid a few inches to one side of his head and bunched up against a large round ear. "Th'fuck, Deet! What kind of game are you playing at? Redhorn's dead? You spring this on us after two hours of questioning? What were you hoping for, that my client would break down and confess to doing him in? Well, fuck that! My client had no knowledge of Redhorn's death until you mentioned it just now."

Deet's gaze slid off me and settled on Lubank. Costano was staring at the agitated gnome, too, her lips showing the hint of a smile, and it occurred to me that my clever pint-sized mouthpiece had staged an overreaction to Deet's bombshell in order to draw my interrogators' attention away from me.

It was Costano who spoke. "Sit down, Robby. No one is accusing your client of killing anyone. Initial reports indicate that Redhorn died in his sleep of natural causes. A heart attack, most likely."

Lubank glowered at Deet. "Then what the fuck's all this talk about alibis?"

Deet's eyes remained locked with Lubank's. "Mr. Southerland went to The Green Olive hoping to meet Mr. Redhorn. He believed that Mr. Redhorn's life was in danger, and he felt responsible. He'd exposed Mr. Redhorn to his boss and was looking for a chance to give Mr. Redhorn a head's up. And if he was right about an impending threat to Mr. Redhorn's life, he wanted to make sure that he was in a public place so that he couldn't be pinned with the murder."

"Bullshit!" Lubank sat back down in his chair. "If my client had wanted to contact Redhorn, he would have called him."

"He didn't want to be that obvious about it. He was torn. He had been hired by Mr. Leaflock to expose the person selling the company's secrets. Warning Mr. Redhorn would have betrayed Mr. Leaflock's interests. But Mr. Southerland felt guilty. He was hoping for a 'chance meeting' with Mr. Redhorn. If Mr. Redhorn had been there, Mr. Southerland would have done something to help him. He wasn't. So Mr. Southerland tried to drown his guilt in alcohol."

Lubank wasn't buying it. "Th'fuck you sayin'! My client doesn't need any bullshit excuses to drink himself into a stupor."

I'd had enough. "You all might feel less reluctant to talk about me if I weren't here. How 'bout you send me home and continue this deep analysis of my inner psyche without me?"

"We'll let you know when we're done with you," Costano said.

I felt, rather than saw, Deet's eyes turn toward me. "No, that's okay, A.D.A. Costano. I think we can release Mr. Southerland on his own recognizance as long as he promises not to leave town for a while."

Costano looked like she wanted to object, but whatever she was going to say died on her lips after a pointed glance from Deet. An officer came into the room and uncuffed me, and, after retrieving my phone and other valuables from the front desk, I followed Lubank out of the station house and into the lit streets and free air of downtown Yerba City.

When we were half a block from the station, Lubank grabbed me by the elbow and stopped me. "Th'fuck, Southerland! What was all that about? Did you know that Redhorn had bought it before Deet decided to drop it on our heads like a safe falling out a fourth-floor window?"

I pushed my hands into my coat pockets. "No, but I can't say that I'm all that surprised."

Lubank looked up at me. "What d'you mean? Counselor said that he had a bad ticker, right? Did he look all right to you when you saw him yesterday?"

"He'd been drinking, but that's all. But, come on, Lubank. I give him up to Leaflock and his heart just happens to shut down on him? Coincidences happen, but this would be a big one. It's a little too convenient for me."

"You think Leaflock had him knocked off?"

I shrugged. "Sounds more plausible than 'natural causes.' And Leaflock's an excitable little prick."

Lubank's eyes narrowed. "Nah, I don't see it. *I'm* an excitable little prick. That doesn't mean I have anyone knocked off for looking at me cross-eyed. Besides, what does Redhorn's death get Leaflock? Redhorn owes him bigtime. You don't bump off a poor sap when you've got him by the balls—you squeeze him for everything he's got!

Alive, Redhorn can help you get the goods on the competitor who was buying the company info. You can bury them! Dead? Redhorn's no good to anyone dead."

I pulled my hat brim down in the face of a gust of wind. "I don't know. Leaflock doesn't think like you. Revenge might have been all the motivation he needed."

"You're assuming the sap was murdered. We don't know that. And, anyway, it's none of your concern. I know what you're thinking. You're thinking that Redhorn is dead because you ratted him out. Nuts to that! All you did was your job. Whatever Redhorn did, it was his own choice, and you aren't responsible for it. Get yourself some takeout calamari and go home, peeper. It's over."

Lubank went off to find his car and go home to Gracie. I decided to walk to The Acorn Grill, a cozy diner across the street from the police station that offered a decent cup of joe and appetizing fare at prices that wouldn't threaten my ability to pay the month's rent, especially if I skipped on the dessert. My last meal had been a bland chicken salad sandwich at the station almost eleven hours earlier, and my stomach was as empty as a grifter's promise. I was craving a tuna melt with some chowder. And coffee. Lots of black coffee. I could still smell the sour odor of the previous night's cheap whiskey coming out of my pores.

I'd settled into a booth and was sipping some of that coffee when I became aware of a figure sliding into the seat across the table from me.

"We're off the record now," said Deet. "Relax and drink your coffee. Have yourself some dinner. Take your time. We're going to have a nice quiet chat about RAA."

Chapter Four

"You should try the tuna melt, Deet. It's pretty tasty."

"Thank you anyway, Mr. Southerland, but I'm on a special diet."

"Let me guess. You eat private investigators for breakfast." I took another bite of my sandwich and tried not to let any of the filling drop to my plate. Manners, and all that. Deet almost smiled. Maybe. I was pretty sure that I saw the LIA agent's lip twitch just a little, but it could have been a trick of the light.

"You're avoiding the point, Mr. Southerland."

She was right, of course. Rather than deny it, I took another bite of my tuna melt. A tough looking punk in a black suit and matching fedora was sitting on a stool at the counter watching me and not trying to hide it. When the counter man tried to get his attention to offer him coffee, the punk ignored him and kept his eyes on me, as if daring me to do something about it. He had professional muscle written all over him, and I concluded that he belonged to Deet.

I turned my attention back to Deet, who continued to stare at me with peepers that would not blink. I swallowed and used a napkin on the corner of my mouth. Then I looked up and met those peepers. "First, there's no such thing as 'off the record' when you're talking to the LIA. Second, that assistant D.A. questioned me for nearly two solid hours, and the initials 'RAA' never came up until after you talked to her during a break in the questioning. She's a competent professional, so my guess is that she doesn't know what RAA stands for, and she doesn't know what it does. It must be a pretty sensitive piece of information if you didn't share it with her. What makes you think I know any more about it than she does?"

Deet's head cocked to one side a bit before straightening. The movement seemed unnatural and reminded me of something, but I couldn't put my finger on what it was. "You know it exists, Mr. Southerland. You know that it's a formula, and that it's an essential working part of Leaflock's new cell regeneration device. You know from a discarded email message that someone wants to buy it. You had a conversation with Mr. Redhorn yesterday afternoon in his office. Did he discuss RAA with you then?"

"He mentioned it. We didn't discuss it."

Deet's head cocked and straightened again, a movement that seemed almost mechanical. "I believe you, Mr. Southerland. He had no reason to. But then you found the email, and you knew that someone was willing to pay a lot of money for the RAA formula. And Mr. Leaflock told you to search Mr. Redhorn's office for a distinctive green USB memory drive, or flash drive. I'm told that you are a smart man. Did you conclude that the flash drive contained information about the RAA?"

"It seemed like a good possibility," I admitted. "Leaflock asked me if I was sure that I hadn't found a response to the email asking Redhorn to name his price for the RAA formula, and then he asked me about the flash drive. It's a reasonable assumption that the flash drive probably contains the RAA formula."

"Mr. Leaflock expected that flash drive to be in Mr. Redhorn's office."

"He seemed to, yes."

"But you didn't find the flash drive in Mr. Redhorn's office, even though you conducted a thorough and professional search."

"That's correct." Deet's style of questioning was direct and relentless. I took a bite of my tuna melt, if for no other reason than to try to slow Deet down.

It didn't work. "Mr. Southerland, did you go to The Green Olive to discuss RAA with Mr. Redhorn?"

Deet's eyes bored into me like a hanging light bulb in an interrogation room as I took my time chewing. I endured that gaze as long as I could before swallowing and responding to the LIA agent's question. "No. I didn't. I had no idea what RAA meant, and I didn't care. I still don't know what it is, and I still don't care. My involvement with Redhorn ended when I gave him up to Leaflock. Like I said before, I went to The Green Olive because I wanted a drink, and the bar was right down the street." I took another bite of my sandwich.

Deet's expression didn't change, and those eyes still didn't blink. I didn't think it was possible for humans to hold their eyes open that long. The agent waited for me to finish chewing before speaking. "Let's be clear, Mr. Southerland. You went to The Green Olive because you hoped to find Mr. Redhorn there. You felt guilty for giving him up to Mr. Leaflock, an odious little man whom you do not respect. Maybe it wasn't a conscious decision on your part. Perhaps it was your subconscious mind that pushed you into that bar, seeking forgiveness.

Either way, you wanted to warn Mr. Redhorn that he'd been exposed. If that's true, then your only motivation was wanting to atone in some way for ruining Mr. Redhorn's life. A foolish notion. Mr. Redhorn is responsible for ruining his life, not you." Deet finally blinked, once, slowly, before continuing. "But I need to be absolutely certain that you did not go to The Green Olive with the *conscious* purpose of meeting with Mr. Redhorn. More to the point, I need to know whether you *did*, in fact, meet him there, and, if so, whether he discussed the RAA with you. I want to know whether you made a deal of some kind with Mr. Redhorn. And I want to know whether Mr. Redhorn gave you the flash drive, or revealed to you where he hid it. I must tell you, Mr. Southerland, at this point I'm not convinced of your innocence in this matter, and it would be beneficial to you if I were."

I shrugged. "Talk to the bartender. He'll remember me."

"I did. He remembers you. He told me the truth to the best of his knowledge. But you're a clever man, Mr. Southerland, and Mr. Redhorn was a desperate one. It's entirely possible that the two of you managed to meet without the bartender being aware of it. In the restroom, perhaps. The bartender recalls you spending extended periods of time there."

That was more than I remembered, although I didn't doubt it. "Did he tell you how plastered I was?"

"He did. Again, though, a clever man can fool a bartender."

I actually knew a number of ways to make someone believe that I was drinking when I wasn't. My favorite is to throw back a mouthful of whiskey and then pretend to follow it with a chaser from a can of beer. The trick is to not swallow the whiskey, and then, instead of drinking the beer, spit the whiskey into the beer can. When you have a chance, you throw the beer can into the garbage. But that's not what I'd done at The Green Olive. What I'd actually done was to get myself so polluted that I puked all over the back seat of my beastmobile. Worse, most of the vomit had wound up on the carpeted floorboard. It occurred to me then that I hadn't properly cleaned the car yet, and that I was likely going to have to replace the carpeting. I wondered what carpets were going for these days. Maybe I'd—

Deet interrupted my reverie. "Got something on your mind, Mr. Southerland? Mind sharing it with me?"

"Just wondering about my car. I might have to trade it in." I picked up my coffee cup and took a sip.

Deet blinked again. This time it was so rapid that I wasn't certain that I'd actually seen it happen. "Mr. Southerland, did you meet with Mr. Redhorn and discuss RAA?"

I swallowed my coffee. "No, I did not."

"Do you know what the initials RAA stand for?"

"I do not."

"Do you have the flash drive, or do you know where it is?"

"No and no."

"Do you have any knowledge of RAA that you have not revealed to me?"

"I hear that its cost is apparently difficult to put into a cost analysis report."

Deet's expression remained blank. "Nothing else?"

"Nope. That's it."

"You're certain?"

I put one hand on my heart and held the other up with a three-fingered salute. "Scout's honor."

After a short pause, and without so much as a nod, Deet began to slide out of the booth.

"Wait," I said. Deet stopped moving. "Redhorn didn't die of a heart attack. That's hooey."

Deet's pursed lips spread into a brief thin smile. "He's dead, Mr. Southerland, and you didn't kill him. Don't look into it any further. You would gain nothing by it." And with that, Deet slid out of the booth and started for the front door. The punk in the black suit rose from his stool and reached the door in time to hold it open for Deet. He followed the LIA agent out of the diner.

When the agent was gone, I drew in a slow breath and pushed the rest of my tuna melt to the edge of the table. Then I propped my elbows on the tabletop and let my head fall into the palms of my hands. Leea was on my ass. That was fucking terrific.

I spent some time thinking about my interrogation by Assistant District Attorney Costano and my further, more intense interrogation by Agent Deet. I'd spent the whole day cooling my heels in a cell, then questioned for more than two hours, and as far as I could see it had all been a big waste of time. Costano had been going through the motions. Leea was interested in me, but I wasn't really on the district attorney's radar, at least not in any significant way. What had been the point of it all?

And then it hit me. The point had been to keep me on ice while the LIA searched my office and apartment for the missing flash drive. Lubank's office, too? Probably. I'd gone straight to Lubank's after waking up in the Leaflock Services parking garage, and the LIA might have known that. I hoped that Leea had gone easy on Gracie.

I thought back to what must have happened while I was getting pickled at The Green Olive. After I'd left Leaflock's office, he'd called the cops. No, not the cops. He'd bypassed the YCPD and gone directly to the District Attorney's office itself. And then they'd sent assistant D.A. Costano to handle the interrogation, because a mere cop wasn't good enough for an elite citizen like Leaflock. But where did Deet fit into the picture? What was Leea's stake in this matter?

What concerned Deet most was that I might have learned something about RAA, or would learn about it after reading the files on that flash drive. But Costano didn't start questioning me about anything called RAA until we'd all returned from our break. During the break, Deet must have directed Costano to ask about RAA, but the Leea agent hadn't told the A.D.A. what it was. It wasn't likely that Costano knew what RAA stood for, and she probably had no idea what it did. That's why Costano had seemed to be a little off her game. She was as much in the dark about what was going on as I was.

Which meant that Leaflock hadn't called the D.A.'s office after all, any more than he'd called the YCPD. Instead, Leaflock had gone straight to the LIA, maybe directly to Deet. And that could only mean that Leaflock didn't want any law enforcement agency except Leea to know about RAA. Did Leaflock and the LIA have a pre-existing arrangement? It was something I'd have to think more about later.

I recapped my conversation with Deet. Was I worried about the so-called 'liaison from the Office of the Tolanican Attorney General'? You bet I was! Worried wasn't close to the right word. Terrified was more like it. I didn't know exactly what position Deet held in the LIA, but Deet was Leea, and Leea meant trouble. The LIA didn't operate under due process, and it didn't need anything as trivial as evidence or proof to act. If Leea regarded me as an inconvenience, then Leea would brush me aside or swat me like a fly. Deet was concerned that I might know something that Leea didn't want me to know. I didn't, but I wasn't confident that Deet had bought my story even though it was the righteous truth.

That was a problem. But as far as I was concerned the real problem was that a man was dead, and regardless of what Lubank or

Deet or anyone else could say to me, I felt like I was responsible, at least to some degree. I had exposed Redhorn to Leaflock, and Redhorn had died. I'm no wizard when it comes to math, but that wasn't a difficult equation to follow. It was hard for me to believe that my actions hadn't played a part in Redhorn's death, and I wasn't going to be able to look at myself in the mirror again until I knew for sure one way or the other. And that meant that I needed to know all about the information that Redhorn had been peddling. I needed to find out everything I could about RAA. And I needed to do it without falling into the clutches of the Lord's Investigation Agency.

***

A thick mist had settled on the dark downtown streets of Yerba City when I walked out of The Acorn Grill. The nighttime traffic was thick as drivers strained to make sense of the chaos of reflected headlights, taillights, streetlights, and traffic lights clashing together in the fog. It was a Saturday night, and the sidewalks were teeming with pedestrians, hands buried deep in pockets and hats pulled low over foreheads, moving with purpose in every direction and somehow managing to sift smoothly through the disorder without serious incident. I made my way into the crowd, picking up the rhythm of the street, heading for nowhere in particular but wanting to roll with the tide of pedestrians and breathe in the night air.

The elf's magic had left me acutely aware of my surroundings wherever I happened to be, and yet I never heard or otherwise sensed the creature soaring through the air behind me until I felt my fedora plucked off my head. I looked up and spotted a graceful pair of wings soaring away from me, my hat dangling underneath. As I watched through the fog, my hat fell from the air toward the sidewalk, and the bird that had taken it from my head glided to the top of a streetlamp. The bird twisted its head halfway around its body and stared back at me with huge round eyes. An owl! Was it the same owl that I'd seen earlier that evening? It looked the same, but I didn't know if I'd be able to tell one owl from another if they were the same breed. As I stared back in amazement, another owl, identical to the first, appeared out of the fog from higher up and perched on top of the corner stoplight. Now two owls were staring at me, studying me, as if curious to see how I would respond to losing my hat. I'd lived all my life without seeing an owl, and now I'd seen at least two, maybe three, in one night. I wasn't sure what to make of it. Then again, maybe there was nothing to it. Just a couple of birds in the night.

I tore my gaze from the owls and began to search for my fedora, hoping that it hadn't blown off the sidewalk into the street. The hat had sentimental value for me. It had once belonged to a friend I'd made in the Borderland, one of my fellow grunts who hadn't made it out alive. It had taken me a number of years to take the hat out of my closet and start wearing it, but it fit perfectly, and I'd come to think of it as a part of who I was. I pushed my way through the pedestrians, upsetting the rhythm of the street, until I found the fedora. It had fallen upside down onto the sidewalk, and I scooped it up before anyone could step on it. It felt heavy, and I became aware of something lying inside. I turned the hat over, and a limp brown rat plopped unmoving to the sidewalk, causing a group of young men approaching from the other direction to skitter away in surprise. I kicked the dead rat into the gutter, and began scrubbing out the inside of my fedora with a handkerchief. I studied the handkerchief, looking for blood—or worse—but it appeared to be clean. I scrutinized the hat, and once I was satisfied that it had suffered no damage, I pushed it down onto my head and looked up into the foggy night sky, searching for the owls. They were no longer perched on the streetlamp, however, and, even though I stretched my elf-enhanced awareness as far as I could, I was unable to detect any sign of them. Shrugging, I resumed my walk. It had been a strange day.

***

When I got back to the beastmobile, I was disappointed, but not overly surprised, that the elemental was gone. That's a problem with elementals. Most of them aren't too bright—in fact, a good many of them are barely sentient—and they tend to be unreliable and difficult to control. I'd commanded the elemental to keep blowing the stink out of my car until I returned, but then I'd been away for a lot longer than I'd anticipated. At some point the air spirit must have broken free from my command, or maybe just forgotten about it, and gone off to frolic in the air currents. It happens.

I got into the beastmobile and felt my nose wrinkle. It was going to take more than a continuous jet of air to eliminate the stench. I drove to the nearest filling station, and wiped the back seat and carpeted floor down with a wet rag while the attendant was gassing up the car. I also bought one of those pine-scented air fresheners that come in the shape of a tree and hung it on the rearview mirror. The damned thing looked ridiculous and smelled worse than the barf, and five minutes away from the station I flung it out the window.

The people who had tossed my place had been real pros. They hadn't left any drawers hanging open, and they'd made an effort to leave all my stuff where they'd found it. They'd even left behind the extra bills that I keep stuffed in a sock for emergencies, like if I ran out of booze on a cold night. They'd probably cracked my safe, but I didn't see any evidence of it. Nothing was missing from it, and the safe hadn't been damaged. All in all, my place was none the worse for wear. I could tell that they'd been there, though, because after climbing the stairs to my upstairs apartment I discovered a clue. A business card was sitting on my kitchen counter. It was a simple card, plain white with no logos or fancy borders. The name "DEET" was typed in all caps in the center of the card with a phone number underneath. Using my keen powers of deduction, I concluded that Deet had sent agents into my apartment. Sure, maybe I didn't need to be a trained investigator to figure that one out. I'll give you that. I turned the card over and read a handwritten note that consisted of three words in neat printed letters: "Don't leave town."

Fine, I thought. It wasn't like I had any vacation plans at the moment anyway.

I took off my hat and coat and threw them onto my sofa. The best thing I could have done then was to put the day's events out of my mind, take a shower, and climb into bed for a good night's sleep. What I did instead was to fill half a water glass with some bargain-bin rye whiskey. I carried the drink into the living room, sprawled out on my sofa, and thought about Redhorn. Deet had been right. I had gone to The Green Olive at least half hoping that he'd be there. I'd needed a drink after leaving Leaflock Services, and it wasn't because I'd been feeling festive after a job well done. Not that I hadn't accomplished what I'd been hired to do. No, I'd fulfilled my contract to the letter, and if my client and I hadn't parted on the best of terms, well, that was his problem. I'd done a professional job, concluded our arrangement, and walked out the door. Everything should have been copacetic.

But it wasn't. The truth of the matter was that I'd plucked a poor, down-in-the-mouth guppy out of the pond and fed him to a shark. So what had I intended to do about it? Why had I hoped to find Redhorn at The Green Olive? To apologize? Fat lot of good that would have done. To ask for forgiveness? Why? To make myself feel better about gutting him? Alkwat's balls, I hoped that wasn't the case. I didn't want to believe that I was that kind of pathetic asshole. I put my glass to my lips and started to take a drink of the whiskey, but stopped when I realized that I didn't want it anymore. I set the glass down on my coffee table and pushed it away from me.

Redhorn wasn't an innocent man. I knew that. He'd been guilty of corporate espionage, selling his company's secrets to get back at a heel that he'd thought was his friend, but who instead had been using him to benefit himself. Regardless of his reasons, what Redhorn had been doing was a crime. It was unjust. I'd handled a few other similar cases, and I'd never regretted the results. This one bothered me, though, and I couldn't quite put my finger on why. Maybe turning thirty had made me sentimental. Maybe I was getting soft in my old age.

Well, nuts to that! It had been a hell of a day, and it had begun with me face-down in my own barf in the back seat of my car. I wasn't going to end it by drinking myself into oblivion on my sofa. It was past midnight, but I had things that needed doing. It was time to get off my duff and move. I hauled myself to my feet, slipped back into my coat, grabbed my hat, and headed for the stairs.

***

Redhorn's midtown apartment was an upstairs unit in a gray concrete two-story complex that looked like a storage depot. It was a place where the residents went home alone to eat a microwaved dinner, unwind with a drink and a little television, and crawl into a single bed after working an eight-hour shift in an office cubicle. The complex held twelve apartments, and I doubted that any of the people who lived there knew each other's names. I parked the beastmobile a block away from the complex and walked back down the quiet, unlit sidewalk until I reached the building and climbed to the second floor.

I tore the crime tape off the door to Redhorn's unit, picked the lock, and stepped inside. Ever since the old elf had pressed a sliver of crystal into my forehead the year before and changed the way I perceived my surroundings, I'd no longer needed light to get around in the darkness. My enhanced awareness superseded my vision in a way that was beyond my comprehension, and it was easier for me to think about what I was doing as simply seeing in the dark. I closed the door behind me and began to search the apartment.

I figured at this point the odds were long against me finding Leaflock's enchanted flash drive, or anything else of value, in the dead man's home. The cops had already been there, and maybe the LIA, too, and I had no illusions about them leaving anything interesting for someone like me to find. Mostly I wanted to get a sense of how Redhorn had been living in his final days and to open my awareness to anything that seemed significant for some reason, maybe because it was odd or out of place. And, you never knew. Maybe Redhorn had hidden the drive before he died. Maybe the cops and Leea had missed it. Maybe I'd have better luck. Sure I would.

The apartment was small, not much more than five hundred square feet. The only living room furnishings were an overstuffed chair, a small side table, a folded TV tray leaning against the wall, and an eighteen-inch television balanced on top of a four-legged wooden stool. The walls were bare and uninteresting: no paintings, no family photos, and no wall safe. Just a window overlooking the street. I did a quick job on the room, making sure to look under the chair and to dig into its cushions, but nothing leaped out at me. Nothing in the room suggested that Redhorn had intended to stay in the apartment for any length of time. He had watched some television there, but he hadn't left anything of himself in the room, nothing to make him feel at home. It wasn't a *living* room at all. It was a waystation, and nothing more.

The kitchen told me a different story entirely. Like the living room, it was small, but it had a lot of belongings packed into it. The first thing I noted was the fully stocked spice rack and a variety of pots and pans hanging over the counter. The spices seemed exotic and expensive, like they'd come from a specialty shop. At least they weren't the grocery store variety that I was used to. A plastic tub filled with rice sat on the counter beneath a wok hanging with the other pots and pans. I enjoyed Huaxian food, and the sight of the rice and the exotic spices caused my stomach to growl. I wished that I had finished that tuna melt sandwich.

I opened the cupboard under the sink and found a trash container. I didn't relish rummaging through Redhorn's kitchen garbage, but a snoop can find a lot of interesting treasures in another man's trash. This container had been recently emptied, however, and all I found was a used paper napkin and a wadded up plastic wrapper.

The wrapper turned out to be an empty rice bag whose label indicated that Redhorn's preference was for the local grocery store's generic brand of "Extra Fancy White Rice," grown locally in the central valley of our own Caychan Province. I made sure that no flash drives had been hidden under the plastic lining of the waste basket. Satisfied, I returned the basket to the cupboard.

    I opened the oven door and breathed in the lingering scents of baked dinners. I ran my fingertips over the grill and along the bottom of the interior and felt the traces of grease and food crumbs. It was an oven that had seen a fair share of use. I opened drawers and cabinets and found more dishes, eating utensils, cups, and glasses than anyone would expect to find in a single man's kitchen, certainly a lot more than you'd find in mine, and all of the items were carefully arranged and organized to make efficient use of the small amount of space. I noticed the absence of an automatic dishwasher, which meant that Redhorn washed his dishes by hand. The sink was empty, and all of the dishes had been dried and put away. A dish towel hung on a rack that was attached to the oven door. I felt it and noted that it was too dry to have been used in the last couple of days. Finally, I moved to the refrigerator, debating whether or not to peek inside. I wanted to see what was in it, but I didn't want light to spill out and illuminate the inside of the apartment. I settled for cracking the door open a couple of inches and blocking the light as best I could with my body. A quick look showed me that the refrigerator was well stocked with a variety of food, and, judging by the brand names, Redhorn had been something of a gourmet. Interesting. Whereas the living room contained next to nothing of Redhorn's identity, the kitchen was filled with the man's personality.

    I tackled the bedroom and bathroom next, although the latter had only a shower stall with no bath. The washcloth draped over the spout inside the shower was still damp, and the towel hanging on the rack outside the shower was damp enough to indicate that it had been used the night before. In contrast to the kitchen, where everything was in its proper place, various items in the bathroom, including a double-headed safety razor, a can of shaving cream, a tube of roll-on deodorant, a toothbrush, a tube of toothpaste, a roll of dental floss, a comb, and a bottle of hair tonic were scattered on the counter next to the sink. I also found some nail clippers and a few stray clippings. It looked like he was going all out to be presentable. In the bedroom, I found a nice suit, along with a belt, a shirt, a silk tie, and a hat laid out over a chair, with a pair of shoes and one sock on the floor in front of it. The bed was made, but the covers were wrinkled in the way they would be if someone had been lying on top of them. I went through Redhorn's closet and drawers, but found nothing noteworthy, other than an unopened box of condoms alongside his underwear and handkerchiefs. At one point he'd been hopeful about his prospects as a newly liberated bachelor, but evidently his optimism had been unwarranted.

The last remaining point of interest in the bedroom was a small desk. A space on the desktop indicated where a computer had been, but it was gone now, undoubtedly in the hands of the coppers. I rifled through the desk drawers, not expecting to find anything, and I wasn't disappointed when I didn't. I checked to see if Redhorn had taped a flash drive to the bottom of any of the desk drawers, but I came up empty. I went through the waste paper basket near the desk, and found nothing of interest. A portable shredder stood next to the desk, and I checked the receptacle. It was empty, though I could smell the dust of shredded paper. Either Redhorn kept a clean workstation, or the police had taken everything that might be important.

As I'd expected, I hadn't run across any green flash drives, or any flash drives at all for that matter, regardless of color. I felt like I'd seen everything there was to see, and it hadn't been much. I took one last look around the bedroom and living room, and headed for the front door. Except for learning something about Redhorn's eating habits, my trip had been a waste of time.

As I passed by the kitchen, I felt something nagging at the back of my mind. Something about eating habits.... Something I'd seen.... Something that didn't feel quite right....

The rice! Exotic spices in the spice rack, gourmet food in the refrigerator—and locally grown generic white rice in a plastic tub? Not pearl-grained Arborio? Not long-grained Sindhu basmati? Not wild Ghanaian brown rice from western Ghana? Not fragrant jasmine rice from the Spice Islands in the Huaxian Empire? I went back into the kitchen and emptied the tub of rice into the wok. I dug around in the rice grains and found two objects of interest: a cheap off-brand cell phone and a bright green USB flash memory drive stamped with the logo for Leaflock Services Corporation. Fucking lazy coppers, I thought to myself, and dropped the drive and the cell phone into the inside pocket of my overcoat.

Chapter Five

I got out of the apartment and headed down the stairs. When I reached the sidewalk, my attention was drawn by a motion somewhere above me and off to one side. I jerked my head around, but saw nothing. I stood silently, listening to the night and sniffing the air. Nothing seemed out of the ordinary. I scanned the night sky, but whatever had caught my attention was gone. I shrugged, thinking that lack of sleep was making me jumpy.

I'd parked on the street down the block from Redhorn's apartment complex, and I hadn't walked far when I spotted a dark shape the size of a small boulder leaning against the driver's side of the beastmobile. As I approached, the shape began to stir. I saw a flare of light as the "boulder" struck a match across the tread of the beastmobile's rear tire and lit up a hand-rolled cigar. Closing the distance until I was standing in the street next to the squat little man, I glared down at him from a three-and-a-half-foot height advantage, knowing that the pint-sized motherfucker wasn't the least bit intimidated by me. He was covered to the ankles in a broad, but otherwise child-sized, overcoat, and the brim of his hat was pulled down over his eyes. All I could see of his face was a pug nose and a wide smile filled with teeth that had been filed to razor points. He stuffed the cigar into those teeth and tilted his head to meet my glare.

"Find anything interesting?" he asked in a voice that sounded like a twelve-year-old with a chest full of barbed wire.

"What are you doing here, Ralph?"

"Taking in the night air." The stumpy creature pulled his coat tighter around his bulky body. "Brrr, it's chilly! I'll never get used to this fuckin' fog. It's like breathing ice-cold seawater. How do you stand it?"

"This is summer haze. The real fog comes in winter. You'll love it, if you're still here."

"Let's hope not. Answer my question, jughead! Find anything interesting in Redhorn's apartment?"

"Redhorn? Never heard of him. Times are tough. I was doing some B and E trying to supplement my meager income."

"Sure you were, Southerland. That doesn't sound like something you should be admitting to the LIA, though."

"That right? You gonna run me in?"

"I'm gonna whap you upside the head if you don't tell me why you're wasting your time investigating a death that isn't any of your business instead of doing the job you're supposed to be doing." Ralph pulled the stogie from his lips and blew a stream of foul-smelling smoke in my direction.

"Redhorn's death *is* my business. It's connected to a case I'm working on."

"It's connected to a case you finished up yesterday." Ralph gestured in the general direction of Redhorn's apartment. "No one is paying you to investigate that sap's death."

"No one is paying me to do a favor for you, either."

"You're not doing it for me, dumbshit. You're doing it for the elf. You owe him, and you know it."

I looked away, frustrated. Ralph was a nirumbee, an odd creature native to the Baahpuuo Mountains in the province of Lakota. Never numerous, the nirumbees had been driven to near extinction more than a century ago with the coming of the large-scale timber and oil industries to Lakota Province, and the ones who had survived had been herded into poor isolated villages. Ralph was a throwback to the time when nirumbee warriors protected a tribal community of their people in the mountainous regions of what became northwest Tolanica. Shorter than a dwarf, Ralph was broader and more muscular than any dwarf I'd ever seen, with a chest like a beer keg and biceps as big as grapefruits. He was agile, too, capable of acrobatic feats that would dazzle a monkey, and fiercer in a scrap than a jungle cat. The first time I'd seen Ralph, he had brought a troll to his knees, leaped ten feet into the air, and dropped face first into an earth elemental, which, at his command, had whisked him away under the surface of the earth.

After that, Ralph had revealed that he was a high-ranking member of the Lord's Investigation Agency and was now working in Yerba City. He'd also revealed to me that he'd been secretly embedded in the LIA by the elf who had given me my enhanced awareness, and that the elf had given him the same gift. The nirumbee warrior was playing a dangerous double game, heading up LIA activities while furthering the elf's complicated long-range scheme to overthrow the Dragon Lords, who had been ruling the Seven Realms since they had conquered and nearly obliterated the elves from existence thousands of years before.

"I'm not sure what you expect me to do," I told Ralph. "I don't know who that heartstone belongs to."

"You're an investigator. You're supposed to investigate. Isn't finding people one of the things lowlife punks like you do?" Ralph waved toward the apartment again. "You found out where Redhorn lived, didn't you?"

I shoved my hands into my coat pockets. "That was a tough one. I looked him up online."

"And that was fucking brilliant! Now do something equally brilliant and find out whose heart is trapped in that stone. You've had a month already. You'd'a found him by now if you'd'a been tryin'. Instead, you're out here in the middle of the night wasting everyone's time screwing around in places where you don't belong. You need to get your ass in gear! The elf says that we don't have a lot of time."

"So you keep saying. But he hasn't told *me* anything. And I've got to earn a living, which means I've got to take jobs. Rent and whiskey aren't free."

"Yeah, well bad news, chump. You aren't gonna get a dime from your last job. Leaflock thinks you betrayed him, and he ain't paying you jack shit."

"We'll see about that. And how do *you* know about it, anyway?"

Ralph snorted. "I'm Leea, you nitwit. We know everything."

"You don't know whose heart you've got locked away in that heartstone."

"Yeah? Well that's your fault. Tell me that you've at least got a lead."

I shrugged. "I'm working on some things."

"Quit tryin' to bullshit a bullshitter. That shit ain't nothin' but code for 'I ain't got nothin'.'" The nirumbee took the homemade stogie from his lips and spit specs of torn leaf into the gutter. He returned the cigar to his mouth and its tip flared red as he glared up at me.

I glared right back. It was turning into a regular glare-fest. "How do I even know he's still in the city?"

"The heartstone would let me know if he's moved on. We've been over this, bright boy."

"Yeah, yeah. When the body moves too far from the heart, the body slips into a coma. But the body sends out some kind of signal that attracts the heart and tries to pull it back into range. That's how you were able to trace the body from Lakota to Yerba City: the heartstone let you know which direction to go. But how does that work?"

Ralph shrugged. "Fuck if I know. I touch the heartstone and I can feel something pulling me in the right direction. I'm a warrior. One of our shamans could explain it to you if you ever get out to the Baahpuuos. If they felt like it, that is, and if you could understand it. It's a lot of mumbo-jumbo to me."

"But the heartstone isn't pulling you now?"

"Nope. Which means that the heart is in range and the body is awake. It doesn't need the heart to be any closer, so it's not pulling at it anymore."

"And there's no chance that the heart's owner is dead?"

The nirumbee waved that idea away. "As long as his heart is safely locked in the heartstone, the body can't die. You could run it through a meat grinder and it would be good as new by morning."

"Neat trick."

"Sure is." Ralph looked up at me and winked. Although he had never come right out and confirmed it, I was sure that the nirumbee warrior was speaking from personal experience.

Ralph pointed at me with his cigar. "But the heartstone isn't much of a help anymore now that it's in range of the body. I can't be using up my time looking for the mug it belongs to without blowing my cover at the agency. The elf had a feeling that whoever took our mystery boy would bring him to Yerba City, and he told me to look you up if that was the case. He said that you were capable of finding our boy, but I'm beginning to wonder. Tell me you're at least making some progress."

I let out a breath and prepared to summarize the situation. "Somebody snatched our boy in Lakota Province, right? We don't know who our boy is, but we know he's somebody special because at some point his heart had been magically taken from his body and put into a heartstone for safekeeping. That basically makes our boy immortal as long as the heartstone is secure. Anyway, our boy gets taken somehow and transported out of range of his heart, which puts him in a coma. The kidnapper drives sleeping beauty out here to Yerba City, where he would have remained in a coma. The elf, for reasons he hasn't shared with either of us, sends you with the heartstone to find our boy and bring him back to Lakota. Using the heartstone to guide you, you made your way here to Yerba City in that rattletrap van of yours. How it made the trip in one piece is anyone's guess."

"Hey!" Ralph interrupted. "That van is a classic!"

"It's a bucket of bolts. Be that as it may, once you brought the heartstone within range, the owner of the heart would have regained consciousness, right? I've checked with every hospital and private clinic in the city looking for a recent comatose patient who suddenly woke up. I've also put the word out with a few of my shadier contacts to see if they've heard anything. So far it's no soap. Like I said, I'm working on it."

"You call that working? A few phone calls?"

"Yeah, well I don't do miracles. You don't like it, get someone else."

Ralph pulled himself up to his full height, all thirty-something inches of it. "Here's the deal, tough guy. Stop wasting your time with these side jobs. Concentrate all of your efforts on finding our boy, and start getting some results or I'm gonna have to kick your sorry ass all the way to next Tuesday. And just in case you don't think I've got what it takes to cut you down to size...."

Ralph held up a hand and snapped his fingers. As soon as he did, I felt the ground disappear from beneath my feet, and I fell straight down into a hole. Before I could even get my hands out of my pockets, the ground clamped shut around my waist, halting my fall and pinning my arms to my sides. I was now eye-to-eye with the nirumbee, unable to move no matter how hard I strained.

The nirumbee stepped toward me until his face was an inch from mine and smiled, showing me his pointed teeth. His breath could have stunned a troll. "You find our man, Southerland. Don't take any other jobs until you finish this one. The elf is your only client now, and I'm the elf's representative, which means you're working for me. If you need beer money, you let me know and I'll see what I can do. You owe the elf a debt, and it's time for you to start paying it off. Do we have an understanding, big man?"

I nodded. "Fine. We have an understanding. You wanna get me out of here? My face itches."

"I'll let you out when you answer my question."

"What question?"

"Did you find anything interesting in Redhorn's apartment?"

I looked Ralph dead in the eye and shook my head. "Nah, man. Wasted trip."

The nirumbee took a puff from his cigar, pursed his lips into a circle, and blew a long stream of smoke into my face. Then he stepped back a pace and I felt the earth elemental that he commanded push my feet back up to ground level. I brushed loose dirt off my coat.

Ralph flipped his cigar butt into the street. "Better watch your step, Southerland. You never know what you're gonna fall into."

***

Life can humble you sometimes, even when you're six-one, two-ten, battle-tested, and hard as rocks. Sometimes a little humility can be a good thing. But as I made my way back home through the fog-shrouded night after my meeting with Ralph the LIA agent, Ralph the nirumbee warrior—Ralph the motherfucking runt!—I wasn't seeing it that way. I was pissed off, and I wanted to take it out on someone. Ten years earlier, I would have walked into the diviest dive bar I could find, knocked down a couple of pitchers of beer, looked for the toughest pug in the joint, and broken a pool cue over his head. I like to think that I had matured a bit now that I was thirty, so I settled for going home and pounding the shit out of the homemade heavy bag that I'd hung from the ceiling in my laundry room.

I'd been at it for fifteen minutes when Chivo came wandering in from wherever he'd been roaming and started slurping down the bowl of yonak that I'd left for him next to the washing machine. At that point, I don't know who smelled worse, him or me. Sure, I'd been sweating out the last of the previous night's cheap whiskey, not to mention all the jailhouse coffee that I'd poured down my gullet at Clubhouse Copper, but Chivo reeked perpetually of roadkill and the garbage that he'd rooted through in neighborhood trash cans. Syphon, a willing air spirit under my command, did all it could to push the foul odors out an open window and into the night, but, together, Chivo and I were more than the determined elemental could handle. It could have been worse. At least we were both housebroken.

Even though Chivo had found a home in my laundry room, I still kept a watchful eye on him whenever we found ourselves in close quarters. I'd been told that the goat-headed rat-tailed monster was the legendary Huay Chivo, an ancient sorcerer who had lost his mind resisting the conquest of his territory by the armies of Dragon Lord Ketz-Alkwat. He had disappeared for centuries, only to turn up in my back alley rooting through my garbage can. I'd called Animal Control to come and get him, but the critter had escaped the clutches of their agents. I hadn't cared for the puffed-up blowhard who'd arrived at my house with his team of eager tin soldiers, so, later, when the Huay Chivo returned to my laundry room, I'd decided that Animal Control didn't need to know about it.

The creature rose up on his hind legs, grasping the bowl with hands that appeared to be human if you ignored the lethal-looking claws. He tipped his head back and poured the yonak down his open snout. Well, most of it, anyway. The rest of it ran down his chin and into his whiskers. If the old sorcerer had ever had table manners, he'd lost them along with the last traces of his humanity. He was ninety-nine percent beast now, albeit a clever one, with only the dimmest memory of ever having been anything else. Chivo spotted me watching him and lowered the bowl from his mouth. He leveled a stare at me with red eyes that glowed like a troll's, and the spikes that ran down the center of his back snapped to attention.

I clenched my jaws at the wave of nausea that passed through me, and then took a deep breath until it subsided. "Knock it off, Chivo. You know that has no effect on me. Anyway, don't you know that you're not supposed to bite the hand that feeds you? Or make him sick with your death stare?"

Chivo lowered his eyes, and his spikes relaxed back down on his back. I chuckled. "Good boy," I told him. He dropped to all fours, carefully placed the bowl on the floor, and began scraping the remains of the bloody soup off the sides of the bowl with a long, thin tongue.

I shook my head. I had no idea why the legendary monster had decided that I was a "friend." I had no doubt that he could rip me to shreds with his horns, claws, and teeth if he'd a mind to, and he had a set of magical skills that I didn't understand. He could open a locked door, for one thing, and leave it locked when he closed the door behind him. I'd seen him stop a bullet in midair. And when he locked eyes with someone, he could make them instantly and violently ill. Except that he couldn't do that last thing to me. I was immune to that bit of sorcery for some reason, and I suspected the healing powers that came with the elf's gift to me had something to do with it. Maybe it was the fact that he couldn't inflict me with his whammy that made Chivo treat me with respect. I'd come to respect him in return after he saved my life a month earlier when I was staring down the cold steel barrel of a forty-four, out of time and out of ideas, waiting to be put down like a sick dog by the murderous loogan on the other end of the gat. So I set a bowl of food out for the mange-infested critter every night, and I gave him space to sleep in my laundry room.

But I wasn't going to make him my pet, even if he would allow such a thing. I thought of Chivo as a lodger, free to come and go as he pleased, which was something he was going to do anyway whether I wanted him to or not. But I didn't hinder him. As long as he needed me to, I would ignore his fetid body odor, tolerate his occasional displays of crazy, give him free room and board, and hide him from the government authorities that were searching for him. I owed him that much.

I left Chivo curled up in the bed I'd made for him under the window and went upstairs for a shower. When I was done, I put on a robe and went back down to my office with the flash drive and cell phone that I'd found in Redhorn's apartment. It had been a long day, and sunrise wasn't that far off, but I was invigorated after my workout and shower, and I knew that sleep wouldn't be in the cards for another hour, at least. Besides, I was curious about what might be on the flash drive. Redhorn had taken pains to hide it, and I wondered what he had been so anxious to keep secret. The disgruntled engineer had been living a lonely life since separating from his wife, and I hoped that the drive contained something more significant than a collection of dirty videos. Well, only one way to find out. I sat at my desk and plugged the drive into a free USB port on my computer.

The drive was passcode protected, of course. I'd been expecting that, but I was still disappointed. It looked like I was going to have to contain my curiosity for a bit. Or would I? Hey, it had worked before, so why not give it another go? What would be the harm? Shrugging, I typed in R3d&Horny! and hit the enter key.

My screen went black. A second later, the stylized leaf/padlock logo for Leaflock Services appeared in the center of the screen. One second after that, a single word appeared above the logo: "Congratulations!" Two seconds after that, two words appeared below the logo: "You're fucked."

I stared at my screen, waiting for something else to happen. Nothing did. I hit the escape key, but it had no effect. I pulled the drive out of the computer. I tried the function keys. I tried control-alt-delete. I clicked my mouse button a few times. The screen remained unchanged. I turned off my computer, waited sixty seconds, then ten more just to be sure, and turned the computer back on again. Congratulations! I was still fucked.

***

As I expected, I was able to catch Lubank and Gracie at their office the next morning. It was Sunday, but neither of them knew the meaning of "a day off." The reception room was empty when I walked in, but Lubank's inner office door was open and, even without quite knowing how, I knew that they were both inside.

I announced myself from the entryway: "It's me, Lubank. You busy?"

Lubank shouted back at me from inside his office. "We're having breakfast. Grab a bottle from Gracie's desk and come on back."

I selected a half-filled bottle of rye from the drawer where I knew Gracie kept her supply of beverages and brought it with me into Lubank's inner sanctum. The attorney was sitting at his desk munching on an egg-and-sausage sandwich that had come out of a vending machine while he studied something on his computer screen. Gracie was perched in a chair that she had pulled up to the desk and was making some handwritten notes on a printed form in a manila folder. She held a coffee cup up to me when I came into the room.

"Be a dear and sweeten this up for me, will ya honey?"

"Say when," I told her. She waited until I'd poured half a finger of rye into her coffee before stopping me with a "When!"

Without looking away from his screen, Lubank waved an arm at the coffeemaker on the far side of the room. "Grab some coffee for yourself, peeper. Then grab a seat. I'll be with you in a minute."

After hanging my fedora on the rack next to the office door, I poured myself a cup of morning pick-me-up, added a splash of the rye, and parked myself on Lubank's leather sofa. Gracie crushed out the cigarette she'd been working on and took a sip of her coffee. She favored me with a coy smile. "Get some Saturday night action last night, champ? You look like some cute number put you through the wringer! And here I thought you were saving yourself for me." Her eyes drooped and her lips curled into a pout.

I shook my head and held the hot coffee cup against my temple. After giving up on my computer a few hours earlier, I'd had a couple of drinks to make myself drowsy, but sleep had proved to be elusive, and I'd only managed a few brief minutes of shuteye in the midst of a lot of fitful tossing and turning. I wasn't exactly hungover, but things weren't all peaches and cream, either.

Gracie rose from her chair and walked over to sit next to me on the sofa. She put her cigarette in her lips and began massaging my shoulders. "You poor baby. You've got too much tension in you for someone who got lucky last night. You must have struck out again, you poor dear."

I made an effort to relax and give myself over to Gracie's tender ministrations. I had to hand it to her: the gal really knew what she was doing. I think I must have groaned, because Lubank looked up from his computer screen with a smirking smile.

"Th'fuck!" The lawyer shook his head. "You two want me to step out for an hour or two?"

Gracie pressed her fingers gently into my trapezius muscles on both sides of my neck. "Don't be silly, sweetie. I don't think we'd need more than five minutes. This poor darling hasn't had a lot of opportunities lately. He's probably primed to pop."

I glanced sidelong at Gracie. "Gee, thanks, doll. 'Preciate the shoulder rub, though. Tough day yesterday."

Lubank snorted. "And now I suppose you need me to bail you out of another jam. What'd you do this time, besides call your latest client an asshole?"

I took a long sip from the coffee cup and let the hot liquid roll down my throat. Gracie stood, gave my cheek a little pat, and walked back to her chair.

I sat up in the sofa and turned my attention to Lubank. "I need Leaflock to pay me what he owes me. I did the job for him. Just because I told him what I thought of him doesn't give him the right to withhold payment for my services."

Lubank looked up from his computer screen. "Who told you that he wasn't going to pay?"

"Just a little something I heard through the grapevine."

Lubank thought for a moment and then waved a hand in dismissal. "I'll get you your money. He's got no proof that you took his flash drive, and I'll explain that you're too much of an imbecile to know anything about whatever's on it anyway. You'll owe me fifteen percent of your fee, though."

"Two percent," I countered.

"Ten percent, and I'm only going that low because you need the rest of it to pay off what you already owe me."

"Fine." I didn't feel up to arguing about it any further. "I've got other problems to deal with."

Lubank stuffed the last of his breakfast sandwich in his mouth and talked around it. "Fuggin' righ' you do. You're on Leea's radar, and that's never good."

"Yeah. After you left me out in the cold last night, I ran into Deet again."

Lubank gripped his temples with both hands. "Alkwat's fucking balls! Tell me you kept your trap shut, at least. You're still here, so I guess it can't be all that bad."

"I don't know. It's hard to say." I told Lubank all about my conversation with Deet.

When I was done, Lubank leaned back in his chair with his hands behind his head and looked off into nothing. After a few moments, he sat back upright and lit himself a cigarette. "Any idea about what this RAA shit is?"

I scratched at my unshaven chin. "Not really. I gather it's some kind of formula. It must be a key component of Leaflock's cell regeneration gizmo, but I have no idea what it does, or what it looks like. Deet was very concerned about it, though. Someone searched my apartment yesterday, probably looking for the flash drive."

Lubank nodded. "That must have been Leea. They searched this office, too. I think that Deet knew that your apartment was clean before the interrogation started. And did you notice that Deet stopped the session when Costano started pressing you about possibly meeting Redhorn at his favorite watering hole?"

"Yeah, that occurred to me."

"And then Deet came up with that bullshit about you going to the bar to establish an alibi."

I nodded. "I think that Deet knows all about RAA, what it stands for and what it does. But Deet didn't tell Costano anything about it. It must be highly sensitive information. Think about it. Deet is LIA, Lord Ketz-Alkwat's own private elite security force. Deet is trying to contain any knowledge about RAA, which might mean that Lord Ketz himself doesn't want anyone to know about it. Deet was afraid that I had met Redhorn at the bar and that we'd talked about it, or made some sort of deal." I thought for a second. "It would be interesting to know when Redhorn actually died. Was it early in the evening, or later on? It must have been later, or Deet would have known that I couldn't have met him in the bar."

"And if it was later, then Deet knew that you couldn't have killed him, because you were in the bar all night."

"And by the time I left the bar I was in no shape to kill anybody."

Lubank took a drag on his pill. "It's a safe bet to assume that Leea knows everything."

I thought about it. "Deet told me that he doesn't.... I mean that she... they.... Deet doesn't think I killed Redhorn. So we can also assume that the LIA isn't thinking about me for Redhorn's murder, if he was murdered. I mean, he might actually have had a coronary."

Lubank nodded. "So does this mean you're done with Redhorn?"

"Well...." I told Lubank about going to Redhorn's apartment and searching it.

Lubank didn't seem surprised. "And you found no evidence of murder?"

"No. It looks to me like he was getting ready to go somewhere fancy. He'd showered, shaved, and brushed his teeth. He had a suit of clothes laid out, but it looks like all he managed to get on was his underclothing and one sock. Then, I think he might have had a seizure of some kind and fallen onto the bed." I shrugged. "A heart attack fits the scene that I found."

I leaned forward on the sofa. "I found something else, though. And this might be big." Lubank and Gracie gave me their full attention, and I told them about finding the cell phone and the green flash drive.

When I was done, Gracie's only reaction was a wide-eyed, "Wow." Lubank leaned back in his chair and puffed his cigarette as he thought about what I'd told him. Then he turned back to me and asked, "I don't suppose you've seen what's on that flash drive, have you?"

"Well, funny thing about that...."

***

"Alkwat's flaming pecker! Th'fuck, Southerland! Of all the lamebrains I've ever run across, you've got to be the fuckin' lamest."

Gracie was more sympathetic. "Oh, sugar. Don't bother buying a new computer. At least not before you pass a competency test." Well, okay, maybe she wasn't more sympathetic, but somehow it sounded nicer coming from her.

I squirmed in my seat. "It seemed like a good idea at the time. I mean, that passcode had worked before. How was I to know that the flash drive would react to a wrong passcode by turning my computer into an expensive paperweight?"

Gracie sighed. "Honey, plugging a strange flash drive into your computer is like drinking from a bottle that ain't got no label. And if it asks you for a passcode, you better know what it is before you try to enter it. You're lucky it just froze your computer. It could have stolen all your files or secretly embedded some spyware that would have copied all your keystrokes and transmitted them to some other user. Say, buster, don't you have any virus protection?"

"Sure, I think so."

"Yeah? What kind do you have? And when's the last time you upgraded it?"

"Uh, I'm not sure. Doesn't it upgrade automatically?"

Gracie slapped a hand on her forehead. "I hate to say it, sweetie, but you kind of brought this on yourself. You would think that a lug in your line of work would be more careful. When you get around to buying yourself a new computer, let me set it up for you."

"You think I'm going to need a new computer?"

"It had a good life, baby, but it's gone now. Sorry."

Something cold grew in the pit of my stomach. "All my financial records are on that computer."

Lubank smiled in the direction of his wife and then turned back to me. "Let me guess. You didn't back any of it up."

My failure to respond gave him all the answer he needed.

The gnome reached up and casually adjusted his hairpiece. "Well, my friend, you'd be truly fucked except for one thing. A few months ago I had Gracie install some spyware into your computer so that it would send backups of all your files to a private server that we keep in a secure location. So your files are all safe, and you can download them to your new computer as soon as you get one."

A wave of anger rose from my chest. "You've been stealing my files?"

Lubank leaned back in his seat, and his mouth widened into an expansive smile. "Not stealing. Backing them up. And you're welcome."

I felt a surge of blood swell the veins in my neck, and my hands clenched into fists. "You son of a bitch! Those files are private!"

"And thanks to me, they're safe. Don't worry. I've been giving you a discounted rate to back up your files, since I didn't ask for your permission. It's all itemized in the statements that Gracie sends you. You know, the ones you don't bother to read. I think that it's listed under 'Client Protection Services.' Of course, now that you know about it I'm going to have to stop giving you the discount. That's okay, Gracie will take care of it starting with your next bill."

A thought struck me. "Wait a minute—when did this happen? I never brought my computer to you."

Gracie waved her hand in dismissal. "Of course you didn't, silly. I let myself into your office one day when you were away. I was only a minute, though, and I didn't disturb anything."

I felt my jaw drop, and I couldn't think of anything to say.

Gracie laughed. "Oh, sweetie." She crossed one leg over the other at the knees and favored me with a smile as bright as the morning sun.

Lubank reached across his desk and handed his wife a lit cigarette before turning back to me. "What can I say, Southerland. You can be a real blockhead sometimes, but Gracie likes you. That's why I extend all this extra service to you. And it's a good thing that I do, too, or you'd be shit out of luck with your financial records. As it is, we've got them stored, safe and sound."

I finally found my tongue. "You could have at least asked me."

"You kidding me, peeper? Number one, you're too protective of your privacy. You would never have agreed to having copies of your computer files sent off to a server that I controlled. Number two, you would have objected to my fees. I'm not cheap, and you're a fuckin' tightwad."

I turned my steeliest glare on Lubank, the one that brings weaker men to their knees. "If I find out that you put hidden mikes or cameras in my apartment...." I left the threat unspoken. I thought that it would sound more menacing that way.

Naturally, Lubank was unfazed. "Fuck that. Those devices are expensive, and I'm not going to waste that kind of dough just to watch you sit around in your undershorts drinking beer and eating frozen pizzas."

I continued to stare at the slimy gnome, telling myself that I would go over my office and apartment with a fine-toothed comb the first chance I got.

Gracie brought my attention back to the problem at hand. "What are you going to do about that flash drive? You still want to see what's on it, doncha?"

I tore my stare away from Lubank and looked over at Gracie. "Yes. I do. Leaflock's company logo was on the message that the virus left behind. He told me that he'd had the drive enchanted. I think that he also protected it against breaking and entering. The idea was that if some dumb sap stole the drive and tried to open it with the wrong passcode, he'd get hit with a virus." I slouched into the sofa. "Which is exactly what happened." Another thought struck me then. "I hope that the data on the drive is still good. Could the virus have wiped it?"

Gracie nodded. "It's possible. Especially if it was part of the enchantment that protected it against screwing around with the data files." She turned to Lubank. "What do you think, dear?"

The gnome shrugged. "Maybe." He turned to look over at me. "If Leaflock was worried about someone trying to steal data from his special drives, he might have programmed the virus to wipe the data from the drive, just in case. On the other hand, he might have wanted to make sure that he didn't lose any of the files on the drive, in which case he would have installed a virus that only attacked the intruder's computer, rather than the data on the drive. There's only one way to find out. You'll have to get past the passcode and try to access whatever is in it."

"Great. Got any ideas?"

It was Gracie who answered. "Sure do, sugar. Walks in Cloud."

"Uhhh.... Come again?"

Gracie slid her cigarette to the corner of her mouth and smiled. "Walks in Cloud. She's a computer tech that I work with sometimes. A real wizard, and I mean that literally. If anyone can help you, she can. Believe me, honey, you've never met anyone like her."

Lubank was shaking his head. "Forget it, doll-face. There's no fuckin' way that Southerland can afford the likes of that broad. I mean, you've seen his finances."

Gracie turned to her husband. "I'm sure we can work something out, sweetie. I'll give her a call and see if she's available." Gracie rose from her chair and walked to stand over me. She leaned down, kissed me on the forehead, and then reached up and gave my cheek a pinch. "Don't worry, honey. Gracie will take good care of you, just you wait and see." She winked at me and disappeared through the door.

Chapter Six

"Something I can help you with?"

I looked down at the heavyset woman inside the doorway. "Are you Walks in Cloud?"

"Yep. Walks in Cloud..." the woman slapped at the side of her wheelchair, "...and Rolls on Land. Are you Southerland?" I nodded, and she pulled the door open as she wheeled herself back. "Come on in."

I stepped through the door into a dimly lit workshop. "Thanks for seeing me on a Sunday."

The wheelchair-bound computer tech that Gracie had referred to as a "wizard" pushed the door shut behind me. "No problem. I work when I feel like it, which is one of the benefits of being my own boss. Besides, weekends are just an arbitrary designation. Who came up with that idea, anyway?"

"The Dragon Lord, probably. He must have realized at some point that we would all be more cooperative if he didn't work us to death."

"Well, I'm sure the old lizard meant well." Walks in Cloud held out a chubby hand, palm up. "You got the doohickey?"

"Doohickey? You mean the flash drive?" I pulled the drive out of my pocket.

"Whatever, Jack. Gimme."

I handed over the doohickey, and she studied it through glasses as thick as cola bottles. "Hmmm. Mm-hm. Hmph!" The tip of her hand-rolled cigarette flared and sputtered as she filled her chest with sour-smelling smoke that was neither tobacco nor cannabis. After blowing the smoke out the side of her mouth, she looked up at me with a discerning eye. "Pretty. And interesting. Hold it for a sec." Walks in Cloud handed the drive to me and used both hands to wheel her chair to a table at the back of the room.

I followed her, and when she once again held out her hand I returned the drive to her. She plugged it into a small tablet, and after a few seconds the passcode page appeared on its screen. She looked up at me. "This drive is enchanted, you say?"

"Uh-huh. And any attempt to open it with the wrong passcode launches a mean virus."

"Yes, Gracie mentioned that on the phone. Hmm. Okay, pull up a seat and keep your trap shut. This will take a few minutes, and I need to concentrate."

"I could come back later," I offered.

"No. I need you here."

"What for?"

Walks in Cloud ignored my question. "Would you like some coffee? The sludge in the pot's been there since sunup, but I can whip up a fresh batch for you if you want."

"I'll take what you've got. Black."

Her lips widened into a smile. "A man after my own heart. Do you mind getting it yourself? One for me, too. No sugar, lots of cream." I crossed the room to a coffeemaker that appeared to be in its second decade of heavy service and poured us each a mug of high octane swill strong enough to lift an SUV. I placed a mug on the tech's worktable and perched myself on a nearby wooden stool.

After we'd put away a few swallows of the bitter brew, Walks in Cloud began staring at the passcode screen on her tablet. Following instructions, I kept my trap shut while she stared and stared, grunted occasionally, and stared some more.

Fifteen minutes passed. I should have been bored into a stupor, but I actually found myself fascinated. I spent the time studying Walks in Cloud, looking for evidence of who she was. Her long hair, so black that it seemed to absorb light, was tied into a single braid. It hung from the back of her head and over her shoulder to her lap and reminded me of the thick ropes I'd seen on the fishing boats hauling squid out of the bay. The stub of her cigarette, no longer burning, dangled from the corner of her mouth as if attached to her bottom lip. She was wearing a pink flannel robe that covered her shapeless body down to her toes like a blanket. Her fleshy arms and chubby hands rested on the arms of her wheelchair and never moved. I got the impression that nothing below the tech's neck mattered to her all that much, at least when she was focused on her work.

Nothing was happening on the screen, which was blank except for a box waiting for a passcode, but the tech's mahogany-brown eyes moved back and forth behind her specs as if she were speedreading a digital novel. Remembering what Leaflock had told me about the enchantment on the drive, I asked, "Did you get past the encryption?"

In response, she shot me a brief, but meaningful look that conveyed her strong opinion concerning foolish questions from uneducated laymen before resuming her work.

When Walks in Cloud finally tore her eyes from the screen and turned toward me, I realized that I'd barely been breathing, and I felt like a man waking from a trance. She frowned then and snatched a pad of paper off her worktable and wrote something on the top page with a ballpoint pen. She ripped off the page and handed it to me. "I can get you to the information on that drive if you want me to. That's what it'll cost you. Payment up front."

I looked at the figure and choked on my coffee. "That seems a little steep to me."

The computer wizard shrugged. "Suit yourself. You know the way out."

"Whoa now, hold your horses. If I can get you the dough, what do I get in return?"

"All of the information on the drive."

"That's the problem. I don't know for sure what's on that drive. It might be useless to me. For all I know, it's someone's secret porno stash. I don't want to have to pay a fortune for something without knowing what I'll be paying for."

"Then don't. Ain't no skin off my nose."

"But what if the data is worthless?"

"You're going to have to pay to find out."

"And what if the data is corrupt?" I continued. "For all I know, anything that was on that drive was wiped out by the virus."

"I can assure you that the files on that drive are intact."

"Can you? How do you know that? All I saw you do was stare at a screen that displayed nothing except a passcode box."

The computer wizard gave me a quick smile. "Then you didn't see very much."

I took a sip of scorched coffee and considered my position. Redhorn had taken pains to keep that drive hidden, and I was reasonably sure that it contained information about RAA. About what it did, and maybe even the formula for it and how to make it. But how much was it worth to me to find out?

A lot, apparently. I found myself wanting that data like a dog wants a hambone. "What about the virus? Can you download the files without the virus coming along for the ride?"

Walks in Cloud sniffed. "I've met the virus, and it obeys me now. You don't have to worry about it anymore."

I stared at the tech. "What do you mean, 'it obeys you'?"

She shrugged. "I mean that it won't bother you no more if I tell it not to."

I continued to stare at the woman. "Gracie said that you were literally a wizard."

"Did she?" The tech took a sip of coffee and peered back at me through her thick specs. "Gracie is a sweet lady. But while I may be a wizard, I'm not quite a witch. I can't defeat the enchantment on this drive. Which means that while I can read the contents, I can't do much with them. It will be the same for you. You'll be able to plug the drive into a USB port on your computer and access the files, but you'll only be able to read them. You won't be able to edit them or move them."

"Can I copy the files?"

Walks in Cloud relit her dead cigarette and took a puff. "Normally, if you can read a file, you can copy it." She pointed the revived cigarette at her screen. "In this case, though, the enchantment won't allow you to, and I won't be able to do anything about that." She took another puff and blew smoke out of the corner of her mouth. "Take it or leave it."

I considered what she was telling me. "I'd like to be able to see that data. I want to know if the data is going to be worth anything to me once I get access to it. You're asking me for a lot of dough, and I feel like I'm walking in blind. Are you sure you can't download a sample so that I can see whether I want the rest?"

Walks in Cloud's face twisted into a scowl. "You're not listening to me, Mr. Southerland. I agreed to see you because Gracie assured me that you were a serious man. But if you can't work with me on my terms, then beat it. I've got work to do, and I don't need you wasting my time."

I gave up. "I'd love to get into that drive," I admitted, "but I can't come close to scratching up enough dough to pay your bill, especially when I don't know if it will be worth it. I'm sorry. Thanks for the coffee. What do I owe you for the consultation?"

Walks in Cloud's scowl turned into a sympathetic smile. "My treat. It was a pleasure." She hesitated, as if a new thought had come to her. "Listen. I told you that this drive was interesting, and it is." She leaned her head so that her braid fell to one side, and then she reached back, pulled it over her shoulder, and began fiddling with it. I could see that she was working something out in her mind, and I waited to see what would come of it. After a few moments, she lowered her eyes and began murmuring to herself. "Yes... mm-hmm.... It *is* very interesting.... Very, very interesting. Truth is, I wouldn't mind.... And then there's.... Hmmm...." The tech seemed to come to a decision. She looked up at me, her eyes absurdly magnified behind the thick lenses of her specs. "Tell you what, Jack. Let's crack that thing open, just for shit and giggles. Let's walk right into it. Together. Then we'll come to some sort of fair arrangement once we've seen what we've got. Okay?"

"What kind of arrangement? Some kind of installment plan?"

The tech's smile broadened. "Maybe. Or maybe we can work out an exchange. You seem like a decent enough fellow, and I hate to see you leave here unhappy. It could be that I might have a need for someone like you. And...." The tech frowned in thought for a moment. "And maybe you can help me with the drive."

I hadn't expected that. "Help you? How?"

Walks in Cloud blinked once, slowly, before she answered me. "Mr. Southerland, I wasn't entirely honest with you. I told you that I can get you the data, and I meant what I said. I can do it, but... but the truth is that it's going to be a little more complicated than I let on. This is a tricky little nut, and, working alone, it will take me some time. Days... weeks maybe. But we might have an easier time cracking it if we try something more... unconventional." She smiled. "If we work together, you might even be able to get what you need before the end of the day. Tell you what.... Help me out, and no charge until we see what we've got. Then maybe we'll work something out. Can you follow instructions?"

"Depends on the instructions. I'm no techie."

Walks in Cloud laughed, and the laugh lit up her face. "Oh, I can see that. Don't worry, soldier. It won't be more than you can handle. At least I don't think so. And you might even enjoy the experience. You won't forget it, that's for sure."

***

"You're sure about this?"

"Quit being a baby, Southerland. Sit still."

I had switched over from the wooden stool to a faded, but comfortable padded chair. Walks in Cloud was taping something that looked like a computer chip to the back of my neck. She had wheeled herself right up against me in order to position the chip, and I could feel my nose flare at the sour odor of the smoke coming from her cigarette. When the chip was secure, she attached one end of a thin cable to it.

"I'm not going to get electrocuted, am I?"

Walks in Cloud shrugged. "Probably not."

"You're not very reassuring."

She wheeled herself to her worktable and plugged the other end of the cable to her tablet. I brushed some cigarette ash off my chest, noting that it had left a gray smear on my shirt, right next to the brown one. Then she wheeled herself directly in front of me and looked her setup over with a critical eye. "Okay, that should work. Just sit back and relax."

I took a breath and leaned back. The relaxing part was going to be more difficult. "What happens next?"

Walks in Cloud smiled. "The fun part."

"Goodie."

The tech wheeled herself to the side of the room and came back with what appeared to be a three-foot long wooden pipe, the kind we used to use in the Borderland after lights out for smoking hashish. The mouthpiece seemed odd to me, however. It was much narrower than I expected, almost coming to a point. Walks in Cloud filled the bowl of the pipe with some kind of dried herb that smelled like something you'd step in while mucking out a barn.

"You know, actually, I don't smoke."

"Oh, hush, Southerland. You won't exactly be smoking it. Before we get started, you'll need to switch off your cell phone. You won't want to be disturbed." I pulled my phone out of my shirt pocket and shut it down. When she was satisfied that I wasn't going to be bothered by any outside communications, she lit the herb in the bowl of the pipe with a match and gently blew on it until the flame died down. Then she extended the mouth-end of the pipe to me. "Put it in your nostril."

"Huh? My nostril?"

"Lean your head back and stick it up as high as you can. Quickly now."

I hesitated, wondering what the hell I was getting myself into.

"Trust me, Southerland. Gracie has done this with me several times, and she's still around to talk about it."

She'd never talked about it with me, I thought to myself. I wondered how much her husband knew about it. I took a deep breath, leaned back, and slid the end of the pipe up my nose a half inch or so.

Walks in Cloud lifted the bowl of the pipe up to her mouth and wrapped her lips around it. Before I could say anything, she drew in a deep breath through her nose and forced it out her mouth in a sudden violent puff.

A bomb burst in my head. White light poured out of my eyes, ears, nose, and mouth. At least, that's the way it felt. I think that I probably screamed, but all I could hear was the sound of the blast. I became aware of a chaos of colors, every color that I'd ever seen and maybe a couple that I hadn't, swirling, shifting, colliding, blending, separating, and speeding away in every direction. I was unaware of my body; I was a wave of energy shooting and twisting my way through the colors at an impossible speed. The effect was dazzling. I didn't lose consciousness—if anything, I felt more conscious than I ever had in my life—but I ceased to think. I just... existed, and I reveled in my existence, in my... aliveness. I was, and would ever be, alive, gloriously alive, endlessly alive, life itself, life living, life existing, life being. I was life with one purpose, and that purpose was to live. Fulfilling that purpose was satisfying beyond measure, beyond comprehension. I lived in timeless, placeless existence, and I was life itself.

And then I became aware of another life, and, with that awareness, I was dismayed. I wasn't life, I was only *a* life. I became aware of... not so much space, or borders, but of the concept of separateness, of the existence of a living thing that was not me. And with that, I became conscious of myself as an individual existence. I was overcome with sadness and a sense of profound loss. I tried to turn inward and find the place where I had once felt whole, with no sense of anything separate from me.

An emotion touched me from outside myself, a feeling of comfort and assurance. The feeling began to register as words: "It's okay. Don't run. Stay here. Stay calm. Everything is happening the way it's supposed to happen. Stay here with me. It's okay. I brought you here. Let me guide you now. It's okay to trust me. You'll see."

The comforting continued until I began to accept it. It was okay for another living thing to exist. We could both live. We could share the experience of living. I'd been wrong to resent this other living presence. I began to crave the presence, to embrace it in order to be whole. I wanted to absorb it, to merge ourselves into something larger. I began to reach out.

"Easy there, Jack. It's not that I'm not flattered, but let's not get carried away."

I backed off then, and felt a rush of thoughts and memories flooding my consciousness. I had a name. I was Alexander Southerland. And with the memory of my name, I regained not only my sense of self, but my desire to remain an independent entity.

I formed a thought. "Where are we?"

I heard a thought. "We're in a place that's not a place. I call it the Cloud. It's not the *cloud*, I mean, that's really a series of storage devices located... well, don't worry about it. Just do what I tell you and you'll be fine."

"I feel like I'm dreaming."

"We need to ground you before your mind wanders too far down la-la lane. Think about some place you've been where you were happy. Any place will do."

"I've got a place."

I did, in fact. During my days in the service, I'd undergone a series of hypnotherapy sessions involving meditation, sedatives, and a lot of psychobabble that I didn't fully understand. Probably some magic, too. Anyway, I'd learned how to call up my "happy place," a memory of a real place where I'd once felt a sense of profound peace. The place was a waterfall in the jungle that I'd run into while on a patrol detail in the Borderland. I'd somehow been separated from my unit and found my way to a narrow stream of water plunging down a twenty-foot incline into a dark pool before continuing on its way into the brush. I'd seen the waterfall during a break from a solid week of heavy rains, and I imagined that the fall was reduced to a trickle during most of the year. I'd been lucky enough to see it at its peak, and I'd spent at least an hour listening to its roar and watching the water roll over the rocky face into a swirling pool.

After my sessions, I'd been able to call up a vivid vision of the place in my mind in an instant any time I needed to. It was a handy skill, especially during times of stress, or when I was lost in a hallucinogenic non-place of bright light and chaotic swirling colors. I found myself sitting on a rock near the stream, listening to the fall and breathing in the thick smells of jungle growth. I could even feel the sweat beading up on my face and neck in the humid tropical air. I drew in a long, slow breath and marveled at the sensation of moist air rushing down my throat and into my lungs. The place felt more real to me at that moment than the day I'd actually found it.

I don't know how long I watched the water pour over the top of the cliff and down into the pool. Time didn't seem to exist in that spot. The flow of the water seemed eternal, with no beginning or end. While in this timeless state, I became aware of a change in the mist at the base of the fall where the water plunged into the pool. The mist was growing larger and thickening into a cloud, and with this change came the consciousness of the passage of time, measured by the perceptible increase in the size and density of the cloud. Time passed, and I began to see a new thing, a shadowy form in the center of the thickening haze. The form grew more substantial, until it resolved itself into a human figure with long, black hair tied in a braid that hung over the figure's shoulder. The figure grew more familiar until I remembered a name: Walks in Cloud. And, indeed, the figure *was*, in fact, walking in my direction.

I saw the figure smile. "Hi, Jack. Nice place you've got there."

"You are..." I started, realizing that I had spoken the words.

"Rolls on Land..." she slapped the side of her leg, "and Walks in Cloud. How are you feeling? A little spooked?"

How was I feeling? I thought about that for a few seconds, conscious of the fact that I was sitting on a rock next to a waterfall that was the product of my memory, and taking a measurable amount of time to gather my thoughts before speaking. "My brain is trying to tell me that I'm dreaming. But everything feels real."

Walks in Cloud lifted her eyebrows, and I noticed that she wasn't wearing glasses. She tilted her head to one side and nodded her approval at me. "Not bad! I'm impressed. A lot of people would be melting down and screaming right now, but you're doing a bang-up job of accepting what your senses perceive to be real."

"A part of me feels like panicking," I admitted. "But I've been drugged before, back when I was in the army. This is different from that, but it's not an entirely new experience. And it's only temporary, right? I'll get back to reality at some point.... Won't I?"

Walks in Cloud smiled. "Do you want to? This place is just as real as any other place. It's a nice place, too. No problems. No stress. Just everlasting peace."

"Everlasting? I mean, I like to retreat here from time to time, but I've got things I want to do. Everlasting peace isn't what I want. It sounds pretty dull to me."

Walks in Cloud shook her head. "Some people might say that you want the wrong things. But I'm with you, Jack. I love euphoria as much as the next guy, but too much of it starts to feel like death, and I ain't done living yet, not by a long shot. Anyway, we can't stay here for too long. She won't allow it."

"She?"

"The Cloud Spirit. Although you might see her differently. She might even be a he, or an animal, or something else. Everyone sees the spirit in their own way. But you probably won't see her at all. She'll send another spirit to guide you to where you need to go, and, when your time here is finished, I'll guide you out. Are you game?"

"I guess I'd better be. What's the worst that could happen?"

"Don't ask. Your guide is on the way now. Good luck. I've got a few things of my own to take care of now that I'm here. I'll be back in time to bring you home from the other side."

Even before she'd finished speaking, the figure of Walks in Cloud was already disappearing into the darkening mist. When I could no longer see her shape, the mists began to swirl and coalesce into a new shape. The color changed from dark gray to a light bronze, and when the transformation was complete, I found myself face to face with an enormous cougar the size of a horse.

I didn't move, and the cougar regarded me with feral eyes. I felt the part of me that wanted to panic seizing command of my brain functions, but, with an effort, I forced myself to remain calm. The trick, I discovered, was to not care. I could do that. I breathed in the feline odor and the tropical air and allowed myself to smile.

The oversized cougar sat back on his haunches, and a thick soothing voice like melted chocolate sounded inside my head. "Welcome, Alexander Southerland. The priestess of the Cloud has done well to bring you to me. I have studied you, and I know and accept you. Will you receive a name from me?"

How was I supposed to answer a question like that? Especially from an oversized mountain lion that was speaking inside my head. I took a look at the cougar's massive claws and forced myself to redirect my gaze into the creature's eyes. "I don't know. I'm kind of attached to the name I've got. I'm used to it. It suits me fine."

"You need not give away one name to receive another. One may have many names, each to be used in the appropriate circumstance."

"What would be the appropriate circumstance for the name you want to give me?"

"That will be for you to decide."

"Uh-huh. And will I be able to pronounce this name?"

"Of course. Otherwise it would be useless to you."

I felt my head start to spin. I reminded myself that I was under the influence of a hallucinogen and forced myself to passively accept the reality of my current experience without fighting it. When I had calmed myself I asked, "What would I owe you for this name?"

"A promise."

"Naturally. And what would I have to promise?"

"When it is in your power to do so, you must promise to protect the boy who talks backwards."

Okay, this hallucination was starting to get downright goofy. "The boy who talks backwards. Sure. Is he worth protecting?"

"He is."

"And protecting him will resolve my debt in full?"

"It will."

"And what will this boy do for me in return for my protection?"

"He will preserve your life."

That sounded fair. "So let me get this straight. You'll give me a name. I will promise to protect the boy who... talks backwards. And he will preserve my life. So what do *you* get out of this?"

"Satisfaction. And sustenance."

"I see. You aren't going to eat me, are you?"

The Cougar's tongue rolled out of his mouth and he flicked it over one side of his snout. After a beat the chocolate voice sounded in my head. "Not in a way that will bring you harm."

I guessed that would have to do. "And what if I don't accept the name you want to give me?"

"Then I will be displeased."

The tone of the voice in my head didn't change, but the sudden sense of menace that assaulted my senses spoke volumes. I supposed that there was a time and a place to resist a god, but this didn't seem like one of them. And besides, the deal seemed solid enough. "Okay. I will accept a name from you."

"Then I name you 'Speaks with Wind.' Will you receive this name?"

Speaks with Wind? Ehhh.... Well, it could have been worse. "Fine. Sure, I'll take it. Why not."

The cougar's jaws parted and his mouth stretched into something that sort of resembled a toothy smile. "That is good, Speaks with Wind. And now, you hunt something beyond the falls. Follow me, and I will show you the way through."

The giant cougar rose to his feet and began padding his way toward the waterfall. I stood and followed him. When the cougar reached the edge of the pool, he didn't stop, but instead waded into the water until he was standing directly in front of the tumbling waterfall, the surface of the pool rippling against his haunches. I hesitated at the side of the water, but then walked in. When I did, the water melted away, and I found myself standing alone in front of a wall of solid iron.

The cougar was nowhere to be seen, but I heard his voice in my head. "Step up to the wall, Speaks with Wind, and place the palms of your hands against it."

I did so. The wall was cold and solid against my skin.

Again, the voice sounded in my head. "You know the one who built this wall?"

An image of Leaflock sitting behind his desk came to me. I remembered him telling me that he'd protected the flash drive with his own security software. I began to recall every encounter I'd ever had with him. I remembered the way he moved, the way he expressed his emotions, his pent-up energy, the manner in which he spoke, and his hair-trigger temper. I didn't hear his words, but I relived the way he had made me feel when I was in his presence. In a flash, I remembered every conversation I'd ever had with anyone who had known Leaflock, again, not the words, but the way the conversations had helped me form a picture of the gnome. I recalled every impression I'd had of the brilliant, arrogant, autocratic Leaflock, every sense of who he was, and I began to grasp the essence of his identity to the extent that I could. And then I closed my eyes and pushed against the wall.

I felt the strength of a mountain cat pouring into my arms, wrists, hands, and fingers. The wall resisted at first. I pressed harder, grabbing at the iron with claws that extended from my fingertips. The claws sunk into the iron, which melted, and then parted like a curtain. I stepped through.

I walked into swirling mists reflecting a green glow that seemed to come from everywhere at once. Walks in Cloud was standing in front of me. She was flanked by two lean gray wolves, one sitting on either side of her. The wolves stared at me with evil thoughts, and each one curled its lips back in a snarl as they showed me their teeth. Walks in Cloud put a hand on each of their heads, and, when she did, the wolves stopped snarling and looked up at her with adoring expressions. Walks in Cloud smiled at the wolves in return. "Don't worry about these fellas, Southerland. It's the virus, and I've got it under control." She looked over at me. "Congratulations, Jack! You're in. You've eliminated the passcode from the security software, and in record time, too. It most likely would have taken me weeks to knock it down myself, or to socially engineer it, but since you were able to get to know the man who wrote the security program and learn how he thinks to some degree.... Well, I won't go into all of the technical mumbo-jumbo. It's a complicated combination of technology and mysticism, and I want to maintain a few secrets, but together, with the help of your spirit guide and the Cloud Spirit, we were able to clear the barrier away in just a few hours. You'll be able to access the flash drive now with no obstacles."

"Hours?"

"A few, yes. Time is a little wonky in this place. The drug will be wearing off soon. Let's take a look around and see what we can learn about the data files."

She reached for me and took both of my hands while the wolves crouched down and watched us without interest. Together, bathed in green light, we walked through the mists.

"This green all comes from the enchantment," Walks in Cloud told me. "We can't turn it off, but it shouldn't affect us in any way. I don't think."

I jerked my head toward her, and she shrugged. "There could be some side effects. I wouldn't worry about it. I deal with this shit all the time, and I'm fine. Mostly."

My eyes dropped to her legs, but I decided not to say anything. No risk, no reward, and I had more or less volunteered for this ride.

When I looked back up, the mists parted to reveal a cluster of thin jagged spires that appeared to be made of smoky-colored glass and varied in height from a few inches to between fifteen and twenty feet tall. Set apart from the spires was a smooth block of smoky glass or crystal about the size and shape of a shoe box. I followed Walks in Cloud to the spires.

"This is the data," the tech explained to me. She reached out to touch one of the spires, and I did the same. "What do you feel?"

I closed my eyes and concentrated on the tactile sensation of the glass spire on my fingertips. "It's cold, almost freezing. It's not smooth. I feel... not a vibration, but a tension, like something inside the glass has been wound tight and is waiting to spring loose. It feels... dense. Tightly packed."

"Try listening to it."

I put my ear against the glass. "It's faint, but I hear a high-pitched hum, like a machine at rest."

"Do you hear anything more specific?"

I channeled all of my concentration into my hearing and kept my ear pressed against the freezing cold spire as long as I could stand it. At first I couldn't distinguish anything inside the humming sound, but just as I was about to give up I thought I could sense a subtle arrhythmic pattern in the humming, not quite words, but a message. I focused on the sound for a few seconds, and then pulled back.

"Anything?"

I shook my head. "I'm not sure. Maybe it was just my imagination, like seeing images in clouds, but I thought I could hear... numbers, like mathematical equations. I don't know. Like I say, it might have been nothing."

Walks in Cloud nodded. "Okay, try this box over here." She led me to the block that was set apart from the spires.

When I reached the block, I knelt down and touched it for a few seconds, then lowered myself farther to rest my ear on the surface. I pulled back immediately.

"What did you hear?" Walks in Cloud asked me.

"A voice! Robotic sounding, and I couldn't make out the words, but it was definitely a voice."

Walks in Cloud smiled. "Try to see if you can hear any of the words."

I pressed my ear to the block again, bracing myself against the freezing cold of its surface. A few seconds later, I pulled back, my ear numb with the cold. "I can almost get it," I told Walks in Cloud. "It's like a radio with the volume loud enough to hear, but too low to make anything out. I thought I heard a word or two. 'Alpha,' I think. And 'engineers.' And, I think, 'formula.'"

Walks in Cloud raised an eyebrow. "What do you think, Jack? Think you'd be getting your money's worth?"

"It doesn't seem like porno. Okay, you've got a deal. Can we get out of here now? I've had about all of the weird I can take for one day."

Walks in Cloud smiled. "Sure, Jack. Coming down can be a little rough. Stay with me and listen to my voice, and with a little luck you'll come out of it with little more than a headache."

Chapter Seven

As it turned out, the "little more" involved a good deal of disorientation and nausea, but Walks in Cloud brewed a fresh pot of coffee, and that, along with a little something from my flask, went a long way toward restoring me to something approaching normal. By the time I'd finished my second cup, I believed that a decent meal and a good night's sleep would bring me back the rest of the way.

In retrospect, that belief might have been a little naïve, but it was a comforting thought at the time.

We were "back" in the computer wizard's workshop. I mean, technically we'd never left, but it felt like I'd traveled to somewhere far away and taken an even longer road home. After we'd settled, Walks in Cloud wanted a detailed account of my experience, and I gave it to her, holding nothing back. She interrupted me often with questions.

"A cougar?"

"Yeah. A big one."

Walks in Cloud frowned. "Makes sense."

"Yeah? What do you mean?"

She shook her head. "Let's get back to that. Did the spirit give you any advice or instructions?"

I told her about the deal I'd made and the name I'd accepted. She maintained a continual frown of concentration as she listened, but shook her head when I asked her if she knew what any of it meant. "The boy who talks backwards? I don't know anything about that. I'm afraid you're on your own, Jack."

Her expression gave nothing away, but I thought, or imagined, that I had seen something in her eyes. Something that looked a little like... fear? Or amazement? But maybe I was reading something into her response that wasn't there. My head was still a little jumbled after my excursion into weirdsville. "You're sure about that?" I asked her.

"I guess you'll know more if you actually run across a child who talks backwards." The corners of her eyes crinkled as her lips broadened into a genuine smile. Whatever I'd thought I'd seen was gone, and I figured it would be a mistake to draw hard conclusions given the state of my mind. I shook it off as she continued speaking.

"Cougar has given you a path to follow, and you've agreed to follow it. He has selected you. He's your spirit animal now. It's a great honor."

"Yeah? If you say so. All I know is that I owe him, and I don't like being in debt."

"You owe me, too, Jack. Don't forget it."

I might have groaned a little, but the expression on her face remained inscrutable. I continued telling my story, and when I was finished we both sat in silence for a while to soak it all in.

After a time, I asked the question that was uppermost on my mind. "How much of that was real? I mean, you say that I have a 'spirit animal' now. What does that even mean?"

"It means that Cougar has chosen you. He's your guide in matters of the spirit." Walks in Cloud lifted her eyes until they met mine. "You need to understand something, Jack. When I asked you to help me get you into the drive, I didn't expect you to receive a spirit guide. That was a surprise. My people are descended from the oldest people on this continent, people who were here before the coming of the Dragon Lords. Throughout centuries of changes to our world, many of our families have managed to hang on to some of our most ancient traditions. One of these traditions is that when we come of age, we go on quests to contact the spirits and find our designated purpose in this world. Originally, only young men went on these quests, but eventually that changed, and women undertook these quests, too. These quests require much preparation, including several days of fasting."

"And a good dose of mind melter?"

"Sometimes. More in some families than in others. My family was a big believer in the use of herbs and potions to open doors that would otherwise remain closed."

"So you starve yourselves and give your brains a jump-start in order to push your way through locked doors. Then what?"

"Then we are sent out of the settlements and into unspoiled nature to seek the spirits."

"And the spirits tell you about your designated purpose?"

"That's the general idea. But it doesn't always work, or at least not in the way you might expect. Sometimes these quests last for days before the seeker receives a sign from the spirits, and the designated purpose might be nothing more than 'teach your child good manners,' or 'be sure to preserve the stories of your people.' A lot of trouble for something you were probably going to do anyway. Sometimes the seeker fails to make contact with the spirits and receives no sign at all."

"That must be disappointing."

Walks in Cloud smiled. "Do you really think so? For a lot of people, it's a relief. If the spirits have no assigned purpose for you, then it leaves you free to live your life as you please."

I nodded. "I suppose so. But you still haven't told me about spirit animals."

Walks in Cloud feigned annoyance. "I'm getting to it. Drink your coffee and let me finish. Anyway, sometimes during these quests, the seeker is visited by a spirit animal, like Cougar. It's a big deal to be chosen by one of the spirits, but the spirits don't think like humans. Their intentions aren't always clear."

"In other words, you don't know. You could have told me that when I first asked about it."

She looked me up and down. "Do you have indigenous roots?"

I shrugged. "Truthfully, I have no idea."

She nodded. "You might. The old bloodlines have long blended into the larger population. But it's not necessary that you do. Many things have changed over the centuries, and the spirits have adapted themselves to the changing world." Walks in Cloud chuckled. "It turns out that the spirits of this continent are surprisingly progressive. Anyway, the spirits choose whomever they please. But what you have to realize is that what happened to you today was rare. I don't know what the consequences for you will be, but spirits choose people for a reason. That reason may become apparent at some point. Or you may never know why you were chosen. All I can tell you is that Cougar has put his mark on you, and he will always be with you."

I thought about that, and then shrugged. "It sounds like I should just go on with my life like nothing happened and keep my eyes and ears open. If my...spirit guide..., if Cougar...," I hesitated. The words sounded strange coming out of my mouth. "Lord's balls! Look. I didn't ask for this. I just wanted to get into that fuckin' flash drive! If this cougar spirit wants something from me, I guess he'll let me know. And if he's just fucking with me, then screw him."

I'd expected Walks in Cloud to take offense at my lack of respect, but I was mistaken. Her broad eye-crinkling smile made another appearance, and she choked back a laugh. "I like your attitude, Jack. Who the fuck do these fuckin' spirits think they are? What gives them the right to assign us a purpose in life? I'll bet you didn't wake up this morning expecting to have a conversation with a giant mountain lion, am I right?"

I smiled back at her, shaking my head. But the truth was that I was fascinated by all this talk about ancient spirits, and I couldn't stop myself from being curious. I could pretend to dismiss all this talk of spirits and spiritual quests as a load of hooey, or a product of mind-fucking drugs, but who was I to be skeptical? A few weeks before, I'd watched a vengeful demon drag the mayor into an abyss. And a few weeks before that I'd seen a human figure with the head of a hummingbird crawl down from a world with a greenlit sky and try to pull my heart out of my chest with its three-foot beak. Had those been hallucinations? I took a sip of my coffee and asked, "What does it mean that Cougar is my spirit animal?"

Walks in Cloud folded her hands in her lap. "It reveals a lot about you. The animal spirits accept spirits that are similar to their own. Cougars are solitary animals with the ability to adapt to a wide variety of surroundings. But once they establish a territory, they don't tend to wander beyond its borders, and they become very protective of that territory. They maintain an emotional balance, although they can be pushed into great anger if they lose control of their temper. They are aloof. Loners. Most people see them as dispassionate, but the truth is that they keep great passions bottled up inside them. When they allow free rein to their desires, look out! They are hunters by nature, and they are subject to a sometimes insatiable curiosity. You've heard of how curiosity kills the cat? That's something that cougars have to watch out for. Cougars are confident animals, and they depend more on their instincts than on their reason. They don't overthink the details. They have great pride, and they have to be careful to keep that pride in check. Their pride can be a weakness. It can make them foolhardy, and it will drive them into unnecessary danger if they aren't careful, especially if they are crossed and become angry. They are powerful creatures, both strong and stealthy. They are intelligent, and, when on the hunt, they are patient. Cougars are dangerous, and yet they can be surprisingly gentle."

Walks in Cloud's face broke into a smile. "Any of this sound familiar?"

"Sounds like a lot of bunkum to me. You hear stuff like this from the card-readers on the wharf."

I caught an amused gleam in Walks in Cloud's eye as she pursed her lips and nodded. "Yep. Just a lot of hokum. Tell me, are you married?"

"No."

"Live alone?"

"Yes."

"How long?"

"Ever since my discharge from the army. About nine years now."

"You like it that way?"

I shrugged. "I guess so."

She settled back in her chair. "Women need to be careful with cougars. They tend to be overly selective and don't form relationships easily, but, once they are in one, they tend to be over-protective and extremely possessive. On the upside, their single-mindedness makes them faithful. At least until they get tired of their mate. Then they ditch them and seek out someone else."

"What are female cougars like?" I asked.

"Pretty much the same. Cougar pairings actually work rather well."

"Because they smother each other with single-minded attention?"

"Because they'd rather be alone with each other than with anyone else, and because they watch each other's backs."

"Until they get tired of each other."

"True. But at least they don't cat around while they're together."

"Cat around. I get it. Cute."

Walks in Cloud lit one of her sour-smelling cigarettes and shook her match until it went out. "So... Speaks with Wind?"

"That's the name he gave me." I shrugged.

The tech stared at me while she smoked. After a couple of puffs, she asked, "You're an elementalist, right? You summon and command air elementals?"

"I guess that explains the name."

Her mouth formed into a knowing grin as she nodded. "I had a feeling that you were gifted in some way, and my feelings are rarely wrong. You've visited the spirit world, and you may find yourself more attuned to the world of spirit now. Your abilities to communicate with the spirits of the air may be changed in some unpredictable ways. Or maybe not. Not everyone is affected by their experiences in the spirit world in the same ways. But you formed a relationship with a spirit guide, and that will have some intriguing benefits. It may also have some equally interesting consequences. Or maybe you won't be affected at all."

"Uh-huh. That's mysterious, but not really helpful."

She shrugged. "We'll see."

"And what about you? Your spirit animal is, what, a cloud?"

In response, she lit up a fresh cigarette and breathed a double stream of smoke out her nostrils. "You might say that I'm a priestess of the Cloud Spirit, which means that I can communicate with her. But she isn't my spirit guide. Not all of us have spirit guides. Not everyone who seeks a spirit guide finds one. Some of us are given a different kind of choice. Accepting the choices offered by the spirits can come with a price." She slapped the side of her wheelchair. "Sometimes that price can be a heavy one."

She took another draw on the cigarette, and then placed it, still smoldering, into an ashtray. She wheeled herself until she was directly in front of me and met my eyes. "You may have some unexpected reactions to your experience today. Vivid dreams, lack of focus at times, that kind of thing. I wouldn't be surprised if a crowd of nightmares are lining up in your brain, just waiting to come out and show their stuff. Probably nothing serious, but if it's worse than that, call me anytime, day or night. I put you up to this, and that makes me responsible for any aftereffects you may suffer as a result. I want you to know that I take that responsibility seriously."

She turned herself back to her worktable and picked up the green flash drive. "This is ready for you to use. The old passcode is gone, and you can enter in your own now if you want. I'd recommend it. Once you do, be careful. The wolves are still in there, and they will attack if the passcode isn't entered accurately." She plugged the drive into her tablet and waited for it to load. After a few seconds, she typed some commands on her keyboard and then handed me the tablet. "Type a passcode into the box. Make it something that you'll remember, but don't make it anything obvious, like your name, or your birthday. And don't write it down anywhere. Ever."

"You're forgetting what I do for a living," I said. "Trust me. My job would be a lot tougher if no ever wrote their private passwords down and taped them to the bottoms of their keyboards." Too bad Redhorn hadn't done that, I thought to myself; I could have saved myself a lot of time and effort. I pondered for a moment, and then entered a string of characters, which showed up as asterisks in the box. When I was done, I hit enter, and another box appeared, along with a command to retype my passcode to verify it. I did so, and the files were now protected with a code known only to me.

When I was done, Walks in Cloud unplugged the flash drive and held it out for me.

"Wait. Aren't we going to see what's on it?"

The tech shook her head. "Not here, and not on my equipment. My guess is that whatever's on that drive is hot, and I don't want to know about it. It will be safer for you, too. If anyone asks me, I can truthfully deny all knowledge of its contents."

I took the drive and tucked it away in my pocket. "I'll have to buy a new computer before I can look at this thing. You don't sell computers, do you?"

"I'm strictly tech, Jack. I don't do retail." She started wheeling herself to the front door, and I took the hint.

At the door, Walks in Cloud smiled up at me from her chair. "I hope you'll be able to make use of the information that's on it. As for compensation? Let's hold off on that for a while, Speaks with Wind. I might be calling on you for a favor, maybe later, maybe soon. It won't be anything that you can't handle, but it won't be easy, either. I'm not going to try to deceive you on that score. But I'll expect you to fulfill your obligation to me to the best of your ability when I require it. Deal?"

I nodded and held out my hand. "Fair enough, Walks in Cloud." We shook on it.

***

I kept the beastmobile parked at Giovanni's Auto Repair, which was located a block up the road from my place. I paid out a good chunk of change every month for the privilege, but, given the going rates for parking garages in the city, I was happy to do it. Gio, the owner, was a good working-class mug, and as part of the service he and his fourteen-year-old son Antonio kept the beastmobile polished up and in good working order.

When I walked into the lot first thing Monday morning, I could see a tall skinny teenager standing outside the open back door of my car scratching his thick mop of dark brown hair and looking puzzled. "Big problems, Antonio?"

Antonio looked over my way and wrinkled his nose. "I think something crawled in here and died during the night. I'm looking for the dead body."

I grimaced. "Shouldn't you be in school, kid?"

"It's summer break, Mr. Southerland."

"Summer break! We never got summer breaks when I was your age. We stayed in school all year long and loved it."

The kid's face broke into a grin. "Sure you did. And you had to walk five miles to school every day. Uphill, both ways."

"In the snow! You kids got it easy these days."

Antonio smirked. "Ri-i-gghht.... Seriously, what happened in here? Did someone get drunk and puke all over your back seat?"

"Something like that. What do you think, am I gonna have to trade this thing in, or do you think we can save it."

"You ain't gonna trade the beastmobile in to anyone, unless it's me! Yeah, we can save it. I think." The kid scratched his head again. "It's gonna take some work. I don't think that cornstarch will be enough to do the trick. We're probably gonna have to take the carpet out and give the floorboard a good scrubbing. How long ago did it happen?"

"Saturday night."

"You should've covered it up with some baking soda or kitty litter. Or, better yet, crushed charcoal."

"I didn't happen to have anything like that on me at the time."

The kid shook his head. "I wish I'd'a seen this yesterday, but I was out skateboarding all day. Sorry."

"Don't apologize. I'm grateful for all the attention you give to this beast. Your dad in?"

"Huh? Yeah, he's in the garage doing an R and V. We'd probably best leave him to it, though. I can handle this myself. If that's jakeloo with you, I mean." He looked up at me.

When I was fourteen, the last thing I would have wanted to do with my summer break was clean the vomit out of some old man's car. Of course, I would probably have spent it breaking someone's window or picking a fight with some other bored kid, but that's another issue. I shrugged at Antonio. "Wouldn't you rather be out skateboarding?"

"Nah, not today." He turned back to the beastmobile, and I'd be lying if I didn't say that I would have given my left arm to see a good-looking dame gazing at me with that same adoring expression.

"Okay, kid. Knock yourself out. How long do you think you'll need?"

Antonio looked back at me, grinning from one ear to the other. "Can you give me the day? I'll have it ready to go by tomorrow. I'd like to take a look at the fuel intake filter, too, if that's okay. I started her up this morning, and she seemed a little sluggish."

"Fine with me. Let me just have a chat with your old man."

I found Antonio's pop leaning over the hood of a dinged-up ten-year-old so-called "economy" car. The repairs it would require until it broke down completely would set its owner back enough dough to buy a vehicle with some class. "Busy day?" I asked Gio, just to let him know I was there.

"Busy month," came the reply. "People neglect their cars all year long and then bring them in during the summer to catch up. By then, their oil has turned to sludge, their cooling systems are shot, and their fuel lines are clogged." He waved at the beat up little four-banger. "This is my third ring-and-valve job in the last two weeks. Summer months are the golden months for a guy in my racket."

"Your boy wants to check my fuel filter."

"Good idea! It seemed a little sluggish when I started it up yesterday." He pulled his bald head out from under the hood and wiped oil off his hands with a grease-stained rag. "What happened to your back seat? Someone get sick in there?"

I groaned and pulled my hat down over one eye. "Don't ask."

The burly mechanic's lips spread into a toothy grin. "Fu-u-uck.... You didn't."

"It was a bad night. I slept it off in the back seat, but sometime during the night, well...."

"Alkwat's balls, Southerland! I thought you could hold your liquor."

"Like I said, bad night."

Gio shook his head. "I'll get the kid to clean it up."

"He's already on it. He wants it to be clean when I give him the pink slip."

"*Hell* no." Gio grabbed a cup of coffee from a nearby shelf. "No way I allow that kid to cruise around in a fuckin' pimpmobile."

"Beastmobile. I had the decal of the naked nymph scraped off the hood the day I bought it."

Gio wiped sweat from his forehead with the rag. "Don't get me wrong, I love that car, but it's a pimpmobile. You bought it from a pimp, didn't you?"

"He doesn't run hookers on street corners. He owns an expensive high-end escort agency."

"Just because I can't afford his joy girls doesn't mean he ain't a pimp. Anyway, that kid's probably going to get himself in enough trouble without cruising the streets in a man-juice machine like that. The dollies will all want to ride with him and the punks will all want to kick his teeth in."

"Antonio's a good kid."

"Sure, just like his old man was a good kid. But he's better looking than I ever was. He's already got the little girls hanging all over him. He starts picking them up in a crate like that beastmobile and their daddies will be waiting outside my door so they can punch me in the nose! I check his drawer every day looking to see if he's got rubbers. If I find some, I don't know whether I should be happy because he's playing it safe or furious because he's still just a kid."

"How old were you your first time?"

Gio smiled, and his eyes grew dreamy. "Nona Sue. I was, let me see...." His face hardened. "Shit! I was fourteen!" The hardness left his face. "Alkwat's balls, what am I gonna do. That kid can't be fourteen already. Why did I ever become a father? I'm not ready for this."

I tried to think of something encouraging to say, but never having been a father I didn't think that I was qualified to give any advice. "Well, it looks like he'll be busy with the car today, so you probably won't have to worry about anything until tomorrow."

"Gee, thanks pal." He brightened. "Hey, maybe I'll crack your engine block with my sledgehammer. That'll keep the kid busy for the rest of the summer!"

"Nix on that idea, pal."

"Eh, it's a thought. Anyway, what's shakin' with you? Still working that case? We missed you at poker night last week."

"Yes and no. Technically the case is done with, but some things have developed from it. Unfortunately, I need to get me a new computer before I can get much farther with it."

"What happened to the one you got?"

"I got hit with a virus that pretty much fried it."

Gio's eyes narrowed as he grinned. "Ahh, I get it. You need to lay off those jerk-off sites, champ. Don't you know that kind of thing makes you go blind?"

"Very funny. It was work. I was a little careless opening a flash drive that I ran across."

Gio wasn't going to let me off that easily. "Oh, it was *work*. *That's* what you call it. It never seemed like work to me."

"Screw you. I'll tell your wife that *you* gave me that drive."

"Oh, right. Like she'd believe that. She thinks that you're living the life of a swinging single. Booze and broads every night."

"She's been watching too many detective shows. Those actors are all a lot better looking than I am."

"That's true. Still, she's afraid you're going to try to lure me away to an orgy."

"It might not be a good idea to tell her that I got drunk and passed out in the back of my car the other night."

"Don't worry, my lips are sealed." He frowned. "Does Antonio know about it?"

"I didn't tell him it was me."

"Yeah, well let's leave it that way."

"Sounds good to me. I don't feel all that great about it. I don't plan on it ever happening again."

Gio nodded at me, expression serious. "That's a good plan. But you know what they say about the best of intentions...."

"Yep. The road to ruin is paved with them."

Chapter Eight

I slept in fits and starts that night. I remember having a lot of strange dreams, but by morning they had all fled my memory. Too bad. One or two of them might have inspired a fantasy novel some day when I had the time to write one. I'd never read that trash myself, but I figured it couldn't be all that hard to write, and I'd heard that some of those writers made a ton of dough. On the other hand, if I'd remembered some of those dreams too well, they might have driven me out of my mind. Maybe that's why I'd forgotten them. My brain was trying its best to preserve as much of my sanity as possible.

After a hearty breakfast of a fried egg on top of a slice of sourdough toast smeared with creamy peanut butter, which I washed down with a cold beer, I took a cab to an electronics store and bought the cheapest computer I could find that met my limited needs. The eager-beaver acne-scarred sales clerk warned me that I wouldn't be able to play any of the latest games on it, and I told him that it wouldn't be a problem as long as it could load a spreadsheet and get me on the internet. He didn't even try to hide his disgust. I turned down his generous offer for an extended warranty and carried the package out of the store without assistance.

Once outside, I called for another cab and sat down on a bench to wait. The sun had found an opening in the midst of the heavy marine layer, and it was bathing me in its light. I was halfway in the act of pulling my hat brim down to shade my eyes when I froze. Something about the clouds, the patches of blue sky, and the partially obscured sun seemed... off. I couldn't quite put my finger on what it was that looked different to me. Were the clouds a little whiter? The blue bluer? The sun a little brighter? I examined the cars parked along the street, and it seemed to me that the colors of the vehicles were crisper than I'd ever seen them before. I closed my eyes and pinched the bridge of my nose with my thumb and forefinger. Then I rubbed at my eyelids and opened them. Not only did the world appear to be brighter and more sharply delineated, but the sounds I heard seemed unusually distinct, as if I'd been walking around with cotton balls in my ears, and the cotton had dissolved. I breathed in the air and felt the tang of salt in my nostrils like tiny pinpricks.

I figured that I was either having a stroke or I was experiencing some of the aftereffects of my trip to narco-land that Walks in Cloud had warned me about. I took a mental inventory, and outside of a slight headache and some passing dizziness, I felt that I was doing an okay job of coping with the effects.

The leaves of a bush that had been planted in front of the beauty salon next to the electronics store in order to introduce a patch of nature into the property began to rustle as a gust of wind swept by. I blinked, and I was looking into the world of air elementals, watching spirits of air swirl as they caught the passing wind currents. I started in surprise. About a year earlier, when the elf had favored me with his gift (not that I'd had any say in the matter), I'd discovered that if I called up the proper sigils in my mind I could see the normally invisible air elementals that were traveling nearby. As far as I knew, no other elementalist had the ability to do that. The standard way of summoning an elemental was to write down a sigil that would send a blanket call into the winds and wait for a response from whatever spirit might be close by. Or we could send out a call for a specific elemental that we had previously worked with and named. The elf's gift allowed me to form the sigils in my mind, rather than write them out. But this was new: never had the world of elementals flashed into my vision unbidden, and I hadn't used any sigils at all.

I wondered how much control I had over the phenomenon. I closed my eyes, willing the vision to disappear. When I opened my eyes, the world appeared to be "normal" again, except that the unusual clarity had remained. I stared into the sky, willing the world of air elementals into my vision. The elementals appeared. I blinked them away again, and they disappeared from view. I decided that this was very cool.

I blinked the world of elementals back into my vision again and scanned the skies. Off in the distance, high above me, was a familiar blob of air drifting in the breeze like an oversized soap bubble. I sent out a summons for it, and the blob floated swiftly toward me. When it was hovering fifteen feet over my head, I held up a hand, and it stopped. Remembering how my conversation with Cougar had taken place in my head, I "thought" words in the direction of the elemental: "Hello, Badass."

Words that sounded like the moans of the wind blowing through a forest formed in my head: "Hello, Alex. You are different."

Extremely cool.

Badass was one of my two favorite elementals. I had found and named it a year or so earlier when I'd needed some muscle to use against a troll that had been bouncing me around like a human punching bag. The elemental stretched anywhere from six to twenty feet tall and could produce whirling winds with enough intensity to overturn a small car. Before the unnamed elf had done whatever he'd done to me, an elemental the size and strength of Badass would have been too much for me to summon and command. Elementals with that much power tended to hold me in little regard, but Badass was special. The big spirit had some kind of connection to the elf himself, and it followed me everywhere, making itself available whenever I needed it. I suspected that the elf had provided Badass to me as a kind of guardian, though it only acted on my behalf when I summoned it. It had proven to be useful on a number of occasions, and, although I knew that my debt to the elf was increasing every time I called on the potent bag of wind, I was grateful to have it handy.

And now I could communicate with the elemental—and presumably other air elementals—without having to speak to it out loud. I saw any number of ways in which that would be convenient. Speaks with Wind, indeed!

Using only my mind, I spoke with Badass until the cab arrived, just because I could, and then sent it on its way. The cabbie dropped me off in front of my building, where two cop cars were double parked, and four of the city's finest were waiting for me outside the door to my office.

I smiled at the coppers, all dressed up in their blues. "One, two, three…four. Huh! Must be serious."

The lead bull took a step in front of the others. "Alexander Southerland? We're taking you in for questioning."

"What for?"

"Police business." Which meant that he hadn't been told.

"Can I put my new computer in my office?"

"We'll need to take that with us." The officer waved at one of the other bulls. "You wanna take that, Wildfire?"

I kept a grip on the computer. "I just bought this. You got a warrant?"

"Sure," said Lead Bull. "I think I left it in the car. Or maybe I forgot it on my desk back at the station."

Officer Wildfire, if that was his real name, grabbed at the boxed-up computer. I pulled it away from him. "This is new. I just bought it."

Wildfire smirked at me. "Don't worry, sir. We'll take real good care of it." I let him wrench the computer from my arms. They were going to end up with it anyway, and I was curious to see why the YCPD was interested in me.

I objected when one of the other officers tried to cuff me, though. "Nix to that," I told him. "I'll come along quiet, but try to put those bracelets on me and I'll shove them up your ass."

The officer reached for me. "Go ahead and try, motherfucker."

But Lead Bull stepped in. "No need for that. Mr. Southerland isn't going to give us any trouble. Are you. Sir."

"Not me," I told him. "I've got nothing but respect for our boys in blue."

The coppers drove me to the familiar downtown clubhouse. I'd been a guest at the station just two days earlier, and it was starting to seem like a second home to me. If they kept bringing me back, they were going to start charging me rent. The officers told me to wait in the waiting area, and after a few minutes they led me to one of the interrogation rooms. At least they didn't stuff me into a cell this time. They even gave me a cup of coffee. It was weaker than dishwater, but I considered it to be a good omen.

After what seemed like an eternity, but was probably less than ten minutes, the door to the sweatbox opened and Detective Laurel Kalama stepped in. She closed the door behind her and nodded at me. "Hello, gumshoe. Having a nice day?"

"Peachy. I almost made it into my office before your boys put the arm on me. They took my new computer. I'd just bought it and was bringing it home. They insisted that I should give it to them, and I did because they assured me that they had a warrant. You got a copy of it by any chance?"

"Not on me. I'm sure it's laying around here somewhere."

Detective Kalama was one of the good guys. She was dedicated, competent, and professional. She and I had found ourselves working with each other a couple of times earlier that year, and I'd found her to be a smart, tough cookie whom I could rely on when the excrement was hitting the fan. She had gained my respect, and I was certain that the feeling was mutual. We were even something like friends. She and her husband, Kai, had had me over for barbecued steaks and beers not long before, and we'd stayed up most of the night talking and getting to know each other. Kai was a history professor at Yerba City U who supervised an archeological dig near Tenochtitlan, and I was fascinated with his stories of pre-Dragon Lord Tolanica. The detective had asked me questions about elementalism, and I told them stories about Smokey and Badass. They asked me for a demonstration, so I summoned Smokey and introduced the Kalamas to the tiny air spirit. It had been fun, and we had enjoyed each other's company, but Kalama was a cop through and through, and, for her, that came before anything else.

And not just any cop. She worked in homicide.

I sat forward in my seat and leaned my forearms against the table. "So.... Who got killed?"

Kalama's eyebrows arched. "I was hoping that you could tell me."

"Can you give me a hint?"

"Let's hold off on that for now. I brought you here because I might have a lead on the killer."

"I didn't do it."

"You didn't do what?"

"Never mind. What's this about a lead on a killer?"

Kalama's eyes met mine and held them. "You might have received an email from my prime suspect yesterday."

That was news to me. "Me? I didn't see it. Come to think of it, I haven't seen my emails in a couple of days. My computer got fried by a virus Saturday night, and I was busy all day yesterday. That's why I had to buy a new computer today, but I never got the chance to hook it up, thanks to the fine folks in blue. What do you think you're going to find on it, anyway? It's brand new."

"Don't you get emails on your phone? I know you've got a phone. I've called you on it, and you've answered. In fact, I called you on it this morning. But you didn't answer. Which is why I had to send some officers to pick you up."

"Oh. I guess I haven't checked it."

The detective waved a hand at me. "Well? You've got your phone on you, don't you? Check it now."

They hadn't taken my phone from me at the front desk, and I pulled it out of my shirt pocket. I realized that I hadn't turned it back on after leaving Walks in Cloud. "Uh, yeah. I've got some voicemail messages from you."

"Don't bother listening to them now. I know what they say. Check for emails."

I pulled up my emails, and in the midst of a cluster of ads and requests for political contributions I saw one from a login name I recognized.

"Any idea who that is?" Kalama asked.

"Nocturnal? How would I?"

She nodded. "Read the message."

I read it out loud. "R is dead. We need to talk."

I looked up at Kalama. She looked back at me. "Well?"

I shrugged. "It's a mystery to me."

"Who's R?"

"I'm guessing someone whose name begins with R?"

"Like maybe Inyon Redhorn?"

"That's a possibility."

Kalama pulled up a chair and sat across the table from me. She gave a quick sidelong glance in the direction of the one-way glass at the side of the room before turning her eyes back to me. "As you know, Inyon Redhorn died Saturday night."

"So I heard."

"And someone calling him or herself 'Nocturnal' sent you this message yesterday afternoon."

The detective hadn't asked me a question, so I didn't say anything.

"Do you know who Nocturnal is?"

"No. Are you going to tell me?"

"He or she had your email address."

I shrugged. "I'm in business. I make my email address available to the general public. It's on the internet. It's even on my business cards, which I hand out for free to anyone who wants one."

The detective's expression didn't change, but she flicked her eyes ever so briefly toward the one-way glass. "Whoever it is, he or she is connected to you through Redhorn."

"And yet, I don't know who he or she is. As far as I know, we've never met, online or off. As far as I know."

Kalama kept her eyes locked with mine. I got the feeling that she was performing for an audience, and I gave her the slightest of nods to let her know that I was telling her the truth. Which I was, technically speaking. I recognized Nocturnal as the login name of the person who had messaged Redhorn, asking him to name a price for the RAA formula, but I honestly did not know who Nocturnal was.

Eyes still locked with mine, the detective reminded me of the contents of the message. "R is dead. We need to talk." She leaned forward over the table. "Why do you suppose that this mysterious messenger needs to talk with you?"

"Maybe I've inherited some dough. This R might be a long-lost uncle."

"Or maybe someone thinks that you're involved in Redhorn's death. Maybe someone wants to blackmail you."

"Good thing you put a stop to it. Which reminds me, detective. How did you know about this email in the first place? And what makes you believe that R is Redhorn?"

Kalama didn't answer. Instead, she turned toward the glass and pushed her chair back from the table. "Okay, gumshoe. I won't keep you any longer, but don't leave town. Thanks for coming in."

Like I'd had a choice. She stood and opened the door for me. As I passed, she grabbed me by the arm. "Don't neglect your phone messages. You wouldn't want to miss out on any new business."

I nodded, and she released my arm.

**

In the cab on my way home, I checked my phone mail. I had three messages from Kalama, two from earlier in the morning, and one from just before I'd been picked up by the cops. In her first message, Kalama had told me to call her as soon as possible. Her second message was that she was sending some officers to escort me downtown. The third message consisted of five words: "Smokey's place. Tonight at eight."

I put the phone back in my pocket, leaned back in my seat, and closed my eyes. Then I snapped them open and mentally kicked myself. I'd forgotten to ask for my computer back! I still wasn't going to be able to see what was on the green flash drive! I wanted to tell the cabbie to take me to the electronics store, but I wasn't making the kind of dough that would allow me to buy two computers in one year, much less one day. Besides, I realized, I still hadn't taken a look at the cell phone that I'd found with the flash drive. I had no doubt that it was a burner, and I'd bet a month's wages that it was Redhorn's connection to whoever was offering to buy the formula to RAA. And I'd bet another month's wages that this prospective buyer was waiting for me to call him on that burner.

When I was back in my office, I opened my wall safe and removed the burner phone that I'd put there along with the for-the-moment frustratingly useless flash drive. Like most burners, this one was a cheap, no-frills cell phone with an anonymous phone number and a limited amount of pre-paid call time. I checked the call history and saw only one display: an outgoing call made on Friday afternoon soon after I'd left Redhorn's office after we'd had our little chat.

I called the number. The call connected midway through the sixth ring, but I heard nothing but silence. I broke it after waiting for what I felt was an appropriate space of time. "Nocturnal?"

A sleep-deprived male voice responded. "You must be Southerland."

"And you are?"

"Barely awake. You obviously received my email, and you have Redhorn's burner. Do you have anything else for me?"

"I don't know. Should I?"

"Depends. Would you like to be rich?"

"I could live with that."

"Then let's get together and talk about it. The Diner Forty-Niner. Do you know where that is?"

"Sure. It's over on Shell Street."

"That's the one. Shall we say... one-thirty?"

"One-thirty! It's after that now. Wait.... You mean in the morning?"

"I find it distasteful to do business when the sun is up. I guess you could say that I'm a bit of a night owl. Indulge me."

"All right, whatever you say. One-thirty at The Diner Forty-Niner. How will I know who you are?"

"Don't worry about that. You will."

I started to say something more, but the call disconnected. I guess I didn't rate a chipper "goodbye." Maybe Mister Nocturnal would be less grumpy after nightfall.

I had a few hours to kill before I would be meeting Kalama at "Smokey's place," which was code for The Black Minotaur, a neighborhood watering hole. Smokey, my favorite air elemental, could usually be found haunting the rafters of the joint, basking in the smoke from cigarettes and the kitchen. That's where I'd first summoned the diminutive air spirit, sending it off to tail a troll. It had proven itself to be exceptionally intelligent for an elemental, and the little puff or air had become an essential asset for me in my investigations. Kalama had something that she wanted to tell me in private, and that made me wonder who had been sitting on the other side of the one-way glass when she'd been questioning me at the station.

I was restless. Too many things had been happening, and they'd been happening too fast. I needed to process it all, so I changed into my sneakers and an old sleeveless hooded sweatshirt, because nothing clears my head and allows me to focus like a good run.

It was a typical Yerba City summer day: cool and breezy with just a hint of drizzle in the air, a perfect day for pounding the pavement. As I ran up and down the sidewalks of the neighborhood, turning at random, using my instincts to thread through pedestrians, children, and dogs along the way, I concentrated on my form, my heartbeat, and my breathing, and all extraneous thoughts fell away. I shortened my stride and increased my turnover going up the slopes, and I stretched out and let gravity do the work when I ran downhill. I leaned into the wind when it was in my face and broadened my shoulders to catch the breeze when it was at my back. I ran without keeping track of either miles or time, taking care to remain within the bounds of the Porter District, with its working-class houses and apartments, its corner markets, gin mills, chilidog stands, strip malls, filling stations, and hash houses, opting for a meandering course that never left me more than a mile from my own building.

At some point during the run, I began to notice my heartbeat slowing and my stride becoming more fluid. I was able to take corners sharper, turning on a dime. I also detected a faint wild feline odor emanating from my pores. Looking out at the world, I perceived the same crispness in my surroundings that I'd noticed that morning outside the electronics store. Though the sun was obscured by a thick marine haze, the world seemed as bright and clear as it would on a cloudless day. On top of that, certain places seemed even brighter, as if shining with their own light. I ran straight through one such spot, a short stretch of pavement in front of a used clothing store, and for those few yards the world smelled cleaner, the air felt warmer, and the hairs on my arms stood up as if they'd been charged with electricity. It was like passing through a pocket of time and space in a different world. I stopped running and walked back to the spot, but it no longer seemed any different than the rest of the street. I continued my run, thinking that I must still be having flashbacks from my hallucinatory joy ride.

As I ran, I began to feel pressure building inside my head, as though someone was pumping steam into my skull. I experienced a bout of vertigo, and, even though I quickly recovered, I had trouble regaining my earlier rhythm. I was beginning to notice more of the otherworldly pockets blinking in and out of my vision. I tried to concentrate on one and nearly ran into an elderly woman walking her dog. I grunted out an apology, and the woman pulled her dog back by its leash as it snapped at me. I ran on, but my breathing had become ragged, and I was starting to feel lightheaded. Colors were too bright, and I sensed movements just out of my range of vision. I became aware of voices, loud enough to hear but too low for me to distinguish individual words. I was hot. Sweat was pouring from my body. I felt myself becoming dizzy. The horizon began to tilt....

I woke up on the sidewalk in front of a gin joint. Pedestrians breezed by me without pausing. This was Yerba City, and the sight of a body sprawled against the front of a bar was not an unexpected sight, even in the middle of the day. I dragged myself to a sitting position and leaned back against the outside of the bar, holding my head in my hands. At least the vertigo had subsided. When I was sure that I hadn't suffered anything more serious than some scrapes and bruises from my fall, I rubbed the sweat out of my eyes and took a look around.

I recognized the gin joint and calculated that I was about three-quarters of a mile from my apartment. Colors still seemed brighter and edges crisper than they should, even after I blinked and rubbed my eyes a few times, and I acknowledged that this was going to be the new normal for me. Fine, I thought to myself. Brighter and clearer. Got it. I'd adjust to this new reality, just as I'd had to adjust to my new sense of awareness after the elf had worked his magic on me. Things change. The key was accepting things as they were, instead of trying to force them to be something they weren't, even if that's what they'd always been before. Or something like that. It probably sounded wiser when coming from the mouths of the ancient Huaxian philosophers.

I tried to pull myself to my feet, but a new wave of vertigo put a stop to that idea. Shit, I'd thought I was done with that. I wondered if I'd suffered a concussion. I didn't remember hitting my head, but who knew. Closing my eyes made the vertigo worse, so I popped them back open again. I found myself staring into the old paving stone that made up the front wall of the gin joint. I blinked a couple of times and noticed that some marks had been scratched into the stone with a small blade. The scratches were thin, but after focusing on them I realized that the marks spelled out a question. Some of the words had been reduced to letters or numerals, some of the characters were written in reverse, and some of the words were spelled wrong, but the question was clear: "Are you looking for me?"

"Sure I am," I muttered to the wall. "I'm looking for you and the bus that ran over me." I breathed in and out slowly, and, fighting off more dizziness, pulled myself the rest of the way to my feet.

I was dusting myself off when I noticed sunlight glinting off something metal on the sidewalk where I'd been sitting. With a start, I realized that it was my house key, which I'd pinned inside the pocket of my sweatpants before starting my run. Figuring that it must have come unattached and popped out of my pocket when I fell, I bent down and retrieved it. While still crouched, I noticed that the tip of the key was shinier than it should have been. Examining it more closely, I could see that the surface had been scratched off. I looked at the writing on the wall. Using the tip of the key, I underlined the question. The scratch mark appeared to match the width and depth of the scratches used to form the letters. Had someone taken my key out of my pocket and used it to write that question? And was the question intended for me?

I shook my head, rose to my feet, and started for home.

**

Once I was cleaned up and dressed, I punched in a number on my cell phone and hit call. A peppy voice jumped on the line in the middle of the first ring. "Nautilus Jewelry and Novelty, how can I help you?"

"Business must be slow."

"Ehhh, Mondays. What can you do. What's the haps, Jackson? Staying out of trouble?"

"You know me."

"That bad, huh? Anything a drink can't fix?"

"Wouldn't hurt. I need a favor."

"That right? The last time I helped you out you ruined my snazzy hat, you bastard! I still haven't been able to find a replacement."

"That's hard to believe. You wouldn't think that pink and white fedoras would be that hard to find. Its loss has left a real void."

"You mock, but that hat was a gem. They don't make them like that anymore."

"It's a wonder they ever made them at all."

"Hardy har har, motherfucker! So what's this favor you want?"

I was relieved to hear an upbeat, almost manic note in Crawford's voice. He'd lost more than an ugly hat the last time I'd needed his help. A particularly nasty witch had possessed him and left him shaken up but good! At the best of times, Crawford's grip on his sanity required an extraordinary amount of self-discipline reinforced by a mundane life of quiet routine. Few people knew that Crawford was a were-rat, a shapeshifter who transformed into a swarm of more than a hundred rats, and, as he had explained to me, were-rats were psychotic by nature. The hints that he'd dropped on occasion spoke of a sordid and depraved earlier life, although anyone would be hard-pressed to imagine the middle-aged, apple-cheeked, balding, little pixie of a shopkeeper having an interesting and checkered past. Maintaining an ordinary life was a strain on the little shifter, and he sometimes needed to, as he put it, let the rats run wild for a spell. It had been several weeks since his ordeal with the witch, and I'd seen him a few times afterwards for casual lunches and a few drinks. It seemed to me that he was mostly over his case of the heebie-jeebies, and I hoped that he'd be willing to do another service for me, especially since this time if everything went according to plan I wouldn't be placing him at any real risk. I wanted to be careful, though. The little bundle of rats was probably the closest thing I had to a best friend, and I wasn't going to ask him to do anything that either of us would be likely to regret. Unless he insisted.

"Would it be all right if I came out to your shop? I'll explain it all when I get there. It's nothing much. I just need you to hold on to something for me."

"Yeah? Is it shiny?"

"It's small and valuable. And some nasty people are after it."

"Cool! We'll negotiate terms when you get here. And pick up a bag of cheese balls on your way over. I'm fresh out!"

***

A few hours later, having somehow missed out on lunch and left less than satisfied by a handful of cheese balls, I decided to get to the Black Minotaur early so that I could feast on the specialty of the house—a plate of deep-fried calamari, soaked in garlic sauce, on a bed of rice—before my meeting with Detective Kalama. I was pleasantly stuffed and nursing my third mug of beer when the detective arrived at a little after eight. The Black Minotaur was a popular place, cleaner and classier than most of the night spots in the Porter, and the joint was jumping, even on a Monday night. As usual, the crowd was diverse: business men and women smoking cigarettes and sipping cocktails and single-malt whiskeys, working-class stiffs salting their beers, street people passing around joints and drinking from flasks, humans, gnomes, dwarfs, nymphs, some shady characters who I thought might be shifters of some sort, and even a couple of trolls. Kalama spotted me, and I made room for her in my booth.

The detective's eyes were drooping, and perspiration caused her short dark hair to stick to her neck. "You look tired," I said.

She glared at me. "You have no idea."

But then her face softened, and I saw the hint of a smile come to her lips. She glanced upwards toward the ceiling. "Your elemental, Smokey... is she here now?"

"It. I keep telling you that elementals aren't animals. They don't have genders. And, yes, Smokey's up in the rafters, soaking up the whiskey fumes."

Kalama's smile broadened. "Can I see her?"

I sent out a summons, and a heartbeat later a two-inch gray funnel of whirling wind appeared out of nowhere to hover an inch above my beer glass. "Greetings, Aleksss." The voice coming out of the funnel sounded like the hissing of wind over reeds. "Howsss tricksss?"

I'd taught it to say that.

A delighted gasp came from Kalama, and her face lit up in childlike wonder. I held out my hand, palm up. "Hello Smokey. Stay away from my beer." The elemental hopped up from over my glass and landed on top of my palm.

"Smokey, do you remember Detective Kalama? You met her when I was at her house."

"Smokey rememberss. Greetingsss, Detective Kalama."

The detective couldn't stop smiling. "Hello Smokey. It's nice to see you again."

Smokey jumped out of my hand and lowered itself carefully onto Kalama's shoulder. My heart leapt a little in surprise. In theory, Smokey shouldn't have had the wherewithal to initiate such an act unless I commanded it to. The general consensus among the authorities was that elementals were barely sentient forces of nature that could mimic speech and obey simple commands, but which were incapable of any real independent thought. But in the year or so that I'd been working with Smokey, it seemed to me that this particular tiny force of nature might be a little more sentient and possess a bit more intelligence and self-awareness than most of the experts in the field considered possible. I suspected that the same was true of other elementals, too. I wondered if the established authorities were reluctant to accept a higher level of intelligence in elementals because the idea of fully sentient, self-aware beings with the ability to think for themselves threatened the status of elementalists as masters and the role of elementals as mere animated tools.

Kalama arched her neck so that the wind from the elemental would cool her neck. "Mmmm...," she murmured. "That feels good, but I think I could use a beer."

I nodded at the elemental. "You can go now, Smokey. If Detective Kalama comes back here again, you come to her and say hello."

The tiny twister hopped off Kalama's shoulder and hovered over the table for a beat before launching itself to the rafters, where it disappeared in the smoke-filled haze.

Kalama arched an eyebrow. "She's cute."

"It," I corrected.

"I think she's a she. And weren't you going to get me a beer?"

I signaled for a waitress, who took Kalama's order. I ordered a fresh beer for myself, even though I was only half finished with the one I had. When the waitress was gone, the detective frowned at me.

I frowned back at her. "What have I done this time?"

She shook her head. "You have a habit of getting in over your head, don't you."

"What do you mean?"

"There was that business with Captain Graham."

I shrugged. "Like I told you, I wasn't the one who killed him."

She ignored me. "And then there was that mess with the Barbary Coast Bruja."

I felt an involuntary shudder that I hoped didn't show. "Yeah, that was weird."

"Weird! It almost got me killed!"

"Sorry." In point of fact, it had almost got *me* killed, too. A couple of times. At the very least, I'd been on my way to a very dark and mysterious place before I'd been snatched back to what we like to refer to as reality.

"And then there was that child-killing demon a few weeks back."

"So what's your point?"

"My point is that the kind of trouble that follows you around isn't your ordinary kind of trouble."

I took a sip from my beer glass. "That might be true, but I still don't know where you're going with this."

The detective leaned toward me over the table, and her voice was barely more than a whisper. "Leea." When I didn't say anything, she elaborated. "You've got the LIA on your ass." She held up a hand and indicated a half-inch space with her thumb and forefinger. "And they're this far from making you disappear from the face of the earth."

Chapter Nine

"What in the world have you gotten yourself into, gumshoe?"

"Does this have to do with Redhorn?" I shook my head. "I don't know. I did a job and Redhorn turned up dead. I don't even know for sure if his death was connected with the job I did, although it would be quite a coincidence if it wasn't. But I don't know what Leea's role is in all this. It seemed like a routine job, and it's over and done with now."

Kalama's eyes narrowed. "You better give it to me from the beginning. And don't hold anything back. None of this 'protecting your client's interests' bullshit. A possible murder suspect got in contact with you, and right now you're my only link to this suspect. Or maybe you did it, and this other guy knows about it and wants to blackmail you. You're up to your eyeballs in hot water, and you think you're taking a bubble bath."

I shook my head. "It doesn't work that way, detective. I'll tell you what I can, but I've still got a duty to my client." Even if I didn't like the son of a bitch, but I kept that part to myself.

Kalama arched her eyebrows at me, waiting for me to continue. I gathered my thoughts and obliged her. "I fingered Redhorn for something that he shouldn't have been doing. I didn't feel good about it, but I caught him red-handed. A few hours later, he dies. I don't feel so good about that, either, but that's the breaks. You probably heard that a prosecutor from the D.A.'s office questioned me for a couple of hours in one of your sweatboxes. Deet was there, and we both know that Deet is LIA." I shrugged. "Deet talked to me afterwards, too, at The Acorn Grill. Deet seemed to think that I knew something about something, but I'm still in the dark about that. I don't know if Deet is convinced, though."

I stopped talking then, and Kalama continued to stare at me. "You're holding back, gumshoe. I don't like it when you hold information back from me."

"I've told you more than I needed to. Why don't you let me know what this is all about, and maybe we can go from there? That's why you wanted to see me, right? Because you've got something to tell me, and you don't want your bosses to know that we're talking."

Kalama's voice was a hiss. "I don't want *Leea* to know that we're talking!" She leaned back in her seat and nodded. "Okay. You're right. I don't make a habit of discussing my cases with persons of interest, but I expect some quid pro quo from you. Got that?" She took a deep breath, glanced at the crowded lounge, and began to tell her story. "We got an anonymous call just after midnight on Friday night. A request for a welfare check on a man named Inyon Redhorn. Officers are dispatched to his apartment, and they find him in his bed, dead. Doesn't look like there's any foul play involved, so they scoop him up, put some tape on the door, and bring him to the coroner, where he gets put in line for an autopsy."

The waitress came by with beers, and Kalama paused to take a sip before continuing. "A couple of hours later, I hear that our officers are looking to bring you in for questioning. I ask around, but no one knows why. Then I get wind that the D.A.'s office is going to send someone to question you, and I'm thinking, okay, you've been a bad boy, but Lubank will handle it." The detective smiled. "Our brass is scared to death of that slimy weasel." She held the smile for a beat before her lips pursed and she grew serious again. "And then I hear that Deet is going to be in on the questioning, and I'm thinking that you've been more than just a bad boy. I'm thinking that you've been poking your nose where it doesn't belong. So I'm starting to get a little interested, because, you know, Kai thinks you're a swell guy to have a drink with. Or to invite to a barbecue. He likes it that you have an interest in pre-Dragon Lord history. Most people, including a lot of his students, are bored to tears by the subject."

Kalama paused to empty half her glass of beer in one long gulp. "Then this morning I get word that a swell named Inyon Redhorn *might* have been murdered, and that you *might* be connected to his death." She turned her head to fire off a belch. "So I dig around, and find out that Redhorn was a bigwig at Leaflock Services, and that he was selling company secrets, and that you're the one who caught him at it. I know that Leaflock hired you, so we can stop dancing around with that. My Lieutenant wants to know if Leaflock hired you to put Redhorn's lights out, but I'm not buying that, and he doesn't really buy it, either. Besides, we did a quickie autopsy on Redhorn, and all the coroner can come up with is heart failure."

"All deaths are heart failure, aren't they?"

Kalama's smile came and went. "Yeah, but it's generally caused by something. And in this case, we don't know what caused it. Coroner says the heart appeared to be reasonably healthy. Right up until it stopped, that is."

I nodded, and Kalama continued. "Next thing you know, the lieutenant tells me that we've got a suspicious email delivered to you, and it's connected to Redhorn's death in some way. He tells me to bring you in for questioning, which I try to do as quietly as I can. You don't answer your calls, so I have to do it a little noisier than I wanted, but that's on you."

I waited for her to go on.

"And then, who do you think shows up for your questioning?"

"Let me guess. Deet."

"Deet. So what does Leea want with you, gumshoe? Look, I get it. I know that you're a big strong hardass who can take care of himself and who doesn't need help from anyone, least of all the coppers, but something is going on here. And if Leea's involved, then it's something you're not going to be able to handle by being strong and silent." She leaned back. "Okay, your turn. I want to know about Redhorn. Specifically, I want to know if he was murdered. You're in it somehow, and I want to know how far."

I took a sip from my beer while I thought about how much I wanted to tell the detective. Kalama was looking out for me, but I wasn't going to be doing her any favors by dragging her any further into this mess. On the other hand, she was a big girl, all grown up and capable of making her own decisions about things. I set my glass on the table. "Once I start talking, you're going to know things that Leea will find interesting. Are you sure you want that? Think about how badly you value your career before you answer."

"I don't have to think about it, you dumb palooka. You know how I feel about Leea. Spill!"

I nodded. "Okay. This Leaflock character is a real prick, but he's also the genuine article, a real genius. He's developed some sort of cell regenerator that he thinks is going to revolutionize the world and make him a fortune. A key component to this gizmo is something called RAA, and it has Leea's attention for some reason. Don't ask me why. I don't know what RAA stands for or what it is, but I'm pretty certain that Redhorn downloaded information about it, including a formula for it, to a special enchanted flash drive."

I told the detective what I'd discovered about Redhorn's illicit activities and why I believed that he had intended to sell the flash drive to a mysterious buyer. I described my questioning at the hands of

A.D.A. Costano, and my later conversation with Deet. "Leaflock must be working with Deet. Deet must have found out from him that Redhorn was negotiating with someone calling himself Nocturnal for the info on RAA. The LIA must have uncovered Nocturnal's email to me. They're good at that kind of thing. Maybe they know who Nocturnal is, I don't know, but it's hard to hide anything from Leea. So Deet has the coppers haul me in and then watches you question me about the email. Did Deet say anything when you were done with me?"

"Not to me." Kalama's shoulders hunched, and she drew her arms to her sides as if she were fending off a sudden chill. "I get the same feeling around Deet that I get around those witches you introduced me to."

"I don't disagree."

I went on to tell Kalama about finding the flash drive in Redhorn's apartment, and the detective didn't bat an eye. She didn't arrest me for B and E, either, so I went on to tell her how the flash drive had reduced my computer to slag when I'd tried to access it. She sighed and shook her head at that, and my attempt to freeze her with my steely glare had no effect.

"I went to a computer tech who got me past the passcode, but I haven't been able to access the drive because your bulls confiscated my new computer. You think you can do something about that?"

She shrugged. "Maybe."

I told her about the burner phone and my conversation with Nocturnal. That got her attention.

"And you're going to meet with him tonight?"

"Early tomorrow morning, technically."

"Alone?'

"I should be okay."

The detective's eyes narrowed. "And you base that assumption on...."

I tried to sound cheerful. "He seemed to be a right enough gee on the phone. I'm not expecting any trouble from him."

Kalama's glare could have sliced a diamond. "I'm touched by your warm and fuzzy view of human nature. Your mystery man may have killed Redhorn, but somehow failed to come away with the flash drive. Either that, or he believes that you killed Redhorn and stole the flash drive from him."

"That's what I'm thinking, too. Five will get you ten he'll offer me money for the drive."

"And you intend to sell it to him?"

I shrugged. "Depends on what he's offering."

"You know that selling stolen property is a crime, right?"

"Is it? Well, if it belonged to Redhorn, I doubt that he'll be pressing any charges."

"That flash drive is evidence."

"Evidence of what? Redhorn died of natural causes, right?"

"Sure he did." Kalama finished off the rest of her beer. "And what about Leea?"

Before I could respond, our waitress came by and asked if we needed anything. I lifted my glass, and Kalama nodded at me. "Two more of the same," I told the waitress. When she was gone, Kalama caught my eyes and raised her eyebrows. "Leea?" she prompted.

"What about them?"

"Think about it. How did Nocturnal get your email address?"

I shrugged. "No idea."

Kalama frowned. "There's too much we don't know. Do you think Deet knows you're meeting with Nocturnal tonight?"

"I don't have any reason to think so. The LIA might be watching me, but, if they are, I haven't spotted them."

Kalama scowled. "And you think you would? You're good, but they're the LIA."

I had to admit that she had a point. I tried to look confident. "It's a chance I'm willing to take."

Kalama looked less than convinced. "Uh-huh. And has it occurred to you that this Nocturnal joker might be LIA?"

Actually, it hadn't. I'd figured Nocturnal either as a representative from one of Leaflock's competitors, or as a free-agent of some sort. But I had to admit that the detective might be on to something. Had Redhorn been dealing with Leea? Had Redhorn been dealing with Leea and not known about it? "It's possible," I began, putting pieces together as I spoke, "that when Redhorn started selling off proprietary information, Leea got wind of it. An LIA agent, Nocturnal maybe, was then assigned to contact Redhorn and make a deal for Leaflock's cell regenerator. Redhorn sold the blueprints of the device to Nocturnal, but Leea still needed the formula or schematics or whatever for the key component: RAA." I paused, thinking about it. "But why would Leea be interested in Leaflock's device? What use would they have for it? And why wouldn't they just wait for Leaflock to build the thing and then buy it, or confiscate it for reasons of 'national security'?"

Kalama thought about it while the waitress came by and set us up with fresh beers. When we were alone again, Kalama shook her head. "I don't know. Who knows why Leea does what it does. All I know is that the agency is all over this. Nocturnal might be Leea or he might not be. He might even be a foreign agent, maybe from Qusco, or the Huaxian Empire. If you're smart, you'll assume the worst."

We picked up our glasses and tilted them at each other as if making a toast. As we drank, dark thoughts slipped unbidden into my brain. Kalama was right: I should assume the worst. But what if there was something worse behind all this than the LIA, or foreign agents? I failed to suppress the shudder that ran down my spine.

**

Kalama left the Minotaur once she'd finished her beer, leaving me to ponder my upcoming meeting with the mysterious Nocturnal, who may or may not have iced Redhorn. I considered the possibilities. Possibility number one: Mister Nocturnal was going to make me an offer for the flash drive. Would I accept the offer? Why not? I didn't know what was on the flash drive, and I couldn't think of any reason why I should care. And what if it was information about the mysterious RAA? I still didn't care. It was nothing to me. I could sell the information to Nocturnal and put the whole matter out of my mind. That seemed like the ideal option to me.

Of course, Kalama was right: I'd be selling stolen goods. Well, what of it? Lubank was the cleverest mouthpiece in the city. He'd figure out a way to keep me from going down for it. Did anyone have any proof that I'd stolen the flash drive? Sure, I'd told Kalama, but that had been off the record, and neither of us had been recording the conversation. Besides, she was homicide, not theft, so I doubt that she'd even care all that much. She had other fish to fry. She hadn't tried to stop me from going to meet with Nocturnal, had she? No, outside of making sure I was aware of the potential dangers to me, she'd been jake with it. So, yeah, maybe I'd take the money and run. Especially if the only person who'd be hurt by it was Leaflock. I slapped the table with the palm of my hand. The arrogant little gnome could fuck himself!

Some of the other patrons shot quick frowns my way, and it occurred to me then that I should probably slow down on the beers.

Okay, possibility number two: Leea is in the diner, ready to swoop down on me as soon as I produce the flash drive. Maybe, despite my attempts to be cautious and attentive, they'd manage to follow me to the diner, or follow Nocturnal. Except that I wasn't going to have the flash drive on me. I'd left it with Crawford, a man whose special talents made him uniquely suited to hide small items of value, and it was going to stay with him until I figured out what I was going to do with it. The truth was that I wasn't going to let Nocturnal or anyone else get their paws on it until I knew what was on it. It wasn't just that I wanted to make sure I wasn't unleashing something dangerous on the world. No, it was more a matter of my insatiable curiosity. The simple fact was that now that the drive was in my hands, I needed to know what I had. I thought about what Walks in Cloud had said about curiosity killing the cat. Well, I thought to myself, I am what I am.

Possibility number three: the man calling himself Nocturnal was an LIA agent, or an agent from another realm. It made a certain amount of sense, especially if one or more of the Seven Realms had an interest in obtaining Leaflock's gadget. I had no idea why they'd want it, but then I didn't really know what it did, either. Was Nocturnal working with Deet? Deet had been ready to remove me from the playing field if the agent had been convinced that I knew anything about RAA. It occurred to me that the only reason why I was still in the game was that Deet had been waiting to see if I could make the missing flash drive appear. Or maybe Nocturnal and Deet were working against each other. Even if Nocturnal was LIA, rumors were rampant of rival factions within the agency.

My head started to spin. There were too many loose strands in this tapestry, and I didn't have enough information to know how they were all supposed to weave together into a recognizable picture. Well, fuck it. Planning wasn't my strong suit. I'd simply have to go meet the mysterious Nocturnal and wing it. That was me all over. Lead with the chin and see who tries to take a poke at it. Throw a counterpunch and see where it lands. Everything was gonna be swell. Another beer and a shot or two later, I put on my hat, left some bills under my glass, put a smile on my face, and strolled out of the joint, making sure not to stagger into anything or anyone on my way to the street.

I had some time to kill, so I decided to take a walk and let the night air drive some of the alcoholic fog out of my brain. I put my back to the wind and let it push me up the hill to the next intersection. The light was green, so I pressed forward. I caught a red light at the next corner, so I made a right turn and breathed in the competing smells of bus fumes from the street and barbecued beef from a restaurant with a line hanging out the door. I heard the buzz from a neon sign over the entrance to a cocktail lounge farther up the street and watched the glaring blue outline of a squid blink on and off, on and off as I made my way toward it.

As I drew close to the cocktail lounge, a bird—an owl, I realized—dropped from the sky to land on the roof of the building above the sign. Another owl landed next to the first, and then a third one descended to join the other two. Three owls, with identical coverings of orange, black, and white feathers on their bulky bodies and orange feathers circling large orange and black eyes, sat side by side and swiveled their heads to stare down at me with unblinking eyes.

When I was standing beneath the owls, I stopped in my tracks. An approaching couple saw me looking up and glanced over their heads to see what was attracting my attention. Without stopping, they looked back down and continued walking, uninterested in the sight of three birds of a type not often seen in Yerba City. I kept my eyes on the owls, a part of me half expecting them to open their beaks and begin speaking, perhaps to impart some secret words of wisdom to me. As I stood in the middle of the sidewalk I became aware of a deep blackness forming behind the birds, an absence of light darker than the night. The blackness grew until it surrounded the owls, and then the blackness—along with the owls—vanished in the blink of an eye.

In that same instant, a gust of wind blew my fedora off my head and sent it flying up the sidewalk. I broke into a run and caught the hat just before it skidded into the intersection. I dusted it off and started to jam it onto my head when something caught my attention. Tucked into the outer band of the hat was a lead pencil that had been sharpened to a stub and a folded piece of plain white paper. I plucked the paper out of the band and unfolded it. It was blank on both sides. Curious, I freed the nub of a pencil from the band. Before I could think about what was happening, I fell to my knees and slapped the paper down on the sidewalk. As if it had a will of its own, my hand began printing letters on the paper with the pencil. When I was finished, I dropped the pencil and read the message that had been printed in large, shaky handwriting that was not my own: "U R luknig em 4?"

I stared at the paper until a gust of wind sent it shooting into the intersection, where it was pulled beneath a passing bus. I put my hat on my head, making sure that it was snug against the wind, and got to my feet. Pedestrians passed by without giving me a second glance. I looked up, but saw no owls, or any birds at all for that matter. I didn't see any black voids, either. It was a typical evening on the streets of Yerba City. Fine, I thought to myself. Everything's fine. I pulled out my cell phone and placed a call.

"Hello?"

"Walks in Clouds? This is Alex Southerland."

"Speaks with Wind! Good to hear from you. Doing okay?"

"To be honest? I'm not sure. That's why I'm calling. I know it's late, but..."

"I told you to call me anytime, day or night, remember? So what's up? You experiencing some aftermath from your journey to the spirit world?"

"Probably. Everything looks a little different to me now. Colors are brighter, and sometimes I see patches where reality seems to have, I don't know, shifted or something. It's hard to explain, but I'm guessing you're familiar with what I'm describing."

"You're a different person now, Jack. You're more sensitive to alternate realities. There are places that act as gateways to other places. Some of these gateways are more or less stable, but other gateways come and go. You'll get used to it."

"Earlier today I collapsed while I was running. But I think I'm starting to adjust. Anyway, that's not the problem. A few minutes ago, my hat blew off my head. When I caught up to it there was a pencil and a folded piece of paper stuck in the hatband. They hadn't been there before."

"That's weird."

"Yeah, well it gets weirder. I unfolded the paper to see if anything was written on it, but it was blank. Then I took the pencil out of the hatband, and I started writing a message against my will in someone else's handwriting. Please tell me that's a normal side effect of whatever it is I'm going through."

Walks in Cloud made a hmphing sound. "Nope, that's a new one on me, Jack. Your hand moved on its own? Like you were possessed?"

"Like my hand was possessed. I'll admit that I've done some drinking, and if I'm not three sheets to the wind, I might be at least two. But I was still in control of myself. Except that my hand had a mind of its own."

"I've heard of that. It's called automatic writing. Someone or something took control of your hand in order to send you a message. What did it say?"

"It was jumbled up a little. Some of the characters were reversed, and some of the words and letters were written in the wrong order, but I think that the gist of the message was, 'Are you looking for me?' But here's the thing. Earlier today when I collapsed while I was running? When I came to, I saw the same message scratched into the side of the building I woke up next to. I found my house key on the sidewalk below the message, and it looks to me like the key had been used to write it. At first I thought that someone had taken the key out of my pocket while I was unconscious and written the message. Now, I think I must have written it myself."

"Are you by any chance looking for someone?"

I looked around to see if anyone was listening to my half of the conversation, but this was Yerba City, and anyone passing by was either involved in their own lives or being extra careful not to seem to be involving themselves in mine. "Cougar told me to protect the boy who talks backwards."

"You think that this message is from this backwards talking boy?"

"Could be. Or I could be going crazy. I'm trying to keep an open mind."

"You're not going crazy, Jack. Or maybe you are, but that might be totally unrelated to what's happening here. I mean, I'm an information tech, not a headshrinker. Look, our people tell stories about boys who talk backwards. In the stories, these boys have certain connections to the spirit world. It sounds to me like your own connections to the spirit world have put you in touch with this boy."

I rubbed my eyes. Either this conversation was making me a little woozy, or I was still trying to shake off the effects of too much drink. "Is there anything I can do to stop him from grabbing control of pieces of my body without my permission? It's intrusive."

Walks in Cloud laughed. "Welcome to your new reality, Jack. Find this kid and talk to him. I'm sure you can teach him some manners. In the meantime, you might try writing him a message and see if he responds. Could work. You never know."

"Thanks, I might try that. I want to be good and sober first, though. Hey, listen. You've been a big help. Thanks."

"No problem, Jack. You all right now? I need my beauty sleep."

"I'll manage. As long as the kid doesn't take control of my fist and start punching me in the face."

"My advice? Don't piss him off. Goodnight, Southerland."

"Goodnight."

I disconnected the call and resumed walking, breathing in as much of the cold night air as I could and hoping that it would clear the dizziness out of my head before I met with the man who may or may not have murdered Redhorn.

Chapter Ten

A hack dropped me off at the Diner Forty-Niner a little after one. No one seemed to mind that I was early for my meeting with Nocturnal. I'd've been lying if I'd said that my head was clear, but I figured it wasn't nothing that a gallon of black coffee couldn't handle.

My senses were overwhelmed with the fragrance of that coffee when I walked into the diner, and my stomach began to clench in anticipation of the dark elixir. The joint was less than half filled with workers coming off the night shift, a cabbie on a break eating by himself, a couple of uniformed cops, and a solitary street bandit that I had pegged as a dealer in black-market something or another waiting for a customer. A hostess in a brown and white uniform that was supposed to be reminiscent of the Old West led me to a vacant table that sat four. A harried-looking waitress with a nice set of gams came by as soon as I had settled in and filled my coffee cup. I told her that I was waiting for someone and to top off my cup whenever she was in the neighborhood.

One-thirty came and went, but I saw no sign of anyone who might be my mystery man. At one forty-five, I decided that I was hungry and ordered a tuna steak with rice. When it arrived, I spent a few moments wondering how tuna could be that greasy. By two-fifteen, I'd finished as much of the fish as I could stomach and was thinking about leaving. The place was filling up with the after-hours crowd, and I was starting to feel self-conscious about hogging an entire table to myself. It looked like my meeting with Nocturnal was going to be a bust.

As I picked up my hat and started to rise from my chair, the door to the diner opened and an odd-looking gentleman slipped inside. He was short for a human, not much over five feet tall, and his large top hat somehow made him seem even shorter. His round, clean-shaven face was neither young nor old, and a monocle was fitted over one of his large pale brown eyes. A diamond the size of a golf ball was affixed to the lapel of his tuxedo jacket, whose tails hung down past his knees. A cummerbund stretched over a torso the size of a beach ball. He carried a thin ivory-handled cane in one hand like a wand, and he showed no indication that he needed it for walking.

Once inside, the rotund little man spotted me right away, and his face lit up with something that appeared to be genuine delight. He removed his hat, revealing a head as bald as a cue ball, and approached my table with a distinguished stride, as if he were making his entrance at the Dragon Lord's annual New Year's Eve ball. All at once, I realized that I recognized this man. How could I not? Armine Clearwater was an eminently familiar face in Yerba City.

Clearwater had a reputation as one of the richest men in the city—possibly the richest—but no one could tell you exactly what it was he did to earn all that dough. Investments, some said. Others said gambling. Probably both, since they amounted to the same thing. A mainstay in the Yerba City nightlife, the press described Clearwater's occupation as "professional socialite," and stories of his late-night and early-morning drinking and dining exploits were legendary. His critics declared that one of his secrets for maintaining his wealth was that he never had to pay for his own drinks. Any one of a group of sycophants, hoping to hang on to his place in the prestigious swell's orbit, was always there to place a full glass in his hand, or to set it in front of him at his table. No social event could be considered top drawer unless Clearwater was invited, and he could make or break an event by choosing whether or not to be present.

I rose as the grandly dressed dandy drew near and offered my hand in greeting. Clearwater passed his cane from his right gloved hand to his left and shook my hand with a firm grip. "Good evening," he said in a wine-soaked tenor voice that sounded much clearer than the one I'd heard on the phone earlier. "I can see by the expression on your mug that you know who I am. Good. It will save us a lot of questions about my credibility." He released my hand and indicated my chair. "Shall we be seated?"

We sat and Clearwater placed his hat upside down on the chair next to him, then took off his gloves and placed them inside the hat. He turned to the waitress with the shapely gams, who seemed to have materialized out of nowhere with a coffee pot, and greeted her warmly. "Good evening, dear. I'll have a dolphin steak, rare, with creamed acorn dressing on a bed of dandelion greens."

The waitress blinked. "I'm sorry, sir, but that's not on our menu."

Clearwater favored her with a gracious smile and a twinkle in his eyes. "I believe that your kitchen staff will find that the ingredients are on hand, and I have no doubt that they will have the skill to put the dish together. Off with you now." He feigned brushing her away with the fingers on both hands. "Shoo! Shoo! That's a good girl."

We both shared a long look at the confused waitress's gams as she bustled her way toward the kitchen. When she was out of sight, Clearwater turned his attention back to me, just sitting there at first, a warm smile on his face, looking as if he were meeting his long-lost cousin. From the way he was dressed and the scent of expensive wine on his breath, I concluded that he'd been spending the evening at a much more upscale venue than the Diner Forty-Niner, but far from acting put off by the casually dressed nighthawks, the noisy kitchen clatter, and the odor of stale coffee and deep-fried fat, the professional socialite seemed as comfortable in this working-class bistro as if he were dining at the VIP table at The Gold Coast Club. After a few moments, he reached across the table for a packet of cream and emptied its contents into his coffee. He breathed in the aroma of the hot java, closed his eyes, and took a small sip. Immediately, his whole face puckered, as if the cup were filled with lemon juice. "Oh, that's awful." He took another sip. "Simply dreadful." Then the pucker disappeared as his face lit up in a smile. "Scorched and bitter, just the way I like it." He tipped the cup and took a long gulp, which he punctuated with an "Ahhhhh."

I found myself with nothing to say, so I listened to the scraping of utensils on plates and the raucous babble of conversations from the other tables for a few moments, waiting for Clearwater to tell me why he'd asked me to meet him in this place.

Clearwater placed his cup in its saucer. "So! You're Alexander Southerland. Unless I'm making a terrible mistake, and I don't think I am, you have something I want. Hmm?"

I took a sip of my own coffee, which I was no longer tasting. "I think so. I have a flash memory drive, but I haven't been able to access it. It's passcode-protected, but I'd be surprised if it didn't contain what you're looking for."

Clearwater leaned over the table and lowered his voice. "You took this memory drive from Mr. Redhorn?"

"I didn't take it from him. I found it in his apartment along with the phone that I used to call you. Redhorn was not there at the time."

Clearwater closed one eye and stared at me through his monocle, letting me know how an amoeba feels when it's being studied through a microscope. "Did you kill him?" he asked.

"Would you believe me if I told you that I didn't?"

Clearwater opened his closed eye and smiled. "Actually, I would. I wanted to know how you would answer the question. You didn't deny it, which is interesting. But I know that you didn't kill Mr. Redhorn."

"I hear he died of natural causes."

Clearwater's smile broadened as he sat back in his chair. "I heard the same thing. But, of course, neither of us believes that to be true."

"It *would* be quite a coincidence if it were." I took a tiny sip of coffee. Truthfully, I was feeling like I'd had my fill, but Clearwater's intense scrutiny was making me uncomfortable, and I was having trouble sitting still for it.

"In any case, Mr. Southerland, I know that you found that drive on Saturday night, the night *after* Mr. Redhorn... died." Clearwater let out a chuckle. "And I know that you were in no shape to kill anyone on the previous night."

"You seem to know a lot of things," I said.

"More than you can imagine, my dear fellow. More than you can imagine. My reputation for wisdom is the stuff of legends."

"Did you kill him?"

Clearwater barked out a surprised laugh. "Me? Don't be silly, my dear boy. I was waiting for Mr. Redhorn to meet me at The Gold Coast Club on Friday night, as we had arranged. He was going to give me a memory drive containing information that I desired, and I was going to make him rich. But he didn't show up, and later I found out that he had met an unfortunate end. Unfortunate, I say, not just for him, but for me. Sadly, I never received the memory drive he had promised me. And now you have it. And I still desire it."

He reached for his coffee cup, and as he took a sip something seemed to emanate from the strange figure. It wasn't anything I could feel, like heat or cold, but it seemed to wake something up in my skin. It wasn't anything I could see, either, although the air around the stout little gentleman seemed to be clear of the haze that filled the room, as if his very presence repelled the cigarette smoke drifting our way from the nearby diners.

I met his eyes and held his gaze. "You're not an ordinary man, are you Mr. Clearwater."

He winked at me with his non-glassed eye. "Neither are you, Mr. Southerland. Neither are you. I sense some strangeness in you.

You've been touched by a spirit." His large eyes narrowed. "More than one, perhaps."

I felt twitchy in the light of those narrowed eyes, as if I were naked, and I wanted to draw his attention away from me. "Why do you want this flash drive, Mr. Clearwater?"

He blinked. "Hmm? Why do I want it? What an odd question. I would have thought that you'd ask me how much I was willing to pay for it."

"Maybe we'll get to that. First I'd like to know what you intend to do with it."

Clearwater waved a hand in dismissal. "That's neither here nor there, Mr. Southerland. It's immaterial to our transaction."

"I'd like to know anyway. It might have some bearing on price."

"Nonsense, dear fellow. I'm prepared to offer you a sufficient sum of money for the drive in your possession, the same amount that I was willing to pay Mr. Redhorn. You will either accept that offer or you won't. What I do with the drive afterward is none of your concern."

I shook my head. "I won't sell the drive if there's a chance that you'll use it for purposes I disapprove of."

Clearwater frowned. "I see. And if I assured you that my intentions are completely altruistic? That no one will be harmed? Would that satisfy you?"

"I'd need to know the details," I insisted.

Clearwater shook his head. "I admire your sense of morality, but I'm afraid that will be impossible."

I picked up a napkin and wiped my mouth. "Then I'm afraid that we won't be able to do business. I'm sorry, Mr. Clearwater. No sale."

I pushed my chair back and stood, but Clearwater stretched out a hand as if he meant to stop me. "Oh do sit down, Mr. Southerland. I just got here, and it would be rude of you to leave so soon."

"We don't seem to have anything to talk about, Mr. Clearwater. And it's getting late." But my curiosity grabbed hold of me, and I lowered myself back into my seat.

"That's better." Clearwater took a deep breath and let it out. "Let me ask you a question, Mr. Southerland. What is it that you fear

I will do with the information on that memory drive? It's not a weapon."

"Anything can be weaponized."

Clearwater again closed one eye and studied me through his monocle. "You don't know what's on the drive, do you."

"I'm reasonably certain that it contains information about something called RAA."

"As am I." Clearwater opened his eye and folded his hands over his belly. "But how much do you know about RAA? Do you even know what it is?"

I shrugged. "A key component in some device that Leaflock Services is developing."

He waited a beat. "And?"

I sighed. "I admit that I don't know much beyond that."

Clearwater's face broke into a smile that brought dimples into his cheeks. "I thought as much."

"Do you know what it is?"

"Of course."

"Care to share?"

Clearwater shook his head. "Why should I?"

"Because unless I know more about it than I do, I'm going to get up right now and walk out that door."

Clearwater sighed, a great heaving sigh that started in his belly, pushed its way up his throat with a low roaring sound, like a wave breaking on the shore, and drifted out his nose. "Okay. I'll give you something. You expressed concern that I might use RAA for some nefarious purpose. You implied that it might be a weapon of some sort. Quite the contrary. I'm going to use RAA to save a life."

I looked down at the remains of my tuna steak and listened to the buzz of conversations from the nearby tables while I thought about what Clearwater was telling me.

After a few moments, the gentleman leaned forward in his seat. "So what do you say, Mr. Southerland. Shall we negotiate a deal? What price would you set for the opportunity to prevent the loss of a life?"

"And whose life do you intend to save?"

"Does it matter, Mr. Southerland? Don't you believe in the sanctity of life?"

At that point, the waitress came by with Clearwater's dinner, and he sat back to give her room to place it on the table in front of him.

The odd gentleman savored the aroma of his dolphin steak before slicing off a piece and sampling it. He closed his eyes and smiled as he chewed. "Mmmm," he moaned. He placed his fingers to his lips and then flung them open, releasing a kiss to the rest of the room. "Perfection!"

I got the impression that Clearwater appreciated his food and drink, whether it was a well-prepared dolphin steak, fine wine, or weak and bitter coffee. If he could swallow it, he savored it.

I wondered whether he was human. I was certain that he wasn't.

I watched the man eat for a full minute before responding to his question. "I don't know about the sanctity of life, Mr. Clearwater. I'd hate to see some people die before their time, but there are others that I wouldn't mind helping along. It seems to me that we should take it on a case-by-case basis. You say you need this RAA, whatever it is, to keep someone alive. That sounds very noble, but what if it's someone who the rest of the world would prefer to see dead? I'd have to know who we're talking about and something about the circumstances before I'd be willing to help you. Otherwise, no deal."

Clearwater continued to chew his steak, and the look of deep satisfaction never left his face. When he'd swallowed, he opened his eyes and met mine. "I'm very sorry to hear you say that, Mr. Southerland. Are you sure you don't want to know how much I'm willing to offer you? Can I at least tempt you by telling you how many figures we're talking about?"

I shook my head. "Not even if it were six."

"And if it were more than six?" He spoke the words with such a casual air that I almost missed their meaning.

When I registered what I'd heard, I was stunned. But only for a moment. "Not for any amount, Mr. Clearwater. I need dough as much as the next man, but I won't kill a piece of myself for it."

Clearwater smiled. "Integrity. For many, it's just a word, a vague idea. But for you, it's real. Are you familiar with something called reification?"

I shook my head. "Nope. My education didn't extend past secondary school. And I wasn't exactly an honor student."

The stout man's belly jiggled as he let out a laugh. "It means taking something that's abstract and turning it into something real. There's a long-running philosophical debate about the reality of abstract ideas, such as integrity. My advice? Stay far away from it."

Clearwater lifted a napkin to one corner of his mouth and then the other before carefully laying it down over his mostly intact steak, as if he were preparing the expensive meal for a funeral service. He rose from his seat, put on his gloves and hat, and picked up his cane. Bowing slightly in my direction and tipping his hat, he removed his monocle and looked me straight in the eyes with both of his own. "I gave you a chance, Mr. Southerland. I don't give second chances. I will have that memory drive, and you will wish that you had allowed me to compensate you for it." With that, he straightened, turned, and sauntered out of the diner like a man without a care in the world.

It was only when the waitress came by with the check that I realized that the professional socialite had stuck me with the bill for his dolphin steak.

***

Chivo wasn't in the laundry room when I got home, and the first thing I did was to fill his bowl with yonak, a type of soup favored by trolls. The foul-smelling slop consisted of rancid meat, curdled blood, and some secret spices that I probably didn't want to know about. I bought it in bulk at a corner market a couple of blocks from my apartment. They gave me a discount, and in return I didn't inquire about the source of the meat. I didn't know where Chivo went when he was out, and that was jake with me. But ever since he'd come back to my place hungry one morning and trashed my kitchen searching for food, I'd made sure that he always had a bowl of yonak waiting for him. It was fortunate for me that the creature seemed to love the stuff; it beat having him go for my throat while I was sleeping. To be on the safe side, Syphon, the elemental who kept the laundry room aired out, was under standing orders to warn me immediately if Chivo ever set foot on the stairs leading up to my apartment.

Dawn wasn't far off when I finally hit the sack with every intention of sleeping until noon. It was a good plan, but it fell apart when someone started pounding on my front door a few minutes before sunup. I slipped on a robe and stumbled my way down the stairs to my office. I was groggy from too little sleep, and maybe, despite my best efforts, from a couple too many the night before at the Minotaur. In any case, I wasn't at my sharpest when I heard an unexpected shuffle of feet from behind me just as I was reaching the front door. Whirling around caused some momentary dizziness, and I was distracted by the sight of the lead-weighted sap streaking toward the side of my head. I managed to duck away and take most of the impact on my shoulder, but the blow knocked me off balance, making me a tick late responding to the thug who burst through my door. As he reached for me, I grabbed at his arm and threw him to the floor, only then becoming aware of a stabbing pain in the side of my neck. I had just enough time to gape at the hypo that rolled out of the thug's fist before the world came crashing down around me.

I might have been dreaming, but all memory of dreams vanished in an instant when I opened my eyes and saw darkness. My head was clear and my heart was pounding out the kind of drum solo that drove festival crowds into a frenzy. Because of my elf-enhanced senses, I didn't need my eyes in order to "see," so the bag over my head didn't prevent me from being aware of my surroundings. I knew that the man to my right was withdrawing a hypodermic needle from my arm. I knew that I was propped up in a hospital bed with my arms and legs restrained by metal clamps. I knew that Deet was standing in front of me even before the LIA agent spoke.

"Remove the head-covering."

The man with the hypo pulled the bag from my head, and I confirmed that I was not in a hospital. The bed I was lying on was the only piece of furniture in a room that was nothing but a concrete cube with no windows and just one door, closed, in the middle of the wall on my left. A single lamp with a bright halogen bulb hung from the ceiling.

Deet addressed the man with the hypo. "You can go now." He disappeared through the door and closed it behind him.

"No elemental can reach this room, Mr. Southerland. Magical wards will repel them if they try. No one knows where you are. Your cell phone is still in your apartment, and you have been scanned for tracking devices. No one can contact you or come to your aid. Do you have any questions before we get started?"

"Yes, just one. If pomosexuals reject all gender labels, then do you reject being labeled as pomosexual, too? Because that's essentially a label related to gender. And, if so, what pronoun are the rest of us supposed to use when referring to you? I guess that's two questions."

"You're being childish, Mr. Southerland. Let's begin."

Deet stepped toward me and leaned forward until the agent's face was only inches from mine, but just out of range of a head butt. Deet knew what Deet was doing.

"When you searched Mr. Redhorn's apartment on Saturday night, you found a green USB flash memory drive. Where is this flash drive now?"

I had a burning desire to scratch my nose. "What makes you think I searched Redhorn's apartment?"

"Mr. Southerland, let me clarify your position. I'm not going to waterboard you, hook you up to electrodes, or have you beaten. I'm not going to drug you, at least not any further. I will simply ask you questions until I receive satisfactory answers. If I receive satisfactory answers, I will release you. I will continue to ask my questions until I receive satisfactory answers to all of them, no matter how long that takes. You will receive no breaks, not even toilet breaks. You will receive no food, no beverages, and no sleep until I am finished. You will not be released from your restraints until I am ready to release you, and I will not be ready to release you until I am satisfied with your answers. If you think that you can outlast me, you are mistaken. If you think that you will be rescued, you are mistaken. And if you think that I will lose my patience, Mr. Southerland...."

"I am mistaken."

Deet nodded. "Yes. So now that your situation is clear, let me ask again: Where is the flash drive that you took from Mr. Redhorn's apartment?"

My inability to scratch my itching face was going to drive me insane. I concentrated on Deet's eyes. I wanted to see how long Deet could go without blinking. It turned out to be a long time, several minutes, at least. I tried to count the seconds. For the record, Deet blinked when I reached three hundred twelve, but there were no clocks in the room, and I didn't know if my count was accurate.

Deet continued to wait for my response. I continued to not give one to Deet. Instead, I sent out a summoning call to Badass. When I received no response, I sent one out for Smokey. When that came up empty, I sent out a shotgun summons for any air elemental that would respond. None did.

Switching tactics, I called the image of my jungle waterfall to my mind. It came to me in an instant, and, ignoring Deet, I sat on a rock and listened to the falling water. I knew that going catatonic wasn't going to save me, but it was a good way to think. If nothing else, Deet would be forced to use drugs or torture to snap me out of it, and, right or wrong, I would count that as a victory.

Time passed in that timeless place in my mind. After a while, I was no longer aware of Deet, and the jungle clearing became more real to me than the LIA interrogation cube. The water fell, and mist rose from the pool.

Cougar stepped through the mist and sat on his haunches in front of me. His dark chocolate voice sounded in my head: "You will die if you do not escape that place."

I thought back: "Then I guess I'll die."

"Is that your wish?"

"It's not my first choice. It might be my second, though."

Cougar didn't respond, so I sent a thought his way: "Little help?"

"I can't leap into that room and bite Deet's head off, if that's what you're thinking."

"Then what good are you?"

I sensed quiet laughter. "Why don't you answer Deet's question? Why do you wish to keep the flash drive? Why not simply give it up and go free?"

I thought about that for a few heartbeats. "I don't know. Maybe I don't like the way Deet is asking me for it."

I sensed something that felt like understanding, or maybe even pride, coming from Cougar.

Cougar's voice sounded again. "You will gain your release. But you will suffer first."

"That's the best you can do?"

"No, but it's the best I'm going to do. You should be grateful. Without me, you would either lose your self-respect or your life."

"In that case, I'm grateful. What do I need to do?"

"Talk."

"About what?"

"Anything you'd like."

And, with that, I was back in the interrogation room having a staring contest with Deet, who I knew was never going to lose.

I talked. I began to tell Deet my life story. It kept my mind off my itching face. I told Deet about growing up in a rough neighborhood with a drunk for a father and a mother who had been beaten down by life. I talked about roughhousing with the hoods in the neighborhood and joining the army to do my mandatory three-year stint with the state. I didn't talk about the Borderland. I didn't like sharing details about that part of my life with anyone, and certainly not with an agent of the LIA. I talked about helping old Mrs. Colby discover that one of her prospective tenants was a were-rat, although I didn't identify Crawford by name. If the LIA didn't know about Crawford already, they sure as hell weren't going to find out about him from me. I explained how Mrs. Colby had helped me become a private investigator, and how I'd been operating as one ever since. While I was telling my story, I emptied my bladder and evacuated my bowels. I didn't care, and Deet didn't seem to, either. I ignored my thirst and my hunger. These were small things. I knew that I couldn't outlast Deet, but that didn't mean I couldn't try.

 I talked about a few of my cases, being careful to be vague with the details. I talked about bars, which ones had the best drinks for the best prices, and which ones were just good for getting drunk in while the world turned and burned. I talked about cops, about how some cops were good, but that others were just dimwitted bullies with badges and a desire to buy respect at the end of a nightstick, or through the barrel of a gun. I talked about hope in a hopeless world. I talked about beauty and truth in a world of ugliness and lies, knowing that I was just making noise. I talked about a lot of things, all the time trying to say nothing at all. I don't know how long I talked. Hours. Maybe through the entire day. The outside world was barred from that room. I had no way to measure the passing of time. I talked, and I talked. Eventually, I got tired of talking. My words lost meaning, and I forced them through a throat as dry as the desert sand. But I forced myself to continue.

 Deet never said a word, just waited for me to answer the question. I was worried that I might say something I shouldn't, give up a bit of information that the LIA didn't already know. I kept talking. I couldn't seem to stop. Had I been drugged? Beyond the knockout drops that allowed the thug to bring me to that place and the go-go juice that woke me up, I didn't think so. Cougar had told me to talk. Had he compelled me? It didn't feel like that, but then how would I know? I thought that I could stop if I wanted to, but talking, painful as it had become, seemed like a good way to pass the time, and concentrating on not giving anything up seemed like a good way to keep my focus.

 My thoughts lost coherence, and I began to ramble. Still, I talked. My words became slurred. My mouth was parched, and my head felt like it was going to split like a ripe melon. I began to talk about owls, and how I'd been seeing them over the past couple of days.

I talked about how one of them had stolen my fedora and left a dead rat in it. I talked about how three of them had disappeared into a black void.

"And after the owls were gone, the wind blew my hat off, and the fuggin' thing was rollin' into the street, you know, 'cept I caught it before it did. And then I took the pencil—there was a pencil in the band—did I mention that? Jus' the nub of one, you know? An' I open the paper up, the paper that was folded in the ha'band, nex' to the pencil. An' then I was, I dunno, I was writing on the paper, you know? But it wasn't me doing the writing, jus' my hand. Does zat make sense? Anyway, I wrote sumthin' sumthin'.... You know, it reminded me of sumthin' else, sumthin' I heard.... Sumthin'.... Whad wassat.... Oh yeah, the boy who... the boy who toggs baggwards. Pretty weird. I don' know...."

Deet blinked. Deet did more than blink. Deet staggered backwards, out of my face. Deet stepped purposefully to the door and opened it. "Get in here! Now!"

The man with the hypo came into the room, wrinkling his nose against the smell.

"Put him under," Deet instructed him.

The last thing I remember was a needle punching into the clenched muscle of my upper arm as I struggled against the restraints.

Chapter Eleven

Something was poking at my side. When I tried to push it away, I heard an iron voice. "Get up, rummy! You can't sleep here. Move along now."

Blinding light seared my brain when I opened my eyes. I had never been so thirsty. I forced words past a cardboard tongue: "Need a drink."

"I'm sure you do. Get up! Move along now."

I blinked, and the light faded until it was just the first threads of dawn peeking through the low-lying clouds. I was sprawled on the sidewalk, and someone was trying to roust me with a broom handle. "Get up, rummy! You'll scare away the customers."

Every muscle in my body cramped as I forced myself into a sitting position. I smelled awful, and the stains in my pants reminded me of at least part of the reason why. I grabbed my head with both hands and held it until it stopped spinning.

When I closed my eyes, I felt the end of the broom handle in my ribs.

"Beat it, rummy!"

"All right already!" My voice sounded like a key scraping across the hood of a car. I tried to spit on the man's shoes, but I had nothing in my throat except razorblades.

I got to my feet and stumbled away from the broomstick on legs that were numb from my hips to my toes. After three steps, I stopped and tried to retch, but nothing came up except the dry heaves. The broom handle came crashing down across my bent back, and I'd had enough. I turned and buried my fist into the man's fat stomach. I didn't have a lot behind it, but he crumpled at the waist and the broom handle clattered onto the pavement. His eyes widened, and, with a voice that had lost all its iron, he shouted, "I'm callin' the cops!"

I didn't stick around to see if he'd make good on his threat. I was feeling better now that I was moving. A quick look around showed me that I was in the South Market District, probably about five miles from my office. I patted myself down and found only empty pockets: no phone, no wallet, no keys. A cab was out of the question. Even if I'd had the dough no cabbie was going to let a man in my condition get into his hack. I'd have to hoof it. The morning was young, the air chill, and the wind calm. I felt like I could make it home okay if I could find me some coffee, or even some water.

I needed a break, and, for once, I got one. After walking for three blocks, I ran into a neighborhood park and found a water fountain that worked. My stomach clenched against the first swallow of the freezing cold water, folding in on itself until it was the size of a tennis ball, but it adjusted and allowed me to take in a few more swallows. After splashing some of the water on my face I began to think that I might live through the morning.

The cloud cover had broken, and the sun was fast approaching its zenith when I reached the front door to my building, footsore and stiff, wondering how walking five miles could be more taxing on the body than running. Maybe it was because walking puts a different kind of stress on muscles and joints than running. Or maybe it had something to do with the fact that I'd been pumped full of at least two different kinds of narcotics and had my movements so restricted that I hadn't even been able to scratch my nose.

I was thirsty again, and I was hungry enough to eat yonak. I was considering how to get into my building without my keys. They'd taken my lock picks, too, the motherfuckers. I'd had that set since I was fourteen years old! I'd never bothered to try to hide a spare key under the mat or under a rock, either. Had I locked my window? Of course I had. Too bad Chivo wasn't around. I'd never learned his trick for breezing past locked doors as if they didn't exist. Frustrated, I grabbed the doorknob and gave it a twist.

It was unlocked. Careful as a barefoot man walking through broken glass, I stepped through the door. Once inside, I pulled up short so that I wouldn't trip over the body of the dead man sprawled on the floor in the middle of the room.

Making sure to lock the door behind me, I walked in a circle around the body, examining it without touching it. I didn't recognize the stiff. Maybe it was because he was missing a good portion of the lower part of his face. He was wearing flannel and denim, and the brown flatcap lying next to the body was soaked with the blood that was still spilling from the dead man's lower jaw, neck, and upper chest, which had been ripped open and consumed, leaving the remains of the head dangling from the exposed spinal column. It was a grisly sight, but, on the upside, I wasn't hungry anymore.

I crouched next to the body and went through the pockets of the dead man, searching for identification. I didn't find any. I didn't even find a wallet, nor did I find any keys. I *did* find a set of lock picks when I took a peek underneath the body. I pulled them out, studied them, and then put them on my desk. The universe takes away, but it also gives. I was beginning to think that this was my lucky day! The last thing I examined was the metal attaché case lying near the corpse's feet. I opened it and stared at the portable thermal cutting lance and gas container that I found inside.

The dead guy had picked the lock to my front door with the intention of breaking into my safe, and, unlike the pros who had searched my office last time, this mug wasn't going to be subtle about it. The cutting lance seemed par for the course for the tough-looking customer: finesse wasn't going to be his forte. He'd known somehow that I wouldn't be home. What he hadn't known about was the new lodger in my laundry room, a lodger who liked to sleep during daylight hours, and who got a little cranky when strangers invaded his territory and disturbed him. Especially since I hadn't been home the night before to fill his bowl with yonak.

I left the corpse where it was and went upstairs to clean up. Later, I told myself, I was going to have an overdue discussion with Chivo about establishing some house rules.

***

Chivo was, of course, nowhere to be found by the time I came downstairs to deal with the body. I recognized his work, though. The man's mangled throat told me everything I needed to know. He'd been heading for my safe when Chivo waylaid him. The intruder had locked eyes with Chivo and suffered a paralyzing bout of nausea. Once the man was helpless, Chivo was able to have his overdue dinner.

I needed to get rid of the body before anyone else came calling. I knew that I'd wasted precious time showering and changing clothes, but I'd already spent more time tramping around in my own filth than I'd cared to, or would ever care to again.

I wondered who'd sent the would-be safecracker. Maybe after failing to get the location of the flash drive from me, Deet had sent someone to search my office and apartment. I had my doubts about that idea. Deet struck me as the kind of clinically precise person who liked clean jobs that didn't leave behind a lot of messy clutter. Sending someone to cut into a safe with a torch didn't sound Deet-like to me at all. But I couldn't dismiss the idea entirely. It was possible that when questioning me didn't work Deet could have decided to throw clinical precision out the window. And, sure, I'd spent most of the previous day with Deet, but how well did I really know the agent? After all, Deet had spent exactly zero time talking about him... her... them... it... Deetself.

Could Clearwater have sent the thief? He hadn't been able to buy the flash drive from me, and he'd seemed like a man who didn't take no for an answer. I pegged him as the kind of high-rolling swell who would have cultivated underworld connections to do his dirty work for him, and I doubt that he would have been concerned about his man making a mess of my safe in the process.

I considered the possibility that Leaflock had found out I had the flash drive and taken steps to get it back. I knew firsthand that he was not above hiring a professional to take care of sensitive matters.

I decided to put the matter of who had ordered the break-in out of my mind for the time being. At that moment I had more pressing concerns. While I was pondering how to dispose of the bloody corpse in broad daylight without alerting the neighbors, passing motorists, or a cop on the beat, I heard the chiming of my cell phone from my desktop. Shit, I thought. I'd been out of touch for a full day. My phone was probably jammed with messages.

I picked up the cell phone and read the name scrolling across the top of the screen: Kalama. I couldn't stop myself from groaning out loud. Sorry, Detective. Definitely not the person I needed to talk to at the moment. I let the call go to voicemail.

I checked the phone for messages and found more than a dozen. After sending the ads and solicitations straight to trash without bothering to read them, I was left with seven messages of interest. Officer Wildfire had called to inform me that I could come in and pick up my computer at my convenience. Leaflock had left me a voicemail saying that he wanted me to come into his office for a talk. Kalama had texted me in the afternoon wondering why I hadn't come in to pick up the computer yet. Leaflock had left a second message telling me to call him back immediately. Leaflock had left a third message informing me that if I didn't get my ass into his office with the "you-know-what" within the hour, he'd send the police to my office to pick me up and bring me there. I had a text message from Ralph, my favorite nirumbee warrior and LIA agent, sent late in the evening, telling me to meet him "in the usual spot, tomorrow, midnight."

The seventh and most recent message was the one that Kalama had just left, and my heart sank as I listened to it: "I'm headed out your way, gumshoe. Expect me at your office in a half hour."

I was regretting taking that shower.

I considered my options and took the one I liked least. I picked up the phone and punched in Kalama's number.

She picked up on the second ring. "Hello, gumshoe. Are you in your office?"

"Yes. You're headed over?"

"Should be there in twenty."

"Are you alone?"

Kalama didn't answer right away, and when she did her voice was guarded. "Maybe. Maybe not. Why do you ask?"

"I've got something for you to see, but I'm not ready to show it to just anybody."

I heard Kalama let out a breath. "Anything else you want to tell me before I get there?"

"When did you last eat?"

"A couple of hours ago."

"Good. You're not going to want to see this with a full stomach."

"Don't move. I'll be right there."

***

"Oh for Ketz's sake, Southerland." Kalama stared down at the corpse.

"It was like this when I walked in."

"Sure it was. Any idea what happened here?"

I hesitated. "I'd like to hear your opinion, first."

Kalama scowled at me. "Doesn't work that way, gumshoe."

I sighed. "I don't recognize him, but I'm guessing that he's a professional. Or he was, anyway. I was out, and he seemed to know that. He broke in and it looks like he was headed for my safe. There's a thermal lance in that attaché case. Someone stopped him."

"Looks to me like someone ripped out his throat and ate it."

"Well, it wasn't me. I may be a lot of things, but cannibal isn't one of them."

Kalama nodded. "Good to know. Any idea who, or what, did this?"

I didn't respond.

Kalama glared daggers at me. "Southerland...."

"There's a confidentiality issue at work here."

"Are you saying a client did this?"

"Not exactly." I wasn't feeling comfortable, and it showed.

"Don't make me have to put you in a sweatbox, gumshoe. Some of the guys in the clubhouse are getting tired of looking at you."

"The punk was breaking into my home. I've got the right to defend my property."

Kalama tilted her head a little. "I thought you said you didn't do this."

"I didn't."

"Then what's this bullshit about protecting your property?"

I put on my best poker face. "Someone else might have been defending my property."

Kalama's eyes never left mine. "On your orders?"

"Not exactly."

"I'm getting tired of that answer, gumshoe." The detective's voice was measured. Shouting wasn't her style when she was questioning a person of interest. "I hope you're not going to ask for a lawyer."

"Not if I don't have to. Can we speak off the record?"

Kalama sighed. "Tell you what. You start talking, and I'll tell you when you'd be better off having your mouthpiece present."

"We'd better sit down. You want coffee?"

Kalama glanced at the corpse. "Sure. Make it strong."

***

After I'd finished explaining how a deadly magical creature who had once been a legendary sorcerer was now living in my laundry room, Kalama shook her head. "You can't keep a dangerous animal on the premises, Southerland. You have to notify Animal Control."

"Those clowns at Animal Control can't handle Chivo."

"Bullshit. They know exactly what the Huay Chivo is. They've been hunting it for months, and the department has been helping them. They know what they're doing."

"Anyway, Chivo isn't technically an animal."

"Are you saying he's human? In that case, I need to bring him in for questioning."

"He's not technically human, either. Not anymore."

"Then what is he?"

I shook my head.

"See? This isn't your call, gumshoe. You need to bring in the experts and let them do their job." Kalama drank down the last gulp of her coffee. "Call Animal Control. I'll get some of my people over here. This is a crime scene."

"Don't do it, detective. Those guys will throw Chivo in a cage. They'll poke and prod at him to find out what makes him tick. They might even cut him open."

Kalama stared at me across my desk. "The monster killed a man, gumshoe."

"A man who was breaking into his home."

"Oh, so he lives here then? Does he contribute to the rent? Does he do any of the cooking or cleaning? Or is killing visitors his only job." The detective paused. "He hasn't killed anyone else, has he? Southerland? Lord Alkwat's balls, he has, hasn't he!"

"Chivo saved my life, detective! I was in this chair staring down the barrel of a forty-four, and there wasn't a thing I could do about it. I'd used up every trick I had, and I had nothing left. Then Chivo showed up and... took care of the problem."

Kalama's jaw clenched and her eyes narrowed. "Who was it? Don't lie to me."

I shrugged. "A Hatfield torpedo. No one will miss him. You guys don't even have an open case file on him."

After half a minute Kalama's face relaxed by maybe a millimeter, and she nodded so slightly that I barely detected it. "You lead an interesting life, gumshoe."

I let some of the tension run out of my body. "I owe Chivo. I'm not going to allow him to become some government agency's science project."

Kalama shook her head. "You may not have a choice. What if the next person who walks through your door is a client? Or a police officer? Or a friend?"

"I'll work it out with Chivo. There's enough intelligence in there for me to keep him out of trouble."

Kalama's eyebrows shot up. "You don't know that. Look. If this Huay Chivo was a guard dog, we'd still have to bring someone in to determine whether he's a danger to the community. If he is, then he'd have to be put down."

"Lots of people have dangerous animals in their homes. You and I know someone who lets a manticore run around loose in her back yard. Chivo hasn't attacked anyone who wasn't a threat, either to my life or my property."

"So far." She sighed. "If I keep quiet about this, and he hurts or kills someone who doesn't have it coming, I'll hold you personally responsible. I'm taking a big risk here, Southerland. Don't make me regret it."

"I appreciate it, detective. Now, what about my computer."

Kalama shook her head. "Forget about that. What about this stiff on your floor?"

I glanced at the body and then turned my attention back to the detective. "I guess we'll have to get rid of it."

Kalama leveled a glare at me. "You realize I'm a cop, right?"

"Of course. But think about what happens if you call this in."

Kalama frowned while she considered this. "We'll examine the crime scene and determine that the stiff was mauled by a predatory animal. You'll be questioned, but you'll dummy up. We'll hold you downtown for as long as we can, but eventually we'll have to let you go."

I shook my head. "I'll never make it to your clubhouse. Leea will swoop me up and whisk me away into the night before you coppers know what hit you. I'm surprised they aren't here already, but I figure it's just a matter of time. Somebody sent that palooka to steal the flash drive I told you about."

Kalama nodded. "The one with the skinny on the whatchahoozits?"

"RAA."

"Right. You think it was Leea?"

I shrugged. "Could have been."

"So why don't you just give it to them? Look, gumshoe. I hate Leea as much as anyone. You know that. But if they want something from you, there's not much you can do to keep it from them. It's Leea. You can't fight them. Anyway, I thought you were going to sell that flash drive to that Nocturnal joker. What happened with that? And where were you yesterday?"

"It's a long story, detective. And I've still got a dead body on my floor."

"And I'm still wondering why I shouldn't call it in."

"That's probably what Leea is waiting for."

Kalama's eyes narrowed. "I'm checking my patience meter, and it's right on the edge of empty."

I picked up my coffee cup, but I'd finished it off long before. I put it back down on my desk and leaned back on my chair. "All right, I'll give you the short version. First, you'll never guess who Nocturnal is."

"I'm in no mood for guessing games, gumshoe."

I kept the suspense up for maybe three seconds. "Armine Clearwater."

The look of shock on the detective's face was the best thing that had happened to me all day, although given the way the day had started it wasn't running into a lot of competition.

I filled Kalama in on the gist of our conversation, making sure to mention how the socialite had stiffed me with the bill.

Kalama shook her head at that. "Figures. The richer they are, the less likely they are to pick up a check. Human nature, I suppose."

"Maybe. But Clearwater isn't human. I don't know what he is, but he's from somewhere else. Like the Sihuanaba, or that dog shadow that the Barbary Coast Bruja tussled with. Whatever he is, he implied that he'd be willing to give me more dough for that flash drive than I'd make in five lifetimes of honest work. We're talking seven figures."

Kalama whistled through her teeth. "Lord's balls! What does this RAA do? Blow up cities?"

"That was my first thought. But Clearwater said that he wanted it so he could save someone's life. He wouldn't tell me who. So I told him to forget it."

"You turned down seven figures?"

"Money isn't everything."

"That much money comes pretty close."

I shrugged. "I didn't like him."

"You live with a monster that eats people's necks."

"Clearwater threatened me when he left. A few hours later, someone ambushed me in my office and drugged me. When I woke up, I was strapped to a bed, and Deet was questioning me about the flash drive."

Kalama started. "Lord's balls! You were tortured?"

"In a weird way, yes." An involuntary shudder ran up my spine. "I'll tell you about it some other time. Deet didn't get any answers from me, so I was hit with the hypo again and woke up on a sidewalk over in South Market. I walked home and found laughing boy over there staining my hardwood floor with his blood."

Kalama considered my story for a full two minutes, and I didn't do anything to stop her. "Who do you think sent the safecracker?" she asked at last.

"Could have been Deet. Could have been Clearwater."

"They could be working together. Maybe they're both Leea."

I shook my head. "They might be working together, but no way is Clearwater an agent for the LIA."

The detective nodded. "Yeah, I can't see that, either. But whether it was Deet or Clearwater or both of them, it sounds like you're up shits creek without a paddle."

"No doubt," I agreed. "You coming along for the ride?"

With a sigh, she climbed out of her chair. "All right, gumshoe. We're going to have to hurry. You got anything here to cover that body with?"

Chapter Twelve

I didn't ask Kalama why she'd chosen to help me instead of bringing her fellow coppers in and turning my office into a crime scene. She was a mostly by-the-book cop, a true professional, who believed that the department, flawed as it might be, provided the most effective means of containing the primal forces that were always threatening to boil over and transform the city into anarchy and chaos. But she also knew that rules and regulations were tools, and sometimes they were the wrong tools for the job, especially when the LIA was involved. I knew her decision to bend the law under these particular circumstances had not come lightly, so I wasn't going to press her with a lot of questions. I was just grateful that she'd decided to help me, and, in return, I resolved to do whatever it took to make sure she didn't suffer any professional consequences for her actions on my behalf.

We covered the stiff with my favorite blanket, the only one I had that was thick enough to keep blood from soaking through and staining the trunk of Kalama's car. We drove to an abandoned warehouse in one of the industrial districts in the south of the city and tossed the bundle inside through a broken window. It would probably be weeks before anyone besides needle-jockeys, hopheads, and rock-hounds found it, and by then the rats and other scavengers would have rendered it unrecognizable if the junkies didn't eat it themselves. I still had the problem of dealing with the bloodstain on the floor of my office, and I figured I wouldn't break the bank if I parted with a little dough for a cheap area rug until I could come up with a more permanent solution. I'd write it off on my taxes as a business expense.

We wasted no time putting distance between ourselves and the warehouse. Kalama drove me back to my office, where she left her car double-parked while we made sure my place was free of LIA agents. I walked with her back to her car, and as she was about to head back to the station she leaned out her open window to shout at me over the din of the passing cars. "I'm going to write up a report. I drove out to the Porter District this morning to talk to a snitch about a matter involving a case I'm working on. When I was done, I came by your office, which was nearby, to inform you that your computer was waiting for you at the station. You hadn't come by to pick it up yesterday, and I wanted to know why. During our conversation, I got the feeling that something wasn't on the up-and-up. Copper's intuition. I asked you where you were yesterday, but you dummied up. I grilled you for an hour, but you wouldn't talk. Something smells fishy to me, but I don't have any evidence of a crime at this time. You're a suspicious character, and I'm going to look into it further when I get the chance. If something comes up, I might have to talk to you again. Got it?"

I curled my lip. "Sure, flatfoot. But you ain't got nuttin' on me, see?"

"Knock it off, you dumb lug. And watch your step. I don't like it that someone sent that safecracker to your place right after you rejected Clearwater's offer and escaped Deet's interrogation. Either one of them is more than you can handle. Together, I have a feeling they're more than *anyone* can handle. If you don't have a plan for dealing with them, you better make one."

"Don't worry. I'll figure something out."

"Talk to Lubank," Kalama suggested. "He's smarter than you. If nothing else, he'll make sure that your affairs are in order."

And with that cheery thought, the detective slipped into the traffic and drove away.

Back in my office I was debating whether to walk over to Gio's to see if Antonio was finished with the Beastmobile or to call Leaflock and tell him to fuck off. I decided that I'd better deal with Leaflock before he really did send some cops to bust my balls.

I had Leaflock's private number, which meant I wouldn't have to spend ten minutes winding my way through an automated phone tree. Leaflock picked up the call on the first ring, which made me wonder how much work he actually did.

"Southerland! You motherfucker! Where have you been?"

"Nice talking to you, Leaflock. I'm hanging up now."

"No! Wait! I need to see you. Get over here right away."

"What's this regarding?"

"It's regarding your ass! Just get the hell over here. And bring that motherfucking flash drive!"

"What motherfucking flash drive would that be, Mr. Leaflock?"

"You know which flash drive, asshole! *My* motherfucking flash drive! I know you found it in Redhorn's apartment. That's my property! Bring it over here now or I'll have you arrested for theft!"

"Technically, it was burglary."

"That's it, asshole! I'm calling the cops!"

"Sounds like you need to talk to my lawyer."

"Fuck your lawyer! And fuck you too if that flash drive isn't in my hands by the end of the day."

I considered my position. It sounded to me like Leaflock had spoken with Deet. I'd suspected the two of them were working together, and the more I thought about it the more likely it seemed. Maybe Deet had sent the safecracker to my place at Leaflock's request.

"Southerland! You still there?"

"I'm sorry, Mr. Leaflock, but I'm tied up for the rest of the day. Let me check my calendar...." I held my phone away from my ear and listened to Leaflock scream obscenities for about half a minute. When he began to wear himself out, I returned the phone to my ear and said, "I can be there tomorrow afternoon at two. Will that work for you?"

Leaflock screamed at me for another half a minute, but finally agreed tomorrow at two would be fine. "But if you're not here at two oh one, I'm calling the cops!" he concluded. I disconnected the call without saying goodbye.

I wanted to retrieve my computer from cop headquarters, but I needed to do something about the blood on my office floor first. I scrubbed at it as best I could, but there was no washing out the dark scarlet stain that had set in the wood. At some point, I would either have to replace the wooden floor or paint it over, but for the short term I decided it would be a good idea to cover it with a rug.

A half hour later, I parked the beastmobile in front of a secondhand store. Antonio had done an amazing job of freshening up the vehicle's interior, and I rewarded him with enough dough to keep him in soda pop and cigarettes for a week. I found a used area rug in the store that didn't set me back much and looked like it might work in an office. Unfortunately, I was a few minutes too late.

I was walking down the sidewalk with the rolled-up rug over my shoulder when I spotted the two torpedoes outside my office. The expensive dark suits and matching dark glasses on the well-groomed thugs screamed LIA. Shit, I thought to myself. I didn't have time for this.

I stopped a few feet in front of the two torpedoes. I recognized the taller of the two as the muscle who had held the door open for Deet at The Acorn Grill, and the shorter as the man who had been holding the hypo in Deet's interrogation cube. I decided to call them Bruno and Doc. At least I knew who these knuckleheads were working for.

I turned to Doc. "You aren't going to give me another shot, are you? Are you even a real doctor? My shoulder is still aching from the last two jabs you gave me."

Doc gave me the slightest of smiles. "Mr. Southerland? We'd like to speak with you in your office."

"I'm afraid that won't be possible. I'm booked solid today. You'll have to call for an appointment."

The torpedo reached into the inside of his suit and brought out a leather card holder. "LIA, Mr. Southerland. We don't need appointments."

"Is that so. Do you need teeth?"

That brought a bigger smile, one that revealed a set of obviously capped choppers. "Tell me you're not cracking wise. Are you cracking wise to the LIA?"

"Oh, you're Leea? Well, why didn't you say so!"

The torpedo's smile disappeared, and he slid his card holder back into his pocket. "Let's get inside, Southerland. Unlock the door or my associate will kick it in. Your choice."

Bruno had his hands in his pockets, probably holding some sort of weapon in one of them. Probably not a needle, either. A sap maybe. Or a gun. He stared at me with shark's eyes. Definitely a gun. I scratched my chin and adjusted my hat on my head. "The problem here is that you've only offered me two choices. In my experience, there's always another choice."

Doc lifted his eyebrows. "Oh? Please enlighten me."

I shrugged. "If you insist."

I grabbed the edge of the rug with both hands and snapped it off my shoulders, letting it unroll as I tossed it into the air at the two torpedoes. Bruno's hands came out of his pockets, and I saw the snub-nosed heater in one of them. Time seemed to slow as the gun came up in my direction. While it was still on its way, a fierce gale-force wind that seemed to come out of nowhere plastered the rug into the torpedoes, knocking them off balance. I hit the ground rolling as a shot sliced the air well away from me. When I looked up, I saw that the gale had pasted the rug around both thugs and slammed them against the wall. The heater fell out of Bruno's hand, and both thugs slid to the porch, either dazed or unconscious. A focused seventy-mile-per-hour wind pinned them to the cement.

I'd summoned and commanded Badass using only my mind, and it had worked about as well as I could have hoped. Out loud, I commanded Badass to pull back and drift out over the street until I needed him. I picked up the loose heater and bent over to check on the two LIA torpedoes. I concluded that they would both be nursing headaches for a while, but they'd live.

Doc had taken the least amount of damage, so I pointed the gun at him and said, "Tell Deet that I'll be more than happy to talk with... him? her?"

The torpedo reached up to feel the bump growing on the side of his head. "Deet," he muttered through clenched teeth. "We're just supposed to say Deet."

"Tell Deet that I'll be happy to have a little chat with... Deet. Maybe over a cup of coffee sometime soon. Tell Deet to call me, and we'll set something up. But tell Deet that we play it my way from now on."

The battered torpedo looked up at me. "And what way is that?"

I smiled. "We play nice, like civilized adults. No hypos, no restraints, no home break-ins, and no thugs."

Doc nodded. "I'll tell Deet. Deet will be happy to hear from you. Happy as a clam."

Bruno sat up, groaned, and then pushed himself to his feet. He glared at me. "This ain't over, asshole."

I guess he was supposed to be a tough guy. I sent out a mental shout to Badass, and the elemental whipped itself into a tightly-wound whirlwind and shot over to hover a few feet above and behind me. I put the roscoe in my belt and stared meaningfully at Bruno. "Is there something you want to say to me?"

Bruno's eyes widened, but he decided that he'd said everything he'd meant to say. Tough guy. Right.

"Beat it, you two. Call it a day and consider yourselves lucky. Don't forget to give Deet my regards."

The two torpedoes slid away, giving Badass as wide a berth as they could manage.

***

In my professional judgment, the rug looked good on the floor of my office. Better than a bloodstain, at any rate.

With that problem solved, at least for the time being, I called the YCPD to ask about my computer. After being shuffled around to three different officers, I was told that it was after four o'clock, and I'd have to wait until the next day to pick it up. I was assured that the computer would remain safely stored until then. Swell.

I was halfway through a microwaved frozen pizza and a bottle of beer when Deet called.

"You were quite rude to my associates, Mr. Southerland."

"They caught me at a bad time. Next time you want to send them to my office, you should call ahead to make sure I have an opening in my schedule."

"No need to worry about them. I've decided they weren't a good fit in their former positions. They are in the process of being transferred to another location."

"Is that right. Can you send me their forwarding addresses? I'd like to mail them get-well cards."

"You can send me the cards and I'll forward them for you."

"On second thought, forget it. I'm guessing that mail service won't reach where they've gone."

"Perhaps not. Let's get down to business, Mr. Southerland. I need to acquire Mr. Leaflock's flash memory drive. It contains proprietary information that was never meant to leave the offices of Leaflock Services Corporation. Your possession of this information is unlawful, and the LIA has assumed the responsibility of returning the flash drive to Mr. Leaflock. We also want to ensure that the contents of the drive do not find their way into the hands of Mr. Leaflock's competitors."

I washed down a bite of pizza with a swig of beer and then belched as quietly as I could away from the phone. "Here's my concern, Deet. When you say that you want to keep the contents of that drive quiet, it gives me the impression that you want to make anyone who might know about those contents disappear. Now, I can tell you that I have not seen what's on that flash drive yet, and I'd be telling the Dragon Lord's own truth. But I can't see any way to convince you that I'm not lying in order to save my own skin. You see my problem here, Deet?"

I heard a sigh on Deet's side of the call. "Are you saying you haven't accessed the drive?"

"I'll admit that I tried, but it released a virus that fried my computer. I bought me a new computer, but I haven't been able to install it yet. You're partly to blame for that."

"Mr. Southerland, if you are unaware of the contents of the flash drive, then I have no reason to, as you say, cause you to disappear. Turn the drive over to me and you will not be harmed. You have my word."

"See, you *say* that. But you've had me picked up by the police twice. You've seen to it that I was interrogated by an assistant D.A. and by a homicide detective. You've had your 'associates' kidnap me in my own office. You've had me restrained and interrogated for hours against my will. I pissed and shit myself, and you wouldn't even allow me to scratch my nose. And then you had me pumped full of more sleepy-time juice and tossed into the street. Meanwhile, some thief broke into my office with the intention of slicing my safe open with a thermal lance. Was that one of yours by any chance? Well, never mind, it doesn't matter. Then you sent your two 'associates'... well, I guess you know all about that little dustup. You know, you should vet your associates more carefully. If that's the best you've got then I'm going to start losing my respect for the LIA. Um.... Where was I? Well, the point is, Deet, you haven't convinced me that you are someone I can trust. In fact, at the risk of being rude, you can take your 'word' and shove it up your ass."

If Deet was rattled by my effrontery, I couldn't hear it in the agent's voice, which remained as calm and as precise as the voice that tells you to turn right in three hundred feet. "Mr. Southerland, I wish to meet with you in person to secure the transfer of Mr. Leaflock's flash drive. We can meet at the time and place of your choosing. In the meantime, I ask that you do not try to access the information on the drive. If you will not accept my guarantee for your safety, then you may ensure it in any way you wish. I understand that you have some means for doing that. If you say that you are unaware of the specific contents of the drive, then I will take you at your word. Will that be satisfactory?"

I thought it over for a bit. "Swell. Shall we say tomorrow evening at seven o'clock? I'll need that much time to prepare."

"That is acceptable. And the location?"

"I'll get back to you with that. Expect a call from me shortly before seven tomorrow night."

"I see. I accept those terms on the condition that you make no effort to ascertain the information on that drive. Are we in agreement?"

"We are," I said.

We ended the call, each knowing that the other was lying.

***

Later that night, I was sitting in my office staring at a painting of a crow sitting on a mesa and gazing out over the wasteland. The sun had set, but I hadn't bothered to turn on the lights. In the darkness, I studied the painting, losing myself in the browns and reds of the desert landscape, which was at once both harsh and beautiful. Two feet tall and six feet wide, the painting was too big and too elegant for my office. It had been a gift from someone I probably shouldn't have been thinking about, and who I most likely would never see or hear from again. I wasn't sure why I kept the painting. If it had any special meaning for me, I didn't know what it was. I suppose I just liked it. That was reason enough.

"I am looking for you. Where are you?"

I stared back down at the words I'd written on my notepad a few minutes earlier. I'd written the words consciously and of my own free will. I read the two sentences over and over again until the words made no sense in my head. It wasn't without some trepidation that I let my eyes wander over to my hand, still gripping a ballpoint pen. I breathed in and mentally prepared to see my hand fly up from my desktop and spring into action of its own accord. After a dozen heartbeats, I let out my breath.

Send him a message, she'd told me. Maybe you'll connect with each other through the spirit world. Sure we would.

I let out another breath and shook my head. Alexander Southerland. That's who I was. Private Investigator. That's what I'd been for almost a decade. Speaks with Wind? Who the hell was that? Some kind of wizard who tracks down missing persons by channeling the spirit world? A vessel for ancient animal spirits that I'd only seen or heard while pumped up with happy juice? That wasn't the way I did my job. I was a professional snoop. I searched social media to gather information about people that, if they'd had any sense, they would have kept private. A peeper. I peeked through keyholes and windows and eavesdropped on office gossip. I questioned talkative bartenders about their customers and bitter ex-wives about their no-good ex-husbands. A flatfoot. A gumshoe. I walked through the night and broke into homes, looking for items of interest. I waded into trouble and waited to see who would take a run at me so that I could tell if I was getting close to the answers I wanted. A pug. A rough number. I had scars on my knuckles and on my face, and I was still missing a tooth that a troll had knocked out of my mouth because I wouldn't tell him what he wanted to know. A loner. I drank alone in the corners of bars and observed the other patrons having a good time or watched them settle their beefs with their fists or their knives or their guns because that's the way I liked it. Unattached. I might have loved some women, and maybe some of them had loved me, but none of them were a part of my life anymore and I was jake with that. Just another working-class mug from a working-class neighborhood. Oh, sure, I had my own special gift. I could summon and command air elementals, like Smokey, who I had trained to do some of my peeping and eavesdropping for me. I could weaponize these blobs of air and funnels of wind, too. I smiled to myself, thinking about how useful Badass could be in a scrape, and how I'd once sent Syphon up a nasty troll's nose to keep him from plugging me with my own thirty-eight. But I also remembered throwing bare knuckles with a psycho gangbanger who'd wanted to beat me to death in order to make a point to his posse, and then sharing beers with him when it was over. I was no witch or magician. I'd encountered my share of demons, specters, and spirits—who hasn't? But I didn't move easily through that world. Speaks with Wind? More like Slogs through Alleys.

 I turned my attention back to the painting above my file cabinets and thought about the half-mad artist who had painted it. He had been a man with unique gifts. He'd been a shapeshifter, a were-crow, and I had no doubt that the crow in the painting was a sort of self-portrait of the artist himself. The artist had possessed certain otherworldly gifts, as well, spiritual gifts I guess you could say, and I wondered if that landscape had been his equivalent of my tropical waterfall, a place of rest and peace, a retreat from the turbulence of the everyday world. Maybe that had been the way he'd perceived the realm of the spirit. In the end, his gifts had led him down dark paths and to a bad end. I shook my head and stared back down at the words I'd written on the notepad. I tossed the pen into the air and caught it when it came down. Maybe I should have used a pencil. I stared at the words some more. Then I tore the page from my notepad, wadded it up, and tossed it into the trash.

Chapter Thirteen

At eleven, I picked up the beastmobile from Gio's lot and headed for the old Placid Point Pier in the extreme northern part of the peninsula. The pier had once extended from the city's oldest operating wharf, but it had been abandoned about twenty-five years earlier when it had been replaced by the larger, modernized, and much more consumer-friendly concrete quay and popular tourist site that opened about two miles down the southwest side of the Placid Point coast. The shipping and commercial fishers had all relocated to the new Placid Point Pier, leaving the old pier and wharf area behind. Efforts had been made to redevelop the old wharf, but eventually it was left to rot. Nothing much happened there while the sun was in the sky, but come nightfall the old Placid Point Pier was the focal point for smuggling, drug transactions, and gang bangs. I'd been caught in the middle of a couple of these rumbles, and it wasn't an experience that I wanted to repeat. But I'd also had a strange encounter on the pier the first time I'd been there, an encounter with a creature that, officially, didn't exist.

According to official records, elves had been the dominant sentient species on earth when the seven Dragon Lords emerged from an otherworldly realm called Hell some six thousand years ago. The Dragon Lords wrested control of the world from the elves after humans rose up against their elf overlords and switched their allegiance to the Dragon Lords, who'd been ruling the earth's Seven Realms ever since. Seeing that the Dragon Lords were immortal unkillable hundred-foot long flying fire-breathing masters of magic, it always seemed to me that these ancient humans had made the right call. Official records, the ones written by the victors, refer to the conflict between the elves and the Dragon Lords as the Great Rebellion, and the records described the elves as a malevolent scheming race of oppressors that had subjugated humanity and rebelled against the rightful advent of the Dragon Lords. After the Dragon Lords took control, they launched a genocidal mop-up effort against the elves, and, officially, the elves were hunted to extinction.

The official histories were wrong. About a year ago, I'd met a living elf on the old Placid Point Pier, and I'd met him again a few days later. On the first occasion, the elf had shoved a crystal shard into my forehead, a gift that had enhanced my awareness. That gift had saved my life on more than one occasion, which meant that I was in debt to the elf. The second time I'd met the elf, he'd explained that the few elves who had escaped the attempted genocide had been working ever since on a long-term plan to overthrow the Dragon Lords. Since elves lived practically forever, they could afford to be patient. The elf told me that he would call on me from time to time to help him with the elves' grand scheme, and, since I owed him, I was obligated to extend my services to him even though I had no real feeling toward the Dragon Lords one way or the other.

Ralph knew all about my encounters with the elf, and whenever he wanted to see me he usually arranged for us to meet on the pier where I'd met the ancient creature. Traffic had been light by Yerba City standards, and I turned into the pier's abandoned parking lot fifteen minutes early. Finding a parking place wasn't hard, since mine was the only car on the lot. I pulled the beastmobile in front of the ruins of a once-trendy restaurant, switched off the engine, and listened to the waves rolling through the pilings of the old pier as I waited.

I'd brought two items with me, a flask and a gun. I didn't have a need for the gun at the moment, so I pulled out the flask and knocked back a snort of rye. It set my throat on fire on the way down, and I told myself that I was fighting off the cold. I had to admit that it wasn't as cold as all that, however, so after the one shot, I put the flask back in my pocket. I wanted a clear head when Ralph showed up.

As the whiskey sent its warm glow through my lower abdomen it awakened my bladder, which reminded me that it had been a while since I'd emptied it. Concluding that a clear head might also require a clear bladder, I got out of the car, gave it some room, and hosed down a section of the empty parking lot. When I was finished, I turned back toward the car and nearly jumped out of my skin when I saw the stout figure of Clearwater sitting on the hood. It was a good thing my bladder had just been emptied.

I know that I said something appropriate for the occasion, something along the lines of, "Oh, hello. I wasn't expecting you to be there." Probably not those exact words, however.

Clearwater smiled and tapped the brim of his top hat with two fingers in a casual salute. "You're going to have to answer for Jorgio."

"Who's Jorgio?"

"My associate. I sent Jorgio to your office this morning to retrieve Mr. Leaflock's memory drive."

"I'm afraid we didn't get the chance to meet. You should have let me know he was coming."

"I'll admit to hoping that a meeting between the two of you wouldn't be necessary."

"Uh-huh. How did you get here, anyway?"

"I had you followed, of course. I was curious to see where you were going on such a lovely evening. This is hardly the place I expected, though. What brings you to this forlorn spot? You wouldn't be looking to make a clandestine transaction here by any chance, would you?"

"A what? Wait. You think I'm here to sell the flash drive?" I shook my head. "If I'm not willing to accept what you were offering, what makes you think I'd be willing to accept an offer from anyone else?"

Clearwater put his chin in his hand. "I'm forced to concede that what you are saying is reasonable. Still, I can't help but be curious. You don't have the memory drive on your person, do you? It would make things so much easier for both of us if you did. I assume that if it was ever in your office, you would have moved it to another location after my associate's botched attempt to search for it there. But you realize that I mean to acquire that memory drive one way or the other."

"Well get in line! I've already promised to deliver the flash drive to two of your competitors, and I'm still trying to decide whether I'm going to keep my promise to either of them."

"Is that who you're meeting tonight? One of my competitors? Splendid! By all means, let's wait for this competitor to appear. Perhaps we can work something out that will be beneficial for all concerned."

"The reason I'm here has nothing to do with the flash drive. You followed me here for nothing. I'm giving you one chance to bounce."

Clearwater looked confused. "Bounce? Why would I want to bounce? I'm not a rubber ball."

"Bounce! Beat it! Scram! Take a hike! Take a long walk off that short pier over there!"

"Ah!" Clearwater chuckled. "You want me to leave! You could just say so, you know."

"I'm saying so now. Leave!"

Clearwater shook his head. "You are a most amusing fellow. I don't think that I'll 'bounce' until we've had more time to chat."

We'd see about that. I sent a mental command to Badass, whom I'd summoned while "chatting" with Clearwater. As if a switch had been flipped, Badass transformed itself from an invisible floating blob of air into a very visible fiercely spinning whirlwind. "Badass," I said out loud. "Are you ready to attack?"

A booming sonorous moan emerged from the whirlwind. "Badass is ready." I didn't know about Clearwater, but I was impressed by the amount of volume Badass put into it.

Clearwater's eyebrows raised when he looked over at the threatening elemental, but the smile never left his face. "Interesting!" he exclaimed. "You're full of tricks, aren't you, Mr. Southerland."

"Are you ready to bounce now, Clearwater?"

Clearwater smirked at me. "You don't think I'm bothered by a little wind, do you? Please."

"Don't say I didn't warn you." I issued a mental command to Badass. "Drive him away, but don't hurt him."

I backed away as Badass shot toward Clearwater, who didn't move except to raise a languid gloved hand in the direction of the elemental. A deeper darkness opened in the night between Badass and Clearwater. I watched, stunned, as Badass rushed through the darkness—and disappeared without a trace!

The darkness closed in on itself, and Clearwater rotated his head toward me, still smiling. "You're full of tricks, Mr. Southerland, but as you can see, I have a few tricks of my own."

I couldn't stop staring at Clearwater, perched on the hood of the beastmobile, wearing the same expensive suit he'd been wearing at the Diner Forty-Niner, minus the monocle and cane, and regarding me with an amused little grin that made me want to yank it off his face. I tried to sense the familiar presence of Badass, who had been hovering somewhere near me for about a year, but I couldn't detect the elemental anywhere. A wave of raging anger surged through me, and it took a supreme effort of will on my part to regain control of my breathing and fight back a sudden compulsion to hurl myself at the throat of the grinning little man whose pudgy little legs dangled off the hood of my car.

Clearwater cocked his head, closed an eye, and peered at me through the other. "You know, you could save yourself further trouble simply by giving me the memory drive. It's not too late."

I forced words through gritted teeth. "I don't have the drive on me. And if I did, I wouldn't give it to you." With an effort, I relaxed my clenched jaw by a couple of measures. "I will *never* give that flash drive to you."

"You are mistaken. You'll give it to me in the end. I've foreseen it. The only question is how much you will suffer in the process." He leaped off my car to stand on the pavement, displaying a degree of agility I wouldn't have expected from a fellow with his girth. "Come, Mr. Southerland. You're a reasonable man. I have no wish to see you come to harm. Make it easy on yourself. Tell me where you've hidden the drive, or, better yet, lead me to it. I think you realize now that you lack the power to keep me from getting what I want, as I said before, one way or the other."

A wave of helplessness expanded from my chest, and it reminded me of the same sense of helplessness I'd felt just a little more than twenty-four hours earlier while staring into the unblinking eyes of Deet. Without thinking about it, I blurted, "You might be right. Maybe I don't have the power to stop you. But what about the boy who talks backwards?"

The effect of those words was startling. Clearwater's eyes grew large as balloons, and he staggered back against the side of the beastmobile as if he'd been punched. Just then, Ralph's white van turned into the parking lot. Clearwater's head jerked in the direction of the van. He raised his arms, and, to my utter astonishment, they extended a dozen feet to either side of him, blurred, and became wings. The rest of Clearwater's body changed, too, and, in an instant, it was not a stout little gentleman, but an owl the size of a hang glider that launched itself into the air and soared headlong through an oval of blackness that had opened like a hole in the night sky a few yards above the hood of the beastmobile. I stood rooted to the spot, gawking in amazement, as the blackness dissipated like a cloud of smoke, leaving no trace of the owl when it disappeared.

The van screeched to a stop next to the beastmobile, and Ralph leaped out the door almost before the engine had finished shutting down.

"What the hell was that!"

I came out of my trance. "Looked to me like an owl."

The nirumbee stared at me, his open mouth displaying a mouthful of pointed teeth. "That was one big-ass owl!"

"Biggest I've ever seen," I agreed.

"Where the hell did it go?"

I shrugged. "Let's hope we never have to find out."

Ralph looked like he wanted to ask me another question, but he stopped and pulled the hood of his jacket over his head and tightened it with a draw string. "Okay, never mind. We've got things to talk about. Are we alone here?"

I made a show of looking around. "It's hard to tell these days, but I think so."

Ralph pulled himself deeper into his coat. "We'd better be. Let's walk out on the pier."

"Is that necessary? The wind coming off the ocean penetrates to the bones."

But Ralph was already moving away from me, so I pulled my hat down on my forehead to secure it against the wind and followed.

When we got to the end of the pier, Ralph jammed a stubby hand-rolled cigar in his teeth and fought to light a match. It took him two tries, and his lips stretched into a satisfied smirk once the stogie was fired up. I felt the pier sway with the rolling waves and wondered how much longer the neglected structure would hold up against the elements before it broke apart and washed out to sea. The protective railing had mostly collapsed, and I was partly responsible for that. Badass and me. I called up a sigil in my mind and reached out for Badass, but wherever the elemental was, it was out of my range.

Ralph blew out a stream of smoke and looked up at me from somewhere near my waist. "You need to tell me what you know about RAA."

I looked out over the Nihhonese Ocean. "I thought I was supposed to lay off everything else until I found the person whose heart is in that stone of yours."

"And that's something you should have done already. I'm beginning to wonder about your competence as an investigator."

"Fuck off, Ralph. I'll find him when I'm not busy earning a living."

"Yeah? And who paid you to steal a flash drive with the scoop on RAA from the dead guy's apartment?"

I looked down at the nirumbee. "No one paid me to take it, but I've received a very lucrative offer for it."

"From who?"

"Whom."

"What?"

"It's 'from whom.' Objective case."

"From *fucking* who, wise guy! Who's fucking offering you fucking money for that fucking flash drive? Is that fucking objective enough for you?"

"Why do you want to know? You planning on making a counter offer?"

Ralph sucked on his cigar and took it out of his mouth before blowing a stream of smoke into the night. "Was it Deet?"

"No. Deet didn't try to buy it. Deet tried to torture the location of the drive from me." I leaned on the remains of the railing, checking it first to make sure it was secure, and watched the waves roll in.

Ralph was frowning. "You didn't talk?"

I pulled my coat close against a sudden gust of wind. "No."

"So the drive is still safe, then. You've got it hidden away somewhere?"

I looked back at Ralph. "What's it to you?"

Ralph raised his voice a notch. "The drive is safe, right?"

I breathed in some of the sour smoke coming from the nirumbee's stogie. Bad as it smelled, there was something appealing about it. Maybe it was the warmth. Except for the occasional cigar, smoking was a vice I'd never picked up, but, out on that pier in the icy chill of the wind off the Nihhonese Ocean, I was tempted to ask Ralph to let me give his homemade chest-warmer a try.

I shook off the impulse. I had no idea what was in that cigar, but I knew it wasn't tobacco. After my experience with Walks in Cloud, I figured that swearing off unknown herbs for the time being might be a smart idea.

Turning back to Ralph, I said, "Yeah, it's safe. No one knows where it is but me. Deet isn't going to fuckin' get it. I don't like the way Deet asked me for it."

Ralph looked up and locked eyes with me. "You're sure it's safe? From a top-level LIA agent?"

"Sure as I can be." I stared down at the nirumbee. "Why are you so concerned about it? How do you even know about RAA? And what's your interest in it? What do you know about it that I don't?"

Ralph's eyes dropped. He took another puff of the stogie and flicked a half-inch of ash into the wind. "I've run across some information. RAA has become a hot topic of conversation in the Leea offices. Deet wants it bad, but Deet's not the only one. I'm not sure who the others are. Some might be LIA, and some might not be." Ralph's eyes rose to meet mine. "There are factions within the LIA, and this RAA shit is stirring them up. Now, I don't know what RAA is or what it's supposed to do. But people are willing to kill for it. Powerful people. Including Deet. Especially Deet. A lot of people know you've got a flash drive with information about RAA on it. That's why I called you here. To warn you. You need to be on your game and on your toes." He took one last puff on his cigar and then tossed it over the railing. Red sparks flew off the end of the stogie as it floated down to the rolling waves.

Ralph peered toward the entrance to the pier. I knew that he could "see" in the darkness in the same way that I could. Satisfied that we were truly alone, Ralph turned back to me. "Give me the flash drive, Southerland. I can keep it away from Deet and anyone else who's looking for it. As long as you're in possession of that drive, some very nasty people will be gunning for you. Believe me, you'll be safer without it."

I laughed without any humor. "You're the fourth person who has asked me for that flash drive this week, and it's only Wednesday. Well, Thursday, I guess, since it's after midnight. I've received a seven-figure offer for that drive from one of those persons, and you want me to just hand it over to you for nothing? Why would I do that?"

Ralph shook his head. "If you think that you're going to actually get any dough for that drive then you're a bigger sap than I took you for. Once your 'buyer' has it, it will be curtains for you. You're only alive now because they want you to lead them to it."

I thought about that, and decided that the words rang true. Deet suspected that I knew too much, and Clearwater didn't seem to have my best interests in mind. He wanted the drive at any cost, and he didn't want me to know what he was going to use it for. Ralph was right: the minute either of them got their paws on the drive, my life wouldn't be worth a plugged nickel. I blew warm air into my hands and looked down at Ralph. "And how will that change if I give you the drive? Won't they take me out of the picture just as soon as they know that I've given it to you?"

Ralph nodded. "Probably. We'll have to make sure they don't know you've given it to me."

I smiled. I couldn't help myself. "What's this 'we' bullshit, Ralph? Are we supposed to be a team now?"

"Like it or not, you need me, you dumb fuck. I'm on your side because that's the way the elf wants it. That makes us partners. You don't know what you've gotten yourself into. Trust me, you can't handle this alone."

I shrugged. "Maybe I'm not alone."

Ralph's head jerked up at me. "What are you talking about?"

I stared down and locked eyes with him. "I'm talking about the boy who talks backwards."

Ralph's eyes widened and a choking noise rose from his throat. When he spoke again, his voice was a hiss. "What did you just say?"

***

As the wind gusted off the water, I heard the calling of birds back near the shore. I wondered what kind of bird hunted near the ocean at this time of night. They didn't sound like seagulls. They sounded more like... owls. But at that moment, birds were the last thing on my mind.

My eyes were still locked with Ralph's. "I said—"

"Never mind, I heard what you said." Ralph looked back down toward the entrance to the pier, straining his senses to detect any suspicious movements or sounds. Apparently, he'd also heard the birdcalls. After a shake of his head, he tightened the drawstrings of his hood and looked up at me. "Alkwat's balls! Where did you hear about the boy who talks backwards?"

I studied the nirumbee, trying to decide how much I wanted to tell him. "It's an odd story."

"I'm listening."

I was still hesitant. "If I tell you, you have to help me understand a few things that aren't clear to me."

Ralph nodded. "I'll do what I can."

"All right. A couple of days ago, I took a little journey without leaving my chair. A very strange woman blew smoke up my nose, and the next thing I knew I was sitting next to a waterfall in the jungle. You with me so far?"

The nirumbee's eyes narrowed. "Go on."

"A cougar the size of a pickup truck came up to me and started talking in my head. He gave me a new name: Speaks with Wind. In return for the name, he asked me to take care of the boy who talks backwards."

Ralph pulled out another of his cigars and lit it up, first try. Impressive, given the way the wind was beginning to whip. Smoke rolled out of his mouth as he asked, "And it was Cougar that spoke to you?"

I had thought that Ralph might have trouble believing my story, but I should have known better. Like Walks in Cloud, he was descended from a people with strong ties to an ancient past. "The strange woman I mentioned explained that I had been on a quest, and that Cougar had chosen to be my spirit animal."

Ralph frowned. "Cougar. I'll be damned." His lips twisted into a wry smile. "I was chosen by Badger. That vision drug is some shit, am I right? I guess we'll be all right as long as you don't get in my face." He stuck the cigar into the corner of his smile.

I waved away the smoke that rose to my nostrils. "Lord's balls, man! What the hell is that garbage? It smells like old socks."

Ralph pulled the cigar out of his mouth and studied it. "This? The leaf comes from a type of laurel tree that grows in the Baahpuuo Mountains. It's seasoned with kinnikinnick made from bearberry oil and some other shit. I'd give you some, but you'd probably fly off on another visit with the spirits, and now's not the time for that."

"Great. So what do you know about this boy that I'm supposed to be taking care of? Deet flipped out when I mentioned him."

Ralph's teeth clenched. "What did you tell Deet about him?"

"Nothing. I don't know who he is. A boy who talks backwards? What is that even supposed to mean? Deet had me under restraint and had been interrogating me for hours, but the moment I mentioned the boy, the interrogation was over. I got poked with a needle, and I woke up the next morning on a sidewalk five miles from home."

Ralph nodded. "That's interesting."

"Is it? I also mentioned him to Clearwater—that's the mug I was talking to when you showed up—and he turned himself into a big-ass owl and flew off into a hole in the sky. I don't know who this boy who talks backwards is, but he seems to scare a lot of scary people."

Ralph's eyes narrowed. "Tell me about this Clearwater lug."

"Armine Clearwater. You know. *The* Armine Clearwater."

Ralph's face was blank.

"You've never heard of Armine Clearwater? The richest man in the city? The 'A' in 'A-List'?"

"I'm new in town, remember? A few weeks ago I was running an LIA branch office in Lakota City. Enlighten me already."

I spent the next half hour freezing in the wind and ocean spray, going back to the beginning and telling Ralph the story of Leaflock, Redhorn, "Nocturnal," the flash drive, Deet, and Clearwater, bringing the nirumbee up to date. I didn't mention Walks in Cloud by name, and I didn't mention my meetings with Kalama or Crawford. Ralph wanted me on his team—wanted me to be his partner—and he seemed to mean well by me, but that didn't mean I was ready to embrace him and call him my brother. The elf might have embedded him in the LIA, but Ralph was still Leea. I was certain that he wasn't interested in telling *me* anything that he didn't think I needed to know, and I didn't feel a need to treat him otherwise.

"I'm convinced that Clearwater isn't human," I told Ralph. "He didn't have to turn himself into an owl for me to figure that out. He gives me the same feeling that I got when I was around the Sihuanaba—the Deer Woman."

Ralph frowned. "You're probably right. He's not an ordinary shapeshifter. That owl was too big to have been a transformed human. I didn't get a good look at the man before he grew wings and flew into a hole in the sky. Describe him to me."

"Short for a human. Fat, but carries it with style. Classy dresser. A gentleman. Wears a tux with tails and a fancy top hat. Wears a fucking monocle he probably doesn't need and carries a fucking cane he doesn't use. High roller with expensive taste in food and drink, but he'll settle for what's available. Smiles when he tells you that he could kill you without batting an eye."

Ralph nodded. "Sounds like a spirit to me, and I think I know which one. If I'm right, then your Clearwater is Night Owl. And you need to avoid him at all costs. He's what my people call 'strong medicine' and a real vicious bastard."

"Easier said than done. I didn't exactly invite him here tonight."

Ralph looked up at me, his expression stern. "He's been toying with you, Southerland. That's his nature. He's a hunter, and he likes to play with his food before he swoops in for the kill. But listen to me good. If he gets his hands on that flash drive, you're dead meat. If you're lucky, he'll only kill you. Night Owl's a heavy hitter. Not even Cougar can protect you from him."

"And yet he's spooked by the boy who talks backwards."

"He should be."

"Why? It's your turn now. Who is this backwards-talking boy?"

Ralph's eyes drifted out over the water as he pulled his cigar from his lips. "The boy who talks backwards plays many roles in our stories. He's usually associated with the spirits in some way."

I nodded. "I've heard this much already."

Ralph ignored my interruption. "But if Deet and Night Owl—especially Night Owl—are actually afraid of this boy, then I can only think of one reason why. It doesn't make a lot of sense to me, and if what I'm thinking is true, then it's big. Really big." Ralph shook his head. Then he looked up and met my eyes. "It doesn't seem possible, but this boy who talks backwards could be Thunderbird."

Chapter Fourteen

"Thunderbird? Like the car?"

The nirumbee gazed past the railing into the blackness beyond. A thick marine layer meant that no stars would be shining down on us that night, nor would the moon be making an appearance any time soon. The darkness was complete. Without our elf-enhanced awareness, neither of us would have been able to detect our hands in front of our faces. I hadn't heard any birdcalls for quite a while, and I couldn't sense any movement in the sky.

When Ralph spoke, his voice was quiet and, for the usually feisty warrior, oddly gentle. "My people live close to the spirits. Spirits like Badger, Cougar, and others. They have a big impact on our lives. Thunderbird is the most powerful spirit of all. Or at least the most powerful spirit who walks amongst us. The most loved and the most feared. Also the most mysterious and the most confounding. All of the spirits are strange in their own way. They're unearthly—not of this world—and they don't think like you humans or us nirumbees. But Thunderbird is the most difficult of them all to understand. In the old days, the tribal chiefs were chosen by Thunderbird. Thunderbird brought the wheat from the ground and lightning from the sky. Wars were fought when Thunderbird wanted them to be fought. He raised some villages to power and he turned others to stone. I've seen their remains. He brings life and he brings death, and no one knows why he sometimes chooses one and sometimes chooses the other."

Ralph turned back to look up at me. "When the modern world came crashing down on us, we looked to Thunderbird for protection. But, for reasons we don't know, the twofaced motherfucker refused to help us, and we nirumbees were unable to protect ourselves. We waited for his return, but he stayed away. We looked for him, but he couldn't be found."

Ralph gazed back out over the water, gathering his thoughts. After a few moments, he turned back to me. "It was said that Thunderbird would sometimes manifest himself as a human boy who was destined to be a great chieftain. According to the stories, the mark of that boy would be that he talked backwards."

"The boy who talks backwards," I said.

Ralph nodded. "If Thunderbird has returned, he may have taken the form of a boy living somewhere in our midst."

I thought about that. "I think that he's been trying to send messages to me." I told Ralph about my automatic writing episodes. "Could this boy be the one the heartstone belongs to?"

Ralph frowned. "I suppose it could. The boy who has been sending you messages might not be the same person who was kidnapped from Lakota, but the heart could still be his. It's hard to explain. Thunderbird is as powerful as it gets. He can... change reality. With him, anything is possible."

"In that case, why don't we just whistle for him and tell him to come pick up his heart? Hey, Mr. Thunderbird. We've been looking for you. We've got something of yours. You want it back?"

Ralph scowled. "Because that's not the way it works."

"Then how *does* it work?"

"How the fuck do I know! I ain't a fuckin' shaman. I'm a *warrior*. I'll fight spirits, like I fought the Deer Woman. But understanding what makes them tick? That's not my department."

"Terrific."

Ralph gave me a half grin. "Cougar has instructed you to protect the boy, which means that he knows about the boy's existence. Maybe the other spirits know about him, too. Or maybe some know and others don't. It's impossible for us to get into the heads of the spirits, to know what they know. But Deet and Night Owl are afraid of him."

Something occurred to me then. "Wait. Is Deet a spirit, too?"

Ralph's scowl returned. "I don't know. Sometimes I think so, but... I don't know. If not a spirit, then maybe a shapeshifter, but an unusual one. I've haven't worked with Deet for long, but all I can say is that I'd be surprised if Deet is a normal human."

I thought about that. "Lord's balls."

Ralph nodded. "Yeah."

"I'm in it up to my eyeballs, aren't I."

"Yep."

"Good thing I've got a fierce nirumbee warrior on my side."

Ralph snorted. "Oh, so *now* we're partners. All that means is that we're *both* in it up to our eyeballs."

A gust of wind swept over the pier, and I yanked down on my fedora to keep it from flying out into the ocean. One thing was still puzzling me. "Okay, we're surrounded by spirits, and maybe some other kind of paranormal baddie, too. But where does this RAA come into the picture? Deet and Clearwater are both after it. I thought at first that they might be working together, but after talking to Clearwater tonight I don't think so. I think they're each playing their own game. What *is* this RAA, and why do they want it?"

Ralph shook his head. "Do you know anything about it at all?"

I tried to recall what I'd heard about RAA. It wasn't much. "Leaflock said that it was a key part of a device he was making to regenerate cells. Redhorn was working on the device. He knew what it was, but he's dead. I'm not sure if Deet knows anything about it. I get the feeling that he?... she?... might be acting as an agent for someone else. Clearwater claimed that he wanted it in order to save a life."

Ralph started. "What? To save a life?"

I shrugged. "That's what he said. I figured he was just saying that to appeal to my sense of altruism and make me want to sell it to him. He wouldn't tell me whose life he was trying to save."

Ralph frowned. "Whose life would Night Owl want to save? From the stories I've heard, he's really fuckin' powerful, but hopelessly irresponsible. He's all about night life and parties... eating and drinking... sharp clothes and hot music... living it up and having a good time. He doesn't have a reputation for compassion or caring about anyone but himself." Ralph's eyes widened. "Unless... unless there's something in it for him...." Ralph's voice trailed off.

I looked at him. A wave crashed into the pilings and shook the pier so hard that I had to grab onto the railing to keep from falling. "Ralph? You know something?"

Ralph's jaw was hanging open, exposing his pointed teeth. His eyes were open wide, and he reached out to grab the railing as the pier swayed a little under the force of an incoming wave.

"You okay, Ralph?"

The nirumbee closed his mouth and wrapped his arms around himself. "It's cold out here."

"Really? Well, I'm not one to say I told you so, but...."

"Hmph. You could have tried to be more convincing." He reached inside his coat, and then let out a disappointed sigh. "I could use a drink. I didn't bring anything with me. Do you happen to, uh...?"

I reached into my pocket and pulled out my flask. After knocking back a shot for myself, I passed it to Ralph, who took a drink and grimaced. "You've got lousy taste in firewater, Southerland."

"Bring your own next time."

Ralph choked down another swallow and handed the flask back to me. "Give me the flash drive, Southerland. I think I can do a better job of keeping it secure. The LIA has resources you wouldn't believe."

"Deet is LIA," I pointed out.

Ralph nodded. "That's true. But the LIA is a strange place. Like I said, it's got factions, and factions within factions, and everyone has secrets they keep from everyone else. I can stash that flash drive in places no one else can get to. That's how I'm keeping the heartstone safe. Believe me, I can make that flash drive disappear from the face of the earth and then retrieve it whenever I want."

"That sounds impressive, but I've got some resources of my own."

Ralph made a scoffing noise. "No offense, but what are you, a private snoop? I'm fuckin' Leea! And on top of that I've trained in fighting arts you've never heard of and could never hope to master. I could carry that flash drive around in my pocket and even Night Owl would have a tough time taking it from me."

"If that's the case, then he's not as tough as you've been letting on, little man."

Ralph looked up at me with the light of battle in his eye. "Better watch that mouth of yours, beanpole. You've challenged me before, remember? How'd that go?"

"Yeah, you can take me in a fair fight, I'll give you that. But I've got a lot safer places to keep the flash drive than in your fucking pocket."

"That so? Like where?"

I glanced down at Ralph, at the eagerness in his eyes, and a soft buzz of suspicion streaked its way across my thoughts like the vibration of insect wings.

Ralph must have sensed something in my stare. He looked away and raised a hand in dismissal. "Forget I asked. I'm sure you *think* you've put it in a secure location. It's just that we're talking about a reality-bending spirit, and Deet, a top LIA agent and maybe something more besides. No matter how good you think you are, they're better. If you really want to keep it out of their hands, you should let me do it for you. The drive will be safe, and you'll be safer, too, because you won't know where it is." He paused for a beat, and his voice sunk to a whisper. "Or what's on it."

"I'll know that you have it. They might get your name from me."

"You're a tough guy. You've stood up to both of them. You stood up to the fuckin' Deer Woman. Besides, even if they know I've got it, they'll never get it from me. And I assume you've got it password protected, right? None of us will be able to access the memory on that drive unless you give up the password. Its secrets will be safe from all of us. Come on, Southerland. Be smart. What'd'you say?"

***

In the end, I decided to hang on to the flash drive, much to Ralph's consternation. To keep him happy, I promised I would keep the drive safe from Deet and Clearwater until we'd heard from the elf, which, in truth, suited me fine. I was certain that no one knew I'd given the drive to Crawford, and not even I knew where Crawford had stashed it. That had been part of our deal. Only Crawford knew where the drive was, and only I knew the passcode. If anything happened to either of us, the information would be lost forever. I felt like the flash drive was as secure as anyone, even Ralph, could make it.

When I got back home, I found that my office had been tossed again, and they hadn't been subtle about it this time. My safe had been sliced open and the contents, including my thirty-eight and a round of ammo, scattered around the room. Every drawer had been pulled out of my desk and rifled. Papers and office supplies were everywhere. They had even slashed the painting of the crow overlooking a desert landscape. They had even taken the bottle of rye I kept in my desk and emptied it out on the floor. My apartment upstairs had also been searched, and was in the same condition as my office.

I went back down to the laundry room and found Chivo hunched over his food dish and licking it clean. "Thanks a lot," I muttered at the beast. "Some watchdog *you* are." I could see that Chivo's fur was still moist from the nighttime mist, however, and I reasoned that he had entered the building only minutes before I had. It seemed that my intruders had done their damage and departed before Chivo had come in from his nightly prowl.

Syphon was on-duty, as always, drawing the foul odors from the room and forcing them out the window. Turning to the elemental, I asked, "Syphon, did you see anyone besides Chivo and me come into this room?"

Syphon's response sounded as if it was rising from the bottom of a well. "One human and one dwarf entered room."

"Describe them."

"The human has one head, two arms, two legs...."

"Stop." Elementals. I needed to ask something more specific. "Did they speak?"

"Yes."

"Can you remember what they said?"

"Yes."

"Good. Repeat what they said, please."

Syphon's voice raised in pitch and sounded vaguely trumpet-like. "Go through the clothing. I'll check the washing machine and dryer. And hurry. He should be back any minute now." Then the elemental's voice deepened a bit, and Syphon somehow introduced a growl into the tone. "Nothing here. Phew. It smells like something died in here." Trumpet voice: "Check that dog bed." Growly voice: "This smells even worse. How can anyone live like this." Trumpet voice: "That's quite a statement, coming from you." Growly voice: "The street smells better than this room. I'm tellin' you, if the agency ever fires me I could survive just fine out there." Trumpet voice: "Don't be silly. When the agency fires you, you'll disappear." Growly voice: "There's nothing here. We're wasting our time." Trumpet voice: "Okay, let's get out of here. He should be back here any second. We'll go out the back door so we don't run into him."

"Syphon, describe the dwarf."

"The dwarf has one head, two arms, one leg—"

"One leg?"

"One leg."

I nodded, thinking that the dwarf didn't sound nearly so crazy when he wasn't sleeping on the sidewalk. I wasn't going to look at another derelict without suspecting he was Leea. It was enough to give a guy the yips.

**

Later that morning, I found they'd broken into the beastmobile, too. They must have searched it just after I'd returned to my apartment. They hadn't taken the time to be subtle. The front driver's side door had been forced open, along with the trunk. I found the hood standing open, but at least the engine was undamaged, as far as I could tell. The good news was that they hadn't slashed my leather seats.

Gio was apologetic, even after I told him that there was nothing he could have done. I explained that I was the one who owed *him* an apology, since the LIA wouldn't have invaded his lot if I hadn't kept my car there. Gio volunteered to spend the next night in his office with a shotgun, but I told him it wouldn't be necessary. I told him that Leea had already searched the beastmobile and come up empty, and it was unlikely they'd come back. Gio volunteered to fix the damage free of charge, but I insisted on paying. We bellyached about the Lord's Investigation Agency until the cab I'd called for arrived, but it was a problem neither of us could solve.

The cabbie dropped me off at cop headquarters, where my new unused computer was waiting for me to rescue it and take it home. While I was waiting for Officer Wildfire to retrieve the computer, Kalama spotted me and came by to see what was up.

"You got a free half hour sometime this morning?" I asked her. "There have been some developments concerning our mutual friends that you might be interested in hearing about."

Kalama scowled. "You mean Cousin L?"

I nodded.

"I don't know, gumshoe. I'm interested, but my job is still homicide. You didn't happen to shoot anyone, did you?"

"Not yet. But I still have suspicions about that stiff you've got in your basement. He was in the middle of too much shit for his death to be natural." A thought struck me then. "You've still got him, haven't you? Leea hasn't scooped him up?"

"Last I checked."

"Do me a favor and check again, would you?"

"Sure, gumshoe. We cops do favors on demand for you ordinary citizens all the time. That's what we're for."

"Thanks, detective. Coffee at the Acorn?"

"Give me an hour. Hopefully they'll find your computer before then."

***

I was scanning the newspaper over a cup of coffee with my computer next to me when Detective Kalama slid into the booth across the table from me.

"You were right. Leea's sending someone for Redhorn's body this afternoon. They're going to make it disappear."

"But you guys did an autopsy on him, right?"

"Yes, a quick one. I just got done printing out the report. Leea has a way of making inconvenient police reports disappear from the system, along with inconvenient bodies." The detective plopped a folder down on the table and opened it.

"Let's see...," she began. "Not much here. No sign of injury.... No sign of disease, other than a pickled liver.... Lungs weren't in good shape, but nothing there that would have killed him.... Overweight, but who isn't.... Heart? Not great, but nothing to indicate that he was in danger of a coronary.... Hmmm, the coroner speculates that a blocked artery could have killed him, but there's no follow-up.... Conclusion is heart failure, cause unknown."

"Did they test for poison?"

Kalama scanned the report again. "Tests of the blood and urine came up clean, and there were no needle marks on the body. Not a thorough search, but the coroner ruled out anything obvious."

A waitress came by and filled Kalama's cup. I passed her the cream pitcher and four sugar cubes. She doctored the coffee without looking at it and continued reading from the report. "Looks like Redhorn was going out on the town. He'd showered, shaved, brushed his teeth, put on aftershave, deodorant, hair tonic.... Even clipped his fingernails." Kalama grimaced. "Coroner wrote a note saying that he was the best-smelling stiff in the morgue." She looked up. "Sometimes I think those ghouls like their job a little too much."

Something about the report nagged at me, but I couldn't put my finger on what it was. "All right, detective. Hang on to that. Once Leea takes the body, this will be all we've got."

Kalama stared across the table at me. "You're convinced that Redhorn was murdered?"

I nodded. "He must have been. I just can't figure out how."

"I agree." Kalama blew across the top of her coffee cup and took a sip. "Leea coming in for the body clinches it for me. Why else would they want it? I want to look into it, and, right now, you're my best source for information. You were investigating him, and you were one of the last people to see him alive. You need to spill, and don't hold anything back. I need to know everything. You mentioned some developments?"

I told her that I was meeting Leaflock that afternoon and Deet in the evening. I told her about Clearwater intercepting me at the pier. "He threatened me again. He told me that there was nothing I could do to stop him from getting that flash drive. And then I spooked him by mentioning the boy who talks backwards."

Kalama's eyes narrowed and she gave her head a little jerk. "The boy who what?"

"The boy who talks backwards." I shifted in my seat, trying to get comfortable. "This is where it gets a little weird."

"Oh, *now* it gets weird." Kalama shook her head. "Okay, give it to me from the beginning, and don't leave anything out."

I settled back and told a wide-eyed Kalama about my visit to the spirit world and my encounter with Cougar. Her reaction was about what I expected.

"You're the last person I would have expected to scramble your brains with mind-fucking drugs." She shook her head. "I thought you had more sense than that."

"I didn't exactly volunteer for the trip," I pointed out.

She gave me a thin smile. "Am I supposed to call you 'Speaks with Wind' now? Are you going to sell off your possessions and try to persuade me to join a cult?"

"Come on, detective. How is this any weirder than some of the other things we've seen since we met?"

She shook her head, and the smile stayed on her face. "I'll have to hand it to you, gumshoe. Life around you is never dull. I never expected you to turn into a wet-brain, though."

"Yeah, well you haven't heard all of it yet."

I told Kalama how Cougar had instructed me that, in return for my name, I had to protect 'the boy who talks backwards,' and that the boy would save my life. Then I explained how mentioning the boy had extricated me from two jams, one with Deet and one with Clearwater. I told her about my meeting with Ralph, too, and about how he believed that Clearwater was the spirit known as Night Owl.

"Oh, and Ralph thinks that Deet is some kind of shifter, but not your usual garden variety."

Kalama looked like she wanted to be skeptical, but she nodded. "Gotta admit, I believe him about Deet. Which means that he's probably right about Clearwater, too. You saw him turn into a big owl?"

"And he flew off into a patch of darkness."

"And it wasn't some kind of aftereffect from the hallucinogens? Can you be sure about that?"

"I still can't make contact with Badass. That's real."

Kalama nodded slowly. "Wow. I've dealt with every kind of hophead and juicer. I've had to disarm or defend myself against all kinds of sick-minded humans, trolls, dwarfs, and gnomes. I've questioned or arrested a dozen different kinds of shapeshifters. I've taken a bloody knife away from a half-naked sprite. I can't tell you how many times I've had to run someone in for killing an adaro hooker, or for killing his buddy because they'd been fighting over an adaro hooker. I'd run into a few witches even before you introduced me to Madame Cuapa. But it wasn't until I met you that I had to deal with otherworldly spirits. First that dog shadow—Xolotl? Then the Sihuanaba. And now you're telling me that we've got another spirit running around? Night Owl? And you've got a spirit animal? A cougar?"

"Ralph's spirit animal is Badger," I pointed out. "Everyone is getting a spirit animal these days. You should get one, too. A real tough one, like Bear or Bulldog."

"I'd rather have something with a brain in its head, like a raven. Those are clever birds. They'll be around long after all you boneheaded knuckle draggers have pounded each other into dust."

I nodded. "You could be right. But still, I could do worse than Cougar. I just wish he would be a little more forthcoming. All this crap about a boy who talks backwards.... What I'd like to have is a spirit animal who'll just tell me in plain speech everything I need to know."

The waitress came by then and asked if we wanted our coffee cups topped off, but we told her that we were about done for the night and I handed her a credit card.

When I turned back to Kalama, she was frowning. "A boy who talks backwards.... Hmm.... You know, it's possible that I might have something for you." Still frowning, she finished off the last of her coffee and sat back in her seat. "A few weeks ago, a couple of our officers got called out to break up a disturbance. I don't know the details, but they ran into a young male troll. You don't see many troll children running around, so it got talked about. Word is that the officers had trouble talking with the troll. They said that he had trouble with his speech. At first they thought he was on drugs, but he seemed lucid enough, and he didn't give the officers any trouble.

When I heard about it, it sounded to me like he had some kind of communicative disorder. Apraxia maybe."

"Ah-what? I don't know what that is."

"Apraxia. Some children have trouble forming words correctly. They know what they want to say, but they have difficulty transmitting the information from their brains to their mouths. And sometimes the sounds come out in the wrong order. It's not exactly talking backwards, but it's in the neighborhood."

"What happened to this troll kid?"

"He didn't appear to have a home. Anyway, he couldn't tell the officers where he lived. They concluded that he had a mental problem and dropped him off at a children's center. I don't know which one, but I can find out easily enough."

I felt a surge of excitement. "Would you? I'd owe you one."

"You already owe me plenty, gumshoe. And don't for one minute think I'm just going to write it off. But I'll do this for you. If nothing else, maybe you can find out where the boy came from and who he belongs to. Some anxious parents might be looking for him. In the meantime, try to keep yourself away from LIA agents. And homicidal spirits. And for fuck's sake, stay off the drugs!"

I dumped a boatload of exasperation into my tone. "All right, mom."

The waitress came by with my bill, and I picked up the pen she'd placed next to it. I was calculating the tip when my arm leaped out of my control. Against my will, I began printing letters on the check. When I was done, my hand dropped the pen and I regained control of my arm.

Kalama glanced at me and then looked down at the check to see what I had written. Her eyes widened. "What the fuck is that?"

The hair on my head felt like it was standing straight up from my scalp, and I felt a stream of cold sweat roll down the side of my face. I looked at what I—or someone controlling my hand—had written.

"Ryu luking me 4?"

Chapter Fifteen

I told Kalama about collapsing in the street and finding the message scratched into the side of the gin mill with my key. I also told her how something had possessed me to write the same message on the piece of paper that I'd found in my hatband. After I told her what Ralph had said about Thunderbird taking on the form of a boy who talks backwards, she was convinced that the troll child the officers had found wandering the streets was the manifestation of the greater spirit.

"According to Ralph, Thunderbird chooses human boys," I pointed out.

Kalama shrugged. "Doesn't mean he can't choose a troll if he wants to. I don't think there's a law against it."

After we paid for our coffees, the detective hustled off to the station to find out where the officers had taken the troll kid, and I took a hack back to my place.

I had a two o'clock meeting with Leaflock and a seven o'clock meeting with Deet. Both were under the impression that I was going to give them the flash drive containing information about RAA. Technically speaking, I hadn't actually promised to do anything except meet with them, but I knew that neither of them would see it that way. I needed to plan out some sort of strategy for seeing them and walking away with my skin.

By the time I'd finished lunch, my only plan for my meeting with Leaflock was to show up and play it by ear. So much for strategic planning.

The beastmobile was still a mess when I picked it up at the shop, but Gio at least managed to jury rig temporary latches on the hood and trunk so that they wouldn't fly open while I was driving. The driver-side door closed, but it wouldn't lock. Fortunately, I didn't keep anything of value in the car.

I was only fourteen minutes late when I walked into Leaflock's office, and he'd been gracious enough not to call the cops. I felt like we were getting off to a good start. He greeted me with a cordial smile and even came out from behind his desk to offer me a handshake. He showed me to a padded chair and offered me a drink, which I accepted. He reached for a fancy carafe, which meant that I'd be getting a glass of cheap rotgut all dressed up in crystal, but the price was right so who was I to judge.

My host became a lot less gracious when I told him that I didn't have a flash drive on me. His eyes bulged and his face turned cherry red as he wore a path in his carpet and unloaded a string of invectives in my direction. At least he didn't take back the whiskey.

I sipped my drink and let him vent his rage until he started to repeat himself. As he paused to draw in a breath, I asked him, "Pardon me, Mr. Leaflock, but what makes you think I have Redhorn's flash drive?"

Leaflock's eyes narrowed as his face split into a grin. "Don't play games with me, you snake. I know that you searched Redhorn's apartment and found it."

"Is that what Deet told you?"

Leaflock widened his eyes as he shot for an innocent expression. "Deet? Who's that?"

"Come on, Leaflock. I thought you didn't want to play games."

The look of innocence melted away from the gnome's face, which was fine with me because it hadn't been all that convincing anyway. "Okay, sure. Deet told me that you searched Redhorn's apartment and found the drive."

I leaned back in my chair and crossed my ankle over my knee. "Why do you want the flash drive so badly?"

"Why do you think? To keep it from falling into the wrong hands! How am I supposed to launch a unique once-in-a-generation revolutionary new product if my competitors are already developing their own fucking knockoffs?"

"Is that why you had Redhorn killed? To keep him from selling the drive?"

Leaflock's eyes nearly popped out of his head. "What? Is that supposed to be some kind of gag? You think I had Redhorn killed?"

"Makes sense to me," I said. To be honest, the gnome's confused expression was way too convincing to be anything but genuine. Nevertheless, I plowed ahead. "You had to stop him. You said it yourself: you couldn't have your competitors developing copies of the device you'd staked the future of your company on."

Leaflock shook his head. "Quit cracking wise to me, you shithead. I've been called a lot of things, but I'm no murderer."

"Sure, I get it. You didn't want to get your own hands dirty. That's why you called Deet. You say you're not a murderer, but you knew the LIA would have no qualms about getting rid of Redhorn for you. You dropped a few hints, and then you sat back and let events run their course. That makes you a murderer in my book."

Leaflock turned and slammed his desktop with the flat of his hand. "You're crazy! You're off your damned rocker! The police say that Redhorn died of natural causes. He had a bum ticker or something."

"You really believe that? The day I finger him for stealing your company secrets he just conveniently up and dies? Well, I saw the autopsy report. Redhorn didn't have a bad ticker. It was banging along just fine until someone stopped it."

I didn't know where I was going with this. I just wanted Leaflock to talk. He was more than willing to oblige.

Leaflock waved a hand in dismissal. "Big deal. If someone really did kill Redhorn, I had nothing to do with it. All I did was... was..."

I perked up. "What did you do, Leaflock?"

"Nothing! I didn't do nothing! I just told Deet to get me that flash drive, that's all. If Deet...." The gnome's voice trailed off.

"If Deet what? If Deet killed Redhorn it's not your fault? Is that what you're trying to tell me?"

"No! Get wise, Southerland. Deet wouldn't have killed Redhorn. Not without getting the flash drive from him first." Leaflock had stopped pacing and was leaning against his desk. Tiny little rainbows reflected off the beads of sweat forming on his forehead.

I sat forward in my chair. "Why not? Deet could have killed him first to keep him from selling your info and then cleaned up later. There was no hurry to find the drive once Redhorn was out of the picture. There was no reason to think it was going anywhere. If I hadn't decided on the spur of the moment to search the apartment, I'm sure the cops or the LIA would have found the drive eventually. And if they didn't, chances of it ever turning up were somewhere between slim and none."

Leaflock was shaking his head the entire time I was talking. "No, no. You don't understand. I needed that drive."

That stopped me in my tracks. "Why? What's on that drive that you don't already know? Redhorn copied info about RAA on it so he could sell it, right? But you designed it. I mean, you must have all the specs and formulas or whatever you need in your own company files, or in that genius head of yours. What do you need the drive for? Is there something else on it?"

Leaflock had stopped talking. He just shook his head.

Something began to click, like the square plastic block falling into the square hole. "Unless.... Unless *you* didn't come up with the formula at all.... What was it Redhorn's wife told me? That you were the dreamer, but it was Redhorn who made your dreams real." I pointed a finger at his chest. "You don't know how to make this RAA! It was Redhorn who designed it! Redhorn was the only one who knew how to make it!" I sat back in my seat. "It all makes sense now."

Leaflock walked slowly around his desk and slid into his chair. He stared at his desktop with hollow eyes that saw nothing, and when he spoke it was with none of the arrogant swagger I was used to hearing in his voice. "My cell regeneration device is going to be the biggest thing this world has ever seen. We'll be able to cure paralysis. Restore brain function. Reverse aging—the possibilities are mind-boggling! The test run I've got planned...." His words trailed off, and he shook his head to bring himself back to the present. "This device is going to make me the most important person on earth. I'll be bigger than the Dragon Lords." He put his hands on his desktop and stared at them. "I designed the energy extraction component that connects the device to the special power source the device requires. But Redhorn came up with the working formula for the key component: RAA. I told him what I wanted. I gave him the general specs and parameters. But he devised the final steps. I gave him one of my enchanted flash drives so that he could download a secure backup copy of the formula for me. But the son of a bitch was going to sell it. And he died before I could get my hands on it."

I nodded. "Right. And once you got it, you were going to claim that you were the one who developed it in the first place."

Leaflock looked across his desk at me. "I *did* develop it! All of it but the details. I came up with the idea and told him what he needed to do to make it happen. I left it to him to put it together in its final form. That's the way we always did it. I'd tell him what I wanted, and he'd do the grunt work. The product belongs to the company, and I front the company. It's the way both of us wanted it. Besides, I do all the real work. I'm the one with the ideas. I tell him where to put the nails, and he does the hammering."

"That's not what it sounds like to me," I said. "It's more like you would tell him you wanted a house, and he'd design one for you. And then you'd take the credit for the whole finished product, including the design."

Leaflock glared at me, and the swagger came back into his voice. "You have no fuckin' idea how a successful company like mine works. I provide the vision. I provide the ideas. And I provide the direction. But I'm not a tyrant. I'm more of a hands-off type of leader. I don't micromanage my employees, and they respect me for it. I tell them what I want and they give it to me. Yeah, I take the credit, because I deserve the credit. And besides, Redhorn didn't like the attention. He was a 'back room' kind of guy. Sure, he did good work for me, and I made sure that he was paid for it. Redhorn was a steering wheel, but I drive the car. We had a good working relationship, and it worked fine for both of us. We were a successful partnership."

Sure they were. Except Redhorn didn't know he was a steering wheel. The poor sap thought he was the one building the car. When he found out the true nature of his 'partnership' with Leaflock he got bitter enough to sell his partner out.

I kept that thought to myself. Out loud, I asked, "Isn't the formula for RAA still on Redhorn's computer?"

Leaflock's eyes fell. "We couldn't find it there. He must have erased the file after he downloaded it. Really erased it. We couldn't even find it in his trash. It wasn't on any of his personal devices, either. Now that he's dead, the only place it exists is on that flash drive. And the flash drive has an enchantment that prevents its data from being downloaded anywhere else."

Leaflock rose from his chair. "And you've got that flash drive, you motherfucker! Don't lie to me! That formula is mine! Tell me what you want for it. But do it now, before Deet gets hold of you. Make a deal with me, or deal with Deet. That's your choice, Southerland. Trust me, you'd be a lot better off accepting an offer from me than one from Deet. You won't like what Deet's offering you."

"And what are *you* offering? Besides a lot of hooey about what a big man you are. Bigger than the Dragon Lords. Sure you are. Except that without Redhorn, you've got nothing but dreams and wishes." I rose to my feet. "Good luck, Leaflock. You've had a good ride. It's a nice view from the top. It gets a lot worse on the way down, and the ground rises up to meet you way too fast."

I left Leaflock screaming a lot of bullshit about motherfucking thieves and cops and lawyers and "Wait till Deet gets hold of you" and so on and so forth.... Echoes of it bounced off me all the way to the door, and traces of it followed me out into the street.

***

On my way to my car, I checked my phone for messages and found a voicemail from Kalama waiting for me. She'd found the children's home where the cops had dropped off the wandering troll boy with the speech problem and provided me with the particulars, including the name of the institution's director, a Mrs. Alma Lumpoc. The afternoon was getting on, and I decided I wouldn't be able to get over to the facility and still make my meeting with Deet. Thinking that I'd probably be better off making an appointment anyway, rather than just dropping in, I punched in the phone number.

A voice that sounded like it cared answered my call. "New Horizons Children's Home. Children are our future. Alma Lumpoc's office. Whom may I say is calling?"

"Do you have to go through that spiel every time the phone rings?"

"I'm sorry?"

"Never mind. Is Mrs. Lumpoc available? Tell her it's about the young male troll that the police dropped off there recently."

"And whom may I say is calling?"

"Right. My name is Alexander Southerland. I'm a private investigator."

"Thank you Mr. Southerland. Is that S-U-T-H-E-R-L-A-N-D?"

"S-O-U, like 'south-erland.'"

"Really? Hmm." I got the feeling that she didn't approve. "I'll see if Mrs. Lumpoc can come to the phone."

"Excuse me," I interrupted. "Is that L-U-M-P-O-C?"

After a slight hesitation, the voice said, "That's correct, Mr. *South*erland. Please hold." She pronounced it South-erland, which gained my immediate respect.

I was treated to some familiar-sounding music that rose and fell in a dirge-like rhythm like unceasing ocean waves. After three minutes I recalled that the music was the theme song for a popular children's movie that I'd never seen, something about the daughter of an ancient Adaro king who had fallen in love with a shipwrecked human. The movie was supposed to be based on a grim old fairy tale about unrequited love, needless sacrifice, and disappointment. I guess it was never too soon for kids to learn how unfair life could be. Da-da-*dum*-da, da-da-*dummm*.... Over and over. I groaned to myself. The insipid tune was going to live in my ear for the rest of the week.

After what seemed like an eternity, the melody was cut off by clicking noises. "Mrs. Lumpoc speaking. Is this Mr. Alexander Southerland?" She pronounced it correctly.

"It is," I confirmed.

"And you are calling about Troy?"

"Who? No, I'm calling about the young male troll that the police dropped off at your facility a few weeks ago."

"We call him Troy. I'm afraid we don't know his real name. Do you have information about the boy?" I could hear the hope in her buoyant voice.

"I might know something. I'd like to come by and meet him. He may be related to a case I'm working on."

"I see." The buoyancy in her voice had deflated. I guess she'd hoped that I was the boy's father or uncle or something. "And when were you thinking of coming by?"

I reached my car then and leaned against the bent hood. "Unfortunately I'm tied up for the rest of the day. I was hoping to be able to see him tomorrow."

She sighed. "I understand. Tomorrow morning will be fine."

"I'll try to get there as early as I can, unless you need to arrange for a specific time."

"No, no. Any time after seven o'clock will be fine. Just come to the front desk."

"Seven might be a little early for me. I keep late hours. But I'll do my best."

"That's fine, Mr. Southerland. Um...." She hesitated for a beat, apparently searching for the right words. "Are you familiar with Troy's... eccentricities?"

I frowned. "I'm aware of his speech challenges. I'm no expert, but at least I know what to expect."

"That's very good. There are some other issues, too...." Her voice seemed to trail off.

"Other issues? What do you mean?"

"Troy is... an unusual boy. Perhaps we should hold off talking about him until you get here. Then you can see for yourself."

"Ri-i-ght. Okay, I guess that works for me."

"Then I'll see you first thing in the morning." Again I sensed Mrs. Lumpoc's hesitation. "Excuse me, Mr. Southerland? Did you say that you were a private investigator?"

"That's right."

"That's very good." The buoyancy came back in her voice. "I may have a use for someone in your profession, that is, if you're available. We know nothing about Troy's background, and the police don't seem to have the time or inclination to help us out. You say that you have an interest in him. If you could find out something about Troy.... Maybe even find his parents, or where he comes from.... Well, if you could find out anything about him at all we would really appreciate it."

"That is certainly something that we can discuss, Mrs. Lumpoc."

"Terrific! I'll look for you in the morning."

We disconnected then, and I climbed into the beastmobile. The possibility of a paying job lifted my spirits. As the children's song I'd heard while I was on hold echoed in my brain, I hoped that I'd be free to keep my appointment with Mrs. Lumpoc in the morning, and not cooling my heels in a holding cell waiting to be questioned about the discovery of a dead body, or, worse, locked up in a concrete LIA interrogation cube with Deet staring at me with those eyes that didn't blink.

***

It was six o'clock when I'd finished washing down a roast beef sandwich that I'd picked up from a fast-food joint with a bottle of beer, and I still hadn't decided where to arrange my meeting with Deet. With no better plan, I decided to tell Deet to come to my office. Why not? I was comfortable there, and I figured that Deet would assume I had put some hidden defenses in place for the visit. I hadn't, but I reasoned that the next best thing to having nothing was to convince my opponent that I had everything under control. If you say it often enough, it sounds brilliant.

I even told Deet to feel free to bring along a couple of associates. I thought that would make me sound confident. Deet told me that an associate wouldn't be necessary, which made me believe I'd lost that battle of the minds.

Deet arrived at seven sharp, which seemed very Deet to me.

"Come in, Deet. You can pick one of those chairs up off the floor. Careful not to step on anything."

Deet cast a non-judgmental eye over the mess in my office and nodded toward the floor. "Is this a new rug? It's very you."

"Thanks. I needed to cover over a stain."

Deet glanced at the damaged safe standing open against the wall before stooping to pick up a chair lying on its side on the floor. "Your safe was a poor choice for a man in your profession. Why bother owning a safe that can be sliced open by a portable thermal lance like a knife through butter? I can tell you where to acquire one that is much more secure."

"Thanks, but I never keep anything valuable in it anyway. It's mostly for show."

Deet pulled the chair to a spot across the desk from me and kicked some papers aside to create some foot room. "I see that you have replaced your computer. Have you accessed the data on Mr. Leaflock's flash drive? Please look me in the eye when you answer."

I met Deet's eyes. "No, Deet. It's been a busy day. I haven't even plugged my new computer in yet. I'm thinking of bringing someone in to set it up. I'm having trouble keeping up with all the changes in computer technology."

Deet stared at me for a few seconds before nodding. "I believe you, Mr. Southerland. If you hand me the flash drive now, I will depart and you will be free to live out the rest of your life as you choose."

I glanced away from Deet and blinked. "That's swell. What's in it for me?"

Deet did not blink. "Did I mention that you'd be free to live out the rest of your life as you choose?"

"Stop, Deet. You're scaring me." I sat forward and leaned against my desk. "Like I said, it's been a busy day. If I don't make a phone call at exactly eight o'clock, the information on that flash drive will find its way to the police, the newspapers, and the internet. It will also fall into the hands of seven major engineering firms, one in each of the Seven Realms. Not even the LIA can stop it from happening."

Deet finally blinked. Once. Quickly. Then a crack formed on the front of Deet's face, starting from the top of Deet's head, running down between Deet's eyes and over Deet's flat nose to split Deet's lips, and continuing on down Deet's chin and the front of Deet's neck. As the skin of Deet's face rolled away, the impossibly large insectoid head of a giant mantis the color of dead leaves slithered up from Deet's chest. A thin, bony ridge extended from over the flat nose, back between two bulging eyes, and a foot beyond the top of the head. A pair of hair-like antennae curled up from the head like tentacles. The body of the insect continued to emerge, as if from a cocoon, from Deet's blood-soaked clothing, which ripped apart and fell limply to the floor. Two long, muscular hinged forelegs, lined on their undersides with a row of barbed spikes, appeared, one long, thin talon extending like a needle from the ends of each arm. A thin thorax and a bulbous abdomen rose out of the loose human skin, propped up on four long bony legs. A row of barbs the size of sharks teeth lined the top of the thorax, and triangular wedges rose from the abdomen like a row of bony sails. Wings that looked like the petals of dried flowers opened from the thorax and spread to either side of the mantis's abdomen. One of the wings bumped against my filing cabinets and knocked the slashed painting of the crow overlooking the desert landscape off the wall, shattering the frame. The other wing crashed into my water cooler and coffeemaker and sent them tumbling to the floor. Freed from the shell of Deet's human body, the giant mantis—its head almost touching the ceiling fan—shook itself, sending globs of blood splattering throughout the room.

    I didn't waste any time gawking. I pulled a gat out of my desk drawer and fired three slugs into the chest of the thing that Deet had become. The mantis didn't so much as flinch as the bullets bounced off a layer of carapace as thick and hard as plate armor. Before I could fire another round, the forearms of the mantis shot forward, and I felt the fishhook-like barbs plunge into my shoulders and upper arms. The mantis lifted me up out of my chair and pulled me forward with its barbed forearms until its blunt mandibles were only inches from my face. I fought back a massive wave of vertigo and found myself staring into a pair of unblinking human eyes. Whatever this thing was, those ebony eyes were still Deet's.

    The mandibles opened, and a globule of black viscous liquid, like molten tar, rolled through its fangs and slowly stretched from the bottom of its mouth before finally dripping to the floor. A voice, like Deet's, but tinnier, as if the flesh of Deet's throat had been replaced by metal, emerged from the open jaws. "I don't need to kill you, Mr. Southerland. I don't want to kill you. But if you don't give me the flash drive, I will hurt you very badly."

When the barbs on the mantis's forearms had penetrated into my muscles, I hadn't felt much more than some prickling at first. But as they continued to slice into my shoulders and upper arms all the way to the bone, the pain became excruciating. Something behind my eyes seemed to explode, and animal noises ripped through my clenched teeth. The mantis shook me, and the pain forced a screech from the depths of my lungs. My brain ceased to generate thought. The entire world was obliterated. Only white-hot pain remained.

Then the monstrous insect's head turned away from me as it trained its eyes on something to my right. Some of the pain relented, and I turned my head, as well, trying to focus my blurred vision on whatever had attracted the mantis's attention. Chivo, stretched to his full height on his hind legs, was glaring at the mantis with his glowing red eyes shining out of his goat's face, claws extended, rigid spikes standing straight up along his spine.

I've got to hand it to Chivo. He held the mantis's gaze for a full ten seconds before lowering himself to all fours and creeping away, cringing, spikes flattened on his back, his rat's tail curled between his legs. Poor guy knew when he was outmatched. He was smarter than me, that's for sure.

The mantis swung its head back in my direction, and Deet's eyes locked onto mine. "Let's end this nonsense now, Mr. Southerland. Where is the flash drive? You know you're going to tell me eventually. Why not tell me now while you still have two functioning arms?"

The elf's gift had dramatically increased my body's power to heal itself, but I didn't think I'd be able to replace a limb if I lost one. Or two. An image of myself alive, but without arms, seared itself into my brain. Panic rolled over me like a raging flood, and I reached for the image of my tropical waterfall in a desperate attempt to keep from blurting out where I'd hidden the flash drive. I reached, but I couldn't find it. All I found was more pain as the barbs tore into the bones in both of my arms.

I wanted to surrender. I wanted to lose consciousness. I wanted to die. Anything to put an end to the unbearable pain. All I had to do was tell Deet that I had given the flash drive to Crawford, and the pain would go away. I wanted to do it. But against my desires, almost against my will, something inside me pushed back. A stubborn instinct to survive, maybe. Or maybe just pride. I clamped my teeth together to keep from screaming, glared daggers into the eyes of Deet, and shook my head. The pain in my shoulders and arms jumped up a notch, and I felt the scream I'd been suppressing crash through my jaws and inundate the universe. Yet I couldn't bring myself to say the words that would free me, even though the most rational part of my brain was insisting that it was the right thing to do. I resisted the shooting pain in my arms with everything I had. I allowed the unbearable agony to slash away my rationality so that I wouldn't be tempted by it, and I left myself with only one simple thought: this wasn't the way I wanted to go.

The mantis lifted me higher until my head bumped into the ceiling and began speaking in a calm and reasonable voice. "You are being very foolish, Mr. Southerland. You don't know what RAA is. You don't know what it does. Why does it matter to you? Give me the drive and the pain will end. You have not yet been maimed. Give me what I want, and you will survive, heal, and go on as if you'd never heard of RAA. Continued resistance is not only unreasonable, but insane. Giving me the flash drive will have no impact on the rest of your life at all. Continuing this madness will force me to inflict permanent damage."

It took me several tries, but I finally forced two words through my throat. "Fuck you." What I'd intended to be a shout of defiance came out as a pathetic rasp.

Deet's eyes blinked once. Then another cry was wrenched from my lungs as the barbed forearms sliced into my arms with renewed force.

As I braced myself for more excruciating agony, I was surprised when a wave of calm surged through my body, and the pain changed from a tornado of rusty nails in my head to a steady ache just on the right side of unbearable. I felt, rather than sensed a presence drifting through me like morning fog, dampening the pain centers in my brain like a strong narcotic. I caught a faint whiff of a wild feline scent, and I heard the voice of Cougar emerging from my mind as if from my own thoughts. "That's enough, mortal. Release him."

The pressure on my arms did not relent, nor was I lowered from the ceiling. Deet's eyes bore into my own, seeming to seek for the presence inside me. "Who are you?"

"I am Cougar. Speaks with Wind is under my protection."

The insect's head cocked to one side. "Speaks with Wind? I haven't heard that name."

"No matter. You will release him."

The insect's head straightened. "I think not. You have not been summoned from your realm."

"Speaks with Wind's pain summons me. I am pledged to protect him."

"It isn't enough. You are nothing more than a voice. You have no power over me in this realm."

Cougar let out a growl, and his voice dripped with menace. "I will rip you apart!"

The mantis pulled me close to its jaws, and I felt the heat of its breath pulsing out its nostrils. The stench of that breath was as stomach-churning as the pain from its barbs. "You will be silent, or I will remove this one's head."

I waited for Cougar to respond, but apparently he had nothing left to say. Thanks a lot, I thought at him. At least the narcotic effect was still in place, which meant that, on a scale of one to ten, the pain level had been dialed down from near twenty to about thirteen. I wondered briefly how much more of this my heart could take before it burst from the strain. Staying conscious became too hard, and I felt a darkness descending.

No! I wasn't going to allow myself to go under. I thought at Cougar, "Too numb. I need to feel."

The pain grew in intensity until I felt like my arms were being burned away by thermal lances. But the fog drifted out of my brain until I was fully conscious. I snarled at the mantis and tried to spit in its face. My mouth was too dry to produce anything, but I still felt pretty good about making the effort.

The insect's head drew back a few inches.

"You can't make me talk!" I tried to sound tough, but it sounded like desperation even to me.

Deet's eyes didn't blink. "I'll remove your left arm first. Then the right."

"Eight o'clock." My voice was nothing but a whisper. "I don't make a phone call at eight o'clock, the whole world learns about RAA."

"You're bluffing, Mr. Southerland. The drive is enchanted. It is impossible for you to make copies of the data."

"I copied them by hand."

"I don't believe you, Mr. Southerland." I felt pressure building on my left shoulder as a row of barbs began to sink in deeper.

I'd tried to play poker with Deet. I should have known better. I was holding a weak hand and trying to bluff. But Deet was holding all the aces.

I felt myself rising, pulled by the spikes in the thing's forearms. When my head was inches from the monster's bony mandibles, they opened, and Mantis-Deet's metallic voice rang in my ears. "You know what a mantis does to its mate after they've copulated."

My throat tensed, and I rasped through clenched teeth. "Oh, shit. Don't tell me that you expect me to fuck you."

In response, the mantis began to pull my left arm out of its socket.

Chapter Sixteen

I strained to brace my arm in place with every bit of will I could muster and locked my jaws to prevent myself from screaming again. I dropped my eyes—and my heart leapt! Clenched in my right fist, forgotten, was my roscoe, a thirty-eight handgun. I had started with five rounds and fired three. The slugs hadn't penetrated the creature's armor, but maybe I could still accomplish something with the two remaining bullets if I could put the gat in a position to be fired.

I tried to lift the gun, but my arm wouldn't cooperate. "Cougar?" I called in my mind. "Little help here?"

I gasped as a surge of adrenaline threatened to overload my straining heart, but I was able to bend my right elbow and lift my forearm almost to a ninety-degree angle. I raised my wrist, and when the pistol was pointed roughly where I needed it to be, I squeezed the trigger.

Just as I was firing the roscoe, an electric jolt of agony in my left shoulder caused my entire body to convulse, and the slug flew harmlessly into the wall behind the mantis. I couldn't allow myself to give in to my failure, though. With my heart pounding like an overheated engine, and with every muscle in my body coiled to its breaking point, I re-aimed and fired my last bullet.

And missed again.

But not completely. I'd been aiming for Deet's eye, the one part of the creature's body I thought would be vulnerable. Instead, I'd hit the bony ridge between the eyes of the mantis. The slug bounced off, but the impact staggered the mantis. The creature's head jerked backwards, and it involuntarily flung its arms upward and away from its body in order to keep its balance. I roared as the barbs ripped themselves from the flesh of my arms, and I dropped to the floor in a heap.

The mantis recovered before I did and bent down to try to scoop me back into its embrace. I was able to roll away but couldn't manage to get my feet under me. The mantis lunged at me again, and I scrambled away until I crashed into a filing cabinet. Something poked at me, and I reached down and found a piece of the broken wooden frame from my painting. One end of it was flat and the other jagged. It had been an expensive frame, and the wood was thick and solid. I thought that it would make a nice weapon if I only had enough strength to use it. Unfortunately, my left shoulder felt like it had been torn in two, and the arm on that side hung from it like a dead thing. My right arm wasn't in much better shape, but I could at least get my hand around the jagged piece of wood. I gripped it like it was trying to crawl away, knowing that it was all I had.

The mantis scooped me up with one arm and pulled me close to its head. The creature opened its mandibles to tell me something, probably how it was going to bite my leg off at the knee if I didn't give it that damned flash drive, but I didn't give it the chance. Bracing my feet against the giant bug's arm and the flat end of the piece of frame against the palm of my right hand, I launched myself at the creature, ignoring the lightning surges of pain that shot through my upper arms, and thrust the jagged piece of wood into Deet's widened ebony eyeball, jamming it through the gelatinous matter until the tip of my pointy stick lodged itself into something meaty behind the eye.

The mantis let out a high-pitched keening shriek and arched backward onto its hind legs as I fell to the floor on my damaged left shoulder and let out my own pitiful cry of pain. Our mutual wailing blended into a harmony that could probably have been heard in the depths of the abyss. Somewhere in the middle of our duet, the darkness fell and I blacked out.

***

I woke up in a hospital bed covered in bandages and something dripping into an opening in my arm through a plastic tube. A nurse in a starched white gown and gray streaks in her black hair was studying an instrument panel off to one side of me and making notes on a clipboard. I felt like I was floating in a cloud and wondered whether I was paralyzed. After some reflection, I decided I could live with that as long as I could still sip whiskey through a straw.

When the nurse noticed I was conscious, she stopped writing and glared at me as if I'd spoiled her night by waking up.

"Hello, Mr. Southerland. I'm Talia. Are we in any pain?" she asked me.

"I don't know about you, but I can't feel a thing, doll. I'm not sure I can move anything, either."

A scowl formed on her face to accompany the glare. "You're not paralyzed, Mr. Southerland. In fact, the doctor says you are healing at a rate that could only be possible through some kind of magical assistance."

I tried to stretch, but couldn't. "If that's the case, why am I so numb? I can't even feel my teeth with my tongue."

"The doctor wants you immobile. You suffered a grade three shoulder separation."

"Grade three? Is that all?"

The nurse frowned. "Grade three is as severe as it gets, Mr. Southerland. To put it in layman's terms, your arm was nearly torn from your body. The doctor has reattached it and bound it into place, but you're going to have to keep it immobile until it heals."

"How long is that going to take?"

"For anyone else, it would take six to twelve weeks and about a year of rehab. Longer if surgery is required. For you? Hard to say. If you don't do anything to damage it further, the ligaments will probably heal in a few days. You're still looking at extensive rehab, though. The important thing is not to move it until it's ready to be moved." She paused to glare at me some more. "No bar fights for a while, cowboy."

"Is that what you think happened?"

"You look the type."

I opened my mouth to argue, but decided to concede the point. I gestured with my eyes at the tube. "Is that stuff the reason I'm so numb?"

"You were in a great deal of pain when you came stumbling into the emergency room last night. You're on a heavy dose."

I'd come to the hospital on my own? That was interesting. I had no memory of that.

"I didn't come here in an ambulance?"

The nurse shook her head. "Nope. You walked through the door, took three steps into the emergency room waiting area, and keeled over. I think a cab dropped you off."

A cab? That was swell. It was possible that the cops were unaware of the little ruckus I'd had in my office the night before. I wondered what had become of Deet. I doubted that I'd killed the beast.

I turned back to the nurse, who was regarding me with a scowl. "Okay, Nurse Talia, could you ease up on the joy juice? I feel like I'm having an out-of-body experience."

The nurse rolled her eyes and sighed. "You'll need to talk to Dr. B'Gau about that."

"Well get him in here."

"Her."

"Her?"

"Dr. B'Gau is a her."

"I don't care if it's an it. Get her in here so we can turn off that juice. I can't even tell if I'm breathing."

The nurse turned her glare on me again and then looked me up and down. "Tough number. Just like my kid brother. Until some lug brained him with a lead pipe when he was trying to rob a liquor store. Now he's on the next floor in a coma breathing through a straw. Unlike you, he doesn't have some kind of magical spell to wake him up."

Everyone has a story. "That's a tough break, doll. Tell him I said howdy next time you go visit. Now get me that doctor."

Nurse Talia swept out of the room in a huff and returned a few minutes later with a weary-looking older dame with arms like a dockworker and a stern expression around her mouth that told you to fuck with her at your peril. The bags under her drooping eyes and the sweat stains under her arms told me that she was overworked and nearing the end of another long shift. The cigarette dangling from her lips told me that she didn't give a fuck about rules and regulations, and that the hospital's administrators knew better than to try to make her toe the line. I figured that she must be exceptionally good at her job.

"You been sassing at my nurse, Mr. Southerland?" Some doctors like to cultivate a friendly bedside manner. It was clear that she was not going to be one of them.

"You're Dr. B'Gau?"

The doctor turned to Nurse Talia. "He's a fuckin' bright one, isn't he." She turned back to me and gave me a patronizing look. "Yes. I'm Dr. B'Gau. And you're Mr. Southerland. And I hear that you're feeling so much better now that you think we should discontinue your pain medication. Is that true or did I get bum information?"

"I don't know, doc. I can't feel anything at all."

The doctor narrowed her eyes and pinched her lips around her cigarette in disapproval. "Is that right? You were begging for medication when the EMTs brought you in a few hours ago, which is understandable. Major lacerations in both upper arms, with bone scarring on the humerus, especially near the greater tubercle in both arms. Lots of tissue damage in the delts and triceps in both arms. Looks like someone yanked some king-sized fishhooks out of your arms. Grade three separation in your left shoulder. Both your AC and CC ligaments were severed, and you've got a minor fracture in your scapula. What that means, honey, is that somebody fucked you up but good!" The doctor scowled at me, as if I'd wounded myself in order to ruin her day. "You were semiconscious while I was working on you and talking your ass off. What the flying fuck is a 'deet'?" She pursed her lips around her cigarette and drew in some smoke.

"A deet?" I pretended to think about it for a second. "I have no idea. I guess I was delirious."

"Uh-huh. So is there anything you want to tell me, son? I haven't called the cops in here yet, but if you've been involved in a crime then I am obligated to let them know." She flicked at her cigarette and a quarter-inch of ash fell to the floor.

"No need," I told her. "The LIA already knows I'm here."

The doctor's eyes widened. "Did you say LIA?"

"Don't worry, I don't plan on staying here much longer. You think you can help me out of all these tubes? And get me my clothes?"

The doctor sighed and nodded. "Ordinarily, if a patient came in here as fucked up as you were, I'd be prepping him for surgery, but I can see that you aren't an ordinary patient. You've got some kind of magic flowing through your veins, and it's doing a better job of knitting you back together again than I could. I need to tell you, though, that you're going to be in pain for a while, and you are going to need to keep that left shoulder immobile so it don't heal crooked. Now, it doesn't take a genius to see that you're some kind of hard number. You've got a business card in your wallet that says you're a fuckin' P.I. I didn't think those guys existed except in movies." She smiled for the first time since she'd come into the room, and her eyes took on a dreamy look. "Ever seen that one with that actor... oh, what's his name.... The one who used to be a song-and-dance man in fuckin' musicals and decided to change his image.... Oh, fuck it. I don't have a head for names. I'd forget my own if I didn't have this name tag." The smile disappeared and the eyes went hard again. "Well, it doesn't fuckin' matter. Anyway, what was I saying? Oh yeah." She looked down at me with hooded eyes, her jaws tight. "You look like a mug who gets into scrapes, and from what you were babbling about when they brought you in it sounds like you're in the middle of something hairy. So what I'm saying is that if you don't baby that fuckin' shoulder of yours, it's going to give you grief the rest of your life, no matter what kind of juju you've got flowing through you. So give it a rest for a few days. Let the magic do its job and you should be good as new in a week or so. Get it?"

"Got it."

"Good." The doctor turned to the nurse, who'd been standing slightly behind her off to one side, trying to be unnoticed. "Talia, put this gentleman on saline and get him his clothes. If he still wants to leave when you get back, unhook him and get an orderly to escort him out of here. It's jammed in here, and we could use the bed. Make sure you bring me his paperwork. And if the LIA comes sniffing around, tell them I'm in surgery. Better yet, tell them I'm on vacation." She dropped her cigarette to the floor and crushed it out with the toe of her shoe before walking out the door.

***

A half hour later, I was fitted with an elaborate contraption that reminded me of a straightjacket, or half of one anyway. Some sort of stiff cloth wrapped around my chest, and metal links connected to a sling kept my left arm pinned down tight against my side. At least my right arm was free, though it didn't feel much better than the left one. I was in a hack headed for home, and I could already see the first glow of the morning sun spilling over the East Bay Hills. I winced as a bump in the road set off a minor explosion in the inflamed nerves bundled in my left shoulder. Unclenching my teeth, I drew in a slow breath and told myself to relax. I was due to meet Mrs. Lumpoc at the New Horizons Children's Home in a couple of hours. Good thing I'd had a few hours of drug-induced sleep at the hospital. It wasn't much, but it would have to do.

Chivo was kneeling in the center of my office pulling something out of the inside of Deet's shredded clothing with his teeth when I walked in through the front door. His eyes were downcast, and his rat's tail was curled tightly around his haunches. The spikes along his spine were lying flat, and even his goat's horns seemed to be drooping. The creature turned his head rather than look at me.

"It's okay, Chivo. I forgive you. That thing was too big an order for you. You did the right thing by strategically withdrawing from the battle. I guess it got away?" I couldn't remember anything between blacking out and waking up at the hospital.

Chivo flicked a long, narrow tongue at the blood and gore that covered his humanlike hands. Were those grisly remains the last of Deet? Once the mantis had risen from that flesh could it reverse the transformation? Or did it slough Deet from itself like a snake crawling out of its old skin. I didn't know, but I didn't feel right about feeding the disgusting mess to my lodger. It made me seem like a poor host.

"Leave it, Chivo," I told the dejected goat-creature. "I'll get you some yummy yonak."

By the time I'd settled Chivo in the laundry room with a fresh(ish) meal, flies were swarming over the gory mess on my brand new office rug. I let out a sigh. I had a feeling that I wasn't done with Deet, or whatever Deet was now. Clearwater—Night Owl—was still out there somewhere, and he still wanted the flash drive. I knew that he would make a move on me soon. My left arm was useless, and every time I moved my right arm it felt like it was being carved up for a holiday dinner. I needed to get ready to see a troll child who might be the boy who talks backwards, though I had no idea what I would do once I met him. Cougar had put him under my protection, but what that meant in practical terms was unclear. This mess in my office was just one more thing I had to deal with. I let out another sigh and climbed the stairs to my apartment. The mess would have to wait. At least the flies would be happy.

Standing under the streaming hot water of my shower trying to get as little of it as possible on my straightjacket, I asked myself why I was still hanging on to that fucking flash drive. I couldn't deny that Deet had made a reasonable point. What was the flash drive to me? I didn't know what RAA was, and I had no idea why I should care. Both Deet and Clearwater wanted it, Deet to give it to Leaflock and Clearwater to save a life. Or so they said. Well, who was I to keep it from them? What was I going to do with it? Why not give it up?

The answer was obvious, of course. The only reason I was still alive was because I was the only one who could lead Deet or Clearwater to the flash drive. Once either of them had the drive, they wouldn't need me anymore. Deet had taken a shot at me and would no doubt regroup for another. Clearwater probably had me in his sights already. And I had to stay alive long enough to get myself to a children's home and meet a boy who either talked backwards or couldn't talk at all. Meanwhile, the swarm of flies in my office was growing into a maelstrom. Life was sweet.

***

New Horizons Children's Home looked like a nice place for kids who were headed for prison and wanted to get a feel for what their future held for them. A compound of gray cement buildings was surrounded by a sturdy chain-link fence topped by industrial-grade razor wire. All that was missing were the guard towers manned twenty-four hours a day by government screws with mirrored sunglasses and rifles. I drove up to a security gate and waited for the armed sentry to call the front desk for clearance. The guard looked the battered beastmobile over from one end to the other with a disapproving eye as he awaited instructions. After a few moments he hung up the phone and passed me through, keeping his sidearm holstered, but at the ready. Once I'd parked, I had to pass through another checkpoint at the front entrance, where I was patted down when the metal links in my still-damp straightjacket set off the metal detector. Satisfied that I was unarmed and that I wasn't trying to smuggle a file inside my sling, I was directed to climb the half-flight of stairs in front of me and take the first doorway on my left.

"Will they frisk me again before letting me through?" I asked.

"No sir." The door guard wasn't smiling.

"Do you get asked that a lot?"

"Every day, sir. At least three or four times. You're the first today, though."

I nodded and headed for the stairs.

A well-groomed broad who appeared to be in her late fifties and didn't care who knew it was waiting inside the doorway. She held a folder in one hand and peered up at me over the top of a pair of rectangular reading glasses when I entered.

"Mr. Southerland? I'm Mrs. Lumpoc, the school's director. Very good of you to come." She held out a limp hand and I gave it a light squeeze with my fingers.

"My pleasure. Is the boy ready to see me?"

"Yes, we've informed Troy that he will be having a visitor. Before I take you to him, though, I'd like to have a little chat with you in my office. Would you please follow me?"

Mrs. Lumpoc took me past the front desk and down a short hallway. So far, I had seen no children. "Where are all the kids?" I asked.

"They are not permitted in this part of the building." The school's director stopped in front of a door and pulled out a set of keys. "Here's my office. Please come in and take a seat."

I followed Mrs. Lumpoc through the door and immediately felt a lump grow in my throat as locked-away memories of visits to the principal's office flooded my brain. I fought through a wave of vertigo and managed to sit down on a plastic couch without staggering. I tried to remind myself that I was a thirty-year-old professional investigator, but I couldn't shake the sensation that I had traveled through time and climbed back into my twelve-year-old body to explain why I had been caught on the roof of the schoolhouse lobbing rocks at the cars in the faculty parking lot.

Mrs. Lumpoc took a seat on the other side of a small coffee table, opened the folder in her lap, and leaned in at me to make sure I was listening. "You need to be aware of a few things before I bring you in to see Troy. First, he's a very intelligent boy. But he has a motor skills disorder that makes it extremely difficult for him to speak."

I interrupted. "I heard something about that from the police. One of them suggested that he might have something called apraxia?"

The school director nodded. "Very good. Yes. Troy suffers from a condition called apraxia of speech. What that means is that he knows what he wants to say, but he has a great deal of difficulty shaping his mouth in such a manner as to form the sounds he wants to make. It's very frustrating for him, and, as a result, he is reluctant to speak at all."

I nodded. "I understand."

"You may think you do, but it is a very complicated problem. People who try to hold conversations with children with apraxia of speech usually become very impatient, even to the point of becoming angry. And then the child recoils from the anger and becomes unwilling to associate with other people. In addition, other children are prone to make fun of children with speech disorders, and they don't want to make friends with them. It can lead to a very lonely life for the child who is afflicted."

I shifted in my seat, trying to get comfortable. "I can see how that would happen. Kids can be cruel."

"And adults, too. Both children and adults make the mistake of believing that children who cannot speak properly are unintelligent, and they treat them as if they are. I don't want you to make that mistake with Troy, Mr. Southerland."

I nodded. "I gotcha."

"Hmm." Mrs. Lumpoc looked doubtful. "Along with his speech disorder, I believe that Troy is dyslexic."

"What's that?"

"Dyslexia is a separate neurological disorder that affects the way a person connects sounds and letters. It makes it difficult for the person to read and spell, or sometimes even to form letters. A person with dyslexia will often transpose letters, or even write the letters or numerals backwards, so that some characters will appear as they would if you were holding them up to a mirror. A person with dyslexia may possess above-average intelligence, but appear to be illiterate."

I let out a long breath to slow my heartbeat and tried to keep the excitement out of my voice. "Okay. Is there anything else I should know?"

"Yes." Mrs. Lumpoc pushed the reading glasses up on her nose and glanced down at a sheet of paper in her folder. She looked up again after a moment and repositioned the glasses so that she could peer over them at me. "Troy believes that he is a spiritual being known as Thunderbird."

I smiled. "Then I've come to the right place."

***

In the lobby of the students' dormitory, Mrs. Lumpoc tried once again to convince me that Troy's insistence that he was Thunderbird was a mere mechanism he used to defend himself against the consequences of his affliction, and that I should under no circumstances encourage him in his belief.

"Remember that Troy is ten years old, as far as we can determine, which is young for a troll. And because of his condition, although intelligent, Troy is emotionally immature. I don't think that he truly believes the story he insists on telling. I don't think he's delusional. I truly believe that he tells the story in order to make himself special in a way that doesn't involve his speech disorder. It's akin to inventing an imaginary friend in order to stave off loneliness and to boost one's confidence in oneself. But we mustn't reinforce his pretended belief. To do so would only retard his emotional development. Do you understand?"

"Sure, Mrs. Lumpoc," I assured the director. "I understand. Don't worry about a thing."

The director led me down a hallway past a row of doors. Some were open, and I saw a number of boys in the dormitory rooms sleeping, reading, quietly playing games, and chatting in low voices. In every case, the boys ceased talking altogether as the director and I walked by their open doorways. The boys I saw all appeared to be about ten years old, and it was obvious that the wings of the dormitory were segregated not only by gender, but by age. It was also obvious that the children's home was overcrowded and administered with an iron fist.

As we approached one room, the door opened a crack to reveal a smiling boy with angry-looking burns on either side of his forehead. After we'd passed by, I looked back at the boy, whose smile turned into a scowl. His lips mouthed the words, "Fuck you, Mrs. Lumpoc," and he reinforced the words by pushing an arm out the doorway and extending his middle finger. Then he pulled himself back into his room and quietly shut the door.

I followed the director to a closed door at the end of the hallway, and Mrs. Lumpoc gave it two quick raps. "Your visitor has arrived, Troy." She opened the door herself, and I followed her in.

The room was larger than the others I'd seen, more troll-sized, and the boy sitting on the edge of his bed looking up from the book he'd been reading was decidedly larger than the other boys in his wing. I figured that while I might have a couple of inches on the lad, he outweighed me by a good fifty pounds. Like all trolls, his hairless head was dominated by a pair of large pointed ears and glowing red eyes that burned like warning lights. His putty-like gray skin would become less smooth as he aged, and his pointed canine teeth would become more pronounced. He held his book with the normal (for a troll) four long knobby fingers on each hand.

As soon as he saw me, the boy put the book down on his bed and started to speak. Every sound was the result of concentrated effort, much jerking of the head and blinking of the eyes, and forced exhalations. He had to try several of the sounds more than once, and he didn't always succeed in making the sound he wanted to make. I could see where it might be maddening to listen to, but I couldn't help but admire the determined boy's battle to accomplish what others did without thought.

I tried not to move as the boy asked me, "Ahh-er...... ew... ewya... ewwwy... eeyyyooo...... ull... ull... ullla....... ooolll-ka-ka... ffff-ohhh... eee-mmm... eemmm... eem?" He turned his shining red eyes on me when he was finished, a broad open-mouthed smile on his face. A drop of perspiration rolled down the side of his cheek.

I smiled back at the boy. "Yes, Thunderbird. I am looking for you."

I was still smiling when the boy rose from his bed, walked toward me, wrapped his arms around my waist, and buried his face into my neck.

Chapter Seventeen

"You can't just walk out of here with him!" Mrs. Lumpoc stood in the open doorway, determined to prevent me from leaving with the boy.

"Why not? He's not a prisoner. You don't have the right to hold him here."

"That's where you're wrong. Troy was brought here by the police, and, as a licensed children's home, we are authorized by the Province of Caychan to assume the role of legal guardian to all children who have been admitted into our institution."

"That right? Maybe we should let a judge decide."

"I assure you that the law is one-hundred percent on my side in this matter. No court is going to allow some... some..." The director struggled to find the right word before settling on, "Some *man*—who isn't even a relative—to come waltzing in here and walk out with a child. It's kidnapping!"

I had to admit that she was right. I unclenched my jaw and opted for a different approach. "All right. I see your point. What's the procedure? What do I need to do to get custody of this boy? I've been looking for him, and he's been sending messages to me in his own way."

Mrs. Lumpoc frowned. "Messages? I'm not aware of any messages. The children here are not permitted to have phones, and he's written no letters."

I turned and raised my eyebrows at Troy, who nodded at me in return. Turning back to Mrs. Lumpoc, I said, "It would be easier if I showed you. Let me borrow your pen. Do you have something I can write on?"

With some reluctance, Mrs. Lumpoc handed me a pen and a page from Troy's file. I sat back down on the couch and placed the blank side of the sheet of paper on the coffee table. I held the pen to the paper and looked up at Troy. "Okay, kid. Do your stuff."

Troy nodded at me and closed his eyes. I kept my eyes on the boy as my hand began moving of its own accord, sliding the pen across the sheet of paper. After a few moments, Troy opened his eyes, and I dropped the pen. Beads of sweat were running down the kid's forehead, and a sharp pain was threatening to split my temples, but Troy had a pleased grin on his face. We all looked down to see the shaky characters that had been scrawled on the page. Some words were misspelled, some of the characters were reversed, and some pairs of characters were transposed. The letters varied in size, and they started in the center of the page, moved to the edge, and then curved to run down toward the bottom of the sheet. But the message was clear enough: plese mss lompuc lte me og wiht him.

I looked up at the director to catch her reaction, but didn't get the one I wanted.

"Hmph. That's a cute parlor trick, Mr. Southerland, but the fact remains that this institution has the responsibility for protecting this child. You are clearly not a relative. You have no legal documentation and no legal authority to take Troy into your custody."

"How about we ask the boy what *he* wants. Would that satisfy you?"

Troy looked at Mrs. Lumpoc with hope in his glowing eyes, but she remained adamant. "Troy is ten years old, Mr. Southerland. He is not of a legal age to make the decision."

I felt my jaw starting to clench again. "Are you saying that the boy has no say in whether he can come or go from this place?"

"That's exactly what I'm saying. We don't leave decisions like that to children. It's for their own safety."

I turned to Troy. "Hey, kid. You feel safe leaving here with me?"

Troy nodded his head.

I turned back to the director. "Satisfied?"

Mrs. Lumpoc crossed her arms in front of her chest and stretched to her full height. "No, Mr. Southerland. I am most certainly *not* satisfied. And now I'm afraid that I'm going to have to ask you to leave. Shall I call security and have you escorted to the front gate?"

I was about to respond with a well thought out and well-reasoned argument that would certainly have settled the issue on my behalf when I became aware of a commotion in the hallway behind Mrs. Lumpoc. The kid I'd seen earlier with the burn marks on his temples was running toward us at full speed.

"Mrs. Lumpoc! Mrs. Lumpoc! There are birds in the hall!"

Mrs. Lumpoc turned. "What? Augie, what are you doing out of your room? You need to be getting ready for class."

Other boys were running up behind the first one, who was pointing back down the hallway. "Birds! Big ones!"

I heard yelps and screams from the other boys, and then a bird the size of a cannonball shot through the doorway just over Mrs. Lumpoc's head. It pulled up in front of me, spreading its wings to slow its momentum, and extended a set of deadly-looking curved talons at my face. I ducked beneath the attack just in time to see another of the birds—owls, I realized—sink its talons into Mrs. Lumpoc's back.

The director let out a piercing scream and fell hard to the floor. The owl released her, and she struggled to reach back and stanch the flow of blood that was already seeping through her blouse. Startled yelps and screams from a dozen ten-year-old boys echoed through the hallway.

Meanwhile the first owl had launched itself at me for a second attack. With no better options, I picked up the coffee table by one leg with my only good arm and attempted to use it as a shield. The effort sent waves of stabbing pain up my arm, and I thought that the veins in my temples would burst from the strain. The owl bounced off my makeshift shield with such force that the table wrenched itself from my nerveless fingers and crashed to the floor, banging into my shins. I felt knifelike talons slash at the back of my coat as I stumbled and fell. Rolling onto my back, I looked up to see both of the owls descending on me, talons outstretched. I raised my right arm to protect my face and closed my eyes.

A deafening crash overwhelmed my senses. I froze for a moment waiting for the slash of talons. Nothing happened, and, sensing no movement in the room, I opened my eyes and looked around me. Across the room from me, Mrs. Lumpoc was letting out the choked battleground whimpers of someone wounded and in shock. The odor of ozone and burned flesh reached my nostrils, and turning my head to find the source of the scent I saw the limp forms of two dead owls, feathers blackened by wide scorch marks across their backs. A faint keening sound reached me from another side of the room, and I saw Troy, mouth open wide in surprise, staring at his two outstretched hands and choking back a scream. Little black clouds rose from his knobby, cable-like fingers.

A child's voice from the hallway shouted, "Holy shit! Was that lightning?"

Another voice: "Troy shot the birds with lightning!"

I scrambled to my feet. I caught the attention of the boy with the burn marks on his temples. "Go get help for Mrs. Lumpoc. She's hurt bad. Can you do that?"

The boy nodded and, with a last lingering gaze at Troy, turned to run down the hall. I could already hear adult footsteps moving in our direction, so I figured that the director would be tended to soon enough. I reached over to the troll child and touched his arm to get his attention. "Let's go."

I started for the door, and Troy followed. We ran down the hallway, past the kids and a group of concerned-looking men and women, and on into the lobby, where several adults and kids were walking or running in all directions. A shot from a handgun sounded from outside the building. I held up a hand to stop Troy and went to the door to see what was happening.

Six owls were circling over the lawn area in front of the dormitory, harassing two men with guns. I recognized one of the men as the security guard at the front door who had patted me down and another as the sentry at the front gate. As I watched, one of the owls stopped circling and launched itself at the guard, who fired his roscoe in the direction of the owl, but missed. The owl's legs extended and it plunged its talons into the guard's face. The guard roared in agony as the owl's talons crushed his head like a tin can. Blood shot in all directions from the guard's face, and the gun slipped from his hand as he went limp in the owl's clutches. The owl released its grip, and the guard dropped to the ground.

The other owls were drawing closer and closer to the gate sentry, who was waving a rifle around trying desperately to draw a bead on one of them.

I needed Badass, and the reminder that my trustworthy bodyguard was unavailable to me caused a hollow pit to form in my gut. I opened my mind to the world of elementals and spotted a Badass-sized swirling blob of air in the clouds above me. Hoping for the best, I sent out a summons, but the air spirit tossed it back in my face and drifted away. I'd bitten off more than I could chew and had nothing to show for it but a splitting headache.

Lowering my sights, I searched for smaller spirits that might be able to deal with the owls. I quickly found three fiercely twisting funnels, each about the size of the owls, and they answered my summons without resistance. I sent them after the birds, and they shot into the sky like eager soldiers.

It was none too soon. The rifleman had fired off a couple of rounds, but he wasn't bothering the owls much, and three of them were closing in for the kill. The elementals each picked a bird and attacked. I expected the air spirits to swat the owls out of the playing field, but, to my surprise, the owls evaded the attacks with subtle flicks of their wings and continued to circle the rifleman with deadly intent. My heart sank as I realized that the bursts of wind generated by the swirling elementals were little more than mild inconveniences to these predatory hunters. If the circumstances had been different, I might have enjoyed watching the graceful maneuvers of these awe-inspiring birds for hours on end. But now was neither the time nor the place.

With no better plan, I ran out the door, my eyes locked on the pistol that had fallen from the first guard's hand. I was dimly aware that Troy had followed me out to the lawn, but I didn't have the time to think about him at the moment. Things were happening fast. I scooped the gat up with my good hand, crouched to one knee, and searched for a target. Just then, the owl nearest me raised its head to avoid an attacking elemental. For a brief second, the owl's chest was exposed, and I pulled the trigger. Feathers flew as the owl tumbled backward from the direct hit and then dropped out of the sky. I would never be able to explain how I had pulled that shot off: it had been pure dumb fucking luck. The other owls, perceiving me to be a threat, pulled back several yards and began to glide rapidly around the lawn area, darting back and forth, up and down as they circled, making it difficult to get a good shot at them. The rifleman fired off two more rounds to no effect and stopped to reload.

I heard Troy's agitated voice behind me: "Ahhh... lll... ohhh!"

"Get down!" I yelled back at him. "Stay low!" Hell, it *seemed* like the right thing to say.

One of the owls veered sharply away from an elemental and glided straight for the gate sentry, who had finished reloading. I tried to hold the gat steady, wishing that I could use my other hand to help brace it. As the owl swooped in to attack the sentry, we both fired at it, he with the rifle and me with the handgun. Neither of us so much as ruffled its feathers, and the owl plowed into the rifleman with a thud. The sentry managed to let out a short scream before the owl twisted and snapped the poor sap's neck. I fired off another round at the owl just as it released the sentry's limp body, but the bird veered away and flew off unharmed.

Five owls now circled me, wings outstretched and slicing through the air with a grace that I still couldn't help but admire even as they prepared to slice me up and have me for lunch. I reached up to wipe sweat from my eyes, and it came to me that with my eyes closed I couldn't sense the presence of the owls with my awareness. They were utterly silent as they flew and caused no perceivable disturbance to the air. I couldn't even pick up a scent from the birds. It was no wonder that the efforts of the elementals had been futile against them. These owls cut through wind like hot knives through butter.

Interesting as that bit of information might have been to me, I didn't have time to ponder its implications. As far as I could tell, it was knowledge that I'd be taking along to whatever last stop awaited me when I reached the end of the streetcar line. And the end seemed all too near. The gale-force winds that Badass generated might be able to give them trouble, but no point thinking about that now. Out of options, and with no time to strategize, I aimed the gat and prepared to take out at least one of the birds before my own time ran out.

I sensed Troy behind me and off to my right, and I took a moment to sneak a glance in his direction. I saw him raise both arms and extend his fingers, and then my head jerked back involuntarily as bolts of lightning shot from each of his hands. The thunderous report rang through my head, and I raised my gun hand to shield at least one of my ears from the blast. I at least managed not to squeeze the trigger and put a bullet in my own fool head.

Two of the owls, burned to a crisp, tumbled through the air for several yards before plunging to the earth. The other three birds withdrew with all deliberate speed. I turned to Troy with what must have been a look of bewilderment. The boy had tears in his eyes, and black smoke rose from his shaking fingers. He opened his mouth and a shrill scream poured forth from his throat before he fell to his knees.

I became aware of a new sound, the sound of rapidly approaching footsteps. I looked out across the lawn and saw four more men on the way, handguns drawn and ready.

With no warning, and no memory of how it had happened, I found myself sprawled on the grass. I spotted my hat on the ground next to me and became aware of a dull ache on the back of my head. I looked up to see an owl circling above me. I'd never sensed its attack, but it had somehow decked me from behind. I wondered why I was still alive. My gat was still in my hand, and I raised it in the direction of the owl, but it neatly deflected an attack by an elemental and glided away too fast for me to get a clear shot at it.

A piercing sob took my attention away from the owls. Regaining my feet, I tucked my gat in my belt and walked over to Troy. I put a hand on his shoulders, because I'd heard that was a good way to comfort children. "It's okay, kid," I told him, trying not to sound gruff. "You've done gangbusters. Go ahead and sit the rest of this one out. There's only three left, and we've got help on the way."

Our reinforcements reached the lawn and immediately began firing wildly at the circling owls, who increased their speed until they were nothing but brown blurs streaking through the air. I shook my head. These stooges might have impressed the residents of the children's home with their weapons, but it was obvious they had spent little time firing them in anger at moving targets. I drew my gat, crouched down, braced my elbow on my knee, and tried to focus on the movements of the flying birds.

I thought I had one zeroed in, but before I could squeeze off a shot an oval of darkness, like a hole in the sky, opened above the circling birds. Just a dot at first, it expanded in a hurry, growing larger and larger. The spirit I'd seen Clearwater transform into at the old Placid Point Pier, wings extended a dozen feet on either side, glided out of the darkness until he was hovering just over our heads.

Night Owl, I muttered under my breath. I remembered what Ralph had told me, that Night Owl was a heavy-hitter, and that not even Cougar could protect me against him. Terrific.

The gunmen emptied their weapons into the giant owl spirit, who waited patiently for them to finish firing. When the gunmen had nothing left to do but look at each other with puzzled expressions, Night Owl slashed at one of them with a wing, slicing through his neck and leaving his head dangling from his shoulders. He repeated his maneuver with the other wing, leaving another gunman crumpled in the grass. He reached out with both talons and crushed the skulls of the two remaining armed men. It had taken the owl spirit less than two seconds to dispatch all four of the new arrivals. The green lawn beneath Night Owl was now blotched with pools of scarlet. I fought against a sudden urge to retch and swallowed back a mouthful of stomach acid.

Night Owl pivoted in the sky until he was facing me, wings outstretched, more levitating than hovering. Reaching out with my mind, I directed the three elementals to strike at this new target, hoping to catch him by surprise. As the elementals streaked toward him, Night Owl met them with a casual flip of his wing that dispersed them into the sky. As they disappeared, I felt my contact with the elementals blip away as if someone had switched off a radio.

I raised my hand gun despite knowing it was useless, because I had nothing else.

Instead of attacking, Night Owl spoke in a voice distorted by his bird form, but still distinctly Clearwater's. "Thank you for leading me to this special boy. Thunderbird escaped me a few weeks ago, and I've been looking for his new incarnation ever since. I owe you for finding him for me, so I'm going to let you live a while longer. Well, to be honest, I have to. I still need that memory drive from you, which is why my owls have left you alive. But one thing at a time." The giant owl, still levitating, turned to face Troy. "Come along, my boy. Don't worry. You'll be fine."

Troy stood and tried to answer back, "Nnnn! Nnnn!" He raised his hands and pointed them at the owl spirit, but his eight fingers were blackened, blistered, and powerless.

Night Owl's head cocked and one eye blinked. "None of that, now." The giant owl fell suddenly toward the boy, talons extended. I tried to leap into his path, but he swept me aside with a wing, and I went rolling across the lawn, pain shooting through my arms and shoulders like the points of swords. Helpless to do anything but glare, I watched Night Owl pluck the young troll off the lawn and pull him back toward the black hole in the sky.

The owl spirit shot me one last glance. "I'll be back for the memory drive, Mr. Southerland." His head swiveled on his neck as he turned his attention to the circling owls. "Don't kill him, but feel free to remind him how foolish he's been for denying me what I require." The head swiveled back in my direction. "No one says 'no' to me with impunity, Mr. Southerland. Next time I see you, be prepared to hand over the drive. Ta ta for now." With the struggling Troy in his clutches, Night Owl soared into the darkness.

As the black oval began to close behind the owl spirit, I suddenly felt a familiar presence. In desperation, I sent out a summons, hoping that I wasn't too late. I felt the presence drawing nearer and nearer....

The oval of darkness closed. Defeated, I let my chin drop to my chest. Then I realized I could still feel the presence. I looked up. Bursting its way through the last opening of the black oval was an explosive blast of air. The wind gust twisted itself into a raging whirlwind, which descended in my direction. I felt a smile forming on my face.

"Hello, Badass."

"Greetings, Alex. This one is ready to serve."

I pointed at the three owls streaking toward me through the air. "Get them!"

I allowed myself to sink to the ground, exhausted, surrounded by six dead men who hadn't known what I was bringing their way, and listened to the howling of wind, the shrieking of birds, and the terrified screaming of children.

***

By that afternoon, news of the massacre at the New Horizons Children's Home was all over the media. According to a statement by the YCPD, a heavily armed disgruntled former employee had shot and killed six security guards at the children's home and injured the school's director, Alma Lumpoc, before taking his own life. Mrs. Lumpoc was in critical condition, but was expected to survive. Fortunately, no children had been hurt in the attack.

Wild rumors involving an attack by a flock of owls, or, more correctly, a parliament of owls, were dismissed as the foolish imaginings of frightened children. A wilder rumor, absent from official news reports but gaining traction on the internet, claimed that an unearthly spirit of some sort had been involved in the massacre. By evening, this unsubstantiated but compelling rumor was already the subject of much debate.

I wasn't mentioned in any of the news reports, and, to my knowledge, I wasn't being sought by the authorities. I'd departed the scene before the cops arrived, and I hoped that my presence at the children's facility would remain unreported and unnoticed. Just in case, though, I called Lubank when I got home and told him the whole story. His reaction was about what I expected.

"Lord Alkwat's flaming pecker! You're a fuckin' menace to society, you know that? When the cops find you, I'm going to fuckin' let them put you away for good! It's the only way the rest of us will be safe! Gracie's going to be fuckin' hysterical when she hears about this."

"I'm on the extension, Robby sweetie," Gracie cut in. "Are you okay, Alex? Honey, you really need to be more subtle. I thought you private dicks were supposed to be invisible! You know, you sneak up in the dead of night, you slip in, you slide out, you leave a calling card in case someone needs your services again.... Oh my, that didn't sound at all suggestive, did it! Whew! I think I need a cold drink."

"Gracie, didn't I give you a brief to go over or something? Get off the phone and let me talk to your boyfriend!"

"All right, honey. You boys play nice." We heard the clicking sounds of a landline phone disconnecting.

"How bad is it, peeper?" asked Lubank.

"I think I'm in the clear. I just wanted to give you a heads up in case the heat blows my way."

"Yeah? Well I hope it does! They're already calling this the Children's Home Massacre. It's the biggest story of the year—bigger than the death of the mayor last month!—and you could be my ticket in. If the cops decide you're a person of interest, the billable hours will be off the charts! If they actually accuse you of being involved, I'll be on the fuckin' news for weeks. They'll give me my own fuckin' TV show when it's over!"

"How nice for you. Any advice for me?"

"Advice from counsel costs money, peeper."

"Fuck you. You're already billing me for the call."

"True. You want advice? Turn yourself in. I'll make a fortune!"

"If I turn myself in, I'm gonna hire a different mouthpiece."

"Try it and I'll make sure they throw the book at you. I've got the goods on every judge in this town. You'll never see the light of day again!"

"Come on, Lubank. You're still my lawyer—for now. Help me out here. What do you think I should do?"

"Seriously? Find out what's on that flash drive. Information is power. Once you know what this RAA shit is, we'll have something to bargain with. Right now, they know, and you don't. That's a bad position to be in."

After we'd disconnected, I thought about Lubank's advice, and decided that he was right. Until I knew the secret of this RAA, I was thrashing about in the dark.

Clearwater, or Night Owl, certainly knew about RAA. He needed the information on the flash drive in order to save someone's life. If he wasn't lying, whoever he wanted to help had to be important to him. He certainly had no qualms about killing anyone who got in his way. Was it his own life he was trying to save? I filed that thought away for the moment.

And how did the boy—not just a boy, but the incarnation of Thunderbird—how did *he* fit into the picture? Maybe I'd be able to answer that question if I knew what RAA was all about.

And then there was Deet. I had little doubt that the monstrous shapeshifting were-mantis was still alive. It would take more than a poke in the eye to kill that creature. Deet seemed more interested in restricting knowledge of RAA and delivering the flash drive to Leaflock than in using it for any personal or professional purpose. I wondered.... Leaflock didn't know much about RAA beyond its general function. He didn't know the formula, or how to make it. Did Deet? I wasn't sure. Deet was LIA, which meant that the agency was working with Leaflock. Had the LIA contracted Leaflock Services to build something for them, or maybe for the Dragon Lord? Deet seemed to be the liaison between Leaflock and the LIA. If that was the case, then what was Leea planning to do with Leaflock's cell regeneration device once it was produced?

My thoughts were threatening to spin out of control. I stopped speculating and tried to focus. What was my priority? That was easy: getting the boy back from Clearwater. How was I going to do it? I didn't know yet, but I was convinced that learning more about whatever was on that flash drive was the first step to accomplishing my goal. I hoped it would give me the leverage I needed to use against Clearwater.

I picked up my phone and called Crawford.

Chapter Eighteen

I spotted Crawford sitting in front of an open laptop computer in a back-corner booth moments after walking into the Boatyard Bar and Grill. He saw me, too, and gave me a relaxed wave.

I slid into my seat and watched Crawford do a double take as I took off my coat.

"What the hell happened to you?"

"Oh, this? A giant bug tried to pull my arm out of its socket. It's nothing."

The slight little man shook his head. "You ever think about getting into another line of work?"

"It's crossed my mind. But then I'd lose my retirement plan."

"First, you don't have a retirement plan. Second, you aren't going to live long enough to need one." He sighed and gestured toward the full glass of beer on the table. "I took the liberty of ordering for you."

I noticed that his own glass was less than half full. "Got started without me, I see."

"I wanted to drink it while it was still cold. What kept you?" Crawford picked up his glass and drained most of the remaining brew in three gulps.

I took a healthy sip of my own, closed my eyes, and meditated on the sensation of sparkling cold velvety effervescence sliding down my throat. "Say, this hits the spot," I told Crawford, meaning it. "Next round's on me."

"This one's on you, too. Business has been a little slow lately. I'll make up for it next time out." Crawford signaled a waitress to bring him another glass of the same.

I set my glass down in front of me and glanced around the room. "I had to shake off a tail. A couple of owls watched me leave my office. I called on Badass to deal with them, and then I summoned Smokey to make sure that they didn't have any friends."

Crawford smiled. "How is Smokey? Is he around?"

"Smokey is happy to serve. It's patrolling the area for owls and will let me know if it sees any. Actually, I'm not sure if Smokey has ever seen an owl before, and I was having some trouble describing one. So it's on the lookout for *any* large bird. I hope no innocent hawks happen to be flying by."

"Cool." Crawford shuddered. "I *hate* big birds! By the way, you told me to watch for owls, but you didn't tell me why. Very mysterious. I'm intrigued."

I took another sip of brew and considered the twitchy little man sitting across the table from me. He didn't look any smaller than he had the last time I'd seen him, still around five feet tall, give or take an inch or two, and built like a featherweight, which meant that he most likely hadn't lost any more rats. Crawford could shapeshift into a swarm, or, as Crawford liked to tell me, a *mischief* of a little more than a hundred smaller-than-average rats. He could survive the death of a few rats, but he shrunk a bit in stature with each one. If he was ever reduced to fewer than a hundred rats, he would lose the ability to re-form into a human, and the remaining rats, having lost their psychic connection to each other, would wander off to live their own individual rodent lives. Crawford had lost a few rats over the years, but as far as I knew he still had maybe a dozen to go before he lost his collective consciousness for good.

"I'll tell you about it in a second. But how about you?" I asked. "Anyone try to follow you? Owls or otherwise?"

Crawford shook his head. "Clear sailing. I took a few precautions."

"That's good. You got the dingus?"

A sudden tic in the little man's upper lip caused his nose to twitch. "I've got it. But I want to know what all this is about. Why all the precautions? And how did you get so banged up? I mean, a giant bug? There's a story there, and I want to hear it."

I sighed. "You're right. I'm sorry. I've gotten myself into a tricky situation, and it's blowing up all around me. And I've dragged you right into the middle of it."

I launched into the story of Redhorn and the flash drive, Walks in Cloud and meeting Cougar, Deet and the insect thing that was also Deet, and Clearwater, who was actually Night Owl. Forty-five minutes and three beers later, I finished up by telling Crawford about Troy, who was actually Thunderbird, and how my actions had led to the violence at the New Horizon's Children's Home earlier that day.

Crawford seemed more amused than horrified by my story. He shook his head. "When I heard about the Children's Home Massacre on the news, my first thought was that you had been involved somehow. What does that say about you, Alex?"

"Come on. Not everything that happens in this city is my fault." I finished off my third beer and set the empty mug on the table.

Crawford chuckled in that distinctly rodent-like manner of his that reminded me of his special gift. "You've had quite a week. At least now I know what I've gotten myself into."

I started to apologize again, but he waved it off. "Don't worry about it. I'm happy to help. You can't believe how dull things have been lately. What say we get that item everyone wants and see what's on it."

Crawford gave the room a surreptitious scan. Then he reached under the table near the wall and came up with the green flash drive with the Leaflock Services logo. He smiled as he held it out for me to see. "You'd never know a nice place like this had a rat problem, would you."

I resisted an involuntary urge to lift my feet away from the floor.

Crawford gave another brief chittering chuckle and plugged the drive into the laptop. After a moment, he spun the device around until the screen was facing me. "All yours. Try not to fry it. The laptop is a spare, and there's nothing important on it, but, you know."

"I'll do my best, but can we switch sides? I'd rather have my back to the wall. I don't want anyone to sneak a peek at the screen."

We made the switch, and I leaned as far back into the corner of the booth as I could. A sweet young waitress with blond hair that came out of a bottle of bleach stopped by and we ordered another round of beers. After she left, I gave the room a good look. The place was crowded with boisterous patrons yelling at the television screens that lined the walls of the joint broadcasting a number of different sporting events, and Crawford and I were all but invisible in the midst of the hubbub of glaring screens and earsplitting noise. I summoned Smokey, and, after the elemental informed me that it hadn't spotted any big birds, I sent it back out for more sentry duty.

In short order, the young bleached-blond waitress came by with our beers. The smile she gave Crawford lit up the room, and Crawford's lips stretched into a grin as he watched her walk away.

I glanced at the departing waitress and turned back to Crawford. "Is that your daughter?" I asked.

Crawford winked at me. "Jealous?"

"I like them old enough to qualify for a driver's license."

"She's just baby-faced. You've got to be at least eighteen to serve alcohol in this town."

"That still makes her less than half your age."

"I won't tell her if you won't."

"Sure, but don't be disappointed when you find out that she flirts with *all* of her customers. Big smiles attract big tips."

Crawford's eyes danced. "I didn't notice her smiling at *you*, you big lug."

"That's because I have a face that scares little children."

Crawford nodded. "True."

I sneered at him and turned my attention to the laptop.

A sign-in box appeared on the screen, and, pecking at the keyboard with one finger on my good hand, I typed in the passcode I'd created in Walks in Cloud's shop: 5-p-e-a-k-s-W-!-t-h-W-!-n-6. I held my breath and stabbed at the enter key.

I released the breath when, instead of an error message, a photograph of a page of handwritten notes appeared. I stared at the notes and frowned. "Hey, Crawford. You know anything about mathematical equations and scientific notation?"

Crawford nodded. "A little."

"More than me, I'll bet. I took a little alchemy in high school, but I can't say that I was exactly an honor student. Come around here and take a look at this."

When Crawford was seated next to me, he peered at the screen. I saw his lips move as he studied the notations. "It's definitely some kind of alchemical formula, but it's nothing like anything I've ever seen." He shook his head. "I can tell that it's a formula for something with a lot of juice. I mean, some of these values are huge, but otherwise this is way beyond my skillset. I can't make heads nor tails out of it. Sorry."

I pointed at a symbol on the screen. "That's a symbol for mercury, isn't it? And that's silver, but I don't have a clue what that one is."

"I know the alchemical symbol for almost every chemical on the periodic table. All the minerals, anyway, and most of the gases. Basic stuff every jeweler needs to know." He shook his head. "But that symbol isn't on the chart. It must mean something else. Maybe it's an obscure mathematical sign of some kind. My education only goes so far. This might be an advanced calculus I never got to."

"I don't think so. It looks familiar to me, but I can't place it." I studied the screen. "I think it has something to do with magic. Maybe it's a symbol for a ritual, or an incantation. Or maybe a spirit."

"I think you're right." Crawford leaned back in his seat. "Can't help you there, pal. You need a witch. Sorry."

I felt a laugh make its way to my lips. "Funny. People were afraid that I was going to see this formula and reveal its secret. Well, I've seen it, and I couldn't begin to explain it to anyone."

Crawford gestured at the screen with his chin. "Is there anything else there?"

I extended a finger at the touch screen. "Let's find out."

I scrolled through several pages of photographed sheets of paper covered with the handwritten formula. I wondered if the pages still existed, but, recalling the cleaned-out shredder receptacle in Redhorn's bedroom, decided it was unlikely.

"How long *is* that thing?" Crawford muttered.

I was about to give him some sort of witty response, or maybe just grunt, but then something different appeared on the screen: a typed note. Crawford peered in with interest, and I decided there wasn't any good reason why I shouldn't let him read the note along with me.

> Dear "Nocturnal" or should I say Mr. Clearwater (As you can see, I've deduced your true identity),
>
> If you are reading this, then I have your money and we're square. Too late for either of us to back out now.
>
> I have downloaded the complete formula for Reifying Agent Alpha to this drive. If you don't already have a highly proficient witch at your disposal you'll need one to work with your alchemical engineers in order to decipher some of the components of this formula. The blueprint for the energy extraction device shows where the reifying agent fits into the device and how to activate it for inputting energy from the source—if you can find one! With a little experimentation, any competent genetic engineer will be able to figure out how to use the activated reifying device to regenerate biological cells. If you don't have a genetic engineer

available to you, you'll have to find one. You are paying for the formula and quite frankly getting it for less than it is worth. Finding the people to make it work is your job. I can't be expected to do everything for you.

Your engineers will tell you that this device is completely impractical. They are right. The amount of energy needed to power it is astronomical, especially for what you need it for. Yes, I've figured out what you're hoping to do, although I can scarcely believe it. I will, of course, remain silent about the matter. No one would believe me anyway. The energy extractor Leaflock designed will fulfill your purpose, but I have no idea what you'll be able to connect it to. A volcano? A nuclear reactor? The sun? I've got your money, so it's your problem now.

I've destroyed all other copies of this formula, which only I know. This is the only printed copy of the formula for RAA in existence. Not even Leaflock has a copy. I don't think he has the slightest inkling about what the LIA wanted from him when they contracted his company to build a powerful cell regeneration device. He believes that he is revolutionizing the medical industry and that hospitals wings will be named for him. Poor deluded sap! It has become difficult for him to see anything beyond his own dream to invent something big enough to immortalize the Leaflock name. Well, I'm the one who wound up inventing the device's key active agent, and I am content to let the Redhorn name remain anonymous. Anyway, you've got the RAA formula now. Good luck with it. If you are unable to successfully accomplish your goal, the consequences could be catastrophic. No matter what happens, don't come looking for me! I'm not taking any chances: I'm going to take your money and disappear.

You've got what you wanted from me. What happens next is on your head, not mine.

Inyon Redhorn

Crawford was staring at me openmouthed when I'd finished reading the note. "Lord's balls, Alex—this sounds huge!"

I let out a low whistle. "Sure does." I re-read the beginning of Redhorn's note. "So RAA is Reifying Agent Alpha.... What the hell is a reifying agent? Clearwater asked me if I knew about reification, but I can't remember exactly what he said. The reality of abstractions, or something like that. It was way over my head."

"I can help you there." Crawford cleared his throat and gulped down some beer. He wiped his mouth with the back of his sleeve and launched into the beginning of a lecture. "To reify means to transform something that's abstract, an idea for example, and turn it into something real."

I mulled that over. "An idea. Like having another beer?"

Crawford waved a finger at me. "Nothing like that. More like...." He thought for a second. "Take an idea like justice. To most people, justice is nothing but a vague idea. But a reifying agent would turn it into something concrete."

"Make justice real."

"Make justice a real tangible thing," Crawford clarified.

I was still trying to puzzle it out. "How does it do that? Does it turn the idea into a hangman's noose?"

Crawford frowned. "Something like that. It takes something intangible, and converts it into something tangible."

I considered this. "Like energy to matter?"

Crawford's eyes widened. "Yes, like that!"

I knew when I was out of my depth, and I felt my head start to spin. Seeking something closer to my intellectual range, I reached for my glass of suds. What I really wanted was enough whiskey to dull the throbbing ache in both of my arms, but I wanted to keep my head clear. Well, relatively clear, I thought to myself as I gulped down another swallow of the cold beer. Turning to Crawford, I asked, "How do you know all this, anyway?"

Crawford smiled and reached for his own glass. "The jewelry business is all about reification. We take an idea, like love, and turn it into something tangible—like a ring! Look. That diamond ring you buy for your honey? There isn't anything intrinsically valuable about it. Diamonds aren't rare—the earth is filled with them! But the big diamond cartels get together and work with the governments of all seven realms to hold back the supply of diamonds in order to artificially inflate the value. The cartels sell the diamonds to the wholesalers at the agreed-upon inflated price and kick a portion of the profits up to the governments. The wholesalers mark the price up still further and sell the raw stones to the manufacturers, who cut the diamonds and place them in mountings."

I interrupted. "But the mountings are made of gold or silver, right? Even if the diamonds aren't worth all that much, the gold and silver have their own value, don't they?"

"Sure," Crawford agreed. "But not as much as you'd think. I mean, they're small. There isn't much to them, and, dirty secret, most of them are cut with less expensive material. After all, who buys a ring for the band? It's the shiny rock that matters."

Crawford wet his whistle with a sip of his beer and continued. "Okay, so now we've got a ring. The manufacturer inflates the price and sells the ring to the retailer. The retailer marks the price *way* up and sells the ring to some poor sap who's trying to get laid." He let loose with his rodent-like chuckle and rubbed his hands together. "It's a racket! But it's *my* racket."

I shook my head. "Okay, so where does reification come in?"

"When I sell some poor lovesick sap a ring, the man isn't buying jewelry. He's buying a tangible expression of his love, which he then gives to the object of his affection. He's turned an abstract idea—love—into a concrete object—a ring. Reification!"

I snorted. "And he pays for it through the nose."

"Sure he does, but look what he's getting in return? A tangible expression of his love, a happy partner, and, with luck, a steady supply of good sex."

I shook my head, but I felt like I now had a pretty good idea of what reification was all about. I indicated the computer screen. "So Reifying Agent Alpha is going to take something intangible, apparently some sort of energy, and turn it into something tangible."

Crawford nodded. "Regenerated biological cells, I guess." His eyes lit up with a maniacal light and he pointed at the screen. "And maybe more! Say, you don't think.... You don't think this reifying agent can create life, do you? Or bring back the dead? Redhorn thinks that Clearwater intends to use it for something big. Whatever it is, it shook Redhorn up, but good!"

"Let's not get carried away. If this RAA can kick life into dead or dormant cells, that would be big enough. Leaflock said something about curing paralysis or reversing the aging process. Think what that would mean."

Crawford rubbed his hands together. "Sounds like someone could make a fortune with this stuff." The little man frowned. "But would something like curing paralysis be enough to result in 'catastrophic' consequences if it failed? There's something more going on here than repairing damaged cells."

I couldn't argue with that. "I don't know, but Redhorn seemed to think he figured it out."

Crawford nodded. "And it scared him enough to make him want to pack his bags and leave town."

"Right," I agreed. "And now he's dead."

"Natural causes, they say." Crawford's eyes lifted until they met mine. "Right?"

"Sure. Like that waitress is a natural blond."

The corner of Crawford's mouth twitched. "Maybe Redhorn knew too much?"

"Maybe. But remember, Clearwater never read his note. Redhorn died *before* he could give him the flash drive. I mean, sure, Clearwater might have suspected that Redhorn was on to him, but we don't have any real reason for thinking so."

Crawford gazed off into the distance, thinking. "It sounds like Redhorn was expecting a lot of money from Clearwater for the formula. The note says that he had already received the dough, but Redhorn wrote the note with the idea that Clearwater wouldn't read it until the exchange was made. Maybe Clearwater decided he didn't want to pay him."

I nodded. "That occurred to me, too. Clearwater told me that he was going to offer me what he had offered to Redhorn, and that was more dough than I can get my head around. But Clearwater never got the drive from Redhorn. Killing him without getting the formula first would have been more than a little careless on Clearwater's part. It doesn't seem likely. Besides, money wouldn't be an issue for a high-roller like Clearwater, even if he wasn't actually a powerful unearthly spirit who could probably pull c-notes out of thin air."

"He might have killed him for some other reason," Crawford pointed out. "Maybe they were fighting over a dame."

I shrugged. "Anything's possible. But Clearwater had a deal brewing with Redhorn. It doesn't make sense that he would have murdered Redhorn before getting what he wanted from him."

Crawford sighed. "Yeah, okay. You're probably right." He glanced up at me. "Any other suspects? What about this shapeshifter who did a number on you? You know that shapeshifters tend to be crazy, right?"

"So you've told me." I shook my head. "I don't know. Maybe. According to the note, the LIA was in this with Leaflock from the beginning. But I don't know what motive Deet would have for killing Redhorn without securing the flash drive first. Redhorn didn't give the formula to Leaflock, and it doesn't sound like Deet has the formula, either. Neither of them would have wanted Redhorn dead until they got the formula from him."

Crawford sighed. "So how are you going to find out who killed him?"

I shrugged. "I'm gonna leave it up to the cops. No one's paying me to find out."

"What?" Crawford's jaw dropped. "You're just going to let it go? You're not even curious?"

"Sure I'm curious. But it's not my case."

Crawford's eye began to twitch, and he blinked until it stopped. Since I'd met him he'd struck me as high-strung, but it seemed worse since he'd been possessed by that rogue witch. I wondered if he was feeling a little overwhelmed. I knew that my own heart was pumping. The twitchy little man tapped at the tabletop with the tips of his fingers. "All right, be that way. You're no fun." He pointed toward the laptop. "So now that you know what's on the flash drive, what are you going to do with it?"

I shook my head. "I'm not sure how much I really know. The formula is just gibberish to me."

"True," Crawford agreed. "But Redhorn's note is dynamite!"

I agreed. What was it that Redhorn had figured out about Clearwater's plans for Reifying Agent Alpha? It had to be something earthshaking with potentially disastrous consequences if Clearwater's efforts failed. Redhorn had written that no one would believe him if he told them what Clearwater was up to. I shook my head. Too many thoughts were whirling around in my beer-soaked brain, and I decided to give it a breather for the moment.

I gestured toward the laptop screen. "I've got more questions than answers, and I'm about done in for the night." I turned to Crawford. "I hate to ask more of you than you've already done, but would you be willing to keep this flash drive safe for a while longer? I still need to work some things out."

Crawford smiled. "That's copacetic with me, pal. But you know how I said I would buy the drinks next time around?"

I snorted out a laugh. "Fine. But I'll owe you more than a few drinks."

"Oh, don't worry." The smile on Crawford's lips broadened until his grin stretched ear to ear. "It'll be more than a few. I plan to get good and drunk with you when this is over."

"You're on," I assured him. "Provided we're both still alive."

***

I left the beastmobile at Gio's and walked down the hill toward home. A light drizzle had caused a few drivers to switch on their windshield wipers, and tiny droplets of water drifted through the beams of the passing headlights. I'd left my porch light on, and through the haze I could see the silhouette of a stumpy barrel-like figure that could only be a certain nirumbee warrior.

"I was wondering if you were gonna come home tonight, ace."

"What do you want, Ralph?"

"We need to talk."

"I need to sleep. It's been a long day."

"You going to let me in?"

I sighed. "Let's walk. My office is a mess."

Ralph wrinkled his nose. "I was going to ask about that. You got a dead body in there?"

"Not anymore." I walked back out to the sidewalk and down the hill. Ralph followed. He remained silent for half a block, and then asked, "What happened to your arm?"

"I cut myself shaving." I kept walking. At the corner, the haze formed a halo around a street lamp so covered in grime that it could only emit a pale glow.

Ralph waited until we reached the corner before speaking again. "I suppose you've accessed the flash drive by now."

I whirled on the nirumbee. "What's it to you, half-pint?"

Ralph glared up at me, his lips curled into a snarl. "What did you call me?"

"Oh, did I hurt your feelings? Excuse me all to hell."

Ralph quit snarling. "What are you sore at me for? I didn't do nothing."

"You and that flash drive! If I didn't know better, I'd think you had your own plans for the dingus."

Ralph raised his pointed eyebrows and dropped his jaw in an entirely unconvincing attempt to express shocked innocence. "I don't know what you're talking about."

"Can it, Ralph. Subtlety isn't your style. You couldn't talk me into giving you the drive the other night, and your agents couldn't find it in my house or in my car."

Ralph wasn't ready to let go of the "who, me?" act. "What do you mean 'my agents'? I didn't send any agents to your place."

"Stop. Please. Deet sent professionals to search my place, and they barely left a trace of their presence. Clearwater sent a lone safecracker to my office, but he got stopped before he could get started. So when two trained professional LIA agents trash my office, and my apartment, and my car like a couple of rank amateurs while searching for something that both Deet and Clearwater know isn't on the premises, what am I supposed to think? Why the fucking mess, Ralph? Was that your lame-brained idea? Were you trying to scare me into doing something rash and exposing the location of the drive?" I shook my head. "I'm disappointed in you. You should know me better than that."

All pretense of innocence left Ralph's face. "You're right, pal. That was a dumb move. I should have just beat the location out of you. I let my feelings get in my way. I like you for some reason. We've fought side-by-side, and you seem like an okay gee to me. And, anyway, the elf wouldn't like it if I damaged you beyond repair." He looked meaningfully at the rig holding my arm in place. "Looks like somebody else didn't show the same restraint."

"No, they didn't. But you know what they didn't get from me? The flash drive."

Ralph chuckled. "You've got balls, that's for sure." He lit up one of his hand-rolled cigars and took a puff. "Look. I tried to get the drive from you for your own good. You don't know what's going on here. Your stubbornness is going to get you killed, and I don't want to see that happen. And it's not because I'm all sentimental about you, either. If I let you get bumped off, the elf will have my hide! There aren't too many things in this or any other world that scare me, but the elf is one of them. You've talked to him, but you don't know him like I do. I'm on his good side, and that's where I want to stay, believe me. And he wants me protecting you, not kicking your ass."

I looked down at the two-foot warrior. "I don't need your protection."

Ralph looked me up and down. "Yeah, you're doing fine. If you were doing any finer, you'd be pushing up daisies."

"And then the drive would be lost forever."

Ralph lifted his stogie to his lips and blew smoke out his nose. "Think so? How long you think your rat friend can keep it safe?"

I felt my heart skip a beat right before it started pounding out a drum solo in my chest.

Ralph blew smoke in the direction of my face. "Oh, you thought your little meeting tonight was a secret?" He shook his head. "Southerland, how many times do I have to tell you that you're dealing with professionals? I'm a trained operative for the LIA, and Deet's been in the agency longer than I have. Clearwater is a fucking unearthly spirit—a big one! You? What are you, Southerland? A ferret. A rodent, like your rat friend. You've been lucky so far, but you have no chance. Not against the kind of opposition you're facing. Your elf-senses won't help you. Your little puffs of air won't help you. Not even Cougar can help you. Even I can't help you. Not enough. Not by myself."

"Is my friend okay? If anything happens to him...."

"Crawford? Yeah, don't worry. He's okay for now. I don't think anyone but me knows you met with him tonight. Or that he has the flash drive." Ralph snorted. "He's a clever little rodent, that's for sure. Do you know where he's stashed the drive? I sure don't. But I guess rats are real good at hiding things. It's their nature."

"How did you...?" I didn't finish the question, or expect an answer. Ralph was Leea. Leea knew everything. "And Deet? Does Deet know about Crawford?"

Ralph shrugged. "Does Deet know that Crawford exists, and that he's a were-rat? And that you and he are friends? I don't know, but I sure as fuck wouldn't bet against it. But Deet's been... preoccupied the last twenty-four hours." The nirumbee glanced up at me. "Know anything about that?"

I leaned against the lamppost, and straightened up again when pain ran up my arm like an electric current. I cursed under my breath. I thought I'd been clever when I'd moved the flash drive out of my building, but I'd only put Crawford in danger. I should have known better. Ralph was right. Compared to the LIA and unearthly spirits, I was small change. I considered my current condition. Here I was, half a man, trying to stand up against forces powerful enough to shake the world. Sure, I'd won a battle against Deet, suffering debilitating injuries in the process, but I had no illusions that I'd come close to winning the war. Deet would be back, and next time I'd be lucky to come out of it with my skin. Then there was Clearwater, who had taken Thunderbird out of my arms without breaking a sweat. Now Crawford was squarely in the crosshairs, and I'm the one who'd put him there. Could I protect him? Who was I trying to kid. I hadn't done much of a job of protecting myself. I was treading water in quicksand with one arm, and if I was ever going to get out of the muck alive, I was going to need all the help I could get.

I let out a long breath. "Okay, Ralph. You win. Let's go to my office. I've got something I want you to see."

Ralph dropped his half-smoked cigar to the sidewalk and crushed it out with his toe. "Okay. Just one thing before we go."

I stopped where I was, my good hand in my pocket, and looked a question at Ralph. The nirumbee warrior leaped into the air and sucker-punched me with a piston-like left jab to my nose. I felt bones crunch as I bounced off the lamppost and slid to the pavement in a heap.

Ralph stood over me, scowling. "That's for calling me a half-pint. You need to watch your mouth, motherfucker. Don't you know how sensitive we short people are?" Then he smiled. "That crack of yours was a low blow."

Chapter Nineteen

"Get it? A *low* blow?" Ralph chuckled. "Sometimes I crack myself up."

"You broke my nose, you son of a bitch!" I examined the blood-soaked handkerchief I'd been using on my face.

Ralph snorted. "It'll heal. The elf's magic will see to that. Make sure you pull it straight, though. Unless you think a bent nose will make you more appealing to the ladies." He turned to examine my face. "It couldn't hurt."

I unlocked the door to my office and, thinking it might be Chivo's feeding time, paused before opening it. "Better let me go in first."

The coast was clear, so I waved Ralph into the room. I didn't bother turning on the lights.

Ralph stepped through the door and stopped in his tracks. "Lord's fucking' balls, man! You need to fire your cleaning lady! What the hell happened here?" He tried to wave away the swarm of flies that greeted him.

"Some of this is your fault. Your two agents, the dame and the one-legged dwarf, did the best they could to trash the place."

"They didn't *bleed* in here! Phew! And they didn't die in here, either. What the fuck! This is your office? How do you ever get any clients?"

"Most of my business comes to me over the internet, or by phone. And I do most of my meets on-site, or in diners or bars. Also, it's not normally like this."

"I sure *hope* the fuck not!" Ralph gazed around the office, the darkness no more of a hindrance to him than it was to me. "When did this happen?"

"A little more than a day ago. I spent last night in the hospital, and I haven't had the time to do anything about it since I got out."

"You should have *made* the time." He jerked his head toward me. "Wait a minute! You didn't bring me here to help you clean this place up, did you? I ain't no fuckin' housecleaner!"

"No, Ralph. My mess, my problem. But I wanted you to see it before I told you how it got this way. And, like I said, part of this is your doing."

"Okay, okay.... But can we talk about it outside? I need some fuckin' fresh air!"

"Sure, go on out. I've got a couple of things I gotta take care of. Wait for me. I'll be with you in five minutes."

Ralph wasted no time getting himself out the door and into the open air, and I hustled off to the laundry room to check on Chivo. The critter wasn't there, and his bowl was licked clean. I took it upstairs to the kitchen to refill it.

Once I'd carried Chivo's food back to the laundry room, I took out my phone and punched in Crawford's number. I got his voicemail and left a message telling him that we'd been spotted, and that he might want to lay low for a while. Then I went out to meet Ralph.

As we walked aimlessly up the sidewalk in the direction of Gio's lot, I told Ralph about my meeting with Deet. When I got to the part where Deet transformed into a giant bug, Ralph shook his head and snorted.

"I knew it had to be something like that." He glanced up at me. "I guess that explains the arm. And the blood."

"Only a little of the blood is mine. Most of it is Deet's." I explained how the mantis had shed Deet's body like a skin sack, and how in the course of the struggle I had put a wooden sword through the insect's eye.

"Next thing I knew, I was waking up in a hospital bed with a tube in my arm," I finished. Thinking about the experience made my arm itch inside my sling, and I reached in to scratch it.

Ralph chuckled. "Guess that explains why Deet wasn't in the office today." He stopped walking and looked up at me. "I hate to tell you this, but unless you killed Deet, and I doubt that you did, you're fucked. Deet's going to come after you hard. And I doubt if your rat friend is safe from Deet, either. We're going to have to do something about this."

"We?"

"You and me, bub. Get it through your thick skull. We're partners! You need me. And I need you." Ralph watched the cars pass by through the mist for a few moments before looking back up at me. "Let me put this together for you. The elf sent me here to find the kidnap victim who left his heart behind in that heartstone. He also told me to find you when I got here and get you in on the job. The elf didn't supply me with a lot of details. He's like that. He only tells me what he thinks I need to know." Ralph sighed. "I don't think he understands us all that well. Maybe he thinks we're smarter than we are. Like he thinks we'll know what's going on without him having to explain it all to us." The nirumbee paused, considering the idea, then shook off the thought. "Anyway. Turns out that the kidnap victim was an incarnation of Thunderbird, and it looks like it was Night Owl who took him. I don't know how he got the drop on Thunderbird, but he gets him out of range of his heart and transports him, unconscious, here to Yerba City. The way I figure it, Thunderbird wakes up when I get here with his heart. He... changes reality somehow, so that the incarnation of Thunderbird that Night Owl kidnapped ceases to exist, or never existed, and he creates a new reality in which he is reincarnated as the boy you found at the children's home. The boy who talks backwards."

"Thunderbird can do that?"

Ralph shrugged. "Thunderbird is the most powerful spirit I know about. I have no idea what he is capable of doing, or what rules he has to follow. It hurts my brain just to think about it. But Thunderbird is now this troll kid that Cougar told you to protect."

"And then I let Night Owl get the boy." My arm was tingling. No matter how hard I tried, I couldn't seem to reach the source of the itch.

"Yeah, you really fucked up, pal. You led Night Owl straight to the boy, and after that there was nothing you could do to prevent him from taking Thunderbird back again."

The mist was getting thicker, and I wiped away the beads of moisture that were forming on the brim of my hat. "Night Owl has half of what he needs."

Ralph nodded. "And now he needs the information on the flash drive."

I looked down to meet the nirumbee's eyes. "He needs Reifying Agent Alpha."

Ralph's eyebrows shot up. "Reifying Agent Alpha? That's RAA?"

I nodded. "I accessed the drive tonight. I found a formula for something called Reifying Agent Alpha. The formula itself is way beyond *my* poor brain's ability to grasp, but it includes a lot of alchemical equations and probably some witchcraft. Redhorn included a note. Once the device is put together, it will extract energy to power the RAA, which acts as a cell regenerator. An unusually powerful one."

Ralph frowned. "What do you mean?"

"Clearwater—Night Owl—is up to something big. I don't know what. But it involves converting a shitload of energy into regenerated life."

Ralph wiped mist out of his eyes. "We knew that Leaflock was making a cell regenerator of some kind. What do you mean by a shitload of power?"

"I'm not sure. Redhorn thought that the whole device was impractical. He said that it would need too much power to work. He mentioned a nuclear power plant. Or the sun."

Ralph's eyes widened. "Or something unearthly. Like maybe..."

"A very powerful spirit." I reached inside my sling and started scratching again.

"Then Thunderbird..."

"Must be Night Owl's source for the energy," I finished.

"Lord's fucking balls...." Ralph's voice was little more than a whisper.

"Clearwater—Night Owl—says he wants to save someone's life. Maybe it's his own."

"Maybe, maybe." Ralph looked thoughtful. "So Night Owl has been living it up here in Yerba City as Armine Clearwater for several years. He finds out somehow about Leaflock's cell regeneration device and learns that Redhorn is developing the ingredient that makes it work. He contacts Redhorn, maybe plays on his weaknesses and his resentment toward his boss, and he buys the blueprints for the device and the formula for the reifying agent. But he needs a special source of energy. So he kidnaps Thunderbird and brings him back here where he's been living."

"And where Leaflock's device is supposed to be built." I glanced down at the LIA agent. "You know that your agency contracted Leaflock Services to build the device. Whatever it's supposed to do, the LIA knows about it."

Ralph looked up at me. "That may be, but I sure as hell didn't get the memo. Maybe Deet knows, but Deet's not telling. Anyway, Night Owl probably has his own purpose for the thing."

We walked slowly up the hill, thinking to ourselves. We'd made it all the way to Gio's before Ralph broke the silence. "Night Owl is killing anyone who gets in his way. That's not like him. He's a powerful spirit, but he's not normally so blatantly homicidal, at least not in the stories I've heard about him. He's more known for loving the good life. For him to be so...." He shook his head. "You need to be careful with him. That's all I'm saying."

"Thanks, dad. I kind of already knew that."

Ralph glared at me. "But you don't know the stakes!"

"No?" I glared back at the nirumbee. "Then why don't you enlighten me?"

Ralph looked away. "Just be careful, that's all."

For no particular reason, we wandered over to the beastmobile. I suppose it was just because it was a familiar sight. I leaned against the hood of the car. "Ralph, I don't know what Night Owl is planning, and I'm not sure I care. I've got more immediate concerns. First, I want to make sure that Crawford is safe. I called him while you were waiting for me outside the office and got his voicemail. He's probably all right, but I want to be sure. Second, I need to get the boy back from Night Owl. Cougar told me to protect him, and Night Owl got him on my watch. I'm not going to let that bastard drain the energy out of the boy, no matter whose life he's trying to save."

Ralph cleared his throat and spat off to one side. "He's not really a boy, you know. He's Thunderbird. And Night Owl can't kill him. Not as long as the heartstone is safe, which it is."

I felt my jaw tighten and the hairs on the back of my neck starting to rise. "He was a ten-year-old child when I met him, and he was scared to death. He knows that he's Thunderbird, but he doesn't know what that means. I can't imagine what he's going through now, but I'm responsible for it. I'm going to get him back. You say we're supposed to be partners. Does that mean you're going to help me or is partnership with you just a one-way street?"

Ralph waved a hand in dismissal. "Relax, tough guy. I'm all in on this. The way I see it, getting Thunderbird safely back to Lakota in whatever form he's in is why the elf sent me here in the first place. Tell you what. Go check on your rat friend. I've got a couple of things of my own I need to look into. I'll call you in the morning. Hopefully, one of us will have a brilliant plan of action by then. That suit you?"

I nodded. It wasn't like I had many choices. For the time being I couldn't do anything to help the boy, a boy I thought of more as Troy than Thunderbird. I was a little worried about Crawford. It bothered me that he hadn't answered his phone when I'd called. He was probably fine, but it wouldn't hurt to drive over and see for myself. "Okay, Ralph. I'm too keyed up to sleep, so I'm going to take a drive. But can you do me one favor first?"

"Sure, partner. What'd'you need?"

"Help me get this fuckin' harness off. My arm itches like a sonuvabitch."

***

I tried calling Crawford again on my way out to his place in Placid Point, but the call again went to voicemail, and I disconnected without leaving a message. I told myself that it was well past midnight and that, like any sensible person, Crawford was sleeping off all the beers he'd downed at the Boatyard. But I couldn't shake the feeling of dread that had grabbed me by the throat when I'd found out that our clandestine meeting hadn't been a secret after all. In my mind, I kicked myself for thinking that I could outsmart the LIA. Or Night Owl. Crawford was an innocent bystander in a mess that I'd escalated with my irrational pride and blind muleheadedness. What gave me the right to decide who could possess the flash drive and its information concerning Reifying Agent Alpha? By what right had I stolen the drive out of Redhorn's apartment? What business was any of this to me? I'd only taken the drive because of the guilt I felt when I heard that Redhorn had died. And I'd only kept it because I didn't like the way others were trying to take it away from me. I was like a dog with a bone that it didn't really want, but didn't want anyone else to have. And what had I got from it all? I'd not only been responsible for leading Night Owl to Troy and getting the child kidnapped, but I'd put the life of a friend in danger. Not just a friend, but one of my only friends. Was it any wonder that I didn't have more?

The Saturday night traffic in Yerba City doesn't slacken until just before dawn, and, though I leaned on my horn and gunned my engine to intimidate the drivers in my path, my beastmobile passed through the congested streets like a pig through a python. In the end, it took me forty-five minutes to drive the six miles to Placid Point. I could have run there faster.

Crawford lived in an apartment above the Nautilus Jewelry and Novelty Shop, and his front door was at the top of a flight of stairs leading up from the alley behind the store. I found a parking place near the store and held myself at high alert as I approached the alley. As I walked, I scanned the street for conspicuous vehicles and the sky for owls. Every vehicle seemed suspicious to me, but the night sky was clear of birds. I took a deep breath and turned the corner into the alley.

Directly in front of me, in the center of the alley between the enclosed garage where Crawford kept his car and the stairway leading up to Crawford's apartment, was a pile of clothes that I recognized as the duds Crawford had been wearing in the Boatyard Bar and Grill. In the center of the pile, crouched down and pecking at the clothing, was the distinct form of an owl. The owl and I saw each other at the same time, and the bird spread its wings out wide. A sudden vision of an owl crushing the skull of the security guard at New Horizons Children's Home flashed into my forebrain, and I regretted that I wasn't packing heat. The bird moaned a warning cry at me and flapped its wings. I spotted a broken piece of concrete on the alley floor and scooped it up as I ran headlong at the owl, roaring like a jungle cat. When I got close, I flung the concrete rock at the owl, but the bird was already in flight and hauling ass. Ha! I thought. Not so tough after all!

I hoped that it wasn't going for reinforcements.

With the latter thought in mind, I hurried over to the pile of laundry. The clothes were definitely Crawford's, I thought, holding up the adolescent-sized pair of pants. I went through every pocket I could find. I found his cell phone in his coat, which explained why he hadn't answered my calls. I found his wallet and a set of keys. I didn't find the flash drive.

I examined the area around the clothes, but found nothing of note. I checked Crawford's garage and found his car inside. Crawford had come home and parked his car. Then he'd started to cross the alley to his apartment when he'd spotted something threatening or maybe come under attack. He'd transformed into a swarm of rats and scattered, heading for bolt holes and escape routes in the alley that he knew like the back of his hand. One of the rats had carried off the flash drive.

I looked up at Crawford's front door. Had the rats found their way back into the apartment and re-formed? I didn't think so. It wouldn't be a smart move. If he was going to re-form at all, he'd do it where no one was likely to come looking. I scanned the sky for attacking owls, but didn't see any. The memory of a dead rat spilling out of my hat came to me unbidden, and I hoped that earlier incident hadn't been a portent of disaster now reaching fulfillment.

As I was pondering my next move, I spotted movement on the ground near the back of the jewelry shop. A group of twenty or so rats were scurrying toward the pile of Crawford's clothing. I saw another group of rats heading toward the clothes from near the garage, and another dozen or so were coming up from somewhere behind me. I watched as more and more rats poured out of holes in various walls and from under broken slabs in the alley, all making their way to the pile of clothing. I stepped back from the clothes as the rats merged together inside the shirt and pants, and in mere moments, I was looking into Crawford's grime-covered face.

Crawford reached down to gather up his shoes and socks, and he pulled a set of keys out of his pocket. He looked up at me and grinned. "As long as you're here, you might as well come up for a drink."

***

Crawford, still barefoot, sat in his easy chair and poured a splash of whiskey into a drinking glass. "Not that I mind the visit, but what are you doing here? It's gotta be, what, three in the morning?"

I took the bottle from him with my one functioning hand and poured some into my own glass. "I was worried." I told him about Ralph and how he'd known about our meeting. "I'm sorry. I thought I'd been careful."

Crawford took a sip of his drink. "It's the LIA. You can't hide from them once they're interested. Believe me, I know."

I put my glass on the coffee table. "Look, man. I'm really sorry I dragged you into this. I should have known better. I was worried when you didn't answer my calls."

"Awwww... Isn't that sweet." Crawford took another drink.

"Come on, you dope! I'm in deep. The devils I'm messing with won't hesitate to take you out of the picture now that they know you have the flash drive."

"Once they find it, you mean. And they'll never find it."

I didn't think that Crawford was taking matters as seriously as he should, and I tried to impress upon him the gravity of the situation. "Don't you get it? Deet, the LIA, this Night Owl—they'll use any kind of interrogation technique, *beginning* with torture, to get that drive from you. And then they'll feed your rats one at a time to a flock of owls."

"Parliament. It's a parliament of owls."

I felt pressure building up behind my eyes and reached up to rub the side of my forehead. In a second, I was going to say something that I'd regret.

Crawford chuckled. "You're getting red in the face. And did you get your nose broken? How'd *that* happen?"

"Never mind. What can I do to make you see how serious this is?"

Crawford's smile disappeared behind tightened lips. He took a sip from his drink and put the glass on the table next to mine. "Look. I know you mean well. But do you think you're my big brother or something? You think I need you to protect me? Alex, please. We've been friends for, how long now? Seven years? Eight? And yet, somehow, you don't know a thing about me."

I stopped rubbing my temple. "What are you talking about?"

Crawford pointed a bony finger at me. "You know, you're a very self-centered individual. Anyone ever tell you that? I know a lot about you. What you do, what you think about the world, how you live your life.... What do you know about me?"

I gaped at him. "I don't know. Enough, I guess. I know you're a were-rat."

Crawford made a scoffing sound. "And that says it all, right? Do you even know what that means?"

"I... You... change yourself into rats?"

Crawford's laugh sounded bitter. "Yeah. I turn into rats. A hundred twelve of them. Do you know what I was doing when you showed up in the alley tonight?"

I shrugged. "I assumed you were hiding from whatever attacked you. That owl, I guess."

Crawford shook his head. When he looked at me I thought I detected a strange light in his eyes. "I was getting ready to ambush it. I was going to take it apart. Just like I'd torn up his friend a few minutes earlier. And, after that...." Crawford sat back in his easy chair. "I was going to have him for a midnight snack."

I didn't know what to say, so I grabbed the bottle and put another splash of whiskey into my glass. I didn't take a drink, though. I just stared at the sparks of light reflecting off the brown liquid.

Finally, I looked up to see Crawford draped in his chair, looking like he didn't have a care in the world. "Those owls are big. I watched one crush a man's skull with its claws yesterday."

"Yeah, they're big birds, even for owls. Hunters. The one I caught up to put up a good fight. Scratched me up a little before he died." Crawford sipped his drink. "I've never tasted owl before. Gotta say, it's pretty good!"

"Did you.... I mean, you look... unhurt."

Crawford chuckled. I'd heard that rat-like chuckle of his a thousand times, but it sounded different this time, more menacing somehow. "Ah, Alex. You're a good joe, you really are. But you've got to stop underestimating me. I'm a *mischief* of rats, more than a hundred strong. That's more than a hundred set of sharp teeth and more than four hundred clawed feet. Do you know how much damage a hundred crazed rats can do when they are acting with a single focused mind?" He held out his hand, and six rats leaped out of his palm to the coffee table where they sat back on their haunches with bared teeth and extended their front claws at me.

I picked up my glass and took a sip. "I get your point."

The rats turned around and leaped one by one back into Crawford's palm, the last one launching itself into a showy flip before disappearing with the rest. Crawford's face lit up with a grin that crinkled his beady eyes. "That owl never had a chance. The second one would have met the same fate if you hadn't scared him off. He was right where I wanted him."

"So... what you're saying is..."

"That you worry too much. I've been taking care of myself for a long time now, and I guess I can handle myself for a while longer."

Crawford leaned forward in his chair. "I get it. You look at me and see a harmless looking middle-aged man, less than five-foot nothing, all skin and bones...." He nodded at me with his chin. "And there you are, a big tough bruiser with a cold stare that would intimidate a mob hitter. And you think you need to take me under your wing and shelter me from the meanness in this world. What you don't get, brother, is that I'm part of the meanness. I'm a were-rat, and were-rats are crazy by nature. Sure, since you've known me I've been able to keep my instinctive impulses under control—to keep the rats in line—but it hasn't always been that way. I've told you more than once, if you ever run into a were-rat who isn't me, back away slowly. Don't antagonize it. Most people are uneasy around were-rats—and they should be! Especially young ones who haven't developed any self-control. Well, I was young once, and I haven't forgotten how good it feels to let myself go wild."

I nodded and let out a breath. "You're right. I guess I never really understood. Or wanted to understand. To tell you the truth, I never got over what I put you through that night when we ran up against that witch in the hotel room. I know that shook you up a little. I guess I've been feeling guilty about it."

Crawford shook his head. "Is that why you've made yourself scarce lately? Because you've been feeling guilty?"

I looked at Crawford over the top of my glass. "What do you mean?"

He shrugged. "You hardly call me anymore. You never come around."

"That's not true. I asked you if you wanted to meet for lunch a while back and you turned me down."

He drew in a quick breath and let it out in an impatient sigh. "What are you, a freshman in high school? I was busy that day. I run my own business, you know. Someone's got to man the store, and I didn't have anyone available to cover for me." He smiled and wiggled his eyebrows at me. "That didn't mean I wanted to break up with you, you little bitch."

"I thought you needed a break."

"I admit that it was a tough night. I even had a nightmare or two after that. But I've been through worse in my time. I could tell you stories that would make your hair curl, but... well... let's just say that I'm not ready to yet. Someday, maybe. But those memories aren't good to recall. The point is, I'm not made of glass—I'm made of rats! I'm a lot tougher than I look."

"Well...." I looked him up and down. "You're setting a pretty low bar."

"Hardy har har. Okay, maybe so. But look, man. I went into that hotel of my own free will. I knew the risks. I'm *happy* to help you on your cases when you need me. And the more dangerous, the better. I keep myself sane by living a quiet and routine life, but if I don't bust loose every now and again, I'll *really* go mad! Your little adventures are... therapeutic for me." Crawford sprawled back into his chair. "Tonight, with those owls? Let me tell you—it's been a *gas*!"

Crawford knocked back the last of his drink and turned to meet my eyes. "Sometimes you let yourself get crippled with guilt.

You've got to stop that. You've got to allow people to take responsibility for their own actions. No one made you our daddy. You've got to let us live with the consequences of our own decisions."

I finished off my own drink and put the glass down on the table. "I get what you're saying. I do. But it's not always that simple. I'm responsible for leading Night Owl to the children's home and letting him get his hands on the boy, Troy. He might be the incarnation of Thunderbird, but he's still a ten-year-old child. That one's on me, and I'm going to make it right."

Crawford nodded. "That's fine. And I'm more than willing to help. I'll keep that flash drive safe, don't worry about that."

I studied the little man sitting across from me. I understood that he wasn't an ordinary man, and I accepted that he was a lot more formidable than he looked. But protecting the flash drive from Deet, the LIA, and Night Owl was no ordinary task. "I appreciate your willingness to help me. But Night Owl sent those owls here tonight, and that means that he at least suspects you have the flash drive. Ralph found out about our meeting somehow, and I don't know how I could have been any more careful. He's probably not a threat, but he thinks he should be the one holding on to the flash drive. I wouldn't be surprised if he tried to get it from you. And at this point, I have to assume that Deet probably knows you have the flash drive, too."

Crawford climbed out of his chair and walked over to a drawer on one side of the living room. He pulled something out of the drawer and held it up for me to see.

"This is a gemstone I picked up the other day at a craft show. It's about the size of the flash drive."

"Okay...."

"Try to take it from me."

I frowned. "What?"

"Go ahead. Come over here and take this ring out of my hand. You're a rough number and I'm just a small fry. Come over here and get it. Do your worst."

I smiled inwardly, thinking this might be fun. The little man thought he could outsmart me. Fine, I thought. Let's test him. I started to reach for my glass, moving slow and easy, then I sprang from the couch and launched myself at Crawford, extending my good arm.

Crawford stood stock still until I was almost on him, and then—he vanished! I grabbed at where he had been and came away clutching an empty shirt. At my feet, rats scurried away in all directions and disappeared into the walls of the room. All but one. A brown rat stood on its hind legs about a yard away from me, holding the ring in one of its forepaws. It held up the other paw, clenched it, and extended a single digit in a way I didn't know rats could do. I lunged at the rat, but it darted under the couch I'd been sitting on. I pulled the couch aside and stared down at the heads of five rats blinking at me out of holes in the floor. In half a second, the heads all vanished, leaving me standing in the middle of the room shaking my head and grinning like an idiot.

"Get back here, you goofball! I think I've got a plan!"

I took out my phone and punched in a number.

Chapter Twenty

After the best three hours of sleep I'd had in a month, I got busy and started cleaning up the mess in my office while waiting for Ralph to call. I tried to get Chivo to help, but the creature sniffed at me once from his bed, lowered his head, and went back to sleep.

"When did you become so finicky?" I asked him. "You smell like two-day-old roadkill." Chivo refused to acknowledge that I was still in the room. I closed the laundry room door behind me when I left.

I'd been at it for close to four hours and despite having only limited use of my left arm I felt like I'd made a dent when Ralph called.

He started talking as soon as I hit the connect button. "Let's meet, kid. Drive that tank of yours to the City Hall parking garage. Go to the fourth floor. Someone will meet you there."

"Good morning, Ralph. How's your day been?"

"Shut up, meathead. Leave now."

The call disconnected.

I stared at my phone for a second or two without moving, then, shaking my head, I placed it on my desk and went upstairs. I was at least going to change into clothes suitable for wearing in public before I went running out of the apartment.

It was more than an hour later that I turned the beastmobile into a parking spot on the fourth floor of the City Hall garage. It was the only empty space on the floor, and it was available only because a one-legged dwarf, stretched out on top of a flattened cardboard box, was lying smack dab in the middle of it. I waited for him to haul himself up with what appeared to be a hand-carved wooden cane and clear the space before parking.

The dwarf signaled me to get out of the car, and I did, locking the beastmobile behind me. I caught him studying the damage to the hood of the car. "Admiring your handiwork?" I asked him.

The dwarf glanced in my direction, lips twisted into a half smile. "Follow me," he muttered in the low, gravelly voice that dwarfs all have. He turned and, making adept use of his cane, led me to a spiffy-looking tan SUV farther into the lot.

The dwarf unlocked the driver's side door. "You're driving," he told me, and handed me a key.

I got behind the wheel, and the dwarf pulled in beside me. "Don't go anywhere yet," he said. The dwarf pulled out a cell phone and punched a single number. After a moment, he spoke into the phone. "I've got him. He was late, but he's clear." Then after a pause. "Got it."

The dwarf kept his phone to his ear and turned in my direction. "Take us out of the garage and make a right. I'll give you directions as we go."

"Where are we going?" I asked, starting the vehicle.

He turned away from me, scowling. "Where I tell you. Get a move on."

I sighed. The dwarf was Leea through and through. He looked and smelled like eighty miles of bad road, but he probably thought it was beneath his dignity to talk with a civilian like me.

The dwarf stayed on his phone, listening to instructions and then relaying them to me. Forty-five minutes and a number of right turns, left turns, U-turns, and an interesting two-block side-trip going the wrong way up a one-way street later, the dwarf had me double-park in front of a thirty-floor office building in the heart of the business district.

The dwarf looked up at me, scowling through his matted beard. "Hop out. Leave the engine running. You're going to room fourteen thirty-two. Got it? Say it back to me."

"Kiss my ass." I climbed out of the SUV and walked into the lobby of the building without looking back.

I found the elevator and punched the button for the fourteenth floor. The elevator slowed to a stop at the eighth floor, and when the door slid open, Ralph was standing in front of me.

"Get off here," Ralph told me.

"Is all this cloak-and-dagger shit really necessary?" I asked as I stepped out of the elevator.

Ralph glanced up at me. "Let's just hope we were careful *enough*. You shook at least three tails on the way here. Maybe four. That last one might have been a false alarm, but I'm not taking any chances."

I opened my mouth to say something further, but closed it without speaking.

Ralph led me to an unmarked closed door just down the hall from the elevator and reached up over his head to slide a magnetic card into the slot next to the doorknob. Then he waited. After half a minute, a light next to the slot turned green, and I heard what sounded like a sliding door open just behind the closed door. Ralph pulled the door open, and I found myself looking into another elevator shaft. After I followed Ralph inside, he pulled the door shut and punched a button marked "B1." My stomach rose to my throat as the lift dropped into what seemed like freefall.

The lift slowed to a gentle stop just before we were smashed into jelly, and the sliding door opened. We stepped out of the elevator into an anteroom that was no larger than the lift we'd just left. In the wall in front of us was a door with a metal pad where the doorknob should be. A camera was mounted in the corner to the right side of the door near the ceiling. The walls of the room were steel, polished, and bare.

Ralph reached up and pressed his thumb onto the metal pad. The door slid open, and Ralph motioned me to enter ahead of him. I stepped through the doorway and pulled up short. I now stood in the entry of a windowless gray-carpeted office space the size of a tennis court. An overhead fluorescent lamp bounced harsh white light off four unadorned polished steel walls. A dark red mahogany desk the size of a grand piano dominated one side of the office and contrasted dramatically with the two small metal foldout chairs sitting a few feet away from it, looking as if they'd been hauled into the room from some janitor's closet at the last minute for the occasion. In one corner of the room, a leafy ficus stood tall in a pot that was roughly the size of Ralph. The room was otherwise furnished only with space. Sitting behind the desk in a high-back padded leather office chair, posture rigid, hands in lap and feet flat on the floor, a black patch covering one eye, was the unsmiling figure of Deet.

I turned to Ralph. "What is this, you little weasel. A set-up?"

"Relax." Ralph put a hand on my elbow. "Deet is going to help us." Our voices echoed off the steel walls.

I turned to Deet, who was studying me with one good eye, and looked back down at Ralph. Discarding a number of comments after concluding that no one would find them witty but me, I settled for, "Convince me."

It was Deet who answered. "Agent Ralph and I had a long talk this morning. I think that our interests are aligned. I'm not any happier about Night Owl taking Thunderbird than you are. The two of us decided it would be in all of our interests to help you get the boy back."

I stared at Deet. "Keep talking."

Ralph let out a breath. "Sit down, Southerland. We're all pals here."

I glanced away from Deet toward Ralph. I didn't have to look behind me to know that this room had no escape route. Giving in, I walked into the office and sat down in one of the folding chairs. Ralph climbed up onto the other.

I glared into Deet's good eye. "No one has convinced me of anything yet."

Deet's face was impassive. "You accessed the flash drive, and you know about Reifying Agent Alpha. You left the drive with the were-rat, the one known as Crawford, who has disappeared with it. You are foolish to believe that he can keep the drive safe from Night Owl."

I turned toward Ralph. "You told Deet everything?"

Ralph smiled. "I unburdened my soul."

"Great. I hope you feel better."

"Oh, I feel fine. You should feel fine, too. Deet has agreed to let you and Crawford live."

"How thoughtful of Deet."

Deet cut in. "Night Owl will not be so tolerant. You've seen what he does to anyone who stands between him and what he wants. Crawford is in immediate danger from him. So are you. So is Agent Ralph. And now, because I have agreed to forge an alliance with you, so am I."

"An alliance? What if I decide I don't want your help?"

Deet's good eye didn't blink, not that I expected it to. "Then Night Owl will kill you, and he will kill Crawford. And then, when he is done with him, he will kill Thunderbird."

I tried to keep eye contact with Deet, but I couldn't maintain it for long. I told myself that Deet was wrong, that Crawford was far cleverer than Deet suspected. Was I kidding myself? I had no doubt that Crawford had secured the drive in a hidden rat-hole that not even the LIA could find. But was Crawford clever enough to keep himself hidden from Night Owl? Crawford had proved to be a match for Night Owl's pet owls, but Night Owl himself was another matter entirely. How long would it take for the powerful spirit to wrest the location of the hiding place from Crawford once he had him in his clutches? What were the chances that Crawford would survive the encounter? And what about Troy? Night Owl was going to use him as a power source, like a battery. Troy might be a vessel for Thunderbird, but he was still a child. To be used like that, as an object.... I felt my skin tightening and my teeth grinding.

I reminded myself that I had a plan, one that Crawford and I had put together the night before over a few drinks. Maybe a few too many drinks, now that I thought about it. The plan seemed a little less solid in the sober light of the day, but I still liked it. I just needed to get through the rest of the day without incident. I considered the risks, found them high, but decided they were worth taking. I just needed to improvise a bit.

I turned my attention back to Deet and let my shoulders sag. "All right, Deet. If you're on the level... if you can get the boy safely away from Night Owl.... I'm willing to agree to a truce between us. A temporary one. But once the job is done, all bets are off. And if you're trying to play me for a sucker, then you better play for keeps. I put out one of your eyes, and I can do worse."

Deet actually smiled, a grim smile that promised no warmth. "I look forward to giving you the opportunity."

Ralph snapped his fingers in the air. "Hey! You two lovebirds wanna knock it off? You can flirt with each other later. We got work to do."

Both Deet and I jerked our heads in the direction of the nirumbee, who scowled back at us. "You two are priceless. Are you sure you're not married?"

"Don't be absurd." Deet sounded indignant.

"Knock it off, Ralph." I felt myself bristling.

Ralph at least had the grace not to laugh. "So we're agreed. We've got two primary objectives." The squat little warrior held up a finger. "We've got to secure the flash drive." He gave me a meaningful stare. "That means you've got to get it back from Crawford. No arguments! Your friend is dead meat if Night Owl gets to him first. As long as he has the drive, he's in danger." Without waiting for me to respond, Ralph turned back to Deet. "And the LIA will keep Crawford safe, right? The agency doesn't always need to be so heavy-handed in matters like this. It's no wonder we have such a bad image with the general public. We'll get Crawford to sign a binding non-disclosure agreement promising him eternal ruin if he breathes a word about

RAA to anyone. He's a capable fellow. We might even be able to turn him into an asset." Ralph's eyes narrowed at Deet. "But we let him live. Is that jake with you?"

Deet gave Ralph a curt nod. "If he agrees to keep silent about... certain matters... then I'll agree not to have him removed."

Ralph's smile exposed his razor-sharp teeth. "Good. That wasn't so hard, was it? The other thing we've got to do is secure Thunderbird from Night Owl. Once he's in our custody, the LIA will ensure his safety until he grows into his own powers. Thunderbird is a balancing power in this world. His loss would be a disaster. We don't want a disaster. Again, I see nothing but benefit for the agency here."

Deet looked from Ralph to me, and back to Ralph again, as if assessing our strengths and weaknesses. Turning back to me, Deet said, "Leave reclaiming Thunderbird to me. The LIA has the resources to deal with Night Owl, and you'll just get in our way. I will ensure that the child comes to no harm."

Deet turned to Ralph. "Go with Southerland to find his friend, the were-rat. Secure the flash drive, along with his silence in this matter."

Turning to me again, Deet said. "Stay with your friend until the matter with Night Owl is resolved. I'll make sure that you are continually in the loop. Satisfactory?"

Ralph glanced at me. "How 'bout it?"

I kept my eyes on Deet. "Sounds like the two of you have this all worked out."

It was Ralph who spoke. "Like Deet said, we had a long heart-to-heart before you got here. Face facts, Southerland. We don't actually need you. Deet's right: the agency is capable of dealing with Night Owl. My own priority is to free Thunderbird. With Night Owl out of the way, we can talk about the flash drive, but the fact is if Deet here wants it, Deet will find a way to get it. Be smart. Cooperate with us, and you and Crawford go on your merry way. Refuse, and things won't go so well. For either of you."

"So we're back to tossing threats? How's that worked for the two of you so far?"

"I'm not tossing anything. I'm just explaining the facts. Don't get your panties in a bunch."

Deet forestalled further argument. "Mr. Southerland, you're here now because I promised Agent Ralph that I would endeavor to resolve the issue between us without violence. My initial plan was to seize the flash drive and eliminate you and your friend once I had it. Agent Ralph has convinced me that extreme measures are unnecessary. What assurance can I give you that I no longer intend harm to either of you?"

I slid in my seat, trying to find a degree of comfort in a chair designed to offer none. Giving up, I asked Deet, "How long have you known that RAA was a reifying agent designed to regenerate cells?"

Deet blinked. "How is that question relevant?"

I stood up from the uncomfortable chair, folded it, and tossed it in the direction of the doorway. Crossing over to the desk, I leaned a hip against it and stared down at Deet with my arms folded across my chest. "You want me to trust you? Start spilling. I'm tired of being in the dark. You can start by answering my question. How long have you known about RAA? You didn't just learn about it this morning from Ralph. I think you've known what it was and what it's for from the beginning. If we're going to work together, I'm gonna need the whole story. So let's have it, and don't leave nothing out."

Deet gave Ralph a look that said something like, "I told you this was going to be a bad idea." Then Deet turned back to me and let out a brief sigh. "About a year ago, the LIA learned that Morgan Leaflock was looking into the possibility of developing a cell regeneration instrument with the capability of treating paralysis. The agency, for reasons of its own, was interested. The agency contacted Mr. Leaflock and discussed a contract. Mr. Leaflock was receptive. In fact, according to my sources, he was quite enthusiastic, particularly after learning how much money the agency was willing to offer his company. Mr. Leaflock agreed to turn ninety-three percent of his company's efforts into the design and production of his proposed instrument. At that point, the LIA embedded an agent in Leaflock Services. Our agent reported that Mr. Leaflock had taken it upon himself to design the energy extraction component of the instrument, and that he had delegated the task of designing and developing the active reifying agent for the device to his chief engineer, Mr. Inyon Redhorn."

Deet paused for a beat, and then continued. "To answer your question, Mr. Southerland, I've known about the plans to develop a cell regeneration instrument from the beginning. I also knew from Mr. Leaflock's reports to me that Mr. Redhorn was working on the reifying agent that would make the instrument functional."

I nodded at Deet. "So Leaflock was developing his device for the LIA pretty much from the beginning."

"That's correct. The LIA provided Leaflock Services with the necessary funding. Mr. Leaflock completed his portion of the instrument to the satisfaction of a group of independent engineers the LIA had gathered to examine the results. My understanding is that the energy extraction component is quite sophisticated, but fairly straightforward. Mr. Redhorn was faced with the more difficult task, but, with the help of resources provided by the LIA, Mr. Redhorn was able, in a surprisingly short period of time, to develop an efficient means for regenerating dying—and, in some cases, even dead—biological cells."

"Reifying Agent Alpha," I muttered.

"Precisely, Mr. Southerland."

"Go on."

"Seven weeks ago, our agent submitted an alarming report. Someone at Leaflock Services was selling off proprietary information to rival firms. Nothing directly connected to the cell regeneration project, but the LIA became concerned. After analyzing the situation and gaining sufficient clearance, I personally informed Mr. Leaflock of this development, and he took immediate action."

I nodded. "He hired me."

"Correct, Mr. Southerland."

"Are you saying I owe this job to you?"

The hint of a frown appeared in the space between Deet's eyes. "Indirectly. Hiring a private investigator was Mr. Leaflock's idea. I suggested that the matter be handled by an LIA operative, but Mr. Leaflock turned me down. I confess that I do not know the reasons for his decision."

I smiled. "It doesn't sound like he trusts you."

Deet's frown deepened. "That may be the case. I am told that I lack certain skills when it comes to dealing with other people's emotional responses in stress situations."

I was much more successful in clamping down on my reaction to Deet's self-assessment than Ralph, who forced a cough in an unconvincing attempt to cover up a choked laugh. Deet shot him a quick glance, but let it go.

Deet continued. "After you were successful in discovering that it was Mr. Redhorn who was selling his company's information, Mr. Leaflock called me right away. That's when I learned that Mr. Redhorn had not only sold the blueprints for the cell regeneration device to someone pseudonymously referred to as 'Nocturnal,' but was in negotiation for the sale of the formula for Reifying Agent Alpha, which Mr. Redhorn had, unbeknownst to Mr. Leaflock, completed."

Deet paused. "I gather that some friction had developed in the relationship between the two men?"

Deet raised an eyebrow at me, but I didn't respond. I wasn't going to be an LIA asset. They could do their own investigative work if they were interested.

Deet shrugged and continued. "Under my direction, LIA agents were quick to discover the true identity of Mr. Redhorn's prospective buyer."

"Armine Clearwater."

Deet nodded. "Night Owl."

I considered Deet's story. "How did Clearwater find out Redhorn had been selling company secrets?"

Deet blinked again. And again. I knew what it meant, that Deet was reluctant to disclose anything further.

"Come on, Deet. You're doing fine. We're building trust here."

With another glance at Ralph, Deet continued. "Night Owl was working with us."

Deet paused for a few heartbeats, considering how to proceed, before starting up again. "Mr. Redhorn was aware that the reifying agent he produced would need to be extremely powerful in order to meet the specifications that Mr. Leaflock had provided for him, specifications that I had been given by genetic engineers working for the LIA, and that I passed along to Mr. Leaflock. Mr. Redhorn was dismayed by the amount of energy the instrument would need in order to produce the desired results. It was his opinion that the instrument his company was producing would be impractical because of the lack of a feasible power source. Mr. Redhorn was unaware, however, that Mr. Leaflock had found a way to extract the required amount of energy the device needed from a... *unique*... source of raw power."

"Let me guess," I interrupted. "Leaflock figured out how to extract energy from an unearthly source. From a powerful living spirit. Namely, Thunderbird."

Deet hesitated before responding. "Yes, Agent Ralph told me that you had ascertained this information on your own. I must admit that the process is beyond my ability to comprehend. I'm not a scientist, nor an engineer. But Mr. Leaflock assured me that living energy from certain unearthly sources would be ideal for his device. After much consideration, in a decision made over my head, the agency contracted Night Owl to secure the physical embodiment of Thunderbird, an unearthly spirit of enormous power, and transport it to Yerba City."

I took a step away from the desk. It was getting hot in that steel-walled room, and I fanned myself with my hat. "But after he kidnapped Thunderbird, Clearwater decided to play his own game."

Deet nodded. "Yes. Night Owl contacted Mr. Redhorn on his own and offered him quite a sizable sum—more than the LIA was offering him—to sell him the blueprint for the cell regeneration device and the formula for Reifying Agent Alpha. Eventually, Mr. Redhorn accepted his offer." Deet looked up at me. "And now, Mr. Southerland, I think you know as much as you need to know."

"Not quite." I braced myself on the desk with both arms and leaned in toward Deet, staring down at the agent from what I hoped was an intimidating position. "What does Clearwater want with the cell regenerator? He claims he wants to use it to save a life. Whose life?"

Deet met my two-eyed stare with a one-eyed one. "I don't know. I honestly don't know. I wish I did. But I don't." Deet surprised me by blinking and glancing away. "Let me make a few things clear, Mr. Southerland. The people I work for tell me only what they think I need to know, and, although I am often able to discover information that I'm not privy to, many things are kept secret from me. I nonetheless do my duty to the agency and to the Dragon Lord. That's my job. In this case, I am unaware of the agency's ultimate plans for the cell regeneration instrument. I am equally unaware of Night Owl's personal plans for the device. The decision to seize Thunderbird was not mine, nor was the decision to contract Night Owl for the task. I recommended against both decisions, but, for reasons not shared with me, my advice was not heeded. It is now my task to prevent Night Owl from furthering his scheme, whatever it might be, to secure Thunderbird, and to set the LIA's operation back on track."

Deet glanced at Ralph. "Agent Ralph has convinced me that I can best accomplish my task by bringing you into my plans." Deet hesitated for a beat and met my eyes. "I assure you that our encounters thus far have not been malicious. I bear you no ill will. I have no particular feelings about you one way or the other."

I held Deet's stare for a few more beats, and then relented. I knew I would have to sooner or later, so I elected for sooner. I stood up. "Fine. And thank you. I think I've got what I need."

Ralph, who had been listening to Deet's story with intense concentration, now jumped in. "And?" he asked.

"And, I'm in," I answered. I put on my hat and turned toward Deet. "I'll work with you. Are you going to require me to shake on it?"

Deet didn't smile. "That won't be necessary."

Chapter Twenty-One

Neither Ralph nor I spoke until we'd stepped out of the building and onto the sidewalk. Then I turned and grabbed Ralph by the back of the neck. "Are you insane? You can't be serious about trusting Troy's life to that piece of trash!"

Ralph threw my arm aside. "What are you talking about? You said you were in!"

"Like hell I am! No way am I going to work with that… insect!"

"Don't tell me that you're prejudiced against shapeshifters. Lord's balls—your friend is a were-rat!"

"I'm not prejudiced against shapeshifters. I'm prejudiced against double-dealing secretive LIA agents who try to kill me."

Ralph held up a finger. "First, Deet told you a lot more in there than you needed to know. Probably more than you *should* know." He lifted another finger to join the first. "Second, Deet wasn't trying to kill you the other night. Deet was just trying to scare you a little so you'd give up the flash drive. Okay, Deet might have ripped off one of your arms, just to make a point. But, I don't think Deet would have taken both of them, or let you bleed out. Anyway, if Deet had wanted to put you away for good, you'd be a goner."

"I'll be a goner the minute Deet gets that flash drive, and you know it. Don't tell me you believe all that shit about letting me and Crawford live. We know too much. Deet still needs me to get the drive from Crawford. But once I do, it's curtains for both of us, and Deet will be the one taking the bows."

"You've got Deet all wrong, Southerland. Deet doesn't need you to get the drive from Crawford. I convinced Deet that killing the two of you would be counter-productive. The agency needs to keep this operation as quiet as possible. The Children's Home Massacre has already attracted too much attention. We don't need any more noise. Deet agreed to meet with you today so that you two could bury the hatchet. Bygones be bygones, no hard feelings. Maybe in the future you and the agency could even help each other out from time to time. Why not? I'll take responsibility for your good behavior. Maybe kick a little business your way."

"You want me to stooge for the LIA? You've got to be shittin' me!"

"Why not? We're not the bad guys."

"You think you're the good guys?"

"We're the necessary guys. This realm doesn't run without us."

I felt my eyes roll and told myself to be careful. That kind of tell will kill you in a poker game. "Toeing the company line. You of all people." I gave him a meaningful stare.

"Can it, pal." Ralph glanced around in all directions at once and lowered his voice to a whisper. "Let's take a walk."

The clouds had cleared while I was holed up in Deet's basement office, and blue skies draped over the city like a canopy. Colors were crisp and objects had that hard-edged clarity I'd discovered after my visit to the spirit realm. Ralph turned a corner, and we made our way down a quiet side street. The light descending on the sidewalk ahead of us glowed with an unusual whiteness, as if emanating from a source brighter than the sun. Ralph led me into the patch of brightness, and the sounds from the street dampened to a low buzz.

Ralph pulled up and lit up one of his stogies. "We can talk here."

The air was somewhat thinner than it had been, and it gave me the feeling that we had walked into a different part of the world, or to another world. I knew we were standing in one of those pockets of other-reality that I was starting to become used to seeing, although this one seemed more stable than most.

Ralph puffed on his cigar until the end glowed red, and then he blew out a thick cloud of smoke. "I'm a loyal soldier of the LIA, Southerland. That's the way the elf wants it. It's how I'm valuable to him. You should take note."

"Trusting Deet isn't a sign of loyalty. It's a sign of stupidity. Deet knows more than Deet's telling."

"What do you mean?"

"Deet knows what Night Owl wants with the cell regenerator. Deet knows whose life Night Owl wants to save."

"You can't be sure of that."

I glared down at the nirumbee, whose head was now wreathed in foul-smelling smoke. "You know why Night Owl wants the device, too. Quit trying to bullshit me, Ralph. The only one around here who doesn't know anything is me. Why don't you come clean with me? You expect me to help you, but you won't trust me enough to tell me what's going on."

Ralph put on his best impression of an expression of innocence. As usual, it didn't sit well on him. "Me? What makes you think I know what Night Owl wants? He's a fuckin' spirit! Who knows what those jokers are thinking? I told you, they're not like us. They're not motivated by the same things. He says he wants to save a life? Maybe he does, but it could be anybody. There's no telling."

I shook my head. "You're not nearly as clever as you think you are, Ralph. You've told me what you know in a dozen different ways, both out there on the pier and last night outside my office. I can't work with someone who tries to hide vital information from me." I turned to walk away. "Goodbye, Ralph. We're done. I'll let you explain it to the elf."

Ralph grabbed my arm. "Wait a minute! Where you going? What are you planning?"

"I'm going to get Deet and Night Owl off my back. I'm going to make sure that Crawford is okay. I'm going to see that the flash drive falls into the right hands. I'm going to rescue Troy. Then I'm going to have pizza."

"Wait! Stop! Deet will take care of Night Owl and get Thunderbird back. Quit being such a hardheaded prick. The only way you and Crawford stay alive is by honoring your agreement with Deet. Take me to Crawford. We'll get the drive out of his hands before Night Owl takes it from him. I'll have him sign some agreements, and the LIA will leave him alone. You'll have to sign the agreements, too. It's what's best for everybody."

I pulled my arm out of Ralph's grasp. "I can't trust you, Ralph."

I started away. Ralph's voice trailed behind me, muted by the sounds of the city as I stepped out of the pocket of light, but still clear enough for me to hear. "You walk away now, Southerland, and I can't be held responsible for what happens to you—or your friend! Stop! Please?"

I stopped. I hesitated. I thought about it. Then I walked back into the light. I stood over Ralph, glaring down at him with my best glare. "You want us to be partners? Fine. Talk to me, Ralph. No more secrets. Why does everyone want the formula to Reifying Agent Alpha? What does it do? Don't tell me you don't know, because that's bullshit. And partners don't bullshit each other."

Ralph looked up at me, desperation in his eyes. "Don't make me tell you about this operation. It's too big. The less you know, the better. I'm telling you this for your own good. Because if you knew as much as I know... There wouldn't be anything I could do to keep Deet from taking you out for keeps. I'm trying to protect you, you dumb fuck!"

I shook my head. "It doesn't work that way. Let me worry about Deet. You're not responsible for protecting me. Before I take one more step to help you get that drive, I need to know what it's all for. As someone said to me recently, you're not my daddy. You've got to let me live with the consequences of my own decisions."

Ralph turned away from me and watched a late-model luxury car cruise by. When he turned back, he muttered. "Don't ask. You don't want to know."

"But I really do, Ralph. I left my momma's arms a long time ago. I've served the state in our Dragon Lord's war. I've been running a semi-successful business for nearly a decade. I'm all grown up. Whatever it is, I can handle it."

Ralph shook his head. "If you can handle this, you're a bigger man than me. And I have my fuckin' doubts about that."

"Tell me, Ralph. Too late to back down now."

Ralph stared up at me, doubt all over his eyes and in the curl in his lip. But he nodded. "All right. I'll give it to you straight and you can figure out what to do with it. Leaflock's device regenerates cells, right? And Night Owl says that he needed it to save a life. I think that the LIA wants it for the same reason." Ralph looked away from me, gathering himself for what he was going to say next. He looked up. "It's Lord Ketz-Alkwat. They need the regeneration device for the Dragon Lord. He's dying."

***

"Bullshit."

I'd heard the words that Ralph had spoken, but they made no sense to me. He might has well have told me that the sun was falling out of the sky. I tried to set him straight. "Dragon Lords are immortal. That means they can't die."

Ralph made a scoffing noise. "Immortal only means he hasn't died yet. How do we know he'll live forever?"

"He's lived for at least six thousand years."

"Maybe six thousand is all he's got."

I shook my head. "I've never heard of a Dragon Lord dying."

"There's only seven of them that we know about. Maybe Ketz is the oldest."

I tried to make sense of the inconceivable and gave up. I shook my head. "I don't know Ralph. That's a pretty wild idea."

Ralph shrugged. "Maybe. But I've been hearing some things. You remember the other day when Lord Ketz came out of his hole and graced us all with a flyover? That confused the hell out of the Leea chiefs. I guess it was a last-minute thing, and no one seems to know what got into the old lizard. But I started running across some wild rumors at the office."

"Rumors?"

It was noticeably warmer in this pocket of reality than outside it. I took off my hat and wiped my brow. Ralph reached up and wiped some sweat off the side of his neck before continuing. "The LIA is a strange place. You wouldn't believe how much loose talk floats through those offices. We deal in secrets, but most of those jokers couldn't keep their mouths shut to save their own mothers. I'm the new guy at this branch. I've only been there for, what—a month? But I've already learned just about every personal detail about everyone there, just by listening to the gossip."

Ralph's cigar had gone out, and he took the time to relight it. He shook the match until it was out and tossed it into the gutter. After he'd breathed out a plume of smoke, he continued speaking. "Deet is the subject of a lot of these stories. I've been working closely with Deet. Too close." He shook his head. "Anyway, the scuttlebutt was that Deet was interested in something that was being produced at Leaflock Services. Most of the rumors said that the company had developed some kind of superweapon of mass destruction, and Deet was obsessed with it. Some say Deet wanted to grab it. Others say Deet was trying to prevent the thing from being produced. Others say that the Dragon Lord himself assigned Deet to keep the whole thing secret. I knew Deet had an agent planted in the company." Ralph glanced up at me. "I didn't know the agency had contracted with Leaflock to build this thing. That was one of their better-kept secrets. So I got curious and put an agent of my own in there to monitor developments."

"Your spy was spying on Deet's spy?" I shook my head.

Ralph blew smoke at me. "That's how we do it in the agency. Just another day at the factory." He pulled the stogie out of his mouth and dumped some ash on the street. "Anyway, a couple of weeks ago, my agent told me that some new data-entry clerk was asking a lot of questions about the other employees, especially the muckety-mucks in the executive wing. She thought this guy might be another Leea agent and asked me what was going on. She figured either Deet had sent him, or I had put someone else in the company to check on her. Spying on the spy who was spying..., well, you get the picture. I asked her to describe this lug, and she says that he's a tall dark palooka with an iron bod, menacing eyes, and a rough-looking mug that only a mother could love, so I knew it was you. That got me real curious, because you were supposed to be out there looking for a guy with a missing heart. So I sent another agent in. Or not so much in, but nearby. The dwarf with the missing leg? That's Winston. He's one of our best operatives."

"He's a condescending little asshole. Does a good impression of crazy and pathetic, though. I was ready to take him home with me and give him a bowl of hot soup."

"Yeah, but you went to a bar and got plastered, instead."

Ralph waited for me to respond, but I had nothing to say to that, so he continued. "My agent in the building tells me the company is developing some sort of device for regenerating cells. It's supposed to turn the medical industry upside down. She figures if Deet is interested in Leaflock Services, it has to be because of this device. She says the key ingredient of this device is something called RAA, but she doesn't know what it is. All she knows is that it has some kind of magical component to it. She asks around, and she hears something that doesn't make sense to her. A couple of engineers were talking about this RAA shit, and one of them said that Leaflock was losing his mind. According to my agent, the engineer said, 'Why does this genius think he needs to draw energy from a fucking black hole in order to regenerate a few cells? We aren't talking microbiology here, not with that much energy. We're talking large scale. What's he trying to do, cure paralysis or raise the dead?'"

"That's supposed to mean something?"

"It piqued my interest."

I shrugged. "Okay."

"There's more. A couple of hotshot scientists from back east died a couple of months ago. A Dr. Longwalker and a Dr. Gerta. Know anything about them?"

I shook my head. "I don't think so. Should I?"

"Probably not. Not many people do. They're well known in their field, though. They were specialists in cytology, the study of cells. Gerta won some kind of big award a few years ago. Anyway, a rumor is floating around that they didn't die, but were brought in secret by the LIA to the Dragon Lord's compound to work on some kind of classified project they've got going there."

"Where'd this rumor get started? The internet?"

Ralph scowled at me. "Put it all together, meathead. First, Deet, who, you might recall, is a high official in the Lord's Investigation Agency, has a massive hard-on for a cell-regeneration doohickey with a magical something-or-another in it. Second, my agent tells me that the doohickey in question requires vast amounts of energy, which it converts into enormous amounts of living biological tissue. We aren't talking about regenerating a few cells. We're talking about something on a much larger scale. Third, the Dragon Lord emerges from his lair for a rare unscheduled flyover that couldn't have been for any purpose except a show of strength. Why now? Fourth, a couple of supposedly dead scientists who specialize in the study of cells are rumored to be working on a project in the Dragon Lord's headquarters. Fifth, according to you, Night Owl, one of the most powerful spirits wandering this part of the earth, wants to buy up the blueprints and the formula so that he can build the device. Why? To save someone's life, he says to you, but he won't tell you whose life he wants to save. Why not? Why keep something like that secret from the likes of you?"

I felt my heart start to race. "He won't tell me because it's somebody big. Bigger than he is. So big that if he reveals the name, it would shock the world. Create disruption and chaos." I shot a glance at Ralph. "Does Night Owl like disruption and chaos?"

"Night Owl likes luxury, eating, drinking, partying till dawn. He's a status quo kind of spirit."

"He wouldn't want his lifestyle disturbed."

Ralph nodded slowly. "I know it sounds crazy, but it all adds up to one thing. I think Lord Ketz-Alkwat is dying. Night Owl knows about it. He wants to fix it before anyone finds out about it." He looked up and met my eyes, a grim expression on his face. "And now you know about it."

I shrugged. "I'm still not sure I believe it."

Ralph kept his eyes locked with mine. "It doesn't matter what you believe. If I'm right, and I think I am, then you really *do* know too much. And if Deet finds out that you know, there's nothing I can do to save you." He shrugged. "But it's not my responsibility, right? You have to live with the consequences of your own decisions."

I considered Ralph's points and listened to my heart pound. "Okay, it sounds crazy, and I'm not saying I buy it, but I'll admit it's plausible." I tried to let it all sink in. "So what are we supposed to do about it?"

"We stick to my plan. You get the flash drive from Crawford and give it to me for safekeeping. We don't let Deet or Night Owl get their hands on it until I hear from the elf." Ralph sucked on the stub of his stogie, but it had gone out, and, rather than relight it again, he tossed it into the street. "Look, this is all too big for me. I'm not really a 'big-picture' kind of guy, and I don't think you are, either. We need the elf for this. We both owe him. I'll put the flash drive out of reach until the elf tells us what he wants us to do about it. Let's let him decide. Fair?"

I let Ralph believe that I was considering his advice before letting out a breath of surrender. "Fine. But we do it my way."

Ralph held up both hands. "Sure, sure. Whatever you say."

"Crawford walks away from this clean. I'll get the flash drive from him and turn it over to you. You help me protect him from Deet. Bring whatever bogus non-disclosure form you want if it makes you feel happy. We'll both sign it. But you and I both know it won't mean shit. You help me keep Crawford safe, you hear me?"

"Sure, sure. I'm on your side, Southerland. We're partners, remember? I've got nothing against your friend. I meant it when I said that the agency would be making a big mistake by eliminating you and Crawford. It would be too noisy."

I nodded. "Okay. I'll set things up and give you a call when I know when and where."

"Absolutely. No problem. I'll keep an eye on Deet and wait for your call."

I put a smile on my face. "All right, let's get this done." I waited a beat for effect before adding, "Partner."

I saw Ralph's face light up as I turned to leave. Good, I thought at him. Just keep thinking those happy thoughts.

***

"We got new autopsy results on Redhorn," Detective Kalama told me.

"Murder?"

"Affirmative. But a strange one."

"Can I get back to you? I'm in a cab on my way back to the office, and the hackie is doing his level best to kill us both."

"Sure, gumshoe. It's Sunday. I've got nothing to do but hang around the stationhouse waiting for it to be convenient for you to talk to me."

"Why aren't you home? Hang on.... The cabbie just made creative use of the sidewalk to pass a car on the right. I'm almost positive the pedestrians all got out of his way on time. Don't you ever take a day off?"

"Crime never takes a day off, so why should I?"

"Right. Because you're the only cop on the beat. Refresh my memory: the red light means stop, right?"

"There's a few of us here today, but the bad guys always seem to outnumber us. Even on Sundays."

"How did you get a new autopsy? I thought that Leea was on its way to scoop up the body."

"I convinced the coroner to dive back in and grab some fresh samples before we lost the body. I specified that I suspected poison, probably something exotic. He was happy to do it for me."

"You and he must be tight."

"Tight enough. Let's just say money talks."

"Cost you much?"

"I figured you'd chip in half."

"Why would you figure that?"

"You want the results, or not?"

"That's just evil. I'm going to file a complaint with the police commissioner."

"So you're in?"

I let out a sigh. "Fine. As long as I survive this cab ride. I'll call you back in ten minutes. Tops. If you don't hear from me, check the morgue."

"Whatever you say, boss. I'm just a little ol' public servant."

I disconnected the call.

Twelve minutes later, I punched Kalama's number into my cell phone. I'd made it home alive in eight, but I needed the extra four to pour myself a glass of rye to settle my nerves.

258

Kalama answered after a single ring. "Redhorn was poisoned."

"Poisoned? How?"

"That's the interesting part. He was killed by a tropical toad."

I pulled the phone away from my ear and stared at it for a moment before returning it to my ear. "I think I have a bad connection. Did you say a tropical toad?"

"A rare one, according to the coroner. It's native to the Marajoara River Valley in Qusco. It excretes a toxin that the native pre-Dragon Lord headhunters used to poison the tips of the darts they used in their blowguns. Just touching it can kill you, although it's usually administered either by putting a drop in the victim's drink or by spraying it in the victim's face. It takes hours to kill you if you drink it, but it will stop your heart in a matter of minutes if you inhale it. And it doesn't take much. Nasty stuff, and almost impossible to detect unless you're looking for it. It's got a long technical name, but in elite criminal circles it's known as Frogger."

"Cute."

"Isn't it though?"

I started to take a sip from my drink, stopped myself, and decided to set it down, instead. "How did your coroner know to look for it?"

"Well, that's where it gets interesting." Kalama paused for effect before continuing. "Seems that Frogger is popular among LIA assassins. Allegedly."

"No kidding."

"Yep. Just a little bit of trivia I picked up over the years here in homicide. I gave the coroner a short list of toxins alleged to be associated with alleged murders allegedly committed by alleged LIA killers, and we found a winner."

"Allegedly."

"Right. Because officially, this one will go down as natural causes."

"Frogger?"

"From extremely deadly froggies."

"So how did Redhorn happen to run into this froggy shit?"

"Good question. It has been made very clear to me that there is nothing here to investigate, and that I've already got a full plate of other cases on my desk, and that I'm to forget Mr. Inyon Redhorn ever walked the shining streets of our fair city."

"Mr. Who?"

"Exactly. Have a nice day, citizen. I'm off to protect and serve. Just as soon as I've finished filling out this ever-growing mountain of paperwork on my desk."

***

It took me another few minutes to get the nerve to tackle my glass of rye, but eventually I gathered up my courage and finished it off in one gulp. No one could ever accuse me of being too much of a coward to finish a drink.

Frogger. Sure, I thought—why not? I looked it up on the internet and found a surprising amount of information on the poison. Most of it was technical, but my findings confirmed that the quickest and most efficient way of using the toxin to punch someone's ticket as quickly and efficiently as possible was to get the victim to inhale it. Is this what had happened to Redhorn?

I sat at my desk and considered what I remembered seeing in Redhorn's apartment the night I'd found the flash drive. He'd been getting ready to see Clearwater at The Gold Coast Club, one of the classiest night spots in Yerba City. He had come home from work, cleaned up, and started dressing when he'd collapsed on his bed and died. I remembered the state of his bathroom: damp washcloth in the shower, deodorant, hair tonic, shaving cream, toothpaste still lying out on the sink…. Had the toxin been in one of those items? I dismissed the idea. Whoever had poisoned Redhorn wouldn't have left any evidence of a murder at the scene. They'd been hoping that Redhorn's death would be written off as a heart attack. I thought about Redhorn's clothing draped over his chair. He'd put on his underwear and socks…. No, I remembered. Not both of his socks, just one. Could the other sock have contained the toxin? It seemed an unlikely place to put a toxin that worked best when it was inhaled.

I shook my head in frustration. This was hopeless. Maybe the killer broke into Redhorn's apartment and sprayed him with the toxin, maybe from a perfume bottle. Something from the coroner's original report came back to me then. The coroner had commented on how good the corpse smelled. "The best-smelling stiff in the morgue," the coroner had written.

I sat up straight in my chair, and then rubbed my knee where I had bumped it on my desk. Aftershave! The coroner's report had said that Redhorn had put on aftershave. Had I seen a bottle of aftershave on Redhorn's sink? I called up a mental image, and the memory of Redhorn's bathroom came to me with crystal clarity, as if I were still there. I saw the items, the safety razor, the shaving cream, the comb, the hair tonic, the toothbrush and toothpaste... even nail clippers... but no aftershave! I was certain of it. Someone had put a few drops of Frogger in Redhorn's aftershave, waited until Redhorn was dead, and then come back and removed the bottle from the premises so that it couldn't be recovered and tested.

I was confident that I had discovered how Redhorn was murdered. And, the more I thought about it, the more certain I was that I knew who had done it. I juggled the pieces, tried them in a number of different combinations, and it all made sense.

And now that I knew, I realized just how much trouble I was in.

I picked up my phone and made some calls.

Chapter Twenty-Two

I spent the rest of the day cleaning my office. It was going to be a tough job, and it would take more than a few hours, or even a few days, to finish up. The blood-soaked hardwood floor was destroyed beyond repair. As a tenant, I was going to have to explain the situation to my landlady, Mrs. Colby, and I wasn't looking forward to it. This wouldn't be the first time I'd been responsible for major damage to the building, and I hoped her tolerance for my rough treatment of her property wasn't running thin. As for my new rug, I was forced to conclude that it was a lost cause. It had been in my possession for less than a week, but I had as much hope of restoring it as I did of kicking Night Owl's ass in a fair fight, which was something I hoped I wouldn't have to try to do when we met that night.

Because I had lied to Ralph. I wasn't going to hand the flash drive over to my "partner" later that night. It wasn't that I didn't think the nirumbee could keep it safe. I had no doubt he could. He controlled earth elementals, which meant he could summon one to take the drive to a place far under the earth. He'd never told me so, but my guess was he'd buried the heartstone he'd brought with him from Lakota in this fashion. I had my own ideas about what to do with the flash drive, however, and they didn't involve turning control of the drive over to an agent of the LIA, even if that agent and I were supposed to be operating on the same team.

As I cleaned, I went over the details of the plan I had formed the night before with Crawford's help. It was, I had to admit, an awful plan. A terrible plan, in fact. One with a lot of moving parts and a lot of unknowns. Without trying, I could think of a dozen components of the plan that could—and probably would—go horribly wrong. I'd been reluctant to include Crawford in the plan, but he was eager to play a part in it. In point of fact, the plan wouldn't work without him, and he'd reminded me once again that he was *choosing* to involve himself, and that I wasn't responsible for his choices. So I gave in.

But that didn't keep me from worrying, nor would it prevent me from feeling guilty if my friend got hurt—or worse!

Guilt. Despite my best efforts, I was overcome with it. So many things had been set in motion because I'd felt guilty about exposing

Redhorn as the man selling off his company's secrets. Crawford was right, of course. I hadn't been responsible for Redhorn's poor choices. All I'd done by exposing him was the job I'd been hired to do. But Redhorn was dead, and it was my investigation that had been, if not the direct cause, then the catalyst for his murder. True, he was the victim of his own decisions, but he'd seemed to me like a decent enough joe, for a white-collar criminal, whose biggest crime had been overreacting to his erstwhile protégé's unjustified lack of respect.

Guilt. I mean, sure, Crawford had opened my eyes to how self-centered it was to believe I was the straw that stirred the world I moved through, or that I left such a sizable wake as all that. But I wasn't going to be able to cast the burden of guilt off my back just because I understood how irrational and self-destructive it was for me to carry it around. Guilt was a part of who I was, and I wasn't going to let it go anytime soon. Hell, I was feeling guilty about having to end the short career of an innocent rug that had, through no fault of its own, fallen into the wrong hands. I imagined its hope and optimism at finding a nice new owner and a nice new room to perform its function in, only to see that hope drowned in blood just a few days later. Now it was mortally wounded and headed for a dumpster. Poor thing. And it was all my fault.

Right. Enough of that.

On the plus side, I found that I was regaining more and more function in my left arm. It wasn't close to a hundred percent, maybe half that, but I hoped that I wouldn't need it to be in better condition than that when I met with Crawford and Ralph that night. Ralph was going to be a problem. I wasn't planning on a fistfight with him, and I had no illusions about what the outcome of a violent confrontation with the nirumbee warrior would be, even with two good arms.

On the other hand, I wanted to be prepared for anything. I made a point of taking some time to clean my thirty-eight and make sure it was fully loaded and ready for action.

Because I was a firm believer in heading into a confrontation with a full stomach, I also took the time to prepare a hearty and healthy meal. Earlier that day I'd taken a half pound of ground beef from my freezer and left it out on my kitchen counter. When it was mostly thawed, I slapped it into a hot frying pan and mashed it flat with a spatula. Streaks of burning grease leaped out of the pan like fireworks, leaving a pleasant stinging sensation on my wrist and the back of my hand. After the beef patty had sizzled for a couple of minutes, I flipped it over and doused it with garlic salt. When the outside was good and charred, I threw a slice of yellow cheese on top and let it melt down the sides of the patty into the frying pan.

I was surprised to see Syphon fly into the kitchen from downstairs. Before the elemental could say anything, Chivo barged into my kitchen and sniffed the smoke-filled air. He wrinkled his nose and glared at me, and I felt a wave of dizziness come and go. "Don't look at me like that, you mangy alley rat!" I told him. "I like my meat to be scorched. If you don't like it, find somewhere else to bunk." He sniffed one more time in disgust and slunk back down the stairs, followed by Syphon. Some advance warning system the elemental had turned out to be.

When the burger was done, I scooped it out of the pan and placed it on a slice of sourdough bread that I'd covered in mustard and ketchup, and garnished with a lettuce leaf, a slice of tomato, two pickles that I'd sliced in half lengthwise, and a thick slice of onion. I covered the pile of goodness with another slice of sourdough bread and bit into it. The core of the ground beef might have been slightly frozen, but it was still a meal meant for a lord. To think that people paid a fortune for lesser meals in restaurants! I wiped the juice off my mouth with the back of my sleeve and washed it all down with a bottle of cold beer. All in all, the burger might not have been better than sex, but it was damned close.

When I was done eating, I brushed my teeth, shaved, and took a shower. I even shined my Albions and buffed them to a polished black sheen. I dusted off my best trench coat and put it on, adjusting my shoulder holster so that only a seasoned pro would have been able to detect it under the coat. Finally, I gave the brim of my fedora a good fold and placed it on my head in front of my bathroom mirror, making sure that the front of the hat rested squarely above the midpoint between my eyes. This was going to be a big night, and if it all went belly-up I wanted to be the best-dressed stiff on the battlefield. If I was going to fall, I wanted everyone to know that I had lived my life, such as it was, with pride.

Not that I planned to fall, though. Hell, I'd run like a scalded dog before that happened. Still, the best-laid plans and all that.

Cleaned, dressed, and self-impressed, I sat behind the desk in my office and pulled a bottle of rye out of my desk drawer. The late August afternoon was fading away, and I watched the light coming through the blinds get dimmer and dimmer. When the light faded into darkness, I'd start walking up the hill to retrieve the beastmobile.

As I waited for the night to fall, I sipped from my bottle and let random thoughts about anything except my deeply flawed plan drift through my head. I thought about the latest movies, which I hadn't seen, the latest books, which I hadn't read, and the latest songs, which I couldn't have named if you put a gun to my head. I thought about the mayoral race that dominated the front pages of the papers and kicked off every television news broadcast, but which I'd lost interest in after the incumbent mayor had been officially declared dead. A new night club was going to open downtown, and a lot of people were talking about it. I planned to go there as soon as I could. It probably wouldn't be the kind of place you went to unaccompanied, though, and I preferred to do my drinking alone. My thoughts drifted to my favorite watering hole, The Black Minotaur. It was a popular joint, packed almost every night of the week with a diverse bunch of regular folks. I liked it because it was a place I could be comfortable, whether I was bellied up to the bar enjoying the company of the other patrons staring into their drinks and minding their own business, or huddled into the corner of a semi-private booth observing the people and listening to the shouts and laughter of the noisy crowd.

When the light had faded to a yellow glow, I summoned Smokey, because I felt like having a chat. Soon, the two-inch funnel of swirling gray smoke zipped into the room from somewhere and hovered above my desk.

"Greetingssss, Alekssss. Howzzz trickzzzzz?"

"Hi Smokey. How's the action at the Minotaur tonight?"

"Smokey likes the Minotaur. Smokey likes the smoke."

I smiled. "Guess what, Smokey. I missed poker night again this week. I spent the evening having my arm pulled from its socket by a giant insect."

Smokey continued whirling, but didn't respond.

"I hope Gio forgives me. He's the world's worst card player." I chuckled. "He only breaks even when I'm there to fold winning hands and push the pot his way."

Smokey continued its silent whirling. I knew that the elemental, old as the wind itself, was entirely comfortable doing nothing but spinning.

"None of those mugs know that my awareness gives me the ability to read their faces like the pages from a newspaper. I know all of their tells and quirks. I know which ones will bluff with a jack high—that's Gio—and which ones will give up on a pair of kings if you put a little pressure on them."

I took a sip from my bottle. I didn't want to muss my sleeve, so I tore a sheet of paper from a notepad and used it to dry the corners of my mouth. "Thing is, Smokey, I don't need or want to take their money. I just control the play and try to make sure that no one goes home unhappy."

I looked into the elemental as if I could see a heart beating somewhere inside the whirling funnel of air. "See, Smokey, I'm kind of a loner. That's jake with me. I like it that way. But sometimes I need a little company. That's why I took up Gio's offer to join his Thursday night poker games. I go as often as I feel like it, but sometimes duty calls... or my home gets invaded by a homicidal troll, or a shapeshifter... and then I have to miss a game." I chuckled again. "And then Gio takes a bath. He doesn't mind all that much. Like me, he's mostly there for the comradery." I sighed and sat back in my chair. "Still can't help feeling a little guilty about it, though." I looked back at the patiently whirling elemental. "I know, I know. Crawford tells me the same thing. Other people's choices aren't my responsibility, and I need to stop trying to control their lives. Well, that's just something I'll have to work on during my 'me' time. Right, buddy?"

Smokey stretched itself until it was a spinning straw and leaped onto my shoulder. "Smokey is ready to serve. Smokey likesss serving Alekssss."

I smiled. "Thanks, pal. Good talkin' to you. I hope we can get together again soon. If not, well.... But I'm sure it'll all work out. I've got a plan, see. It's gonna be swell."

The last of the light faded from my window. I sent Smokey back to bask in the haze trapped in the rafters of the Minotaur. I threw back one last swallow of rye, pulled down the brim of my fedora, and walked out the front door.

***

I watched a full moon fight to show itself through low-hanging clouds as I leaned against the beastmobile, now fully restored to greatness by the inestimable Giovanni and Son. The assiduous duo of Gio and Antonio had not only devoted the entire afternoon to smoothing out the dings and wrinkles in the body of the vehicle, but they had waxed and polished it so that it emitted a soft plum-colored glow in the moonlight. Sitting between the front of the stairs leading up to Crawford's apartment and his detached garage, the stately automobile plugged the alleyway like a gleaming steel cork. I gave the moon one last admiring glance as I ran my thumb over the edge of the key fob resting in the palm of my hand.

The night was as peaceful as a night in Placid Point can be. A gust of cold wind blew a greasy food wrapper into the alley, where it plastered itself against the door of Crawford's garage. Tires screeched and horns honked as cars maneuvered their way through traffic on the main drag in front of The Nautilus Jewelry and Novelty Shop. A siren wailed in the near distance, five or six blocks away and waning. Farther off, a small explosion echoed through the air. It may have been a car backfiring, but more likely it was the sound of a robbery going sour.

The sound of suppressed breathing, detectable by me only because of my enhanced senses, vibrated the air from just off the alley entrance.

"Might as well come on over, Ralph. We're just about ready for you."

The squat figure of the nirumbee warrior stepped around the corner and into the alley. "You never called me, Southerland. You were supposed to call me and tell me where to go to pick up the flash drive."

"I was going to, but I spotted you tailing me while I was driving here. You're pretty good, pal, but that white van of yours sticks out like a sore thumb."

"You should talk. I don't even have to keep that tank you drive in view. I can hear it rumbling along from a mile away."

"What are you talking about? The engine in my beastmobile purrs like a kitten."

"Yeah. A monster kitten from Hell." Ralph's eyes scanned the alleyway, from one side to the other. "You got the flash drive on you?"

"It's nearby. Crawford's got it. He'll bring it to me when I'm ready for it."

The nirumbee studied the cracks in the wooden baseboard of the garage and the slim openings beneath the back wall of the jewelry store. "What do you mean, 'when you're ready'? Let's get this over with and get on with our lives. Where's your pal?" He continued searching for rat-sized openings in the walls on either side of the alley.

"What's the rush?" I asked. "Don't you want to wait for the other member of your party?"

Ralph stopped scanning the alleyway. "What are you talking about?"

"Come on, Ralph. Give me some credit. I don't see any non-disclosure forms on you. As soon as I give you the drive, Deet is going to swoop in and mop the floor with Crawford and me. That's the plan, or the essentials of the plan, right? Tell me, are you going to help Deet eliminate us, or were you planning on hitching a ride with an earth elemental and leaving all the dirty work to your boss." I felt my jaws clenching and my lips stretching into a tight grin.

Ralph looked like he wanted to object, but then he shrugged. Glancing over the roof of Crawford's apartment, he called out, "Come on down, Deet. He's on to us." Ralph turned back in my direction. "Anyone ever tell you that you were too smart for your own good?"

I felt a disturbance in the air and looked up in the direction that Ralph had called. A human-sized figure soared over the rooftop, gliding on silent wings that looked like the broad dried leaves of some sort of exotic tropical flower. The mantis that was Deet's alter ego—or perhaps Deet's primary self—parasailed to a stop next to Ralph, one eye opened wide, the other a blind and mangled hole in the insect's head.

Mantis-Deet's metallic insect voice sliced through the stillness of the night. "We're done with the games now, Mr. Southerland. Give us the flash drive, and you and Crawford will live. Refuse, and I'll kill you both."

"You'll never find the flash drive if we're dead, Deet." I pointed out.

"I no longer care. It's true that knowledge of Reifying Agent Alpha will die with the two of you, but Mr. Leaflock has commissioned another design engineer to develop Reifying Agent Beta. I understand that she has a brilliant and creative mind, and that she is already well on the way to creating something suitable. The original formula would speed things along, but if it is lost to us, the delay in the completion of our project shouldn't be prohibitive."

"Let me get this straight. If I give you the flash drive, you'll let Crawford and me live?"

"That's correct, Mr. Southerland."

"Pardon my skepticism, but why would you do that?"

The mantis thing glanced at Ralph. "Agent Ralph is right. Further killings in the wake of the so-called Children's Home Massacre would result in an overabundance of negative attention at a time when the LIA desires an absence of excess social tensions."

I shook my head. "That sounds like a lot of hooey to me. What's the name of this brilliant new engineer that Leaflock has suddenly stumbled on?"

"That is none of your concern."

"Right." I glanced at Ralph, who hadn't moved since Deet's arrival. "You lied to me, Ralph. You said that you were going to keep the drive away from Deet. You were going to take it to a safe place. You were going to... how did you put it? Make it disappear from the face of the earth. That's okay, though, because I didn't believe you. I knew that you were going to hand the drive to your boss all along. A loyal soldier of the LIA, isn't that what you told me? Tell, me, Ralph. Does Deet know about... the you know who?"

That got Ralph's attention. "Can it, Southerland! Not another word!" Deet's insect head jerked toward Ralph, the uninjured eye open wide.

"Or what? What are you going to do, Ralph? You going to kick my ass?"

"You've got a big mouth, Southerland." With that, the nirumbee sprung in my direction.

I punched a button on my key fob, and the trunk of the beastmobile flew open. Chivo leaped out of the trunk and landed on all fours, head lowered beneath his thick curved horns. The goat-creature launched himself at Ralph and, catching the charging nirumbee by surprise, butted him flush in the chest with a head full of horns. The nirumbee flew through the air and crashed into the side of the garage, falling to the alley floor in a heap.

"Now, Crawford!" I shouted.

Mantis-Deet took a step toward me, then stopped as I drew my heater out of my holster and aimed it at the insect's good eye. In the second it took for Deet to start moving again, and for Ralph to spring to his feet, Detective Kalama and three officers came running into the alley, weapons drawn.

"Don't move!" Kalama shouted. "Agent Deet, you're under arrest for the murder of Inyon Redhorn. Surrender peacefully or we'll open fire."

Mantis-Deet whirled to face the cops, poised to launch an attack. Ralph hesitated, assessing the situation, then moved to join his boss.

"Ralph!" I shouted. Ralph turned toward me—and found himself face to face with the Huay Chivo. As Chivo caught Ralph's wide-open peepers with his own fiery red ones, Ralph staggered and fell to one knee. He opened his mouth and let out a strangled cough. Chivo advanced on him, mouth open wide to expose a double row of pointed teeth.

"No, Chivo!" I yelled. "No biting!"

Chivo wasn't that well trained, unfortunately. He sprang at Ralph, who threw up a protective forearm. Chivo clamped down on it and Ralph let out an ear-piercing bellow.

In the meantime, Mantis-Deet had decided to take on Yerba City's finest. Three shots rang out as the mantis leaped forward and came down hard on Kalama, pinning her to the asphalt. Without thinking twice, I charged forward to help the detective, only to be knocked sprawling to the alley floor by a sweep of the giant insect's wing. When I lifted my head out of the cracked asphalt, I saw that two of Kalama's bulls were also on the ground, though I hadn't seen what put them there. The third officer had managed to wrap an arm around the insect's head, but released his grip after the mantis locked its mandibles on his wrist and clamped down hard. The officer screamed in pain and terror as the mantis shook its head back and forth, yanked, and came away with the officer's bloody severed hand in its jaws. Kalama tried to take advantage of the distraction by rolling out from under the mantis, but found herself pinned down by a spiked foreleg.

I raised my thirty-eight and fired into the back of the mantis's thorax. The monstrous insect twisted its head to face me and let out a metallic shriek that sounded like a sheet of tin being ripped in two. I sensed the wing sweeping in my direction but was too slow to avoid it. Stars exploded behind my eyes as the back of my head bounced off the edge of the beastmobile's open trunk. Pain shot through my damaged left arm, and a tortured cry tore through my clenched throat as the reknit fractures in my broken nose ripped apart again. I lifted my one good arm to throw more lead at the mantis, only to discover that the heater had fallen from my nerveless fingers.

I caught sight of Chivo and Ralph rolling over the asphalt as they made savage animal noises. Chivo's teeth were still locked on

Ralph's forearm just above the wrist, and the nirumbee's own teeth were clamped down on Chivo's upper arm.

I turned my attention back to Kalama, who was doing her best to hold off the attack of the mantis. It was clear to me that her best wasn't going to be enough. None of the three bulls she'd brought with her were in any shape to continue the fight, and, tough as she was, Kalama wasn't going to be able to handle the monster Deet had become on her own.

Needless to say, none of this was going according to plan.

I struggled to regain my feet. It was time to bring in the reserves. I reached out for Badass.

In a moment, a twelve-foot funnel of fury descended from the night sky. The air around the elemental began to swirl, and everyone in the alley found themselves in the midst of a maelstrom of blinding dust and flying debris. Holding up one arm to shield my eyes, I raised the other and pointed at the mantis. "Attack!" With a roar, Badass launched itself toward the deadly shapeshifter.

The Deet mantis found itself torn from Kalama and slammed into a wall. Kalama groaned and raised herself to one knee. I fought my way to her through the fierce winds and reached down to help her to her feet. I was feeling good! I was feeling like a damned master strategist directing my forces to a stunning victory. I felt like I had turned the tide. Victory was in sight.

I should have known better. I was up against Deet, and Deet was LIA. Deet knew that I was an elementalist, and Deet had come to the battle prepared to deal with any contingency.

All my good feelings vanished as a funnel three times the size of Badass dropped from the sky, enveloped my elemental, and lifted it high above the alley. The severe winds in its wake ripped me away from Kalama, and, when they subsided, I found myself hugging the alley floor. I rose to my hands and knees and coughed up a wad of dirt-filled phlegm. Shit, I thought to myself. Why is it that the other guys always have a bigger gun?

The two elementals were nowhere in sight, and in the sudden calm I jerked my head toward the mantis, my jaw hanging open in stunned surprise. So much for my vaunted poker face and the professional self-composure I took such pains to maintain in stressful situations. The mantis looked up over its shoulder. I followed its gaze and spotted Winston standing on the roof of Crawford's apartment. Balancing on one leg, the dwarf raised his walking stick and traced a symbol in the air. I recognized the symbol. It was a cute salute air elementalists used to greet each other, as if they were members of some kind of dumbass secret society. I gave him a salute in return, although mine was more universal and available to anyone with a middle finger on at least one hand.

A yelp from Kalama drew my attention away from Winston. The mantis once again had the detective pinned to the alley floor, and black drool dripped from its mandibles to splash on her face. I no longer felt like a high and mighty master strategist. With Badass occupied somewhere in its own battle against a more powerful opponent, it was time to throw highfalutin battlefield strategies out the window and try something more suited to the kind of back-alley brawl I was accustomed to. I let out a roar, hoping to distract the Deet monster, scrambled to my feet, and charged.

I'd only taken two steps when the ground around Deet seemed to ripple. The mantis's head jerked back away from Kalama as more than a hundred rats swarmed over the creature's legs and hindquarters. Hundreds of sharp claws and teeth sought openings in the mantis's layers of spiked carapace. Thick streams of black blood began to spill from the insect's joints and underbelly.

Rats flew from the creature, brushed aside by legs and wings, and Kalama attempted to crawl from beneath the creature. I staggered over to her, nearly collapsing when a leg gave way. My left arm hung from my shoulder like a slab of meat, my numb hand flopping uselessly from its end. I grabbed Kalama by the back of her coat with my good hand and began pulling her away from the flailing mantis.

As I helped Kalama to her feet, we watched as Crawford's rats swarmed over the giant insect, slashing and biting with rabid ferocity. The mantis lurched to its feet and shook rats off in all directions, only to see the rats regroup and leap at its hind legs.

Kalama raised a heater that she had somehow managed not to lose during Mantis-Deet's attack, but couldn't find a clear target as the mantis jerked itself in a spasm of chaotic twists and turns trying to throw off the maddened rodents. Suddenly, Chivo rushed past us and launched himself at the base of the insect's neck. In an instant, the goat-creature's head was covered in black blood that rolled thick as tar down his shoulders and back.

I turned to see what had become of Ralph and saw him leaning against the side of the garage, gasping for breath and holding a bloody arm. Kalama turned, too, and trained her heater on the nirumbee.

"Don't move!" she shouted. Blood had soaked through one side of her shirt, but her eyes were clear, and her aim was steady.

Ralph held up his good arm. "Don't worry, detective. I know when to pull out of a fight."

"Keep him covered," I told Kalama. "I don't trust the son of a bitch."

She nodded. "What's happening with the big bug?"

I glanced over at the mantis, the rats, and the goat-creature, and then turned back to Kalama. "I think you can put away your arrest warrant. There's nothing left of Deet but leftovers."

Chapter Twenty-Three

"Tell me again why I shouldn't report that pet of yours to Animal Control." Kalama had come out of her encounter with the giant mantis with some scrapes and bumps, along with a now-bandaged cut along her ribs that was going to leave a nasty scar. An ambulance had come, and, after gathering up the detective's support crew, raced out of the alley, siren blaring.

"What pet? I don't have any pets." I closed the trunk of the beastmobile, hiding Chivo from view.

"That beast killed an LIA agent! Three of my men are witnesses!"

I stretched my left arm, trying to work some of the numbness out. "I don't know, detective. I think that Deet might have already been dead when Chivo got there."

"Your monster tore that thing's throat out!" She nodded toward the remains of the mantis, which was being examined by an LIA forensics team.

"First, he's not my monster. I don't own him. He just sleeps in my laundry room. And I leave him food so that he doesn't raid my refrigerator. Which, if you think about it, is probably a good thing for the neighborhood dogs and cats, so I'm kind of doing a community service. And second, is biting the throat of something that's already dead a crime?"

"I think it probably is!"

I shook my head. "Do you really want to get in the middle of a legal battle over something so trivial? I mean, think of the paperwork."

Kalama glared at me for another few moments, but then her lips spread into a small grin. "Fuck you, Southerland. You just make sure you keep that thing under control."

Ralph, who had been treating his injured arm by pouring whiskey from his flask over the wound and tying if off with a handkerchief I'd given him, gave Kalama a sharp look. "Hey! What if I want to press charges? That thing nearly tore my arm off. Dangerous animals like that shouldn't be running around loose."

"He's not running around loose," I pointed out. "He's locked up in my trunk."

Kalama glared down at the nirumbee. "You thinking of pressing charges? You can file them after I've questioned you about your attack on four police officers."

"I didn't attack any officers," Ralph protested.

"You were going to," I pointed out. "Until you got distracted."

Kalama pulled a set of handcuffs off her belt. "It's a tough call. Maybe we should settle this downtown."

Ralph backed away, "Whoa, hang on a minute. This is an LIA matter now. You don't have any jurisdiction here."

"YCPD officers were attacked. That makes it a YCPD case." Kalama held up the cuffs and advanced on Ralph.

I stepped between the detective and the nirumbee. "Why don't you leave Ralph with me, detective. Technically, he's right. He *might* have been getting ready to join his boss in an attack on our city's finest, but he never actually did."

Kalama caught my eyes. "You sure about this?"

I gestured toward the remains of the giant insect, which were now being scooped into several body bags by the LIA team. "You got Redhorn's murderer. And now that Leea has taken charge, there won't even be a trial. Why complicate things?"

The detective nodded. "I'm buried in open cases at the moment. It would be nice if I could wrap this one up with as little fuss as possible." She gave me a pointed stare. "But if this comes back and bites me in the ass, you're not gonna be invited to our next barbecue."

"Deal. Your men will be on board?"

"They're fine. Well, except for Littlefeather. The paramedic said that he would live, but there isn't much future in the department for a cop who's lost his gun-hand. Good thing he's got insurance. But the boys will go along with whatever I tell them. They don't like extra paperwork any more than I do."

"All right. In that case I guess it's all copacetic. Thanks for your help out here."

Kalama turned to go, but then stopped. "You going to be okay?" She cast a quick glance at Ralph.

"I'm good. I've got something I need to do."

Kalama raised an eyebrow. "And you don't want any cops around when you do it?"

"Something like that."

"Uh-huh. Okay, gumshoe. See you in the funny papers. Oh, and watch out for the rats around here. They're vicious."

"I think I'll be all right. I doubt that they're all that hungry anymore."

Kalama grunted, watched the LIA team load the body bags onto a wheeled stretcher, and followed them out of the alley.

When the detective was gone, Ralph sighed. "I thought she'd never leave. All right—where's that flash drive? Hand it over and let's get out of here."

"Yeah, about that...." I called up a sigil in my mind and sent out a mental command.

"Southerland...." Ralph's voice broke into a low growl.

"See, here's the thing. You haven't been straight with me, Ralph. I don't like that. According to you, we're supposed to be partners, and partners are supposed to be honest with each other. But you intended to sell me out to Deet from the beginning."

"I've been protecting you from Deet, you dumb fuck!" Ralph pounded a fist into the palm of his hand. "You have no idea what it's been like for me. Deet was my boss, but I work for the elf. I'm a fuckin' double agent! I have to walk a fuckin' tightrope all the time. Deet wanted that flash drive, and it was my job to recover it. So, yeah, I was going to give it to Deet. Because there was no reason not to. What were *you* going to do with it? You put yourself in a position where you had to hang on to it in order to keep from getting killed. I was trying to fix that for you! Thanks to me, Deet was going to let you live. You and Crawford both."

"You'll have to excuse me if I find that a little hard to believe. Deet had no reason to keep us alive once we turned over the drive. You might have thought you had Deet convinced to do it your way, but you're not nearly as charming as you think you are."

"You think I'm stupid? I had a contingency plan, you knucklehead! I had an earth elemental ready to take you to safety if Deet backed out on our bargain. But you had to bring in the cops—and that monster of yours—and ruin everything. You should have left it to me! I had it covered!"

"Gee, that's swell. I had everything under control until that cyclone dropped out of the sky. You never told me that dwarf of yours was an elementalist."

"I didn't know! That was all Deet's doing. I told you that the LIA was full of secrets. Anyway, Winston skedaddled when Deet went down. I'll have some words for him back at the office tomorrow. How's your elemental?"

"None the worse for wear. Badass is plenty tough, but I appreciate your concern. You should have let me in on your plan."

Ralph glared up at me. "Yeah? You've got a plan of your own? Well, clue me in, son. How does it go from here?"

I looked past Ralph toward the end of the alley, where a darkness blacker than the night was beginning to form. "Funny you should ask. I think we're about to find out."

Ralph looked back over his shoulder, and both of us watched a squat figure in a top hat and tails step out of the darkness. Light from the moon gleamed off the monocle that covered one of the figure's eyes. In one hand, the figure carried a cane that he didn't use for walking. His other hand was extended, palm up, and whirling on top of his palm was a two-inch funnel of dirty air.

The funnel rose from Clearwater's hand and came to rest on my shoulder. "Smokey has brought the spirit-man to Aleksss."

"Good job, Smokey. Your timing is perfect."

"Greetings, Southerland!" Clearwater's voice was full of cheer. "What a fine night this is! And this must be Ralph. My, it's been many a year since I was in the presence of a nirumbee warrior. It's a pleasure to meet you, my boy. A genuine pleasure!"

***

Ralph whirled on me. "Th'fuck you doing, Southerland!"

I reached into my pocket and pulled out the flash drive.

Ralph's eyes widened. "Lord's balls! You can't be serious!"

I cast my eyes down on the nirumbee. "I'm dead serious, Ralph. I'm going to give the drive to Clearwater."

Ralph's fists clenched. "He killed those men at the children's home!"

"He's offering me a lot of dough."

Ralph's jaw dropped. "You're selling it to him?" Disbelief flooded his face.

"That's right, Ralph. I'm taking his deal."

The nirumbee warrior's mouth closed. His jaw clenched and his eyes narrowed. "Over my dead body."

Clearwater took a step forward, a cheerful smile on his face. "Oh, come now, Ralph. Don't take it so hard. It's business. Your friend is about to make a great deal of money."

Ralph's face reddened as he glared at me, and spittle dripped from his teeth. "He ain't no friend of mine."

The nirumbee coiled in preparation for an attack, but drew back suddenly when the space between us darkened.

Clearwater gestured at the darkness with his cane. "You won't want to step through that gate, my little friend. You won't like where it takes you."

The stout man turned to me, still smiling. "Let's have it then." He held out his hand.

I stepped toward Clearwater and handed him the flash drive. He held it up in the air and studied it. "So this is the device with the information I've been seeking. Hmm. Seems like such a small thing, and yet it's going to help me perform a miracle. But...." Clearwater frowned. "What's this? I feel a protective enchantment on the device. A ward of some sort."

"The drive is enchanted, but you can get past it with the passcode," I explained. I pulled a piece of paper out of my pocket. "When you're prompted, type this in exactly as it's written. You only get one shot at it, but if you're careful you won't have any problems."

"I see. Still, you understand that I will withhold payment until I'm sure that I can gain access to the desired contents."

I shrugged. "Of course. You know how to get in touch with me if you have any other questions."

Clearwater's smile broadened. "Excellent!" He tucked the drive and the passcode into his vest pocket. "In that case, I believe that we are finished here."

"Until later, then." I extended my hand.

Clearwater gave it a vigorous shake. "Until later. I must admit that I had my doubts about you, Mr. Southerland, but I'm pleased that we have brought our transaction to a satisfactory conclusion. It's been a pleasure doing business with you." The little man tipped his hat, turned, and departed the alley through the darkness from which he'd entered with a dignified strut. When he was out of sight, the darkness faded with him.

The dark space between Ralph and me vanished, also, and I turned to see the nirumbee staring up at me with a scowl. "What have you done?" he asked me. "Have you gone batty?"

"I've done what I should have done from the beginning."

"What about Thunderbird? Lord's balls! Night Owl is going to drain his energy! You know what that's going to be like for him? We might as well destroy his heart so he can die. It would be a mercy!"

"Oh, I wouldn't worry about Thunderbird. He'll be all right."

Ralph's eyes narrowed in confusion. "What? I don't.... What aren't you telling me?"

"A lot of things, Ralph. Let me walk you to your car." I moved past the nirumbee and headed for the street, knowing he'd follow. I glanced toward the bloodstained pavement where the mantis had met its end and spotted a rat sprawled motionless against the edge of the building. I glanced around the alleyway and saw no other sign of Crawford. The still form of the rat bothered me, but Crawford and I had made our plans, so I hardened my heart and shut the sight of it out of my mind for the time being.

Ralph caught up to me. "This better be good. Let me guess. That drive you just handed over to Night Owl is a phony."

"No, it's the real deal."

"Then... what? You just handed him the formula for the reifying agent?" Ralph shook his head. "I'm not buying that. What'd you do?"

"I gave Clearwater the information he wanted. All he has to do is access it. He'll plug the drive into a computer and type in the passcode I gave him."

"And?"

I shrugged. "And then, if everything goes as planned, he'll turn Thunderbird loose."

Ralph grabbed me by the arm. "Come on, Southerland. What's the gag?"

I stopped walking. "I did a little tinkering with the flash drive last night. When Clearwater enters the passcode I gave him, a virus will destroy all of the files on the drive. They'll be lost forever."

Ralph let go of my arm. "Bullshit. Since when did you become a tech jeebo? You couldn't program a virus to give you a cold."

"True," I admitted. "I had some help."

Ralph smirked. "Crawford? I looked into him a little. He doesn't have any more tech skills than you do."

"That's not fair to Crawford. *Everyone* has more tech skills than I do."

"He doesn't have enough to reprogram an enchanted virus."

"You're right about that. I had to call a specialist. Point is, Clearwater is going to destroy the information on that drive. He'll do it himself, or one of his people will. My specialist advised me that Clearwater would know it if I gave him a fake drive, or if I wiped the information off the drive before giving it to him. I had to give him everything he wanted, and that's what I did."

Ralph still looked skeptical. "And you're counting on him to destroy the data? What if he finds out what you've done and figures out a way to get around it?"

I shrugged. "It's a gamble. But I think the odds are in my favor."

"And if this lamebrain plan *does* work, then the formula for RAA gets destroyed?" Ralph's lip twitched. "I don't get it. Wait! You backed up the formula!"

I shook my head. "Nope. The drive's enchanted, remember? It won't allow the information to be revised, copied, or moved."

Ralph gawked up at me. "Then when Night Owl tries to open the drive, the formula is gone?"

"That's right. No one will have it."

Ralph' jaw tightened. "Night Owl is going to piss himself!"

"Yes, I imagine he'll be pretty upset."

"And what about Thunderbird?"

I smiled at the nirumbee. "Clearwater won't need him anymore. He'll let him go."

Ralph closed his eyes and let out a breath. "Lord's balls, Southerland. That's the most fuckin' dumbass plan I've ever heard! Do you understand who you're dealing with? Night Owl is going to flip his lid. He'll keep Thunderbird out of spite. And he's going to come after you hard!"

I nodded. "He might. Good thing I've got a nirumbee warrior protecting me."

Ralph shook his head. "You *have* gone batty. You're on your own, kid. It's been nice knowing you."

We'd turned out of the alley, and now we resumed walking toward Ralph's van, which was parked up the block a ways. "You got anything left in that flask of yours, or did you spill it all on your arm."

Ralph pulled out his flask and shook it. "I've got a few swallows."

He unscrewed the cap and knocked back a shot. I reached out a hand, and he passed the flask to me. "Whew! This stuff really clears the cobwebs!"

Ralph chuckled. "We distill that shit in our village. It sure beats the lighter fluid you usually drink."

I handed the flask back to Ralph. "I'm going to need your help for the next part of my dumbass plan."

Ralph gave me a sidelong glance. "If the next part of your plan is as stupid as the first part, forget it. Like I said, you're on your own."

I shook my head. "Nope. It doesn't work that way. You owe me."

"What are you talking about? I don't owe you shit!" Ralph downed the last swallow of his whiskey and tucked the flask away.

"Oh, you owe me all right. Thanks to me, the YCPD is going to pin Redhorn's murder on Deet and close it."

"Yeah? Well, good riddance to that weird piece of shit. Finding Redhorn's killer and getting rid of Deet was the only part of your plan that made any sense."

I watched a lost-looking lug shuffling in our direction. He was wearing an old army field jacket, probably his own, and a lightly loaded military pack was strapped to his back. He kept his hands buried in his jacket pockets and made a point of avoiding eye contact with either of us as he passed us by. I could smell the cheap booze on his breath and hear the wheeze in his lungs as he breathed. It was a night for night owls, I thought, but this one didn't look like he was going to cause me any problems.

On a sudden impulse, I called back to him, "Hey, buddy!"

The figure stopped and turned. His head was lowered against the wind, and he looked up at me from under the brim of his hat. I took out my wallet and pulled out a bill.

"Here you go, brother." I held out the bill. "From a fellow grunt. Use it in good health."

The man looked fifty. He was probably twenty-five and most likely a drunk. He hesitated, eyeing me with suspicion. He wiped his mouth with a dirty hand and took a step toward me. I met him halfway, and he took the bill from my hand as if he feared I would change my mind. Without speaking, he turned and shuffled away.

"What was that about?" Ralph asked me. He had another of his hand-rolled stogies pinched between his teeth. "He's just going to spend it at the first gin joint he comes to."

"Probably. Or maybe he'll get himself a meal. Everyone lives in his own story. His life, his choice." I watched the veteran of Tolanica's wars move with purpose toward the main street.

After the grunt had rounded the corner, I turned back to Ralph. "Deet may have ordered the hit, but you're the one who carried it out. You're the one who slipped the Frogger into Redhorn's aftershave. I know you killed Redhorn. And I'm going to put that information in my hat and stash my hat in the back of my closet. So, yes, you owe me for that, Ralph. You owe me plenty."

Chapter Twenty-Four

Ralph met my eyes and we stared at each other, trying not to show anything in our faces. After a few seconds, Ralph broke eye contact and let his shoulders slump. "How long have you known?"

"I put you on my list of suspects when I walked out of Redhorn's apartment and found you waiting for me. Seemed like quite a coincidence that you happened to be there, and you didn't answer me when I asked you about it." Ralph nodded and let out a breath. "But it was after we talked on the pier that I started to seriously consider the possibility that you did Redhorn in. You were too anxious to get the flash drive from me. I had to wonder why. I think I've figured most of it out. Deet gave you the order, right? And you carried it out like a good soldier."

We reached Ralph's van, and Ralph leaned against the hood. "You don't know the position I was in."

"I've got some idea. It's the same position we're all in. We're in a spot, and we've got choices. We make the best ones we can. We buy a meal, or we buy a drink. Or we get an order to kill someone, and we carry it out, because we think it's our best option at the time."

Ralph pulled his collar up to his ears and seemed to disappear inside his coat. "Friday before last, I get a phone call from Winston. You're outside of the Leaflock building shouting at birds. A lot of it is incoherent, but you've evidently taken down Leaflock's chief engineer—Redhorn—and you aren't exactly proud of what you've done. I put down the phone and shrug it off. It's your business, not mine."

He looked at his shoes, in no hurry to continue. I decided to push him. "And then Deet calls you."

Ralph glanced up at me and looked away. "Yeah. Deet's in a lather. Says that Leaflock has just discovered that Redhorn is selling him out—literally! He's selling privileged company information to a competitor, and he's about to sell off something big. Deet tells me that I've got to stop him immediately. I've got to put him down and make it look like natural causes. Deet says that Redhorn likely has a flash drive on him, a special one. It's bright green with the Leaflock company logo on it, and it contains the information that Redhorn is going to sell. If I find the drive, I've gotta retrieve it and bring it straight to Deet. Deet makes a point of telling me not to try to access it under any circumstances. Says it's enchanted, and that any attempt to open it will fry the contents."

Ralph had been speaking quickly, like a streetcar rolling down one of Yerba City's famous hills. But now he put on the brakes. He took a puff of his cigar, then pulled it out of his mouth and stared at it. With a scowl, he let it drop to the pavement and crushed it out with his heel. He peered at me from inside the collar of his overcoat, expression flat. "Like I said, I was the new guy at the office. Deet could have assigned any number of agents for this hit, but Deet chose me. It was a test. Deet didn't know if I could be trusted with anything messy. If I do this job, then I'm in. I'm on the team. If I refuse it, or botch it, I'm an outsider. If I'm going to do what I do for the elf, I've got to be as inside as I can be."

"So you did the job."

Ralph nodded. "I did the job. Redhorn wasn't the first joker I've rubbed out. He won't be the last. I'm a warrior. I'm trained to kill, and I'm good at it. And who was Redhorn to me? Nothing." He looked up at me. "It's not something I'm proud of, but I don't have any regrets, either. It's just what I do. It's part of the job. And I could give a fuck what you think about that. Got me?"

I nodded. "Sure, Ralph. I get it. You're a professional, just like me. And you've got people to answer to. Orders to follow."

Ralph's eyes narrowed and his jaw clenched. "Kiss my ass, Southerland. I don't need your fucking approval."

"And I don't have to give you any. You aren't going to try to tell me that you were abused as a little boy, are you."

"Fuck no." Ralph allowed himself to smile. "Eight brothers and sisters, and I was my daddy's favorite and the apple of my momma's eye. I'm the pride of my whole fucking village. They tell stories about me in the school to inspire the kids to think about a life outside the village."

"All right, so you're a hero. Tell me how you killed Redhorn."

Ralph stopped smiling. "Just between you and me, right?"

"Sure," I said. "We're partners."

"Fuck you, Southerland." Ralph sighed, reluctant to begin. I let him take his time. When he began to speak, his voice was little more than a whisper. "Deet tells me that I've got to act fast, because Redhorn might be planning to sell the flash drive that night. Deet also tells me that I've got to make the death look like natural causes." He paused, and when he resumed it was with a stronger voice. "The LIA has a whole library of toxins for a job like this. My favorite is what we call poison dart toxin, or Frogger, since it comes from poisonous frogs down in Qusco. It never fails. All you've got to do is introduce it into the target's nasal passages, and it brings on heart failure that looks just like an ordinary coronary. It's quick, and you can't detect it in the stiff unless you're looking for it, and even then you've got to be pretty skilled to find it. Real nasty shit."

"Sounds like you've used it before."

Ralph shot me a glance, but continued as if I hadn't interrupted. "I get to Redhorn's apartment. I'm about to knock on his door, but I can hear that his shower is running. So I pick his lock and walk in. Sure enough, he's in the shower. He's a real organized guy. He's got his go-out-on-the-town duds all nicely laid out on a chair in the bedroom, and he's got all his cleaning shit lined up on his bathroom counter. All lined up in a little row. So I've got a choice, you know? Where to put the Frogger. I settle on the aftershave, because that's gonna get up into his nose. I put a couple of drops in there, and I go out the way I came in. I figure I'll wait until he's had a chance to die, and then I'll go back in, find the flash drive, and pick up the aftershave on the way out."

"Nice plan. Very professional." I watched the nirumbee, who was looking at the ground. "But it all went wrong."

"Not all of it. Redhorn got out of the shower, did his business, and splashed on some aftershave. Then he started to get dressed. And then his heart gave out. But I didn't think there'd be any hurry to get back inside, and I wanted to make sure that I'd given him enough time. I waited a little too long."

"The police arrived."

Ralph looked up at me. "Who'd'a figured, right?"

I nodded. "Clearwater was waiting for him at The Gold Coast Club. He'd arranged a meeting to buy the formula for the reifying agent. But he got impatient when Redhorn didn't show up right away. Probably called Redhorn, and Redhorn didn't answer. So he makes an anonymous call to the police: 'Check on my friend. He's in bad health and I think something might have happened to him.'"

"And they show up and find Redhorn curled up in his bed, dead as a doornail. But they don't have any reason to suspect foul play, so they do a quick examination of the scene, take the body away, and put up some crime tape in case they want to come back later."

"And when they've taken the body away, you go back in for the flash drive."

"I find it right on his desk, sitting right out in the open. I take it, and I take the burner phone. And you're right, he'd had an unanswered call from an unidentified number. I grab the aftershave, and I'm out of there. Job done."

Ralph glanced up at me and let out a breath. I think he was hoping that I'd heard enough.

I hadn't. "So you tell Deet that you've taken care of Redhorn," I prompted.

Ralph sighed. "Yep."

"But you didn't tell Deet that you'd found the flash drive."

"Nope."

"Why not?"

Ralph's eyes flashed. "I'd passed Deet's damned test! I'd done the dirty work. But I'm not some fuckin' torpedo. If I'm going to be asked to rub someone out, I fuckin' wanna know why. So I decided I'd hang on to the flash drive for a little while. Find out what it was all about. I told Deet that I'd searched the apartment and come up with nothing. I said the dingus must still be at Leaflock Services."

He looked away from me before continuing. "Deet is thorough. Has the Leaflock offices searched. The next day, Deet arranges to have you picked up and questioned by the A.D.A. while our people search your apartment. Late that night, Deet calls me in and reads me the riot act. The LIA has contracted with Leaflock for a crucial device. Orders come all the way down from Lord fuckin' Ketz hisself. The data on that flash drive hasn't been backed up. Leaflock himself doesn't know exactly what Redhorn has put on it, but he needs it to complete the contract. If we don't find the drive, we've wasted tons of dough and valuable time. Time seems to be the most important thing. Whatever the government needs Leaflock's device for, they need it in a hurry. Time's running out. Blah, blah, blah...."

Horns began honking nearby as angry motorists, three sheets to the wind and frustrated after a night of casting their 'surefire' lines at half-buzzed dames with minimal standards and walking away with nothing in their hands but their dicks, asserted their rights to driving space. After the clamor faded, Ralph continued. "So I'm thinking I might have made a big mistake concealing the drive. Turns out it's passcode protected, so I can't even access the info. I tell Deet that maybe we should send a team back in to Redhorn's apartment. 'Maybe I missed something,' I say, which shows how desperate I'm getting. Deet agrees and tells me to take care of it."

I nodded. "And you get there first to plant the drive and the phone."

"Yes, but I want to make sure they get found." Ralph reached for his flask, but then remembered that it was empty. He looked up at me. "You don't have...?"

"Sorry," I said. "Maybe we'll go out for a drink when you're done talking."

Ralph waved a hand in dismissal. "Skip it. Where was I?"

"You planted the drive in Redhorn's apartment."

"That's right. I wanted to make sure it would be hidden, but still get found. I didn't want it laying right out in the open, because Deet would wonder why I hadn't seen it. So I went to the store and bought some rice."

I drew in a quick breath as a piece fell into place. "You bought the cheap generic rice. Because you knew it would be out of place in Redhorn's kitchen."

"He was a real chef, I guess. All that expensive high-end food. Yeah, I dump all his pearly rice in a grocery bag and replace it with the cheap shit that the rest of us eat and don't know the difference. Then I put the bag in his trash can under the sink, just to make sure that any idiot would know where to look." He looked up at me with half a smile. "I guess it worked."

"I would have looked through the rice anyway."

Ralph's smile broadened. "Sure you would've. You're a fuckin' pro." He chuckled. "Anyway, I'm waiting for my LIA team to show up, and fuck me but who do you think gets there first."

I nodded. "And there you were when I came out. I thought maybe you'd followed me there, but why would you?"

Ralph's smile disappeared. "Yeah, I guess I should'a just made myself scarce. But I wanted to know if you'd found the drive. Should'a known you wouldn't tell me. Anyway, after you left, the LIA team showed up and did their search. I talked to them afterward, and when they told me they hadn't found the drive, I knew you had it."

I stared down at the agent. "*You* knew I had it. What I want to know is, how did *Deet* find out I had it?"

Ralph wouldn't meet my eyes. He sighed. "A couple days later, Deet calls me in. Things are getting tense. I can tell that agency people above Deet are putting the squeeze on. Our whole unit is in jeopardy. LIA agents aren't allowed to fail, and when the hammer comes down, we're all nails. And Deet's holding the hammer." Ralph sighed again. "So I weigh my options, and none of them look good. I... suggest... that it might be possible you've got the drive. I tell Deet that I had a chat with you, and you let it slip that you might have found the drive in Redhorn's office the day you exposed him and walked out of the building with it. I tell Deet that I'm certain you don't know what's on it, because it's passcode-protected and enchanted, besides." Ralph glanced up at me. "Deet bought it."

I nodded. "You're a real convincing little shithead when you put your heart in it."

Ralph looked away. "I tried to call you. I left you a message to meet me. It was only later that I heard about what Deet did. How you were taken and narked up, and questioned."

"Yeah. I'm sure you're all broken up about that."

Ralph glared up at me. "What'd'ya want—a fuckin' apology? Well, fuck that. I did what I needed to do, and I'd fuckin' do it again. You had Redhorn's fuckin' drive. You should'a given it to Leaflock. What happened to you is your own fuckin' fault."

We were silent for a while after that. We listened to traffic noises and pulled our coats closed against the chill in the Yerba City summer winds. The mist was thickening, and I knew that it was on its way to settling into a dense morning fog. Traffic was already starting to slow as visibility diminished, and windshield wipers were wiping the windshields of every third or fourth car that passed by. Ralph had not only confessed to killing Redhorn, but to giving me up to Deet. I had every reason to hate him, to want revenge, to want the unprincipled bum dead. But, like it or not, he'd been my partner when the sun rose that morning, and I needed him to be my partner now. And, anyway, I couldn't find it in me to blame him for anything he'd done. He was a professional with something he'd needed to do, and he'd made the choices that he'd deemed optimal at the time. How was I any different, or any better? After an indeterminate length of time I realized, despite all of the night's events, that I still had my own job to do, and nothing in the world was any different than it had been before.

Ralph broke the silence. "All right. You've got a plan, you say? What do you need me to do?"

I felt the beginnings of a smile and hid it with a forced cough. "You're on board? Good. First, I'm going to need you to pick up Thunderbird's heartstone."

"Okay. I can do that. Then what?"

I scratched at my chin. "My plan is more of a work in progress."

Ralph scowled. "What's that supposed to mean?"

"It means I'm not sure what my next step is going to be. It depends on what Clearwater does. I'm hoping that he'll enter the passcode I gave him. If he does, the virus will destroy the files. At that point, I'm hoping that he'll call me."

Ralph shook his head. "He's more likely to ambush you from out of nowhere and snap your head off."

"I don't think so. The virus will leave a note on his screen telling him to call me on the burner phone I took from Redhorn's apartment. He'll assume that I backed up the files and that I'm making some kind of play, like trying to squeeze him for more dough or something. I think he'll call to find out what I'm up to."

"He'll ambush you, string you up, and force you to talk."

I chuckled. "He might. But he'll probably assume I've taken some steps to protect myself."

"Have you?"

"No, but I'm guessing that he'll assume I have."

The sidelong glance Ralph gave me was filled with skepticism. "Wow. I don't know if you've got brass balls or a death wish. How thoroughly have you thought this crazy scheme of yours through?"

"I thought I'd play it as it goes. Once Clearwater makes his move, I'll figure out what to do about it."

"Wonderful. You're a dead man. You know that, right?"

"Clearwater won't kill me. He still thinks he can get the formula for RAA from me."

Ralph shrugged with both his shoulders and his arms. "But you don't have a backup! Once the files on the drive are destroyed, Redhorn's formula will go up in smoke. And without the formula they can't build the cell regenerator. You've really fucked things up, Southerland."

"Fucked things up? For who? If the Dragon Lord is really dying, and I'm not totally convinced about any of this, so what? Isn't that what the elf wants?"

Ralph let out a breath. "I don't know. Maybe. This is all above my pay grade." He shook his head. "I wish we could talk to the elf."

"You don't have any way to contact him?"

"Nope. When he wants me, he finds me."

I thought about that. "What about Badger? I'm brand new to this whole spirit animal thing, but can you, I don't know, conjure him up when you need him? Ask him to take a message to the elf?"

Ralph snorted. "Spirits. In my experience they're mostly good for telling riddles and laughing at our puny efforts to figure them out." He shook his head. "The most Badger ever does for me is make me more aggressive in battle and help me find things. If I asked him to carry a message, he'd probably get offended and tell me to piss off."

I stared out into the street, temples throbbing, trying to wrap my head around the idea of a world without Lord Ketz. After a while, I became aware that Ralph was looking up at me, an odd smile on his face.

"What?" I asked.

Ralph shook his head. "Nothing."

"What!" I demanded.

Ralph snickered. "You're going to trick Night Owl into wiping the drive? Seriously? You're going to get him to destroy the formula that would keep the Dragon Lord alive? You. Alexander Southerland. A lowlife window peeper from a dead-end street is taking down the mighty ruler of the Realm of Tolanica. Alex Southerland, destroyer of empires!" He started to chuckle.

My heart skipped a beat. "It's not like I'm the one who's killing him." A thought struck me. "Besides, Leaflock Services can't have been the only company that the LIA contracted to build the cell regenerator. We're talking about saving the life of the Dragon Lord! They wouldn't have put all their eggs in one basket. There must be dozens of companies working on whatever it is they need."

"Could be. But maybe Redhorn was the first one to come up with a workable formula. Maybe time is running out. Like you said, no Dragon Lord has ever died before. No one has ever had to cure one before. This is brand new ground we're breaking here." Ralph's eyes gleamed with amusement. "And then one guy comes up with the answer... And I kill him! And you—you destroy his work!" He barked out a laugh. It sounded strained, even frantic.

"You all right there, champ?" I asked.

In response, Ralph's strained laughter turned into high-pitched guffaws. I frowned, but felt my lips broadening, unbidden, into a smile, and, with almost no warning, a choked laugh forced its way through my clenched throat. Another one followed, which set Ralph laughing harder. He pointed at me, and laughter began to pour from my chest, and from deep in my gut. Ralph bent over until his elbows were resting against his knees, and I fell against the side of his van to keep my balance. I was standing next to a two-and-a-half foot semi-human tribal warrior who had just confessed to killing a man he'd never met. He'd been ordered to do it by a cold-hearted self-serving shapeshifting mantis, who'd been devoured a half hour earlier by a swarm of rats—who happened to be my best friend—and a legendary carnivorous goat-creature, who happened to spend his days in my laundry room sleeping off his nighttime prowls. An extremely powerful unearthly spirit was about to discover that I had deceived him and deprived him of something he wanted badly enough to kill for. I'd put into motion a plan that, if it worked, would destroy a secret formula that might be the only means of saving the life of the immortal creature who had been bringing order to this part of the world for six thousand years, and whose death might usher in a chaotic age the likes of which this world had never seen. My entire body ached. Burning acid seemed to be running through the veins of my left arm, which I could barely move. Sudden bursts of electricity lit up my broken nose, sending jolts of pain deep into the farthest recesses of my brain. My heart was beating out a rhythm that would have had a medic reaching for a defibrillator, and my head felt like someone was pumping pepper spray into my sinus cavities. And yet, the tension that had been growing in me since I'd exposed a basically decent man, whose horrendous crime amounted to becoming fed up with his disrespectful former protégé, was draining from my body, released by peals of unrestrained laughter, pouring out of me with the tears streaming down my cheeks, and for the next five minutes my howls and Ralph's shrieks drowned out the sounds of the passing cars rolling over the glistening asphalt in the mist-filled night.

Chapter Twenty-Five

I woke up in my own bed the next morning with an aching arm, a stabbing pain under my eyes, and a two-inch whirlwind floating over my chest. Not all of my days start this well.

"Hello, Smokey." My throat was dry and my voice croaked.

"Greetingsss, Alekssss. Smokey has returned as you wissshed."

I sat up in my bed. "Can you take me to where the spirit-man is?"

"Smokey can. It is far away."

"Did you see the troll boy there?"

"Smokey sees troll boy there."

I bounced out of bed. "Then let's take a drive." Okay, maybe "bounced" is the wrong word. "Stumbled" might be more accurate.

When Clearwater had climbed back through his dark portal, I'd mentally commanded Smokey to tag along, not as a whirlwind, but as a drifting drop of air. As far as I know, Clearwater had never detected the elemental. I had no idea what spirit realm Clearwater might be holing up in, but I guessed he wouldn't be spending much time there. If nothing else, he'd be hitting the Yerba City nightclubs sometime in the evening, like he always did. I'd told Smokey to stick close to Clearwater and return to me as soon as the spirit reentered the earthly realm. I hadn't expected that Smokey would come back so soon. It seemed, however, that Clearwater was holding Troy somewhere in, or at least near, the city, something I'd been hoping for, but couldn't count on.

Once in the beastmobile, Smokey perched on the dashboard and leaned in the direction it wanted me to go. Occasionally, the elemental zipped out of the car and into the winds to orient itself, and then returned to continue its navigation. I had trained Smokey to lead me to various destinations in the city, but it was still a little hit and miss, and our trip included a lot of zigging and zagging, not to mention several U-turns. Eventually, though, we wound up in an abandoned electronics plant in the southernmost part of the peninsula, nearly fifty miles south of the city. I circled the vast empty parking lot, which was surrounded by a chain-link fence, and scanned the three-story complex in its center from a safe distance. Everything was still, save for leaves from nearby trees blowing across the lot, and three owls circling the sky above the building like sentries. I parked a half-block down the street from the complex and did some online research on my cell phone.

It took me about thirty minutes to get the highlights of the story of the abandoned plant. Five years earlier, a young electronics pioneer named Truman Swan had revolutionized the home computer industry by designing a magic-augmented silicon semiconductor. Cheap and efficient, the Swanco semiconductor became a mainstay in a new generation of personal computers, and the young pioneer became wealthy beyond his dreams. A vast lemon tree orchard that had been thriving for more than two hundred years disappeared one day, and a giant manufacturing plant and office complex emerged in its place almost overnight, creating tens of thousands of new jobs and a local shortage of fresh lemons. Swan's face appeared on the covers of trade journals and business magazines, and, finally, on the online gossip sites as he became a major player in the Yerba City social scene. The party came to an end before the electronics pioneer turned thirty when it was found that residual magic in his semiconductors was beginning to exhibit some alarming side-effects, the most common of which was erectile dysfunction in males who spent too much time behind their screens. When the story broke, Swan shot himself full of heroin and hung himself from the rafters of his luxury townhouse with a silk bedsheet. Swanco went belly-up the next day. Armine Clearwater bought the remains of the company and liquefied its assets. He still owned the building.

I peered up the street at the complex, pondering my options. I'd planned to meet Crawford for lunch at noon at a diner in Placid Point, and I needed to get moving if I was going to be on time. I weighed my concern for Crawford against the unlikely possibility that Troy might be sitting around in the Swanco building waiting to be rescued and told myself that I'd have to deal with the boy later. I hadn't heard from Clearwater since giving him the flash drive, but I had a plan, and I decided to let it play out. Because my plans never failed. Right.

An hour later I was sitting opposite Crawford at a table in the Shoreline Café, a greasy spoon down the street from Nautilus Jewelry.

"You know, this place isn't anywhere near the shore." I blew over the lip of my coffee cup to cool the light brown brew.

"The tuna sandwich is made from actual fish of some type, and the coffee's hot." Crawford grinned. "And the waitresses are cute."

"The coffee's hot, all right," I admitted. "But I hope it never comes under attack."

"It's too weak to defend itself?"

"It's... Damn, you've heard that one." I sipped enough of the coffee to scald the inside of my mouth.

"A few times, yeah. The first time might have been thirty years ago." Crawford opened several packets of sugar over his cup.

I studied Crawford, trying to be subtle about it. It might have been my imagination, but his cheeks seemed a little hollow, and his neck a little thinner.

I hadn't been subtle enough for the cagey were-rat. "You checking me out? I'll save you the trouble. I lost four rats to the mantis. I'm down to a hundred eight."

I opened my mouth to say something, but Crawford cut me off. "And don't you dare try to apologize. I knew what I was doing, and I knew the risks." He took a sip of his sweetened coffee and smiled. "Besides, that was the best meal I've had in ages."

I'd picked up my tuna sandwich, but decided I wasn't quite ready for it.

Crawford bit into his, and his eyes lit up. "This isn't half bad. It might actually even be tuna today."

I bit back on the apology I had, in fact, been intending to give. "You don't look all that worse for wear."

"I had to go up a notch on my belt, but I'm okay. I was getting a little paunchy anyway."

I snorted. "Yeah, you might have been approaching ninety pounds."

"Little short of that now. But skinny looks good on me." He smiled at a waitress who was passing by at the moment. She caught his smile and returned it. He was right: with her sloe eyes and long gams, she was indeed a cute little doll. I wondered how old she was under all that makeup. About thirty-five, I guessed.

"She looks like your type," I observed.

"They're all my type. And I may have a little more time for recreation pretty soon."

I turned my attention from the waitress's swaying hips. "What do you mean?"

"I'm going to sell the store. I think it's time for me to move on."

I worked to keep my breathing calm. I'd been half expecting this, but Crawford's declaration still sent my pulse racing. "The LIA?"

Crawford nodded. "They know me, and they won't forget what I did to one of their own."

I felt my throat tightening. "Where are you going to go?"

Crawford shrugged. "Don't know yet. I've got a few ideas. Rats always have bolt holes, you know."

"When do you think you'll be leaving?"

"Soon. Gotta take care of the business first, but I don't want to be long about it."

I took a bite of the tuna sandwich without tasting it. "You'll...." I couldn't finish.

Fortunately, Crawford picked up the slack. "I'll let you know when I go. And I'll keep in touch. You won't be rid of me that easily."

"Yeah." I couldn't think of anything to add, so I sipped down some coffee.

Crawford's eyes lit up, and his mouth stretched into a grin that radiated mischief. "So, is everything still on with Clearwater?"

I breathed in, grateful for the change in subject. "I haven't heard from him yet, but Smokey came back and let me know where he showed up when he returned from wherever it is he goes." I told Crawford about driving to the Swanco building earlier that morning.

"You think Clearwater knew Smokey followed him into that void?"

"I don't think so. Night Owl is a powerful spirit, but I doubt that he tracks every puff of air he walks through. Or flies through. Air elementals are all around us, and nobody notices them. Hell, unless I'm looking for one, I don't even see them."

Crawford rubbed his hands together in that rodent gesture I knew I'd miss when he wasn't around anymore. "You think he'll call you?"

"Either that, or he'll show up and rip my head off my shoulders."

Crawford took a big bite of sandwich, and I listened to the clatter of silverware scraping across plates as I waited for him to finish chewing. I looked at my own half-eaten sandwich, but decided I wasn't hungry.

Crawford swallowed twice before his mouth was empty enough to speak clearly. "It's a risky plan," he pointed out.

"Sure," I agreed. "But that's the way we like them, right?"

Crawford let out a squeaky chuckle. "You know, I didn't get any sleep last night. I guess I should be a little upset about my life getting overturned, but I'm actually excited about it! Things were getting stale."

"You always said that the boring routine is what was keeping you sane."

I saw the light in Crawford's eyes again, and he grinned his mischievous grin. It struck me as a little more than mischievous. "I think I may be past that now."

I stared at him, and my expression probably betrayed my concern.

Crawford chuckled again. "I tried dull and boring. It worked for a while. I'm not sure that's the best thing for me anymore."

"Hmm. You sure you're not having a midlife crisis? You aren't going to buy a sports car, are you?"

Crawford grinned. "I bet I could afford a real snazzy one, once I sell off my merchandise."

***

"That's the place?" Crawford peered over the dashboard of the beastmobile past the fifteen-acre parking lot at the Swanco building, barely visible in the dim light of the setting sun.

"That's it. The lot is still empty. I don't see the owls, but five will get you ten they're perched up there on the roof somewhere." I strained my eyes and focused my elf-enhanced senses, but we were simply too far from the building for me to spot any owls, especially if they weren't flying above the building.

Crawford nodded. "Time to bring in the reconnaissance?"

"Yep. Time to call Badass." In my mind, I visualized the sigil that was Badass's calling card and concentrated my attention on it. Within moments, I felt my connection to the elemental and, with a mental command, sent it off toward the building to search for owls.

Badass returned after a minute or so and floated above the hood of the beastmobile, visible to me only as a six-foot bubble of distorted light. A moaning voice sounded in my head. "Badass sees three owls on top of building."

"Did you see any other living things the size of the owls or larger?" I thought at the elemental.

"No."

Crawford pointed at the distortion in the air. "Is that Badass?"

"Yep. It spotted owls on the rooftop. Otherwise, the coast is clear. I'm going to send Badass after the owls now. We'll give the owls a minute to scatter, and then we go in. You ready?"

The were-rat flashed a toothy grin. "I was born ready."

A few seconds later, I saw what appeared to be three specs of darkness circling over the top of the building in erratic spirals. "Badass is taking care of Clearwater's sentries. Fasten your seat belts." I gripped the steering wheel with both hands. "Here we go!"

I fired up the engine and revved it twice just because I wanted to. I shifted into drive, glanced once at the wide-eyed Crawford, and jammed the accelerator to the floor. All four tires squealed as I aimed the car straight for the chain-link fence surrounding the parking lot. Crawford screeched and I let out a roar as the beastmobile plowed over the curb and crashed into the fence doing better than sixty miles an hour. The shriek of metal echoed in my ears like a demonic chorus, and I knew that Gio was going to pick up a gun and shoot me in the head when he saw what I had done to the body of my car. I was relieved when the fence put up less resistance than I thought it would. Rather than entangling itself in a web of steel, the beastmobile ripped through the chain links like a sledgehammer through plywood. I sped through the lot, drove over a concrete courtyard, and pulled up at the main entrance to the building.

I turned toward Crawford, who was grinning from ear to ear. "You all right?"

"Sure. Why do you ask?"

I shook my head and climbed out of the vehicle. Ignoring the broken headlamps and the gouges to the exterior of the beastmobile, I moved toward the front door of the building at a jog. Crawford was right behind me, carrying a gym bag. A quick glance upwards indicated that Badass had scattered the owls from view.

The entryway to the Swanco building's main lobby was a double-paned glass door that had been chained shut and padlocked. Spray-painted gang tags covered the Swanco Semiconductors logo, but the door was otherwise undamaged. Given time I might have been able to pick the lock, but I was in a hurry, and Crawford had brought a crowbar in his bag.

"You want to do the honors?" Crawford asked.

I gestured toward the glass. "No. Go ahead. You know you want to."

Crawford grinned and began demolishing the glass entryway with undisguised relish. Once he'd created an opening that was twice the size we needed, he held out an arm. "After you."

I stepped over the broken glass into the main lobby of Swanco Semiconductors and looked back over my shoulder. "Smokey? You there?"

The tiny elemental zipped through the opening and hovered in front of me. "Smokey is here."

"Good. Show me where you saw the troll boy."

With the elemental leading the way, Crawford and I navigated the maze of hallways to a double door in the center of the complex. "Troll boy is on other side of door," Smokey told me.

"Want me to use the crowbar on it?" Crawford asked.

I ran the palms of my hands over the reinforced metal doors and took my set of lock picks—the ones left to me by my erstwhile safecracker Jorgio—from my pocket. "Better let me handle this one."

It wasn't easy, but seven and a half tense minutes and several false starts later, we were through the door and walking past an entryway that led into an enclosed space the size of an aircraft hangar. I concluded that this had once been a sterile cleanroom. Smokey led us past row after row of empty tables where I presumed that the Swanco brand semiconductors had been assembled and packaged. At the far end of the room, an open doorway led into an office. All of the furniture had been removed from the office, and a hospital bed had been dragged inside. Troy lay uncovered on the bed, naked, eyes closed, cables and tubes running from various parts of his body to monitors displaying data with glowing green LED readouts. His breathing was so slow and steady that without the monitors it would have been hard to tell if he were alive. I had a moment of alarm when I couldn't hear a heartbeat, but then I remembered that his heart was locked away in his heartstone. I wondered how his blood could circulate under those conditions, but shrugged it off. Magic.

I turned to Crawford. "Time to shift. Have a look around. Don't go too far, though."

Crawford gave me a sloppy salute that told me he had somehow managed to evade his mandatory three-year service time in Tolanica's military. "Call if you need me," he said, and a hundred eight rats poured out of his clothing to seek holes, cracks, and dark shadows.

After gathering up the clothes and putting them in Crawford's gym bag, I took out my phone and punched in a number.

Ralph's voice answered. "Talk to me."

"We're in. No contact from Night Owl yet. Badass drove off his owls, so I think we got in unobserved. I made a lot of noise, though."

"Have you found Thunderbird?"

"Affirmative. He's in a coma."

"Then his heart is still out of range."

"How far out are you now?"

"A little more than thirty miles. I'm on the highway and I've got the heartstone with me, but traffic has been murder. I think there might be an accident up ahead. It's stop-and-go."

"Shit. How close do you think you'll need to get before you're in range?"

"Like I told you before, I don't know. I've never been more than twenty miles from my own heartstone."

I smiled. Although Ralph had hinted that his heart was locked away in an enchanted stone, this was the first time he'd actually come out and admitted it. "All right, move in as quick as you can. My guess is that Night Owl will be here soon."

I disconnected and knelt next to the sleeping troll. He looked to be unhurt, but I'd hoped to find him awake. Ralph had needed some time to pick up the boy's heartstone, and Crawford and I had left ahead of him, not wanting to wait. I hadn't accounted for traffic backing up between us. I should have known better. The roads in and out of Yerba City could jam up and slow to a crawl—or come to a complete stop—without a hint of warning.

I considered moving Troy out of the building and driving off with him, but one look at the tubes and monitors nixed that idea. I was no doctor, and I had no idea whether the boy could be unhooked and moved in his condition. Once Ralph got his heart in range, Troy should regain consciousness on his own. Under ideal circumstances, he would wake up before Clearwater arrived, but I knew I couldn't count on it. I tried to calculate the possibilities, but math was never my strong suit, so I decided to go with my gut instincts. I gathered up Crawford's gym bag and left the office.

"Stay close, Smokey." The tiny whirlwind took my command literally and perched itself on my shoulder as I crossed through the assembly area and stepped out into the hallway. I turned left, just because, and found an unlocked office not far down the hall. It had been stripped of its furniture, and the walls were bare of everything except the horizontal shadows cast by the moonlight shining through the half-open window blinds. The floor was carpeted, so I sat down cross-legged with my back against the wall and waited. Smokey whirled on my shoulder next to my ear, but didn't make a sound.

    I didn't have to wait long. I'd been sitting against the wall listening to my heartbeat and my breathing for no more than ten minutes when the hairs behind my neck and along my arms began to stand up. I can't tell you what sensory apparatus was at work in me. It wasn't my hearing or my vision. It was actually something closer to my sense of taste, but that wasn't it, either. It was something I felt in the back of my throat and in my stomach. In any case, I sensed a change in the reality of the darkness that surrounded me. Rather than try to focus on the sensation, I let it sweep over me, and when I did I sensed that the change was emanating from the direction of the assembly room. I remembered other deeper darknesses appearing and watching owls fly in and out of them. Without hearing or seeing anything, I knew that Night Owl had entered the building.

Chapter Twenty-Six

Almost immediately afterward, a tone from my own cell phone, rather than from Redhorn's burner, cut through the silence. I checked the screen and saw the words "Unknown Caller" displayed across the top.

I hit the connect button and kept my voice quiet so that it wouldn't echo down the hallway. "Hello?"

"I'm disappointed in you, Southerland." Clearwater's voice came to me twice, once softly from the direction of the assembly room, and once a split second later over the phone.

"Oh good, it's you. I was afraid it was going to be a robot telemarketer."

"You owe me an explanation."

"You read my note, didn't you?"

"Of course. But that's not what I was expecting to find on the flash drive. You led me to believe that you were selling me the formula for Reifying Agent Alpha. You gave me a passcode that you assured me would give me access to the formula. Imagine my surprise when, instead of the formula, my computer screen showed me highly realistic images of wolves feasting on a deer. I suppose that was supposed to symbolize a virus destroying the files."

"Were they realistic? I didn't know how that was going to turn out. There was some magic at work there that I don't understand."

"It was quite impressive. I don't suppose you'd care to tell me who helped you with that."

"Not a chance."

"Hmm. In any case, I suppose we've reached the point in your little farce where you tell me that you want more money."

"I'm not interested in your money, Mr. Clearwater."

I listened to silence for several heartbeats. Clearwater finally spoke. "I have to admit to being confused. Why did you agree to sell me the flash drive?"

"I wanted to know where you were keeping the boy who talks backwards."

I waited for Clearwater to put the pieces together. "You put a tracker on me! Of course. That cute air spirit of yours, no doubt. Clever of you. Careless of me."

I didn't respond. I wanted him to make the leap. After a few moments, he did. "Which means you're here in the building somewhere. I take it that you are the source of the disturbance that troubled my owls? Another of your elementals?" I heard Clearwater sigh. "Am I supposed to hunt you down, or will you show yourself."

"Depends on what kind of mood you're in."

I heard the beginning of Clearwater's laugh from down the hall before I heard it on the phone. "Yes, you have a right to be frightened. I do not enjoy being deceived. On the other hand, it doesn't happen to me often, and I can't help but admire your audacity." He sighed again. "Fine. You probably know where I am. I can smell you, so I know you're near. Come on in. I promise you a safe entry. We'll talk, and then we'll see whether or not I can afford to allow you a safe exit."

"That's not much of a guarantee."

"You want a guarantee, my boy? Here's one for you. If I have to hunt you down, I guarantee that your suffering will be far more intense than my pleasure, and I will receive a great deal of pleasure from it."

"Well, when you put it that way.... I'll be there in a moment."

My legs were stiff when I rose, and my knees popped. My arms hurt, too, especially the left one. And I hoped that I wouldn't have to sneeze through my aching honker. Either I was still in bad shape from my recent exertions, or I was getting old. Regardless, I wasn't going to be sitting on the floor again any time soon.

Clearwater was standing on one of the assembly tables, reminding me very much of a perching owl, when I walked into the room. I sat on top of a nearby table, bracing myself with my hands, and faced him.

Clearwater looked me up and down. "You, of course, have a backup of the files from the flash drive, correct?"

I shook my head. "Sorry. That flash drive was causing so much suffering and death that I decided to erase the contents for good. Now there's nothing for anyone to fight over. Which means you don't need Thunderbird anymore, so you can let him go."

Clearwater's eyes were as round as saucers. He took off his monocle, breathed on it, and polished it with a handkerchief that he took out of his vest pocket. "Do you know what you've done?" He replaced the monocle in his eye.

"I think so, yes. Please extend my apologies to Lord Ketz next time you see him."

A sad-looking smile appeared on Clearwater's face. "Do you really want to come to the attention of the Dragon Lord? Do you want him to know who you are? He won't be impressed. You won't get the chance to explain yourself to him. He has as much regard for you as you would toward a mosquito that bit you on the arm. You've deprived him of something he wants, but he'll get it another way."

"Maybe. But will it be in time?"

Clearwater cocked his head. "The situation will soon become urgent, that's true, but he still has some time. I'm afraid you've inconvenienced me a lot more than you've inconvenienced him."

I nodded. "I suspected that was the case. I don't get it, Clearwater. You were working with the LIA, right? You kidnapped Thunderbird for them. Why did you try to build the cell regenerator yourself? Why didn't you just let Leaflock Services fulfill their contract to the LIA?"

Clearwater flicked a bit of unseen dust off his lapel. "Because, my boy, I wanted something from Lord Ketz-Alkwat. I wanted him to do something for me, and if I could give him what he wanted before the LIA did, then I had a good chance of convincing him to grant my request."

I stared at the stout little man standing on the table. "And what did you want? Surely not dough! You've got plenty of that. Power? The life you're leading isn't fulfilling enough for you?"

Clearwater smiled at me. "Ah, my boy. You would never understand. You see, a short time ago—short, that is, for me, but well before you were born—I was the most admired social figure in Angel City, the crème of the crème. Yerba City is a nice little burgh, but Angel City is the city of cities. And I owned that city. I ran a swanky little nightclub, which I modestly called The Night Owl. It was a most elegant and exclusive venue. Entry into my establishment was the most sought-after ticket in the city. The Night Owl featured the top names in entertainment, all the biggest and best-known stars. And they worked there for free, too, for the privilege of being there. I established a table on the floor for myself, of course, and the most elite citizens of the city—powerful politicians, judges and commissioners, tycoons of industry, military heroes, heroes of sport, lords of criminal families, the best-known artists, journalists, and philosophers, celebrities of every stripe—they all schemed and clawed their way to greet me at my table, to shake my hand, to speak a few words, to have the privilege of being seen in my company. I was the toast of the town, the most famous name in the city. I brought people together. I drove them apart. Nothing happened in Angel City unless I gave my nod of approval. But was it for the 'dough,' as you so crudely put it? Or the power?" Clearwater made a scoffing noise. "Pish posh. Of course not. It was for the celebrity, my boy! Money and power are mere byproducts of that. It was for pure, unadulterated admiration, respect, and attention. I had it, too. I had it all. And then it was taken from me."

I sat in stunned silence. Clearwater shook his head, sadness in his eyes. "I let slip a word. A word of arrogance. I ridiculed Lord Ketz-Alkwat. It was in jest, but it was, I admit, a tasteless jest. I was in my cups, as it were, and I boasted that while Lord Ketz might rule Tolanica, I ruled its fairest city. I believe that I may have used a disparaging term to refer to the old lizard. Word filtered back to him, through the LIA, I suspect. Before I could understand what was happening, my dear club was closed down. Some trumped-up ordinance violation. I was humiliated! I had no choice; I fled the city, landing in quaint Yerba City, where I rebuilt my reputation, albeit amongst a less distinguished citizenry."

Clearwater turned to me. "But with the formula and a completed device in hand, I hoped to regain the Lord's blessing. I hoped to rebuild my little club—to make it better! I've learned a few things here in Yerba City. A new generation of humans has emerged. You all live such short lives, and you have such a short generational memory. It would be a small matter for me to regain the respect and admiration I once had. To once again gain the one throne that really matters: to be the king and beating heart of Angel City society!" Clearwater lifted his chin and stared over an imaginary crowd of cheering devotees in triumph.

I stared at Clearwater. "You kidnapped an innocent boy and killed the people protecting him so that you could own a nightclub?"

Clearwater's body sagged, and he lowered his gaze. His lips were twisted into a half-smile that looked like a sneer, and his eyes drooped with sadness. He sighed. "You could never understand. It's not your fault, son. You simply lack the wit, the vision, the ambition. You're a small man, even for a human."

"And yet, I seem to have put a halt to your grand scheme to, what, be admired by a bunch of toadies and sycophants? To be popular? I mean... were you bullied as a child? Did your mother not breast-feed you?"

The stout little man's features hardened, and it occurred to me that I might have crossed one line too many with those last remarks. He tilted his head and studied me the way a biologist examines a new species of bug. "My designs are not yet thwarted. Redhorn wasn't my only resource. I've contacted others who are working on a suitable formula for the instrument I need. Redhorn told me he had something, and that is lost to me now, but others are close. It's only a matter of time before I get what I need in order to get what I want." He sighed. "But, alas, I fear you will not be around to see my triumph."

I didn't like the sound of that. "Uhh..."

Clearwater shook his head. "No, Mr. Southerland, short as your human lifespan might be, I can't for the life of me think of any reason why I should let you continue to live another day."

Clearwater spread his arms, and the air around him shimmered and distorted. Where the stout little man had been standing, I was now looking at an oversized owl, about my height, with a wingspan that spread across the room.

Without thinking, I leaped down from the table, pulled my gat from my shoulder holster, and fired three shots into the center of Night Owl's torso. I was struck by the sudden sensation of having lived this moment before, and then I remembered firing three slugs at the chest of the mantis thing that Deet had become. The slugs had as much effect this time as they'd had then, which is to say none at all. You'd think I'd learn, but old habits die hard.

Clearwater's voice boomed from the open beak of Night Owl. "That was rude. Not to mention foolish." The spirit lifted a taloned foot and took a step in my direction.

I forced myself to smile. Night Owl stopped advancing and cocked his head to one side, as if questioning me. I put my useless pistol back into my holster and sat back up on the tabletop, making myself comfortable. I looked up at the big bird. "You're forgetting something."

Night Owl's head returned to its normal position. "Oh? And what would that be, pray tell?"

I made my smile as cocky as I could make it. "The boy who talks backwards."

A shushing sound emerged from the owl's beak: "Shu-shu-shu-shu-shu." I realized that Night Owl was laughing at me. "Mr. Southerland. I assure you that Thunderbird is quite subdued. Your 'boy who talks backwards' is no threat to me, and he will be of no help to you." Night Owl paused, and he folded one wing, placing the tip of it below his beak. "Perhaps.... Yes, perhaps if you were to apologize to me. If you were to beg for my forgiveness. Perhaps then I might let you live."

"You want me to grovel?"

"No, no, no. Nothing like that. Just a dignified apology. From your knees. And, please, make it heartfelt and sincere."

I laughed. "I'd heard that you liked to play with your prey before you swooped in for the kill. You want an apology? Here's one. Sorry, but I won't play your game. If you've got something to do, then do it."

Night Owl's wing snapped out to the side, and I felt the wind of it like a slap to the face. Clearwater's voice emerged, dripping with a menace I'd never heard from him before. "Very well, child. But I don't intend to be quick. I assure you, you *will* suffer."

Night Owl stretched to his full height. The monstrous hunting bird gazed at me with focused eyes, studying his target, before leaping into the air, talons extended, and gliding in for the kill. I drew in a sharp breath and savored it, thinking it was likely going to be the last one I ever took.

***

I had one final card to play. I had no idea whether it would work, but I had nothing left to lose. "Cougar?" Even in my own mind I sounded desperate. "Little help?"

The air around me seemed to grow dim, and the room faded as if a heavy gray fog had descended. My mouth opened of its own accord, and a voice began to speak through it. It sounded like my own voice, but it spoke with a smooth, ancient quality that I couldn't have put there if I tried. "I wish to tell a story," said the voice.

Night Owl pulled up from his attack and drifted to a soft landing in front of me, folding his wings to his side. He cocked his head and blinked his eyes. "Speak, Cougar. I wish to hear your story."

The voice came through my lips. *"Cougar climbed to a mountaintop. He entered a cave and found Thunderbird fast asleep* on a bed of straw. 'Wake, Thunderbird,' said Cougar. 'Why do you sleep on this fine day? Wake now and fly around the mountaintop. You will find Night Owl sitting on its peak.' And Thunderbird began to wake."

A rippling sensation passed through me. Nothing in the room changed, but everything seemed different somehow.

Night Owl responded. "I will also tell a story. My story precedes yours, and is stronger." He cocked his head and began to speak in a storyteller's voice. "*Night Owl flew to a mountaintop. He entered a cave and found Thunderbird waiting inside. 'Sleep, Thunderbird,' Night Owl said. 'Sleep now, for I wish to hunt on your mountaintop. My children are hungry and need me to bring them freshly killed game. Sleep, Thunderbird, so that I can hunt on your mountaintop and feed my hungry children.' And Thunderbird climbed on to a bed of straw and fell into a lasting sleep from which he could not be awakened.*"

I felt the rippling sensation again. It was as if I had been asleep and was now awake.

Cougar, speaking through me, answered Night Owl's story with his own. "*Cougar climbed to a mountaintop. He entered a cave and found Thunderbird fast asleep on a bed of straw. 'Wake, Thunderbird. Night Owl has deceived you. His children have long been fed and are not hungry. Night Owl does not wish to hunt on your mountaintop. Night Owl wishes to sit on the peak of your mountain and claim it for his own. Wake, Thunderbird. Wake and chase Night Owl from your mountaintop.' You are stronger than Night Owl. Undo his spell. And Thunderbird began to wake.*"

It was as if I'd been dreaming but was now awake.

Night Owl spoke. "My story precedes yours, and is stronger." Again he cocked his head. "*Night Owl sat on the mountaintop, for it was now his own. He spied Cougar climbing up a mountain path, seeking Thunderbird. 'Go away, Cougar. Thunderbird sleeps, lulled by my soothing spells. Do not enter the cave. Do not disturb Thunderbird. This mountaintop is my territory now, and you are not welcome here. Go away, Cougar, and do not return until I require your presence.' Go away, or you will join Thunderbird in his sleep. And Cougar departed the way he had come.*"

Again the rippling sensation, and the feeling of reawakening to a fresh new world.

Cougar had no response, and it seemed that his story had come to an end, or, rather, that his stories had failed in the face of Night Owl's stronger telling.

But as Night Owl spread his wings once again, a new voice, one that sounded like Ralph's, only older and wiser, began to speak. "*Badger climbed to a mountaintop. He entered a cave and found Thunderbird asleep on a bed of straw. 'Wake, Thunderbird. Wake, for I have brought your heart, and it beats strong in you once again. Wake, and drive Night Owl from the top of your mountain.' Badger placed Thunderbird's heart upon his chest, and Thunderbird was awakened.*"

Again, the sensation of returning to consciousness. My head was starting to pound, and I rubbed at my temples to settle myself.

Night Owl folded his wings, and the fog in the room dissipated as if blown away by a strong wind. I turned toward Ralph, who was standing in the entryway to the room, and tilted my head in greeting. He nodded at me in return.

Night Owl studied Ralph for a moment before speaking. "Bringing the boy's heart to this place will not rouse Thunderbird from his sleep. I have applied drugs and spells that will keep the boy in an induced coma. Withdraw from the field, Badger. Neither you nor Cougar have the strength to stand against me.

The owl swiveled his head in my direction, and his body turned so that he was facing me fully. "Storytime is over, Mr. Southerland." The bird's eyes opened wide and his pupils dilated.

"Nnnt-t-t. Doh... doh...."

Three heads jerked in the direction of the new voice, and I felt my jaw drop at the sight of Troy standing in the doorway of the office, tubes hanging loose from both of his arms.

"Nnntt... Doh...."

Night Owl seemed to stagger. "How...!"

A small naked man, practically nothing but bone, sinew, and a crooked grin, stepped up behind the trembling young troll. Crawford's chittering chuckle filled the room, and he held up a tube to display its frayed end. "Never hire a cougar or a badger to do a rat's job." He spat a piece of plastic tubing to the floor.

Night Owl recovered his bearings and launched himself at Troy. Crawford drew back into the office, but Troy stood his ground, following Night Owl's flight with his eyes. As Night Owl closed on the troll, Troy raised a finger, and for the briefest of moments I saw a flash of blinding light in the shape of a massive bird's wing slice through the air all the way to the room's ceiling. Night Owl came to a crashing halt in midair, as if he'd flown into the side of a building, and slid to the floor, stunned.

Troy looked down at Night Owl and pointed a finger at his chest. "Nnnn.... Nnnn...."

Night Owl seemed to draw in on himself, and it was Clearwater who lay on the floor in front of the boy. The stout little man sighed, and he placed his monocle, which had fallen to the floor in front of him, back in his eye. He looked up at Troy, and his lips drew back into a tired smile. "Never mind, child. No need for further displays. I know when I'm beat."

Clearwater stood and dusted himself off. He turned to me. "Mr. Southerland. No hard feelings, I hope." He picked his top hat off the floor and put it on his head. He smiled at me and shrugged. "Win a few, lose a few. Am I right?"

***

"You're going to let him go?" Ralph was incredulous.

"What choice do I have? He's Night Owl. Not even the LIA can hold him."

"He was going to kill you!"

"He said he was sorry. He promised he wouldn't do it again."

"He was going to swoop down on you like a... like a..."

"Don't say 'like a rat'!" Crawford, now fully dressed, emerged from the office with his gym bag.

"How's the boy?" I asked him.

Crawford nodded back toward the office. "He's fine. A little groggy from the drugs, but he's a tough little lug. He's taking a nap. A normal one, not a coma. He'll be all right."

"He's Thunderbird," Ralph pointed out. "He makes Night Owl look like a sparrow."

"Don't be insensitive, my little friend. I'm sitting right here, after all." Clearwater's stumpy legs dangled over the edge of the assembly table. Ralph turned and glared at him, but thought better about responding.

Night Owl released a heaving sigh. "It would have been nice to be the king of The City of the Angels once again. But, if I'm to be honest, I've become accustomed to Yerba City. It's no Angel City, but it has qualities of its own. And I'm highly respected here. And, who knows. Another opportunity to ingratiate myself back into the Dragon Lord's good graces could come along at any time."

I glanced at him. "If he survives, you mean."

Clearwater turned to me, a look of confusion on his face. "Hmm? If he survives? Whatever are you referring to, my dear boy?"

I shrugged. "The reifying agent. It went poof, remember? And who knows if anyone will be able to come up with another effective formula before the Dragon Lord kicks it."

The puzzled expression didn't leave Clearwater's face. "Kicks it? You mean *dies*?" He chuckled. "My boy, don't you know the meaning of immortality?"

I glanced at Ralph, whose mouth was hanging open. I turned back to Clearwater. "Isn't that what this was all about? Isn't Lord Ketz dying?"

Clearwater broke into a laugh. "Dying? Oh, my dear boy. Is that what you thought?"

I turned to Ralph and found him looking at me.

Clearwater continued to laugh. "Oh, the two of you. Oh my. Lord Ketz-Alkwat can't die—he's immortal! Did you think him afflicted with a disease? Or worn out with age? And you thought that the purpose of the cell regeneration device was to cure him?" He shook his head, holding his sides. "The Dragon Lord isn't dying—he's trying to reproduce! It's unprecedented, and there's no guarantee that the fetus will survive, especially now that we've lost Reifying Agent Alpha, but the Dragon Lord Ketz-Alkwat, my friends, is attempting to lay an egg!"

Crawford came running out of the office, mouth agape and eyes opened as wide as Ralph's. Opened as wide as mine. The three of us gawked at each other in complete and utter bewilderment as Clearwater roared with laughter.

Epilogue

Walks in Cloud wrapped her arms around my shoulders as I lifted her out of the passenger seat of the beastmobile and lowered her into her chair. She smoothed the wrinkles from her dress and looked up at me with a smile. "Thanks, Jack. I hope that wasn't too awkward for you."

"Not at all," I said, hoping that I wasn't blushing.

Her smile broadened. "You're sweet. Now get behind me and push. That's a good boy."

We had to overcome some minor challenges—a few curbsides, some inconvenient cracks in the sidewalk, a cluster of well-dressed pedestrians who resented having to clear a path for a wheelchair-bound broad—but in due course we made our way to the gaudy neon-lit entrance of The Gold Coast Club. I pushed my guest past a line of perturbed ticket-holders to the entryway, where a doorman ushered us inside. In the lobby, we were greeted by Armine Clearwater himself.

"There you are!" With a gesture I considered more than a little extravagant, Clearwater lowered himself to one knee and bowed in our direction. "Ah, Miss Walks in Cloud." My date for the evening held up her hand, and Clearwater took it in his own and kissed the air a quarter of an inch above it. "It is so good to meet you. And don't you look lovely, my dear! I absolutely adore those pearls. You are much too elegant for this ruffian you've chosen to accompany you."

Sure, it was corny, but some old jaspers have the knack for pulling it off. Walks in Cloud beamed at Clearwater. "Charmed, Mr. Clearwater. But I am Mr. Southerland's guest, not the other way around. He's the one you invited to this shindig."

"Yes, well it was the least I could do after wanting to pounce on him and tear him into little pieces. I'm pleased that you came with Mr. Southerland, my dear. He would have been such dull company if he'd come alone." Clearwater's smile broadened until it crinkled the corners of his eyes. "Even if we found him a proper suit, the poor boy would still be a fish out of water in a refined place like this. But this old palace pales in comparison to the club that I am preparing to establish. Yes, The Night Owl will live again, but this time right here in Yerba City."

Walks in Cloud continued to beam. "Oh, I don't know, Mr. Clearwater. I reckon Mr. Southerland can handle his liquor with more dignity than most of the phony tipplers who frequent gold-plated joints like this."

Clearwater broke into amused laughter. "I 'reckon' he can at that, Miss Walks in Cloud." He turned his attention to me for the first time. I looked for some sign of resentment in the face of the old hunter who just days before had regarded me as prey, but found only joy and delight. For the night, at least, it appeared that bygones were going to be bygones. "A table has been prepared for you, Mr. Southerland. After you check your hat and coat, a hostess will show you the way. Your dinner and drinks will be on me, of course. I hope you like seabass. The fish was swimming merrily up the coast this very afternoon, and I had it set aside especially for you. The staff has been alerted to see to your every need, and, should you require anything, please feel free to mention that you are my guests. I hope you both have a 'swell' time. Ha ha! Cheers!" And with a last nod in my direction, the stubby little gentleman turned on his heel and strutted toward the dining area with a half dozen men in expensive tuxedos following in his wake.

When Clearwater was gone, Walks in Cloud turned her head and looked up at me. "He's a bit of an ass, don't you think?"

I couldn't help but smile. "He certainly is. But he's also an ancient spirit with the power to alter reality by telling a story. I plan on staying on his good side if I can."

"Oh, I'm familiar with the tales of old Night Owl. He's supposed to be a clever fellow. But that didn't stop us from tricking the pants off him, right?"

I glanced around the lobby to see if anyone had heard her. "Careful with the loose lips. We're in his territory now."

A half hour later, when we were well into our seabass filets and spiced coffees, Walks in Cloud raised her eyes to meet mine. "I want to thank you for doing me this favor."

I shook my head. "I told you, I don't consider this a favor. If anything, you did *me* a favor by accepting my invitation. I'm still as much in your debt as ever."

Walks in Cloud reached across the table and put her hand over mine. She gave me a squeeze and withdrew it. "I told you that I would determine how you were going to repay me for getting you access into that flash drive. I told you that it would be difficult, but it would be something you could handle."

"This isn't difficult. It's my pleasure."

Her eyes glowed. "A night at The Gold Coast? Lord's balls! I've been wanting to come here for, well, for my whole life!" She smiled. "Never thought it would happen."

"It's not like I'm paying for anything," I protested.

"Hmph! You earned it."

I smiled back at the computer tech. "You did most of the work. I wouldn't have known how to program a false passcode to unleash the wolves on those files. And..." I leaned forward and lowered my voice so that it couldn't be heard above the music from the band, the conversations of the guests, and the clatter of the dinnerware. "I wouldn't have done it at all if hadn't known that you'd saved a backup of the files in the cloud."

Walks in Cloud smiled. "Pretty clever, eh?" She wiped the corners of her mouth with a napkin. "I was surprised when you called me that night. Well, surprised and a little pissed at first. I know I told you that you could call me anytime, but don't you know most people are asleep at that time of the night?"

I shrugged. "Sorry. I was at a friend's house, and I'd just come up with a plan to deal with a tricky situation. I needed to know for sure whether you had a copy of the files on that drive in a safe place."

She waved a hand in dismissal. "Whatever. Anyway, what made you think I'd downloaded those files? How come you didn't believe me back in my shop when I told you that I hadn't made a copy? After all, the drive was enchanted. No one was supposed to be able to download its contents."

"I never bought that hooey about you not wanting to know what was on the drive. You'd been walking around in the data files, same as me. And I could sense some of the recorded information just by being there. I assumed you were already reading the whole thing like a book. And I figured if you could get me into those files, you could copy them, too, enchantment be damned. Your methods aren't exactly conventional."

The computer wizard chuckled. "Nope. I'm one of a kind. A priestess of the Cloud Spirit. There's not much I can't do with data." She looked over at me. "That's why I'm expensive."

I rolled my eyes. "I told you, this isn't payment. You're my date."

Walks in Cloud's lips pursed into a small grin that was more than a little coy, and her voice came from deep in her throat. "You're a doll, Jack. But I'm going to want more than dinner, you know."

I opened my mouth to say something, but nothing came out.

Walks in Cloud's grin broadened. "Oh, don't worry, dear. I'm pretty much dead from the waist down."

Heat rose to my cheeks, and I started to choke. "I, uh…"

She reached across the table and put her hand on mine. "You're cute, Jack. But cool your jets. All I'm saying is that I wanna dance with you. Right now."

"Dance?"

"Sure, Jack. Carry me out to the dance floor and give me a twirl. That work for you?"

I smiled at her and felt myself relax. "Absolutely. Let's cut a rug."

Circling to the other side of the table, I knelt beside Walks in Cloud and placed an arm beneath her knees. She clasped her hands behind my neck, and I lifted her out of her chair. Cradling her against my chest with both arms, I carried her to the dance floor.

The band was playing an upbeat ballad, and the other guests gave us room as I swayed my hips to the beat and shuffled in circles. At first, Walks in Cloud clung to me like a refugee from a burning building. "You doing okay?" I asked her after a time.

Her voice came from close to my ear. "I should be asking you that. I'm… not a small woman." I felt heat burning from her cheeks.

In truth, she wasn't wrong.

"You're fine," I told her. "It would help if you relaxed a little, though. You're stiff as a board."

I felt the heat from her cheeks increase. "Thanks a lot, Jack! This isn't something I do every Saturday night, you know."

"Me neither," I admitted. "It's been a long time since I went out dancing."

She was silent as the band's piano player finished a solo. As the music continued, she leaned closer to me and asked, "What are you going to do with that formula?"

"I don't know yet. Can you keep it safe for a while longer?"

"It's stored in a place where no one but me will ever find it."

"Good. I may never ask for it at all, but you never know. Information is power, and it might wind up being the key to something someday. In the meantime, keep it where it is in case I need it. It'll be our secret."

The band finished its song, and immediately launched into another, a slow bluesy number. Walks in Cloud wrapped her arms around me and leaned her head into my neck. Her words to me were soft. "Are you up for one more dance?"

"Of course."

I swayed to the new, more languid beat and shuffled my feet one slow step at a time, but I was starting to feel some strain, especially in my upper arms. I could hear my heart pumping, and beads of sweat were beginning to form on my forehead. Desperately, I hoped that the woman in my arms hadn't noticed.

In my mind, I formed a thought: "Cougar? A little help?"

I breathed in the faintest scent of wild feline, and a new strength flowed through my arms, chest, and back. My heartbeat slowed, and my forehead dried. I pulled Walks in Cloud closer to me, tightening my grip under her knees and around her back and pressing her limp body into mine. She let her head relax on my shoulder, and soon I could feel her slow breathing tickling the nape of my neck. She was as light as a feather.

The End

Thank You!

Thank you for reading A Night Owl Slips into a Diner: A Noir Urban Fantasy Novel. If you enjoyed it, I hope that you will consider writing a review—even a short one—on Amazon, Goodreads, or your favorite book site. Publishing is still driven by word of mouth, and every single voice helps. I'm working hard to bring Alex Southerland back, and knowing that readers might be interested in hearing more about his adventures in Yerba City will certainly speed up the process!

Acknowledgements

When I wrote my first book (*A Troll Walks into a Bar*), I never dreamed that it would turn into a series. I'm four books in, and I couldn't have done it without a lot of help along the way. First and foremost, I want to thank my wife, Rita, my full partner in everything I do. She is not only my biggest fan, but my sounding board, story adviser, and co-editor. She is directly responsible for many of the better ideas in my books. She's my best friend and my hero.

I want to thank my parents, Bill and Carolyn, for their unending support and encouragement. Thanks, also, to my sisters, Teri and Karen, who read this book in advance and not only cleaned up a lot of typos, but gave me great suggestions that I incorporated into my story. I also want to thank my cousin Juliana for her continued support and encouragement.

Big shout-out to Assaph Mehr, author of the fantastic *Stories of Togas, Daggers, and Magic* series, for reading an advance copy of this book and giving me the benefit of his expertise, not only as a writer, but as an experienced electronics communications tech. If my story contains errors when dealing with computer technology, they're mine, not his. I mean, he tried!

I'm extremely grateful for the enthusiastic support of a number of authors in the writers' community on Twitter and Instagram. The story of how writers support writers is remarkable. It would take too long to acknowledge all of my social media friends by name, but I appreciate all of you (including Ziggy, whose reviews of my books on Goodreads and Amazon are incredibly fun reads). At the risk of leaving any deserving people out, I want to take the time to single out five of my fellow storytellers who have gone out of their way to drum up enthusiasm for my books: Peter Hartog, author of the *Guardian of Empire City* series, an exceptional scifi/fantasy/hardboiled crime novel mashup; Zamil Akhtar, author of the

Gunmetal Gods novels, a fabulous dark fantasy series with a Middle Eastern milieu; Mary (M.C.) Hunton, whose debut novel *Resurrection* is a terrific start to what is sure to be a wonderful dark urban fantasy series; DuVay Knox, whose gritty dark fantasies are revolutionizing the pulp fiction sector; and Stephen J. Golds, master of the brutal noir urban drama, who was kind enough to publish an interview with me and promote my books in his online *Punk Noir Magazine*. I have tremendous respect for the works of all of these authors, and I'm deeply appreciative of their support. Do yourself a favor and check them out.

A special thank you goes out to the affable and tireless Duffy Weber, an all-round great guy whose fantastic production and narration bring the audio versions of my stories to life. Thank you, buddy! And get some sleep! Rita and I worry about you!

I thank anyone who ever gave me the slightest bit of encouragement or support. If I left you out, please let me know. I've received a lot of great advice, and, if I didn't take it, that's my fault, not yours.

Finally, a big thank you to anyone and everyone who has read my books and taken the time to rate or review them. Every review—good or bad—helps me in the end. Readers have an abundance of choices, and I appreciate every one of you who chose to read something I wrote. I hope you'll stick with me.

About the Author

My parents raised me right. Any mistakes I made were my own. Hopefully, I learned from them.

I earned a doctorate in medieval European history at the University of California Santa Barbara. Go Gauchos! I taught world history at a couple of colleges before settling into a private college prep high school in Monterey. After I retired, I began to write an urban fantasy series featuring hardboiled private eye Alexander Southerland as he cruises through the mean streets of Yerba City and interacts with trolls, femme fatales, shape-shifters, witches, and corrupt city officials.

I am happily married to my wife, Rita. The two of us can be found most days pounding the pavement in our running shoes. We both love living in Monterey, California, with its foggy mornings, ocean breezes, and year-round mild temperatures. Rita listens to all of my ideas and reads all of my work. Her advice is beyond value. In return, I make her tea twice a day. It's a pretty sweet deal. We have a cat named Cinderella who is happy to stay indoors. She demands that we tell her how pretty she is.

Printed in Great Britain
by Amazon